The Human of All

Ryan Parrett

Grosvenor House
Publishing Limited

This book is published by
Grosvenor House Publishing Ltd
Link House
140 The Broadway, Tolworth, Surrey, KT6 7HT.
www.grosvenorhousepublishing.co.uk

A CIP record for this book
is available from the British Library

ISBN 978-1-83975-807-2

Contents

CHAPTER ONE
- AN UNFORGETTABLE DAY 1

CHAPTER TWO
- SOME THINGS NEVER CHANGE 61

CHAPTER THREE
- ANNIE 120

CHAPTER FOUR
- NOT EVERYONE CAN BE SAVED 180

CHAPTER FIVE
- REVELATIONS 241

Thank you Dad.

This book wouldn't have been possible without you.

Chapter 1 – An Unforgettable Day

John Campbell is a most unusual and unique individual. On the surface, simply a normal, hard working, healthy six feet two inches man. By profession a Marine Engineering Officer who works for a fleet of support ships. It is, however, that which is unseen, or deliberately hidden, that perhaps makes him the human of all. That is to say, he is possibly the most knowledgeable and physically capable person alive today. This level of knowledge and his intelligence has been gained through reading and learning, coupled with an eidetic memory, not by creative thinking or his own deductive scientific methodology. His physical attributes are almost incomprehensible: He can lift massive objects; move at incredible speeds and, the scariest part; appears to be invulnerable to any form of physical harm.

For John, this whole voyage of discovery began three weeks ago and not a single tiny thing has been forgotten by him since. This level of memory retention has been quite the burden at times, considering some of the incidents that have occurred since that fateful accident in Miami. It is well known that a famous fictional character refers to himself as having a mind palace. For post-accident John that is an appropriate analogy. Without doubt, it makes sense being able to dive into one's consciousness and retrieve information at will. After all, the mind is an incredibly vast place. So much so that John, initially, actually found himself lost in his own mind after the accident. So how did this all happen? How has John become, possibly, as strong as a comic humanoid alien? Or how has he gained such extensive knowledge, that a baker street dwelling detective's mind palace now looks like a matchbox by comparison? Well, he was injured in a freak accident in Miami.

The accident occurred whilst he was at work as he walked along a dockside admiring a vast cruise liner. He remembered thinking how the ship was an incredible feat of marine engineering and a splendid piece of naval architecture when suddenly, the ship appeared to be creeping forward, straining against all the mooring lines. Shouts were ringing out all over and the lines were groaning under the immense tension they were somehow withstanding – until they weren't. John had been slowly, apprehensively, backing away from the edge of the dock, mindful of snapback, when an impact to his safety helmet knocked him flying off his feet into the clear blue Miami water. One of the mooring lines, relieved of its burden, had parted with a black scorch mark and scored an incredulous direct hit. John had felt a numbing sense of dread spreading like wildfire, as he watched the white and pale blue behemoth continue to creep forward, in spite of the mooring lines best efforts. John, gripped by dread and awe, remained frozen within the infamous snapback area - an area that had claimed many casualties before him. Then, the huge ship inexplicably stopped as mysteriously as it had started. A stunned silence and eerie stillness prevailed throughout the dock area. Nobody, not Dock Workers or Ship's Staff, could even begin to fathom what had just happened. The event was so terribly captivating that the sudden disappearance of a man wearing a white boiler suit went completely unnoticed. As did the sound of the splash and the ripples that were slowly dissipating from its source.

For John there was only a void, a nothingness. That is until chaos reigned. In the beginning there was no sensation of pain, no shock, no apprehension or feelings of any kind for that matter. There was also no sense of oneself - in the beginning at least. After a tortuous, chaotic and unintelligible time of images and sound, during which John simply couldn't cope and just wanted it all to end, he somehow latched onto something that gave him hope. It was an image he recognised. The image was of a dark star lit sky. There was a silhouette of hills below it, with lights poking through the darkness under the jagged peaks. These lights reflected in the far edge of the water, stretching out from the beach at the low point of the image. Then everything happened at once. Sight was now joined by sound, feelings and then movement, for the image pitched violently upwards becoming only sand. The sound was of a high-pitched shriek of laughter, along with waves ebbing and flowing across the sand. The feeling was a growing sense of embarrassment, reddening and warming John's cheeks. This was because he'd tripped over something protruding from the sand. His attention had been solely on the beautiful woman walking beside him. Instinctively avoiding a face full of sand, by bracing himself in a push up position at the last moment, John noticed that Annie was in hysterics. Adjusting his position, he let his knees rest on the sand and sat upright with his hands on his thighs, eyes closed, mouth in a tight line and head forlornly bowed. The date with Annie had been going really well up until that point. At least that's how he felt. Now this first date may well be the last too. Unexpectedly, he was nudged on the shoulder and lurched sideways - his hand shot out and braced him against the damp sand to prevent another comical fall; thereby surprising him out of his rueful reflection. He stared up at Annie; she was struggling to contain her mirth with her arms folded tightly across her chest and he realised that she'd playfully nudged him over with her hip. She inclined her head along the beach towards the small lighthouse on the rocky shore at the end. Her eyes twinkled and her teeth shone bright from the wide smile John glimpsed as she turned away. John sprang up and quickly fell in line beside her and they both walked towards the lighthouse. Annie seemed cold so he stepped closer and placed his arm around her shoulders, gently drawing her to his side. John had a brief flutter of panic, fearing he'd overstepped, as she tensed up and drew her arms tighter across her chest. Indecision froze his arm in place and his eyes darted anywhere but towards Annie. Just as he was about to recover and remove his arm and flee to a dark corner of anywhere, Annie relaxed and rested her head on his shoulder. He still had the urge to bolt, but now it was to whoop and cheer. Happiness bloomed, making his fingertips tingle and butterflies flutter in his stomach. He couldn't believe his luck and chanced a look towards Annie. She was looking up at him, her wonderful pale grey eyes locked onto his. She was smiling and he couldn't help but smile too. Now it was her turn to trip over as her foot caught the bit of driftwood they'd both failed to notice. Her eyes widened in surprise and her jaw dropped open letting loose a yelp as she pitched forward, her arms struggling to free themselves from her own embrace. John reacted in the blink of an eye, diving forward, pushing off with the foot closest to his falling date in order to complete a half pirouette and land on his back under Annie, cushioning her fall. Well, days playing football as a goalkeeper in his youth suddenly seemed very worthwhile. As she landed on top of him Annie managed to free her arms and place her hands either side of his chest, just as he hit the damp sand. He tucked his chin to his chest, to avoid hitting his head an something else that he may not have noticed, and protectively wrapped his arms around Annie. They both lay quiet in stunned silence for what seemed like a long time. Then, just as the long, drawn out, silence was about to become uncomfortable, John started to laugh and he noticed that Annie was laughing to, albeit slightly muffled against his chest. With both of them almost in tears after a good long laugh, he relaxed his arms from around Annie's shoulders, placing both hands lightly on her waist as she leaned up and placed both hands under her chin on his chest. After a long moment of simply staring and smiling at one another, with their faces only inches apart, she tilted her head up a fraction in what he thought was an impatient gesture. "Are you going to take the hint and kiss me?" She finally said after rolling her eyes up. John couldn't help but break out into a huge smile - happily obliging he kissed her and time stood still. With both of them utterly lost in the moment, not caring for what was to be or what had already been. After what felt like a long time they surfaced for air, although still close as the tips of their noses were touching. Still both smiling, he noticed that Annie's shoulder length dark brown hair was draped either side of his face, with some strands tickling his cheeks and interrupting his thoughts. He was pondering how to ask what he wanted to ask her so very much. Noticing that her eyes were focused on his, with what he hoped was an expectant gaze, John swallowed down his nerves and gathered up his resolve. This was the moment. Time to ask Annie if she would be his girlfriend. John cringed inwardly at how childish that thought was. "Annie ..." - her eyes widened ever so slightly and she raised her head a fraction

- "... would you like to be my girlfriend?" John cringed even more upon actually hearing and realising the words he'd just spoken. Annie turned her head a touch and took on a look of deep contemplation. "Hmm. . . I suppose so." She finally said with her eyes closed, pouting comically ever so slightly. John was beside himself with joy and then the image of Annie's pouting face was frozen in front of him. He was suddenly conscious of a startling realisation. This was a memory. John realised that his recognition of that indeed being a memory meant he was still cognitive, thinking, and thus apparently alive for now at least in some manner. Was he dying though? Was his life flashing before his eyes? What is going on? It didn't make sense, for that memory literally felt as it were happening right then in the now, rather than in the past on that cold September day over seven and a half years ago. The memory was now becoming lost in a sea of other moving images spreading out, distinct from one another akin to a giant ultrawide screen. He was looking around in all directions. No that cannot be, he remembered thinking, how is this even possible? For John now knew where he was. John now knew what all the other multitude of moving images were, along with the snippets of sound accompanying them. He focused his thoughts just to be certain of his hypothesis. His first dog BP, the creatively named boy puppy in full, a black and tan King Charles Spaniel, running around as real as can be, when it had been years since his passing. Then there was his wife Annie, walking down the aisle towards him between their friends and family, beautiful and radiating happiness, as if it was happening now and not four and a half years ago. Next was Annie in Labour, giving birth to their three-year-old son Stewart. John was certain now that his hypothesis was indeed correct. He was somehow stuck in his own mind with all of the memories of his life up until that very moment spread out before him. He was suddenly completely terrified beyond all manners of expression and felt lost in the sea of what he knew to be true. What felt like a million thoughts were going through John's mind and he wondered if anything was real and happening now. Was this his death? Was death to remain conscious and present in amongst all the memories of life and that was simply that? A spark appeared, interrupting the troubling thought, in the distance amongst all the memories of his life. It moved in an erratic manner but only around a certain area. He could ignore it, turn away from it, and then look around again to see it. The luminescence of the spark was fluctuating. Dimming to a small point, almost as if to hide again amongst the surrounding memories. Then becoming incredibly bright and vast, obscuring many memories: demanding attention. John felt the spark could no longer be ignored so he tried to focus on it. Could he and should he try to grasp it? Never had he seen anything like it except perhaps for lightning. That immediately made him dubious as to whether touching, or reaching out to, this mysterious bolt of lightning was entirely sensible. After some internal conflict, the winning side of “what could possibly go wrong” triumphing over the losing “this place is peaceful and safe” side, he set about moving towards the lightning. This proved incredibly difficult as he couldn’t see, or feel his limbs, going so far as to question whether or not he even had a physical presence at all. His will to move, the desire to leave this nothingness, seemed to propel him forward at what felt like the slowest speed conceivable. It was a battle. The strangest battle he'd ever fought. The lightning was there in the distance but now getting closer. In front of it was seemingly everything John had known. Random sentences floating in the air, some of them looked very familiar. Maybe they were from books? A constant stream of moving imagines, making it nigh on impossible to make out what was going on. Just snippets of memories it seemed. It was moments when john stopped, that's if he were ever actually physically moving, that these images became clear. It was tempting just to stay forever. To enjoy these happy moments from times gone by over and over, like re-watching a favourite film. He thought to himself if this was his existence now, maybe it wasn't so bad. Then again, that's not to say this was all pleasant - absolutely not: for there was trauma. Memories of painful moments, such as a car crash whilst driving past loch Lomond, in Scotland, felt like an actual electric shock. And there was emotional trauma as the image of his dying mother sprang up from those times everyone wishes were bad dreams. Onwards towards the lightning John went, for this wasn't living. He knew that. Life had to be the lightning. It was the only thing in this space that hadn't already happened.

Finally, he reached the lightning and there was a burst of blinding light, his eyes flew open and his mind registered an uncomfortable sensation in both them and his hand. At last, John had awoken to find himself underwater, at the bottom of the docks in the sand; thank God, back to having a physical existence in this world again. There was, however, a bull shark shaking his hand, with its sharp teeth and strong jaws no less, as if rudely welcoming his return to the place where all things lived. Curiously, his immediate thoughts were of the lack of blood, and how was it his hand was still attached to the arm that was being roughly shaken by this rude fish, considering a bull shark can bite with the force of a grizzly bear's weight. Surprisingly though, he wasn't thinking of why he wasn't drowning. Nor was he thinking "Oh my god there's a shark attacking me!" Actually, curiosity was reigning over all other considerations at that moment and John was utterly perplexed by it. Eventually, he gathered his senses and pushed the shark away, only to stare incredulously at his miraculously undamaged hand - “What the hell?” He thought. It was then, and only then, that he wondered why he wasn’t struggling to breathe. In addition, his vision underwater was becoming clearer. Amazingly, he could see clearly and admire the shark's individual denticles, even though the shark was now at least 100 metres away from him - such was the clarity of his vision. Furthermore, the ship's mammoth hull, from the tip of its azimuth thrusters, to the end of its bulbous bow - just over three hundred and sixty meters distant, were also clearly visible. It seemed that there was no restriction on what he could see. Sounds had also become enhanced too, although this was quite disconcerting. There were hundreds, if not thousands of sounds, all vying for his attention, all competing to be heard first. It was a struggle to focus, to try to identify different sounds and where they came from. He focused hard and decided to look ahead at the grey coloured large fish swimming away from him. Now he could make out the shark's receding heartbeat, calming after trying to get a little snack. He now sat motionless, wondering why he wasn’t drowning was the thought that was lurking at the back of his mind. His attention now switched to the hum of the cruise ship's powerful diesel engines and the indistinct voices of dock and ship workers talking on the jetty - and now even cars moving along the Miami Port Boulevard Road. Well, with all these thoughts and his new found sensory awareness kind of under control, he decided it was best that he headed to the surface. He stood up, surprisingly gracefully considering his current whereabouts, and took a last lingering look through the water, marvelling at just how incredible his vision was now. John looked up, bent his legs to kick off from the sandy bottom only to burst free of the water and find himself standing on the dockside once again, several meters above the circular ripple of waves that he'd just flown out of. He found himself equally impressed and confused at this surprising turn of events. He still had no idea what was going on until quite suddenly, with the considerable force of his palm striking his head, it all clicked into place. The nothingness he had been in turned out to be his very own mind. The only information there was his own thoughts and memories. An involuntary shudder racked his body as he recalled the more morbid ones. The lightning show had initially been a mystery, as it was completely out of place, but he realised it must've been his brain's pain receptors lighting up, receiving signals from the shark munched hand. That's what set him free from the vastness of the mind. It was the only external input his brain had received during his entrapment within the endless confines of the mind. For some reason being underwater hadn't registered as a stressful or dangerous situation, so there was no fight or flight reflex sparking away. It was only the shark's attack that triggered a response. The body was manically sending electrical nerve signals to his brain, screaming it was being harmed. Or, at least, the shark was trying to harm him. No wonder john took so long to wake up. The mind is an incomprehensibly massive place. All of his memories; yesterdays' general musings during a boring meeting; random thoughts from years ago; the annoyance of having to wait another month until British touring car racing resumed; and so much more is all in there. He had to wade through all of this just to reach the lightning show of his body's pain receptors in the brain. Like those nightmares when you find yourself running, only to be moving agonisingly slowly. It seemed that he was now somehow making more use of his brain. Or at least better use of it. Similar to that of a Mathematical Savant, only his brain was not just better at Maths. Simply everything seemed now vastly improved. This was evident to him by his analysis of what he is now capable of. It appeared that there was much, much, more within his mind, whilst he was trapped inside of it. John now knew comprehensively that there was so much more potential within his brain that he could explore and now make use of. Feelings, moving around, memories, taste, talking, bodily functions - such as breathing - although John actually no longer felt the need to breathe weirdly enough. Also, it appeared that all routine functions controlled by his brain were now more familiar, as if specific areas within the brain had been designated to deal with them. To John it was as if his brain was now an infinitely long book. The initial pages were those functions already mentioned, they were there clear as the Miami sky and would always be there as normal. But new pages were being written as his brain developed further and made better use of those one hundred billion cells that make it up. Now John knew his body was able to change its cellular structure in order to cope without oxygen. He was underwater for over hour, as it transpired. Also, he had withstood a shark attack – with no physical harm evident (a bull shark attack can be deemed as pretty substantial) – in normal circumstances he should have been either seriously injured or dead. And then there was the exponential increase to the amount of force his muscles could exert. It must have been the blow to his head that came from the end of the mooring line when it parted. This blow must have triggered a unique mutation within his brain, allowing for the greater use of those one hundred billion cells. "Wow", he thought – the odds of such a blow striking his head with the exact amount of force, at the exact angle, in the exact spot to trigger this metamorphosis made his head hurt when he thought about it. It appeared that making greater use of these billions of cells has allowed his body to adapt, almost instantaneously, to seemingly any given scenario - such as oxygen deprivation. Looks wise though, nothing had changed; he still had short hair, with a receding hairline; there was still a bit of lazy stubble; he still had sandy blue eyes, was reasonably fit looking and six foot two inches tall. He also still weighed about fourteen stone. "Changing my appearance at will to look like a movie star is out of the window then," he mused. Everything else though, how his body actually worked and functioned, was now able to be changed and adapted. He could feel it and it was incredible. The best way of explaining it is as an extreme form of photosynthesis, brought on by new signals, which evidently altered his skin cells to absorb light like Lego absorbs money. The resulting changes originating from previously underused parts of the brain. His body gained its now incredible energy from the sun, much like a plant. For the sun and it's radiating energy would appear to be, at present at least, his body's most effective way of generating energy. It was no longer sustenance from food and drink. In a weird way he also now felt like a battery. He knew how much energy he had and exactly how his actions affected it. The possibilities of what he could now do were mind boggling. He thought to himself, could his body now adapt at will and do whatever it was called upon to do? What if there was no sunlight? Would his body then find a new source of energy? The possibilities, and the accompanying questions, were becoming a very long list indeed. A shout broke into these thoughts. "John, where on earth have you been!? The ship is going crazy, emergency stations the works, all looking for you!" John smiled, it was Callum Hill, his friend from the ship they were on. Callum was taller than John at six-foot five inches tall, slimly built, with dark brown eyes and black hair in a tapered style hair-cut. They were two of the ship's three Third Officers. Disturbingly, Callum seemed to be genuinely terrified. John could hear his elevated heartrate. But Callum was also relieved, at the same time, judging by the look in his eyes. Looking down at his watch John realised it had been just over an hour since he left the ship on a simple errand to the Seaport Operations Bureau, Port Miami's law enforcement facility. He was to sign for a delivery of parts. A mere ten-minute task, or even fifteen if you felt like admiring the various other berthed ships. Before John could reply, Callum noticed his cracked helmet and blood covered face. "Holy crap - what the hell happened to you!? You're covered in blood and your helmet looks like it was hit by a sledgehammer!" Callum blurted out. "It was a mooring line from that Royal Caribbean cruise ship" was John's monotone response. He was reeling from learning just how long he had been in the water. He then noticed the blood covering his, what were, white overalls. Reaching up he felt his cracked helmet, and the new half circle shaped scar on the right side of his head, one tip looping down to his temple, the other end stretching upwards creating a neat curve a couple of inches long. 'The impact did leave a mark then, before my brain went all turbo charged' John thought. Callum looked like he had suffered a hit to the head himself such was his incredulous expression. "I'm actually OK, it's far worse than it looks" John quickly said, trying to keep the awkward moment from spiralling further. The fact that John didn't have a hole in the side of his head, or the fact that he had a head at all, for that matter after such a blow, seemed to be causing Callum quite some distress. "Shall we head back to the ship and have everyone stop looking for me?" asked John. "Uh . . . yea sure . . ." came the far from settled reply. "Callum, I'm fine honestly. I know it looks like I lost a fight with a shark, but it's honestly far worse than it looks." John had to stifle a smirk as he realised perhaps, he did actually win a fight with a shark. "Oh, silly me. I thought a bird had flown into you and was apologising profusely for knocking you into the water. Hence why you've been gone so long. Did that mooring line there hit your head? Were you just having a nice dip in the water to sooth the little scratch it must've caused? Why didn't you just come back if you're 'fine?" Callum's voice was now dripping with sarcasm, he was even using his fingers to form quotation marks, obviously still stunned by John's appearance. "Well, what do you want me to say? I'm in agony? My head feels like it's splitting in two? I need to-" "Go right to the hospital as a mooring line just smacked you for a home run? Yes!" Callum said butting in. Oh God, he's really not taking this well at all. How on earth can I calm him down before we get back to the ship and he tells everyone what really happened?' John thought. "Callum, we've known each other for twelve years now - since we met as cadets at Fleetwood - have I ever given you any reason to doubt me?" John realised too late, the can of worms he'd just opened. "You kept quiet when the others had put loft insulation in my boxers for my date with Lauren at college. Funnily enough that didn't go well as it's quite rude to keep scratching your nether regions. Also, the time I crashed out on our first ship, after that night out in Weymouth so it was, and you wrapped me in clingfilm to my bunk in our cabin. Seeing as it was a weekend, it was assumed that I had stayed in the cabin to complete my task book, so nobody bothered to look for me until you came back in just before lunch! Oh, and let's not forget -" "OK, OK so I've given you a couple -" "A COUPLE?!" "- Of reasons to be a tad suspicious at times. But this is not one of them though. And come on, you've more than got me back for some of those little incidents. Remember calling Annie to tell her I'd been out and had come back late smelling of perfume, when you knew full well, I'd been in my cabin all day playing that racing game on my laptop. She went crazy! If I'd been home, I'm pretty sure she'd have killed me!" "Yea that was pretty funny." John allowed Callum to chuckle at that indignant memory of his for a little bit as it was calming him down. They walked on towards their ship for a few moments in silence. "Don't you think you should get rid of that helmet and clean up a bit before we get back?" Callum seemed to be calm again now and that was an excellent point. John didn't feel like being interrogated about his grizzly appearance on top of why he had been missing for so long. If possible, he wanted to avoid a trip to the ship's Med-Tech or even to the hospital. Those would be awkward questions he didn't want to answer. John knew full well why he wasn't a head shorter, and felt that explanation was best left to himself for the time being. He dreaded to think of the consequences if people discovered what he was now capable of. This disturbing train of thought was thankfully interrupted by Callum. "Wait there for a bit" Callum pointed to a gap between the cruise ship passenger terminals. "I'll go back to the ship, grab you another helmet and boiler suit, then come back for you." "Take care, the MEO might be angry at you for leaving me ashore when she sees you back again alone." "Not half as angry as she'll be with you when I tell her you'd talked your way into a tour of that massive cruise ship's engine room and were now only just heading to sign for the delivery." John's rude reply of one word was obscured by a truck driving by. Even though it was a complete fabrication and would result in a lot of trouble for him, he still preferred it over the truth. The Ship's Marine Engineering Officer (MEO), their head of department Katherine, was usually very friendly and approachable but, she could terrify a dragon if you crossed the line. And this would be deemed a line jumped over moment. The inevitable meeting with Katherine waiting for him back on board was not a pleasant thought for John. 'Maybe this is an ideal time to see if I can run fast now too? In any direction that doesn't lead back to the MEO' he thought ruefully. He now had to endure an uncomfortable wait trying to hide himself from prying eyes. A man standing in a secluded spot wearing blood-soaked overalls could be deemed as rather suspicious. John shuffled slightly further back, willing himself to disappear in the shadows. He was furtively looking around, hoping to remain inconspicuous, when his eyes picked out a tall man standing three hundred and forty-two meters away looking right at him. John's eyesight was simply incredible now and continued to surprise him. It seemed that if something was in his line of sight, then he could clearly see it, right down to microscopic details. Quite unnerving initially actually. Although, he quickly grew accustomed to the ability to zoom in and out per say, he had a little more trouble comprehending he was physically distant from whatever his eyes could see. Then there was the fact he knew precisely how far away the man was, making the stare coming from his startling bright blue eyes that much more shocking. Not only could the man seemingly see him, he seemed to be intently observing him for some reason. John was starting to doubt himself, surely the man couldn't even see him standing in the shadows from such a distance, let alone be observing him. Another truck went by, obscuring the mysterious stranger, with the black buzzcut and casual suit, briefly from view. In that brief moment though, the stranger was gone. John was still pondering this strange incident when Callum, true to his word thankfully, returned within ten minutes with a new helmet and one of John's clean boiler suits. Once he had made himself look reasonable again, rather than the loser of a boxing match, it was time to head back to the ship. "Katherine is going to rip you a new one, sew it up and rip you another when you get back John - you know right?" John simply nodded, accepting his fate.

As they reached the gangway to board the ship, a tanker with a few tall rigs used to fuel other ships whilst at sea, Callum stopped briefly with a serious expression. "I know you John and I believe we're closer than simply friends - well at least that's what I think seeing as I was your best man, but I know you're hiding something right now. Something to do with that happened back there. If you wish to keep it from me then cool, I'll accept it, but don't keep it from Annie, ok?" John knew that must've been hard for his close friend to say and he was filled with gratitude for it. "Thanks Callum. I mean it. You've always been there for me. I will tell you what's going on soon. I just need to survive Katherine first, then talk to Annie." Although John decided then that this particular talk with Annie may have to wait. This will need to be a conversation in person, such was the magnitude of its potential repercussions. Already worrying now thanks to that lovely thought, he readied himself to face the wrath of what will probably be everyone on board. When a ship is called to emergency stations, it involves everyone having to muster, thus disrupting their routines and jobs, and carry out whatever task they are directed to undertake. And in this case, even though he was pegged off the ship, a wooden board displaying every crew member's name is at the top of the gangway with a peg in an on or off hole, a potential casualty search (it's not uncommon for people to forget to peg in) was never going to be a fun task. Callum nodded and boarded the ship first. John followed and made his way to the Machinery Control Room (MCR). There were a lot of angry faces. He had interrupted everyone's day as the whole ship, as he'd feared, had gotten involved when his absence resulted in the emergency station's muster. An invisible hand squeezed John's heart, as he realised that the shore authorities would've also been contacted to assist with the search for him. He prayed that the Ship's Captain would answer their questions, whilst apologising for the inconvenience caused, rather than having to do so himself. Reaching the MCR was a bit of a relief. The other engineers would be rather annoyed that was obvious, but they would also find it funny in due course. A story to tell of that time John disappeared for a tour. They were a good bunch of people. Friends too. Except for one that is. It was rare that you got on with the majority of the team, well for a normally un sociable person such as John it was at least. John preferred simply being in his cabin watching films, reading or playing computer games. He wasn't one for drinking or going to pubs. He was happiest simply being at home with Annie and their three-year-old son Stewart. Callum was already back in the MCR and led the sarcastic cheers and slow clapping welcoming John back. There were a few chosen words uttered by some of the team, the rudest of which came from Arla Moran, a second officer and one of the three female engineers onboard. She was also a good friend of John's, so she would've been angry and worried too, making her unusually extreme reaction, for she was a very reserved person, understandable. She hadn't cheered, rather just stood with her green eyes staring daggers at him with a face to quell a storm. This look was often enough to frighten most people as, even though she was only five-foot four inches tall with shoulder length brown hair (normally found in a ponytail), she was very strong with a fairly muscular build. John started to head past the first line of consoles to approach her and Callum when he heard Katherine's voice behind him. She had been in the Engineer's Office, which was on the door to the right, just before you entered the MCR. He closed his eyes as waves of dread and nausea crashed over him. Grimacing at Arla and Callum, he slowly turned and walked back to the office, with the air of a man about to face a firing squad. The other engineers remained silent. They were tactful enough to know he was in serious trouble now. They also didn't want to anger an already irate Katherine further with any sarcasm. Smart people. John closed the door and sat in the empty chair across from the seething MEO.

She sat silently for what felt like an age until, finally, she spoke. It was the most uncomfortable ten minutes of John's life. She went on and on, quoting: terms of reference; standards expected of an officer; the stupidity of his actions; the chaos he had caused on board with emergency stations; the involvement of shoreside authorities; and the potential implications this may have if it proceeds to a disciplinary charge. "What do you have to say for yourself?" She asked finally. "I'm incredibly sorry. I know what I did was stupid and completely unacceptable. I've always wanted to look around one of those big cruise ships and I saw an opportunity to do so. It was a stupid spur of the moment action, the first time I've ever done anything such as this. It's not an excuse and it's not a plea for forgiveness, it's simply what happened and I can't express my regret over it enough." said John, talking to floor. Whilst privately thinking that his new found mental capacity was awfully handy. Previously, he would've been lost for words, muttering intelligibly to the floor or the wall after such a tirade from Katherine. "You're right with everything you just said. It was indeed the first of any kind of unacceptable behaviour from you. I also do believe you and accept what you have said as a sincere apology. You absolutely cannot do anything like that again though: EVER AGAIN. You will obviously be called in to discuss this matter with both the Chief Engineer and the Captain. I will, however, be speaking to them first though and mention all that has been said here. Hopefully, this will be the end of it and no disciplinary action will be taken against you. I'd hate to lose you over something as stupid as this. You're hard working and very good at your job. I feel it would be detrimental to the ship if you were suspended and made to leave. Especially seeing as you're only a few weeks from paying off anyway. I'd much rather your relief had a decent set of notes and a good handover from you. I will mention all of this to the Chief and Captain too. You may leave." John looked up, finally meeting her eyes, nodded and left as quickly as he reasonably could for someone who had pretty much dodged a hail of bullets. He took a moment to compose himself at the entrance to the MCR again. He was very lucky. That, for as terrible as it was, it could've been so much worse. Hopefully the Chief and Captain would accept Katherine's opinion of things and that would be this whole sorry affair over with. Entering the MCR again, he once more made his way towards Arla and Callum, who were sitting at the far end of the second row of consoles. They must've been checking some of the day's alarms, or simply trying to avoid everyone else as it was known the three of them were good friends. He stood beside Arla who was sitting in the chair, Callum kneeling on her opposite side, and waited for some sort of recognition from either of them. That recognition came with a swift elbow from Arla to his stomach. She really was upset. Before, this would've really hurt and doubled him over in pain, but now it barely registered as a light tickle. Still, he reacted appropriately and grabbed at his stomach whilst uttering, what he hoped, was a suitably loud "Ooft" sound as he leant on the console. "You're a complete inconsiderate jerk you know that!?" She said in a loud carrying voice, which initiated a chorus of laughs from the remaining engineers that were sitting working at the computers along one wall. The others had left to carry on with whatever they were doing prior to his disappearance. "What were you thinking? Going off on a little wander like that? Oh, I hope you're in a world of trouble! Did the MEO reduce you to a quivering mess? I wish I could've seen that. You idiotic-" "That's enough don't you think Arla?" Callum thankfully intervened. "He's already had a new one ripped for him by the boss, so he doesn't need another one from you." "So, you're on his side, are you? You think this whole thing was funny do you!?" Callum immediately recognised the danger he was now in. Arla was in no mood to be told she was being harsh. Fearing her wrath, he raised both hands and backed off just out of arm's reach. John wasn't the only one to have felt those elbows. She may have only been five feet four, to Callum's six feet five, but she was also a featherweight Mixed Martial Arts fighter. Beyond question, her bite was far worse than her bark, so to speak; and she had a pretty decent bark. She was now looking towards Callum, her eyes flashing dangerously. "I'm most certainly not on that idiot's side" whilst passing a quick apologetic look in John's direction. "I just think he's already had it rough from the boss so maybe he's had enough?" Arla sat quietly seething for a whole minute. During that time neither John nor Callum were brave enough to break this uncomfortable silence. It was a long minute. “Fine. We did hear the MEO's raised voice go on for a good while. You’re still a-” The alarm drowned out thankfully what John was. A high-level bilge alarm was suddenly a very good thing. Callum offered to go and pump out the bilge well in the forward engine room but John seized the opportunity and was pretty much out of the MCR before Callum could even finish his sentence, such was his haste to get away from his angry friend.

As expected, he was called to the Captain’s dayroom for a talk after close of play. The typical working day being eight in the morning until five in the afternoon. This was almost as unbearable as his one-sided conversation with Katherine. Both the Chief, Brian, and the Captain, Robert, were equally unimpressed. Katherine must’ve been very convincing though as, despite their own opinions on the subject, they nonetheless agreed not to take the matter any further. John was banned from going ashore though. He was to remain onboard for the remainder of the ship's visit to Port Miami. A completely fair punishment, but still annoying as there were planned excursions for the ship's company to various places he would’ve loved to visit. Thankfully, the once again one-sided discussions were now complete, with ramifications that could’ve been so much worse, so, gratefully, he left the Captain's dayroom. He noted that it was now dinner time in the Officers’ Mess and his favourite ship combo of ham and leek pie, with bread-and-butter pudding for afters, was the day’s culinary delight. But he didn’t feel like eating at all. He just wasn’t hungry. Actually, he doubted that he would need to eat again, but food was still something he wanted to enjoy. After John had gotten changed into a shorts and T-Shirt there was a knock on his cabin door. It was Arla and Callum dressed in their Red Sea Rig. Shirt with epaulettes, trousers, cumber band and black uniform shoes. "You coming down to dinner?" queried Callum. Arla was still visibly annoyed with John but, at least she was there so it wasn't all terrible. "I don't feel like eating tonight. Guess that I just feel rubbish with all the chaos I've caused today. You know that I'm really sorry you two." With Callum looking significantly at John he continued, "I know you both must've been really worried and I can't even begin to express my regret at putting you both through that." "Well, that was a good start at doing so, but please don't be such a first-class muppet like that ever again, OK?" Arla now seemed to have gotten a bit of her sense of humour back, despite what her body language was saying. Callum looked a little uneasy but quickly re-arranged himself into a relaxed posture with a calm expression. John nodded his agreement, swearing to himself that he would do his absolute best to avoid doing something like this again in the future. With tensions easing, Arla and Callum then both left for dinner. Closing the Cabin door John sighed. He never wanted to see their faces panicked, or angry like that, ever again. He realised that it was only the strength of the friendship they shared that had prevented this sequence of events from being a complete disaster. John noted how grateful he was to have such good friends. So, he decided, he would sit them down together and tell them what was going on. Arla had actually been one of Annie's bridesmaids at their wedding, having met Callum and John on their second ship together with her being a newly qualified officer. That trip had involved a maintenance period at the ammunition docks in Crombie, Scotland, near to where Annie and John lived. Annie and Arla became friends very quickly – probably because they shared many common interests. Mulling over his thoughts, John felt that it was only fair to tell both his good friends about what really happened today together, but first was the daunting prospect of telling Annie. He really wanted to do this in person. But that wouldn't be for a few weeks yet until the end of his trip and he flew home. He didn't think he could, or even should, wait that long to tell her of such an important thing. He was, of course, worried about how she would react. After all, John was still the same person she fell in love with all those years ago. He was just a little . . . different now. He hoped she wouldn't be frightened. Annie and Stewart were the most important things in his life. If he were to lose them … such a thought was unbearable. The fear of losing both of them was now making itself a most unwelcome and prominent thought in his mind. He feared that now the seed had been planted, it would continue to grow until it drove him mad. He had to tell her right away. How though? He was over four thousand two hundred miles away and even flying takes eleven to twelve hours in the air alone. A thought popped into his head. Even though it was a ludicrous idea, was it a plausible one? He asked himself. His body was quite remarkable since the accident had transformed his cellular structure. He knew his cells were capable of wonderous things now, as demonstrated by his leap from the sand in over ten meters of water, onto the dockside. That had been easy. He wondered what else could he do. Could he move quicker? He decided that attempting to run back and forth in his cabin wasn't a bright idea, for fear of breaking down his door or maybe even leaving a John shaped dent in the ship's side. He made his way down to the flight deck, the thought of telling Annie now taking a backseat. John knew no one was in the MCR or on the bridge at the moment, so no chance of being seen by anyone on the cameras. There was no one having an evening walk around the flight deck - presumably all were at dinner he thought. The hangar door was also open so he had more room to run back and forth. So, John went right to the very back of the hangar, which was capable of storing a Merlin helicopter, and braced himself against the bulkhead to sprint towards the end of the flight deck. He closed his eyes and slowed his breathing. In through his nose, out though his barely parted lips. He was nervous and didn't know what to expect. Maybe he should just build up slowly, walk quickly, jog a bit, move up to a slow run and so on. Then his mischievous streak reared its consequences-be-damned head and all thoughts of caution vanished. He opened his eyes and a grin formed. He pushed off the bulkhead and sprinted forward, ready to stop at the end of the flight deck. Only that's not what happened. He had gone for another swim again, only this time he was now a surprising distance from the ship. John was stunned, like he had been at finding himself on the dockside earlier that day. How fast had he been travelling when he reached the end of the flight deck? A spike in adrenaline and the thrill of the moment made him realise it would've been pointless to even try to stop. So, dam the consequences, he didn't bother trying. Although he still didn't expect to have been travelling at what must've been over three hundred miles per hour. John turned a slow circle in the water. The Macarthur Causeway was across from the cruise ship terminals. He was treading water at the Watson Island end of it. In the distance the other end passed by the Miami Beach coastguard station, then onto South Beach. Cruise Ship Terminal A was also in that direction. Looking rather impressive and glaringly reflective with its glass fronted structure. The many cars travelling the causeway were just going about their business. A mild bloom of panic briefly flared up as he wondered if any of the potentially thousands of pairs of eyes had spotted his little adventure. He quickly calmed after deeming it unlikely. Travelling at that speed would've made him out to be a blur, at best, to any wandering eyes that were mainly focused on the road and cars ahead. The docked cruise ships were also a far more interesting sight than the flight deck of a smaller, but not insignificant at around two hundred meters long herself, grey auxiliary tanker. Rotating in a clockwise direction, the many cruise ships currently alongside passed by his vision and he could make out individuals in their cabins. On the Miami side of the causeway came the American Airlines Arena first, with some of the incredibly tall buildings of Miami flanking it, followed by the Maurice A. Ferre Park and finally back to Watson Island as he completed his slow revolution in the water. It had been around five minutes since he had started this impromptu swim, so John felt he could spend a little more time swimming. A little flicker of guilt appeared as he realised he was defying Katherine's order to remain onboard the ship. That guilt quickly evaporated upon diving down towards the sand below as the waters were crystal clear. Kicking his legs, he made his way under the Port Boulevard bridge, moving past Dodge Island on his left and Downtown Miami to his right, out into the channel towards Virginia key. John covered the distance remarkably quickly. Making Sailfish look positively pedestrian by comparison. By the time he'd swam under the Rickenbacker causeway, round Key Biscayne and back towards the port down government cut, Fisher Island flashing by on his left, and found himself staring up at the stern of his ship again, only an additional minute had gone by. John had remained underwater the whole time to avoid causing a mystery wake on the surface. Although he realised later, after stupidly forgetting that even objects underwater create a wake or disturbance, that some pleasure craft felt an unusual swell against their hulls. Eagle eyed observers also noticed a strange disturbance, moving at a scarcely believable speed, on the surface of what had been a very calm day. The witnesses were so few though that the talk quickly faded from downright disbelief and mocking retorts, to it simply being forgotten through the march of time. Putting on what he felt was a modest burst of speed, John once again flew from the water, only to find himself hurtling back down to the top of the ship's bridge, which was seven decks up from the main deck. Seeing as flying was only natural to birds, and with his eyes wide as dinner plates, he felt absurd as his arms and legs flailed in the rushing wind. He gathered up his scattered thoughts and decided the best thing to do was essentially brace for impact, whilst praying the aftermath didn't include a large dent in the roof of the ship's bridge. John knew his body was now incredibly resilient to physical harm, but nonetheless, as with most people he thought, the idea of breaking every bone in one's body after falling from a great height, made him squeeze his eyes shut and throw out his hands ready for the inevitable excruciating pain. He screamed. The wind stopped rushing by and all was quite calm again. Typical port noises came rushing back. Cars driving by, Ship's engines humming away, indistinct conversations, moving cranes and various other sounds were all now present once more. "Eh!?" he thought aloud. He opened his eyes. His arms were still outstretched in front of him bracing for impact, but there wasn't a big crater. He tentatively lifted one hand, still palm down, towards his head and suddenly the world flipped around and he landed with a little thud onto the deck again. This must've been how it felt as a toddler to fall over unexpectedly, with what he suspected was the accompanying shocked expression, after walking around so confidently just moments prior. John realised he now looked like someone directing traffic, whilst lying down, as he still had one hand outstretched and the other waiting for a high five. He sat up slowly, his eyes widening in surprise. There was no dent. No horrible broken limbs. He had stopped himself in mid-air just before hitting the deck. His hands had been outstretched together braced for impact. Then, when he moved one hand, he had lost balance. 'Is that what it really was though? Balance?' he thought to himself. John decided it was a question to ask his commercial pilot friend once back home. Aeronautical definitions and phrases weren't something he was currently familiar with. Then, he burst out laughing. He was howling with laughter thinking about what had all just happened. Worried about leaving a big dent in the ship rather than breaking bones. Fretting about aviation terminology, when he had been hovering mid-air above the deck. Then ending up like a fallen toddler. "What a strange day this has been so far" he said out loud to himself, as no one else was around. It had only been eight minutes since John had left his cabin to see how fast he could run. He pondered the meaning of this as he made his way back down to his private quarters three decks below. It was impossible that time itself had slowed down. 'So that must mean that I can now process information and move with such speed that time is now comparatively slower than it was before' he concluded, entering his cabin again. He came to this conclusion as that little adventure into the water, the swim and the subsequent freefall towards the bridge, had only taken eight minutes. 'Relativity,' John believed was the term. When you're bored, doing very little, time feels like it's crawling by. Yet, when you're busy, or having fun, time seems to fly by. A minute feeling like an hour. An hour feeling like only a minute had gone by. Therefore, the perception of time varied depending on how you were feeling, what you were doing, and how it engaged your mind. And seeing how he was now doing so much so fast; time was now perceptively slower john thought to himself. Admittedly, it was still a bit of a struggle to comprehend all of what was happening to him. This lack of comprehension was a thought that was repeatedly rearing up and jumping to the forefront of his musings. He wasn't even sure these thoughts of his made any sense at all. He hoped someday they would. And soon, as he still had all of it to explain to his wife and his friends! A knock at his cabin door brought him out of his thoughts and into the real world again. It was Callum and Arla back from dinner. "You two weren't at dinner for very long" John said, wondering why they were back so soon. "John we've been at dinner for the last twenty minutes at least. Pretty standard amount of time for dinner you know" was Callum's quick reply. This statement felt like a physical hit to John. He staggered back a little. He had been back in his cabin for around fifteen minutes, he realised. 'Wow, I need to be careful,' he thought to himself. It was so easy to lose track of time within his own thoughts now. With everything that was happening, all his memories and everything he knew, all now readily accessible to look at within his vast new mind palace. John noted that it was easy to spend too much time there and forget the real world existed. The prospect of never leaving his own mind terrified him. It had been a struggle to escape from his mind back in the water. If not for the shark, would he have still been down there in a comatose state? His face must've shown some of what he was feeling as Arla was holding his hand in both of hers talking to him. He snapped out his own head and caught the end of what she had been saying. ".... we're getting worried about you John," Callum nodded vigorously. "You seem to be in a world of your own at the moment. You had an accident, yes Callum told me how he found you. Now you've just been spaced out for a couple of minutes, after briefly losing your balance. Are you sure you don't need to see the med tech or a doctor?" They both looked genuinely concerned for his wellbeing and John realised that he needed to tell them now. He hated the thought of them knowing before Annie, but now that he knew he was literally losing time within his own mind, he would have to rely on them to help him get back to the real world until he was able to easily do it himself. And they deserved to know. He breathed out heavily. "You're right. Something serious is going on and it's terrifying me. Please sit down and just listen. You're probably not going to believe a word I say but again, please, do not interrupt me, OK?" They both looked worried now but, they sat down as he asked. Callum pulled out the desk chair and brought it closer to the bed while Arla sat in the armchair next to the bedside table. John sat cross legged on his bed and started the story. The snapped mooring line, the time in the water, landing on the dock, his run on the flight deck, the long quick swim and finally the fall without the thud. He tried as best he could to explain what was happening in his own head. Why he was acting spaced out. Callum failed to stifle a laugh. 'He obviously thinks I'm lying or crazy' John thought to himself. Arla was more composed but, her expression couldn't quite hide her disbelief. 'Same feelings as Callum then' he thought. "I'll show you", said John. "Arla, can you go and get that book you're reading please. You know, I haven't read it as its … not my kind of book", he said with a tinge of embarrassment. Arla raised her eyebrows slightly. She shrugged, grinned a little and left to get the book. Callum and John sat in an awkward silence. Neither quite willing to meet the others eye. Thankfully Arla's cabin was close so she was back quickly. John accepted the book from her and started to read it. Amazingly, he finished reading it before she'd sat down in the chair again. "OK, first of all that wasn't pleasant" John said with a slight shudder as he handed the book back. "Second, pick any moment, or anything at all from that book at random, and I'll recite the entire page or paragraph it is in." This confused Arla and she looked questioningly at Callum. He shrugged, as if to say 'go on then'. She sighed, with a look of 'why am I doing this' and opened the book to a page just past what looked to be like the middle. "OK, he's just taken her to a door in his house, it's locked. What does he say to her, word for word, and what's inside that room?" Arla placed the book page down in her lap and looked expectantly at John. Callum was like a tennis umpire looking between them. John didn't hesitate. He recited the passage, word for word, exactly what the character had said at that point, and then he spent the next few minutes saying aloud the next few pages from the book which go on to describe, in great detail, and much to John's chagrin, the contents of the room. Arla was staring open mouthed at John now. Callum stopped his umpire routine and asked, "Was he right." Arla nodded her head and quickly looked at the book again to double check. "Yes. Word for word. Exactly as it appeared in the book. He didn't miss a single detail. Oh my god, you were telling the truth!?" She jumped up and was staring awestruck at John with her hands over her mouth. Callum had been so engrossed in what was going on he'd fallen off the chair at Arla's sudden leap up. That in itself was not a good sign for she is normally completely composed and calm, no matter what the situation. Callum stared numbly at John too from the floor. John didn't think it were possible, but now they both looked more worried than before the demonstration. They looked at him as if he were seriously ill with an uncertain prognosis. "Please don't look at me like that. Please, I'm still . . . me". He couldn't exactly say the 'same guy' as John knew he wasn't anymore. Nonetheless, he was indeed still himself. The same person they actually knew. The person they've known for years. They both still looked sceptical. Callum was still on the floor and Arla's hands had yet to uncover her mouth; such was their shock. After what felt like an unbearable amount of time, they both settled themselves back into the chairs they'd hastily vacated. John decided it was best to let them find their own voices again. He settled himself and waited for the inevitable questions. It wasn't too long before Arla found her voice. "What are you going to do now? Let's be honest here, you're not exactly… well… 'human' anymore, are you? Have you told Annie?" 'Ouch that's nice' thought John. Arla's somewhat brutal honesty was usually something he admired and respected. This, however, felt like a bit of a kick below the belt to him though. In her opening words, Arla had struck his biggest concern like a nail on the head. With a Sledgehammer. "That's… strictly speaking true", he eventually replied. "Physically, I am most certainly not a normal person anymore. I am still a person though. I am still the John you both know. I am still… you're friend. I hope…!" He had to pause for a moment in order to reign his emotions in. "Erm… to answer your other concerns. I'm going to simply carry on with my life. I don't want things to change. I haven't told Annie yet. Something like this, I need to tell her in person. I need her to see it's me. Her husband. Stewart's father." Callum was nodding. He still had a sombre look to him. At least he seemed to be coming around though. Arla, on the other hand, was on her feet again. She was leaving. The door closed softly behind her as she exited John's cabin without uttering so much as another word. John put his head into his hands. Tears were forming in his eyes, threatening to spill out. His bed moved unexpectedly. Callum had sat down beside him, bringing him out from the depths of his mind. He felt Callum's hand grip his shoulder. "This is weird man. You're even weirder than you've always been now. You're still my weird little buddy though." This made a little chuckle fight its way from John's mouth. He was pretty tall at six foot two but, to Callum that three-inch height difference meant his buddy was tiny. "You know one day I'm just going to kick you in the delicate place. See how tall you can stand then. Git." Callum guffawed loudly at this. It was a common threat from John. He had never followed through with it though. It was now a little running joke between them. This miniscule moment was like a newly lit flame of hope for John. Hope, despite all that was happening, things could still carry on much as they have been. He couldn't at that moment express how much this meant to him. He just hoped Callum knew. Arla was a different prospect. He appreciated why she reacted the way she did. He would never go so far as to say 'understood' though. He wasn't a mind reader. So, how could he possibly understand how anyone felt? He could only appreciate the way someone felt by rationalising it in his own mind. Callum got up and once again placed his hand on John's shoulder. John looked up at his friend. They exchanged a brief nod, accompanied by a wry little smile. Callum then left as well.

It was just over an hour later when John decided he needed to do something. Even watching British Touring Car highlights couldn't dispel the discomfort crowding his thoughts. He couldn't just sit idly looking at his laptop. He was in danger of becoming lost within his own mind. And it frightened him. Losing track of time was all too easy to do. He got up from his bed and headed out of his cabin. Might not have been his brightest idea, but he needed to speak with Arla, so he decided to go and see her. She opened the door and, after a brief uncertain pause, wordlessly allowed him into her cabin. He nodded thanks and sat down in the armchair beside her bedside table (the cabins had identical furniture and layout, only mirrored on opposite sides of the ship). She sat down heavily on her bed, but close to him. An encouraging sign John thought. She reached out, looking to hold his hand. He obliged by taking her small hand in his own. Their hands were resting on the arm of the chair. It was a little act of solidarity that he appreciated immensely. He didn't care how long the silence would stretch for. She was sitting beside him. She hadn't rejected his friendship, hadn't rejected him. It was another positive sign that things could remain as they are. The silence didn't turn out to be too long. Arla took a long steadying breath. "I'm sorry for how I reacted. Something unimaginable has happened to you and I can see it actually frightens you. You are now capable of incredible things, yet you're frightened. That makes you human if you ask me." Her words - her honest as the day is bright and the night is dark words - were so perceptive and heartfelt as expected. And those few words meant oh so much to John. This was a moment, a good moment that he will always be indebted to her for. "You don't need to be sorry Arla. This is completely unexpected and scary. I can appreciate why you reacted the way you did. I'm just glad we're talking." She gave a small smile in reply. There was, however, a hint of sadness in her eyes. Was it the prospect of potentially losing a friend to the changes he was experiencing? Or was it regret for how she reacted to his news? John didn't want to know the answer. He felt it was best not to dwell on the former as it was a horrible prospect, and the latter he didn't care for. Her reaction was acceptable to him regardless of how she felt about it. "So just how strong are you now?" She asked suddenly, trying to force a conversational tone despite her inner turmoil. The truth was he had no idea. He shrugged with a face that must've looked like someone trying to avoid volunteering for something asked by Katherine, so Arla gave him a playful shove on his arm. "Come on show me I'm curious. May as well see if I can still kick your butt (something she was very capable of doing previously as evident through several painful sparring sessions) or if you're now some sort of superman who can finally keep up with me." John laughed as he stood up. Arla was smiling expectantly now, so he thought it was best to do as she wished to keep her happy. Annie was the only person he knew that was scarier than Arla when upset, so keeping her happy was usually an excellent idea. He looked around the cabin for something to lift. Finding nothing suitable he looked back at Arla. "Hold your ten-kilogram medicine ball (why she insisted on bringing this with her on each ship was a mystery to him as it took up a lot of luggage space) on your chest and lay down at the edge of your bed." She looked mystified at this, but did as he asked. The ball wasn't strictly necessary to test his strength. It was simply to allow him to place his hand higher up her back as the ball would change the place at which she would be balanced on a pivot point, in this case his hand. And he wanted his hand as far from her bottom as he could get it. The last person that touched her bottom without permission, one of the unpleasant engineers sadly still on-board the ship, ended up with two broken fingers. He claimed it was from a heavy section of pipe landing on his hand after he'd removed the bolts holding it in place. John, Callum and Arla knew he was a liar. Katherine was suspicious (she was very good at assessing the team's interactions and preventing any conflicts from getting out of hand), the others just found him to be an idiot for injuring himself so clumsily. John was pretty much certain she couldn't actually cause him any harm now, but was still reluctant to give her an excuse to try. Besides, no matter what the reason or mitigating circumstances, if he were ever to touch another woman's bottom, Annie would murder him. No matter how invulnerable he is now. Arla was now laying at the edge of her bed, the medicine ball held on her chest, looking confused at the strange request. John stood beside her and leant forward, reaching out with his hand. "May I?" he inquired. His hand in line with the point of her back where he knew she could be easily balanced on. She nodded yes, still looking confused. John slid his hand under her back and lifted her easily off the bed. She panicked slightly at being lifted up but quickly tensed up her body to avoid falling off his hand. He kept his arm completely straight, stood up to his full height, and lifted her up until his arm was now perpendicular to his body. It was like lifting a feather to him. It barely registered to him that she weighed anything at all. Arla turned her head to look at him, perhaps thinking what a peculiar sight this must be in her usual calm and methodical manner, but she had the face of someone who had just seen big-foot riding a unicorn. John couldn't help but laugh out loud at the face of his close friend. She looked dumbfounded. Arla looked over her shoulder down onto her bed, her expression changing as it felt like she was levitating above it now, then looking back towards John again. Appearing even more dumbfounded but now with a subtly arched eyebrow included in her expression. She was impressed. "OK you can put me down, gently, please." Putting emphasis on the 'gently' part. John slowly and completely in control, put her back down onto the bed. A curious expression was on Arla's face now, with her eyes a touch narrowed. Before John could decipher the meaning behind her expression, the not-insignificant ten-kilogram medicine ball was flying towards his face after a powerful shove from Arla. If stunningly quick reflexes hadn't been part of John's new repertoire of abilities, the medicine ball would've probably broken his nose and the orbital bones each side of it. Thankfully, those reflexes were now stunningly quick. There was a sudden widening of Arla's eyes, her powerful triceps bunched up then extended with such speed, a striking Black Mamba would be put to shame. The ball then raced towards a facial impact, only to be intercepted by John's hand well before the intended final destination. The loud clap of the impact made them both nervously glance around, for fear of disturbing the other engineering officers in neighbouring cabins. John intently focused on the surrounding sounds. First Officer Thomas Finch wasn't in his cabin, forward of Arla's, and neither was the ship's other billeted Second Officer, Sandra Baker, in her cabin the other side of Arla's. They were both in the Officer's Bar, for it was Friday night after all. After listening for only a few seconds, he realised that the only officer still in his cabin was Callum, who was watching a romantic comedy on his laptop. Other than that, there was Arla, who had a great deal of surprise on her face judging by her expression, as she realised that John had a non-broken face. Everyone else was either in the bar or was ashore sampling Miami's famous night-life. John re-focussed his attention back to his mischievous, to say the very least, friend who had sprung up from her bed and was reaching out to retrieve the heavy medicine ball. 'My turn' was the not quite as mischievous a thought that John had. Arla had taken hold of the medicine ball and went to put it away in her wardrobe again. Only she didn't get that far. The ball stayed exactly where it was in the palm of John's hand. She wasted no time, gripped the ball in her arms, leapt up, looped one leg over and then under his arm with an impressive mid-air half pirouette, hooked her ankle into the crook of the opposite knee and threw her weight forward, going for a flying arm-bar, a move he was painfully familiar with. Rather than ending up on the floor, with Arla's leg across his throat and an arm being hyper-extended, like in those uncomfortable memories, he remained standing this time without moving at all – not even a slight movement. It was hard to decide which sight would've been more curious. The balancing act, or the one where Arla was now wrapped around his arm, again suspended in the air, looking at the blue carpet, with a dawning look of resignation on her face. John ducked his head a little to find her bright green eyes meeting his own. They both burst out laughing. Unfortunately, that meant Arla let go of the arm she had been suspended by and landed in a heap, bent over double in a very awkward looking position. John could've tried to catch her but for two reasons. One, he didn't want to. The medicine ball was still in his hand after all. Two, even if he did, the laughter racking his body rendered him temporarily incapable of doing so. After struggling back to her feet, she did land on her head after all John just realised with a jolt; Arla no longer looked impressed. Nor did she look happy. She looked very unhappy. Now instincts took over. Instincts gained from many years of friendship with the five-foot four mixed martial artist. He held up his hands placatingly and took a step back, whilst maintaining eye contact with what were now bright green irises of fury, hoping the look of contrite would be enough to pacify her. The episode briefly struck John as ludicrous, when considering the immense physical attributes he now possessed. But instinct is hard to ignore and completely dismissed the notion. Arla held out her hand, demanding the medicine ball. John was in no hurry to add fuel to a raging inferno so he placed the ball into her outstretched hand right away. She stepped forward, gripped his shoulder, forcibly turned him around and they both made towards the door. Her grip was unsurprisingly firm on his shoulder and she wasn't letting go, even after exiting her cabin. Arla directed him aft, towards the stern and the flight deck one level below them. They navigated the passageway, the internal then external door, the stairs down which doubled back on themselves, towards the entrance to the hangar, as a pair, with her grip on his shoulder not relenting for one moment. She finally let go of John's shoulder with a shove, moving him towards the centre of the large empty hangar, and stood facing him with the medicine ball ominously still in her hand. "If a bull shark can't even scratch you, despite fancying your hand for lunch, then I believe throwing this ball at your face shouldn't do any harm either". He doubted very much merely 'throwing' the ball was what Arla was about to do. Nonetheless, he meekly nodded his understanding of the situation and closed his eyes ready to accept her actions. The medicine ball was going to smack him in the face, with a great deal of force, delivered by the fearsome fighter. Despite having his eyes closed, he still wanted to brace himself for the impact. John focused to pick up the surrounding sounds, hoping to hear the whistle of the ball as it was hurtling towards his face. The sounds of the running generator, cooling water pumps and the water circulating in the pipework, air compressors and fuel oil purifiers were all easily distinguishable many decks below. Dozens of voices were emanating from the crew bar a few decks above the engine rooms, along with many from the Senior Rate's bar on the same deck near where they currently stood. The noise from the Officer's bar, on the deck above the hangar floor, was also easy for John to make out. With his eyes closed, intently focusing on all of those sounds, he realised that they were all appearing as many individual, but easily distinguishable, wave patterns occupying a certain portion of his mind. Similar to how his pain receptors were lighting up in their own area whilst he was in the water earlier. Curiosity piqued; he focused a little harder on specific sounds. The sound waves of the purifier, rotating at one thousand seven hundred and thirty revolutions per minute, were slightly more distorted than the others he could 'see', for the purifiers were in a separate room within the upper level of the engine room. The rooms fire-retardant insulated metal bulkheads were muffling the sound waves as they resonated throughout the compartment. With a little more focus, those visible sound waves morphed into a very clear monochromatic image of the entire compartment. John could picture the compartment. One purifier for fuel oil, the other for lubricating oil. There were tools on the workbench next to some oily rags. Katherine better not find those, John thought to himself, as ship's husbandry was very important for fire safety. Inboard of the workbench on the aft bulkhead were the starter panels for both purifiers. The various buttons and selector switches clearly visible as if he were standing right there. There are also digital touch-screens on each panel, but as they were each one smooth surface, he couldn't make out the display.

The image grew and spread outward from the purifier room, now more sound waves were morphing, from fluctuating sine waves, into distinct shapes. The entire engine room, along with the multitude of equipment and pipework within it, was there. The Deck above with an incinerator, garbage processing space and a switchboard room came into focus. Like ripples on a pond, the image continued to grow, deck by deck from bottom to top. The MCR came into focus on the next deck up, then the crew bar, and the dozens of rowdy occupants. It was initially quite the blur and took a moment for everything to materialise. Jumping up several decks, he could see Arla and himself standing facing one another in the hangar. She was leaning back slightly, the medicine ball in her hand reaching behind her, like a pitcher going for a strike. Moving past that, the occupants of the Officer's bar, Thomas and Sandra among them, were all standing around talking with drinks of some kind in hand. The Ship's bridge, a further two decks above Thomas and Sandra, was just coming into focus when all of a sudden, a huge spherical shape, whistling through the air obscured everything. The medicine ball hit John squarely in his face. Intently focused on what he could picture from sound, he forgot to brace himself and the ball savagely rocked his head backwards. It didn't hurt at all, but was very much a surprise and his eyes flew open again to greet the real world. He spotted the ball lazily rolling away, then saw Arla with her arms crossed, face a touch flushed from the exertion of launching the retreating ball, with a slightly haughty expression playing across her features. "I secretly hoped that was going to hurt you" was all she said, after huffing some loose strands of brown hair from her face. John was only too happy, for once, to disappoint his friend. "Would you be happier if I asked you to do that again?" He enquired. Arla jerked her head backwards and looked astonished at such an odd request. Her abrupt shift from astonishment to eagerness as she launched herself to retrieve the ball, was a little bit dismaying for him. 'Maybe she landed on her head harder than I realised' was John's interpretation of his friend's willingness to throw things at him. At least that's what he hoped, rather than some deep-rooted desire to hurt him. "Pardon me here, but you seem awfully eager to try to hurt me again." He had to clarify her desire, for the latter scenario was immensely troubling him. Arla had now retrieved the ball and was slowly walking back to him. As she got closer, he noticed that she looked a little taken aback and, shockingly, a little hurt by John's statement. Having returned, she stood stoically in front of him, biting her lip as if trying to figure out how best to say what was on her mind. "I wasn't lying when I said I hoped that it was going to hurt you but, let's be fair here, we both knew that wasn't going to hurt you. Plus let's not forget, you literally just dropped me on my head. So, I think I had every right to be a bit angry with you. That's passed now though - OK? This is me realising I don't have to hold back with you anymore." John's fleeting analysis was that whilst he thought, like Arla, that it wasn't going to hurt, he wasn't actually sure. Notwithstanding, most importantly from her comments, the penny had dropped and John realised that she was holding back all the times they had sparred. John was quite significantly taken aback by this. He had always had a deep respect for Arla, but now – because of her comments - it had grown exponentially, especially realising she could've hurt him far worse throughout all their sparring sessions. "So, John, fair warning, from now on I can train and spar like I do when I'm at home. You know, it's like having a favourite film, but while you're away you can't watch it, so you have to make do with what there is." He fully understood the reference here. There was no denying his fondness for watching films on his laptop. This meant that Arla's sudden shift in temperament made sense to him, her logic expressed in terms she knew he could relate to. Akin to watching a fantastic cartoon for, as a matter of routine, days at home with Stewart were often spent watching animated films. Sadly, only to find later that the sequel is far inferior in terms of the quality of the animation, the vibrancy of the colours and in the storytelling. 'Here's looking at you mouse for that' John thought to himself with an air of disappointment. For as much as he was fond of watching films, Arla was equally as enthusiastic with her training. A wave of shame washed over him for even thinking, let alone actually saying aloud, his friend actually relished the thought of hurting him. "I'm sorry Arla. I shouldn't have suggested you want to -" "It's OK John, I can see why you said it. Even if you were completely wrong as usual." "Hey, I'm only wrong most . . . OK all the time when it comes to being home with Annie at least." "Aha, the two golden rules of the Campbell household. Rule number one, Annie is always right. Rule number two, if in the unlikely event Annie is possibly wrong, rule number one applies." "Annie told you !?" John responded, with his voice being a few octaves higher than normal. Arla just laughed at the obvious deep and murky he was now mired in. "Well of course she did. What, do you think women only talk about shopping, boys, clothes or gossip?" Arla had arched one of her eyebrows, looking at John with feigned dismay for his superimposed stupidity. She didn't let him respond, not even with a curt gesture, and she waited just long enough for the silence to creep towards discomfort, before laughing once again to break it. "I think it's safe to say that despite what happened to you today, you are indeed 'Still you'. For only you could be duped into discomfort like that so easily!" John couldn't help his eyes wondering around, taking in all the little details of the hangar in which they stood. Anything to avoid looking at, well, in reality, what he was actually a little aggrieved by, an excessively smug Arla. Especially as she was once again merrily laughing at the aforementioned discomfort she'd dropped him into, with no apparent desire as of yet to cease it. "OK that's enough now. For goodness sake, cheer up John, you look miserable there." "Oh, I wonder why that is Arla?" "That's quite enough of the sarcasm Mr Supreme human. Actually, that's a point. Seeing as you're now endowed with superhuman abilities, does that make you a superhero? Surely, we've got to think up a heroic alter ego for you. I mean you can't just run around as 'John Campbell'. So, you'll need a secret identity to protect those close to you from harm." "Wow, first of all you're way over-thinking this. Secondly, I'm no hero, let alone any sort of super hero. Finally, I'm not sure the world would be overly enamoured with someone who can do all that I can do now. There are too many people who like things just so. So, as long as it benefits them, no changes, regardless of the consequences for others. Never forget, those are dangerous people who would go to great lengths to keep things as they like it." "You say I'm over-thinking this!?" Arla pretty much shouted, her face arranged in a manner of bewilderment. "Arla please, I don't want anyone else to know. My life has already changed for ever now. If people knew, I would never be able to just live-in peace with Annie and Stewart. Can you imagine what all the attention would do to them?" That did it. The guilt trip. Arla took on a solemn look. She knew he was, for once, correct with what he said. If the world found out there was someone so very different from everyone else, it was impossible to predict with any certainty how it would react. No more words were needed between them. She slowly walked up to John, put the medicine ball down and hugged him. He put his arms around her and they just stood together. Now, John was really thinking about the wider consequences of his accident earlier today. He made a vow to himself, to do everything possible, to keep these super human abilities a secret. The rare gesture from Arla meant she actually understood, and accepted, the unspoken vow. They released each other after a few minutes. Understandably, both had tears in their eyes, with a few breaking free and flowing down their faces. "Thank you Arla" were the words John finally managed to force out past the lump in his throat. "No problem John," she said after taking a few moments to regain her composure. Turning around, whilst surreptitiously wiping away the tears with the back of a hand, Arla picked the medicine ball up again. After such an emotionally draining moment, John was quite happy to go back to what he'd asked before, although he wanted to explain why first. "Right, before you launch that ball at my face again, I'd like to explain why I asked you to throw it a second time." Arla nodded in agreement. "OK, before the ball hit me in the face, I was focusing on the surrounding sounds, so as to prepare myself for what potentially could've really hurt. In doing so, it became clear to me that what I could hear allowed me to form a picture in my mind. It was as if I was standing right beside what was making the noise. I was able to form an image - like a sonar to a certain degree maybe? I need to read up on how bats and marine mammals are able to see sound. Maybe it'll tell me what part of my brain became hyper developed in order for me to see sound too? As for my strength, speed and eidetic memory, I'm certain my brain has adapted specific parts, similar to how some people are mathematical savants. Fundamentally, research is the order of the day to be more certain. Did I mention I'm not hungry or thirsty now, even though I haven't eaten or drank anything since breakfast? Crikey, I think, as crazy as this may sound, that my energy maybe derived from photosynthesis now, rather than nourishment. It's like my brain knew, or at least sensed, a better way to produce energy. Plus, I think that depending on my surroundings, my brain will source the most effective method of producing energy, say if the sun was no longer a viable option. Like, for example, if I were in the frigid ocean depths, where light can no longer penetrate." Pausing for a few seconds after all those words tumbled out of his mouth. One after the other, in an unrelenting narrative as he tried to explain to Arla what had triggered the changes in his genetic make-up. "Uh OK - That's wonderful and all John, but why did you want me to throw the ball at your face again?" "I didn't explain? - Sorry, I got completely side tracked there. I felt I owed you some sort of explanation or theory at least. I'd like you to throw the ball at my face again, a third time, because it completely blotted out the picture I was seeing just then. You know, the picture that I created from sound. I want to adapt to different sounds to see if I can maintain the picture when my concentration is suddenly broken by something that I wasn't expecting. Like a flying medicine ball. Taking an overview, it took a bit of effort to develop that image and a new, more prominent or even threatening sound, completely disrupted my focus and dissolved the image to just that one noise. I think that, with a bit more effort and practise, I'll be able to see by sound alone, without losing focus on the overall image because of sudden changes. Does that make any sense?" "Let's just say you're not exactly brilliant at explaining things. How about you'd like me to repeat the experiment and throw the ball at your face again, so you can perfect your echo location skills?" "Yea that'll work." John nodded vigorously, realising he'd essentially been waffling, rather than actually making any sort of sense. It took three more attempts with the ball before he was satisfied with this new echo location sight. The first test ended up with his head being viscously rocked back again. The second was another crack in the face, but without the nodding dog routine. The third time was the charm, where he successfully avoided the projectile, whilst maintaining the overall image. He couldn't help but feel a little chuffed with himself. Arla remained a little sceptical, so she proceeded to do various additional experiments in order to test John's 'vision'. After a couple of minutes, in which he didn't miss a single tiny thing, the test had to abruptly stop. For there was something he definitely did want to miss.

"Don't you dare lift your top up Arla! That is not something I should ever see, even with my ears! Bloody hell, do you want Annie to kill me!?" Unsurprisingly, John was quite agitated once again, to the point that he was gesticulating furiously with his hands too. Reacting, Arla sheepishly let go of her top and looked around with an air of innocence, tapping her thighs to a random rhythm. He couldn't believe what his friend was about to do as it would've been completely inappropriate. Struggling to contain the fury brewing within, whilst shaking his head as if trying to control the troubling turn of events. He took a few deep breaths and looked towards his friend, who seemed to enjoy causing strife. It was more the fact that he was struggling to figure out the sudden change in Arla's personality. The thought of how the woman in front of him could go from being very modest and somewhat shy, to being incredibly, inappropriately, bold was thankfully de-railed by the same person loudly clearing their throat. "You know I wasn't actually going to do anything there – right?" "I saw an inch of your stomach. Much more than you've ever exposed in my presence previously. That was enough to ring the alarm bells." "Do you really think I'd be that stupid? After Annie had killed you, who do you think would've been next on that particular two-person hit list? So, I'm quite happy to remain breathing – thank-you! If you have to ask, I just wanted to see how you'd react and you didn't disappoint. It goes back to what I said a moment ago, it's safe to say you're still you." John's face fell appropriately into the look of someone who had just been easily duped. Again. It was an expression both Arla and Annie were very familiar with, much to his dismay. Safe to say, he was very much the same person as before the accident. At least, that thought improved his now dour mood a little. Before Arla could attempt to dupe him again, he turned around, shook his head ruefully, made towards the hangar door and out onto the flight deck to admire the now dark Miami Skyline. Quiet footsteps preceded the arrival of his manipulative little friend standing beside him. 'At least it was for entertainment rather than being malicious' John thought. Peering down, displaying a mischievous grin of his own, towards Arla, and knowing full well how she would react, he decided it was time for a little payback. "How is it someone so little, can be so evil?" The word 'little' was all that was required to trigger the desired response: A swift elbow to the ribs. Callum and John had both received a few of those brutal elbows, hence why words that could be loosely likened to short, diminutive or even petite, tended to be avoided during conversation. They hurt a lot. Well, at least they used to in John's case. Arla was never actually evil per say, she rather always thought of herself as just being playful but, she didn't like being described as small either. So throwing in that particular word, or any word of a similar meaning, guaranteed a little extra spite to the inevitable blow. John duly felt a very hard thud to the ribs exposed under his crossed arms. He waited expectantly for the outburst to follow. It was filled with language so colourful a rainbow paled in comparison. Arla was hopping around the flight deck holding her arm, a torrent of ever more colourful language spilling out from her mouth. After a couple minutes, she resumed her place beside him, with a look of utmost indignation, still cradling her arm whilst looking up at the dark star-lit sky. She glanced over and noticed the grin on his face. Before, it would've been safer to try and brush a Great White Shark's teeth. Now however, John felt it was appropriate payback. "Score one to me. Wow, you don't hear that very often." "You git John – you bloody baited me into hitting you! I forgot you're like a man of steel now. Well, you're right - yes, that's a point to you. However, it was a bit harsh though John. You know I hate being called evil, and that it actually hurts my feelings." He was well aware of her feelings on the subject, but nonetheless felt all was fair in this particular instance. She seemed to agree too as nothing further was said on the matter. They both stood in silence for a few moments longer, reflecting on the events that had transpired between them during the evening. John wasn't at all tired, despite the lateness of the hour. Arla, on the other hand, was showing obvious signs of tiredness, failing to stifle an impressive yawn. "I think you best head back to your cabin now. Looks to me like you're about ready to crash out." "I'm not that t-tired-" Another yawn escaping her mouth "Remember, it's half day Saturday tomorrow. So, it's not like I've got a full day of work to survive either." A third yawn was enough to change her tune a little towards sleep. "OK, before I head off to bed, we still have the burning question that remains unanswered. We still don't really know how strong you are. Sadly, I can't kick your butt anymore, that much I do know." Ruefully, she was still holding her arm. "But, what can you actually lift now?" John genuinely had no idea what he was capable of lifting and seeing the vacant expression on his face, coupled with the lack of a response forthcoming, Arla walked back into the hangar to look around for something heavy. Handily, the hangar had a stowage space containing free weights and various other bits of gym equipment. She ignored the weights that were enough to satisfy even an Austrian oak, and continued to walk around the space until she spotted something more suitable to lift. A yellow fork-lift truck had been brought up from one of the holds below, in preparation for main engine spares being craned onto the flight deck tomorrow morning. Arla sat on the driver's seat and looked expectantly at John. Challenge issued and Challenge accepted. He walked up-to the brightly coloured vehicle, gauging where would be the best point to try and lift it. He had to kneel down to slide his hand under it, a little off centre, up to the elbow. Without waiting for any signal from Arla, causing her to panic slightly and grab the steering wheel, he did exactly as earlier in her cabin. Only now it was with Arla on a Forklift-Truck. She leant out slowly and peered down from her unusual perch, mouth agape in shock. John looked up at her, no trace of strain at all visible. He could've been holding up a paper-clip for all the effort it took. It dawned on Arla that they hadn't even scratched the surface of how strong he was now, and it was mind-boggling. Suddenly, she was bright eyed and awake again, there had to be something heavier nearby. Without waiting to be put down she nimbly leapt from the seat, cheekily stepping on John's head, and landed gracefully back on solid ground again. John didn't exactly appreciate being literally stepped on, never mind his head being the step. He gently lowered the Forklift down so as not to damage it. Arla was standing at the port side of the flight deck, leaning on the railing, intently scanning the surrounding docks for something else that could be picked up. There was something very large. Something that was also used to pick things up ironically. It was a large mobile crane sitting patiently near their ship, waiting to lift the main engine spares onto the flight deck tomorrow morning. "Do you think you could pick that up?" She pointed at the crane, eagerly eyeing John for a response. "Well, I guess I could try. Put your phone away though. No videos or pictures. Don't look at me like that, we both agreed to keep this under wraps and the less proof there is floating around, the better. You know I trust you explicitly before you say it, but what if you forgot such a photo or video was on your phone? What if someone else then saw it? I know with it being you it's nigh on impossible, but there is however that very small chance it could get out." Arla reluctantly nodded and put her phone away. John gripped her shoulder and smiled his thanks. He then jumped over the railing, after making sure the flight deck cameras weren't facing him, landing effortlessly on the dockside quite far down from where they were standing. After casually strolling towards the large vehicle, eyes darting around like a child's in a toy store making sure no one was around, he stood in line with its centre and looked back up at the expectant Arla. She nodded enthusiastically and gestured impatiently with her hands for him to get on with the show. John got down onto all fours and crawled under the crane, stopping and laying on his back beneath what he reckoned was the centre of gravity. Lifting one hand, looking like a traffic cop for the second time that day, he pressed it firmly against the crane's stiff chassis. The massive suspension coils groaned as they were eased off their vast mechanical burden. His eyes were wide open in surprise. This was unexpected. He was lifting the huge lump of machinery single-handed and it wasn't difficult. Buoyed by the turn of events, he twisted by the waist and propped himself up onto his elbow, still keeping the crane balanced on the outstretched straight arm. The vehicle was flexing slightly on his hand and he was hoping it wouldn't snap in two, now that it was completely off the ground. John then very slowly, very carefully, leant up and moved his weight from elbow to hand. He rolled a little onto one side, slid one leg up and rested on his knee. Closing his eyes, again hoping there wouldn't be a loud cracking sound, he then simply stood up straight. John was now standing up, as if volunteering to answer a question from Katherine during the morning get together in the MCR. Only now there was large crane balanced on the palm of his hand. "What the actual ... are you kidding me!" Arla was standing with both hands on her head shouting in complete and utter disbelief. After reversing the manoeuvre he'd used to lift the crane, at a painfully slow speed, John crawled back out from under it and leapt up towards the flight deck. Adrenaline can be a wonderful thing, making people capable of heroic acts of strength and courage in dire situations. It can also cause one person to completely miss a ship's large flight deck and land in the water - on the opposite side. Arla had gotten half way across the flight deck by the time John had leapt from the water for the third time that day. She came to an abrupt halt and stood biting her lip, fists clenched standing rigidly as if to attention, trying desperately not to burst out laughing. It was a valiant effort, but ultimately came just short of succeeding. Arla was in hysterics, collapsing down to all fours, bucking and heaving, with uncontrollable snorts and wheezes. It was most undignified. And that was coming from someone drenched head to toe, with bits of sea weed and various other bits of unpleasantness stuck to him. It took a good few minutes for Arla to regain some semblance of composure and stagger back to her feet, tears streaming down flushed cheeks. "You look ridiculous John. And with some of the faces you've had this evening that is saying something. Oh, what just happened, well that alone was worth staying awake for. What an incredible jump though. It must've been at least fifty meters horizontally, never mind the vertical distance you went up into the air too. And the crane. You lifted the massive crane as if it were a toy! It must weigh over a hundred tonnes! Yet you lifted it just like that." She was slowly pacing back and forth in front of him now, expressing herself with her hands too, looking at him every now and again, to emphasise the key points of her little monologue. The hilarity of just moments before was completely forgotten, for Arla was all serious and composed again. Her face lit up with a fresh idea. "We've got to get Callum and show him what you can do. It'll blow his mind. Christ, my mind is blown already!" "I'm not sure Callum would appreciate being woken up. You know he goes to bed early after a duty day." "I know but it's Saturday tomorrow so he'll be fine." "OK, hey I can ask him about the film he was watching earlier. Sounds like a film Annie would enjoy." "You didn't tell me he was watching a romantic comedy!" Arla said with mild indignation. She knew that was Annie's favourite type of film. "I've been a little busy." She seemed appeased by that, nodding begrudgingly, as if it was indeed her who had been wanting to test his strength. "I'm going to tease him something rotten about this. Do you know what film it was?" "I think it was about a young woman who falls for a guy who can turn into a wolf but, she is also in love with a vampire." "Wait, that's not a romantic comedy. That film is a love story!" She pretty much shrieked with glee at the prospect of how badly Callum was going to get teased for this. Then her face darkened a little and she rounded on John. "How on earth did you think that was a romantic comedy?" "It sounded really cringey, so I thought it must've been deliberately bad. Making it a comedy to me." "If Annie heard you describing one of her favourite films like that, I'm pretty sure you'd spend the night on the couch. Besides those are actually really good films." John turned to face Arla, eyebrows pretty much disappearing into his hairline. She caught the look and turned away, putting on what to her must've been a dignified silence, thus cutting the topic of conversation short. They both walked up-to Callum's cabin door and Arla knocked several times. There was a grunt of surprise, an e-reader being put down, fumbling for a light switch, clothes being put back on and then a few of his long strides towards the door, which was opened a fraction, with only an annoyed face visible in the gap. "Do you two have any idea what time it is? And why do you look like you went for another swim John?" Callum immediately noticed the wet clothes. John also just noticed the nice trail of wet footprints too, leading all the way from the door at the end of the passageway. Before Arla could turn round and see the trail, he dashed to the cleaning locker, grabbed a mop and quickly cleaned up his mess. Taking off his wet shoes and socks, placing them back into his cabin a couple doors down from Callum's, in the process. By the time she had turned around the passageway was clear of footprints, John was barefoot and his clothes were steaming slightly. Moving quickly generates a lot of air resistance, which can generate heat in sufficient amounts to dry clothes it seems. John was glad he had very short hair, otherwise he'd look like a spikey blue hedgehog right about now. The speed at which he could move no longer surprised Arla, she just shrugged and looked back towards Callum. He wasn't quite so used to this and was looking like he'd been hit across the head with a mallet. It took a few moments for him to be able to find his voice again. "Whoa, that was . . . fast." Was all he could just about squeak out. He guessed correctly, that Arla and John wanted to show him something. So, after opening his door wider to allow them in to wait, he went back to the desk chair and retrieved the t-shirt he'd yet to put back on. John noticed a slight flutter in Arla's heartbeat, but kept his gaze ahead and decided not to potentially embarrass her by mentioning it. She knew how well he could hear though so still shot him a quick nervous glance as they both stood waiting for Callum to put his shoes on. Despite the invitation to wait inside, they both just stood at the doorway, in a bit of an awkward silence, and waited for Callum to join them. The three of them then headed back out and down towards the flight deck. Arla was telling Callum what she and John had been doing prior to interrupting his reading. He was walking silently beside her listening intently, not bothering to hide his disbelief or surprise. She didn't need to keep her voice down as the Friday night officer's bar crowd, which currently contained all the other officers, except for the duty personnel, was being as raucous as normal. Out on the flight deck, again by the port railing, Arla pointed out the crane John had lifted to Callum, then went on to describe the circumstances behind his third swim of the day. She laughed again at the recollection but only for a short while. Callum was obviously struggling to believe what he was being told, looking somewhat suspiciously between Arla and John. "What you did with the book back in your cabin was pretty amazing. The disappearing shoe act was quite something too. All of that though sounds ludicrous - I'm sorry." He held up his hands as if to ward off the inevitable criticism from Arla. "Come on. Do you really expect me to believe you picked up a massive mobile crane like it were a toy? Or that you jumped so far you flew over this entire flight deck?" He said holding his arms out wide to emphasise the distance. "Callum, you seemed to believe everything John said earlier, so what's so hard to believe about what I've just told you?" Arla asked growing irritable. "I didn't know what to believe then to be honest. It was all kind of shocking so, I just went along with it, hoping to avoid an awkward situation." "You mean awkward like this?" Once again, Arla hit the nail on the head right away and now she had her arms crossed angrily over her chest. Callum nodded, looking apologetically at John while doing so, whilst conveniently avoiding Arla's angry gaze. John didn't mind the insinuation that both he and Arla were essentially lying. It was, after all, quite the extraordinary tale. "Let me show you something, to prove Arla and I didn't drag you out of bed for no good reason." Callum shrugged and nodded again. Arla was looking on with rapt attention, waiting for another spectacle of strength. John looked around for something simpler than picking up the crane again. His eyes lingered on the stern of the cruise ship he'd supposedly toured earlier that day. The one with the fateful snapped mooring line, now removed and replaced by a new one. He shifted his gaze up towards the top of the ship at the weather deck above all the passenger cabins. 'I can jump to that' John thought confidently. Without telling Arla or Callum what his intentions were, he focused on that passenger free open deck, bent his knees and leapt clear of the flight deck, soaring upwards and onwards towards the empty space behind the cruise ship's towering funnels. Such is life and learning though, things didn't quite go to plan. The empty deck zipped by below John, much to his astonishment and growing sense of dread, and the ship's port funnel was getting ominously closer. The word John said aloud before thudding into the funnel, would've been entirely appropriate after hitting a hand with a hammer. There was an incredibly loud crash, like that of a massive bell being struck by a giant, and he tumbled from the new oddly shaped indentation, sprawling haphazardly on the deck below. "Oh dear." Was all he could say, laying on his back spread eagled, looking up at the funnel. Standing up again, he peered around and listened intently for any sign of movement. The thunderous noise had evidently disturbed quite a few people, the fact that the whole ship shuddered perceptibly may have also done so, and they were beginning to move around wondering what on earth had just happened. More worrying though, members of the ship's crew were approaching the doors to the deck he currently occupied alone. Without waiting to be discovered, and not wishing to try and explain how he got there either, John turned and moved quickly to the aft railing, spotting Arla and Callum in the distance rooted to the spot on his own ship's flight deck. Callum had his hands on his head and jaw dropped comically, Arla's hands were covering her mouth but were now waving at John energetically to get back over there. He was stuck momentarily with indecision. Should he just run, find his way through the massive ship towards the gangway, then off and back onto his own ship? Or should he leap into the water for the fourth time that day? The first time on purpose though. A door handle moved in the distance behind him, someone was about to emerge onto the deck he currently occupied alone. The sound brought him back to focus. Water it was. He leapt over the railing, taking great care not to leap too far again, and plummeted once more towards the now darkened Miami water. John remained in the water and slowly swam towards the twin propellers of the ship he was working on. Listening intently, it was apparent that the dent in the funnel hadn't gone unnoticed. There were now several people milling around beneath it, staring dumbstruck at the oddity. Others were looking around in vain, trying to figure out what caused it. Arla and Callum had both darted into the hangar to hide as soon as John leapt over the railing. They stood hidden behind the bulkheads either side of the large open sliding door. John continued swimming, heading towards the bow and port side of the ship, passing between the propellers. He hung suspended in the water next to a ladder opposite the bow thruster tunnel, then cautiously gripped one of the rusty rungs and poked his head clear of the water's surface. Once he was certain no one was looking his way, or towards the gangway back onto his own ship, he raced up the ladder then back along the dockside towards the gangway. Straight up the gangway, towards the stern and the external staircase leading up-to to the hangar, he appeared behind Arla on the port side. She jumped slightly, as the brief gust of wind announced his arrival beside her, and punched his chest angrily for scaring her. Air resistance had once again dried his clothes for him. John grimaced and mouthed 'sorry'. Callum hadn't even noticed his return and only looked towards them at the sound of the punch hitting John's chest.

He quickly overcame his shock, peered around the bulkhead he was hidden behind and, satisfied no one was looking, bolted over to join John and Arla. The three of them stood there in silence, listening to the voices carrying over from the confused crew of the other ship. As the whole situation was so bizarre, they were all grinning and struggling not to laugh. Arla poked her head out from behind the bulkhead one last time, watching with growing amusement as more people gathered around the base of the dented funnel, then gestured with her hand for John and Callum to follow her back into the accommodation area. They hurried as stealthily as possible and snuck into John's cabin, closing the door quietly despite there being no need on account of the ongoing noise emanating from the bar, and dumped themselves into the spots they'd occupied after dinner earlier. "Oh my god!" Arla broke the silence, slapping the arms of the chair repeatedly and stamping her feet at the same time. She then pitched forward clutching her stomach laughing hard, yet again. If laughing really was good medicine, Arla would've been a medical marvel that day. Callum's laughter was muffled by his hands, covering a tear-streaked face, as he rocked back on the chair he occupied. John sat quietly, grinning ear to ear, watching his friends laugh at the misadventure he'd just taken part in. It was going to be a great story between them, of which they would no doubt delight in recalling with Annie back home. A story he was enormously grateful for as despite everything that had happened, Arla and Callum were still his close friends, and they were both sitting there with him. 'Maybe things really are going to be alright' John thought happily. It had been an unforgettable day. The day wasn't quite finished yet though. Before the three of them said their good-nights, there was one last thing to be addressed, something that Arla had only just remembered. “Hey Callum, what film were you watching earlier?” Callum looked confused and a little nervous as he noticed that Arla had a wicked looking grin on her face, eyes wide with merriment. John wished he had some popcorn.

Chapter 2 – Some Things Never Change

A loud ringing phone rudely brought John back to the real world with an unpleasant jolt. He had been reliving a wonderful memory of driving a Mini JCW race car around the Knockhill race track. John remembered it was Saturday, but that was also the problem. His eyes flew open, yep it was Saturday, he was in his cabin, not at the Knockhill race circuit near home as he had been recalling with that memory. "Oh no," he exclaimed loudly, whilst dashing around frantically to get ready for work. In five minutes time, the working day was about to begin at eight am. Less than thirty seconds later he was, as casually as possible, walking into the MCR ready to start the day. Arla was standing by the back door into the MCR still on the phone trying to call him. She noticed him, rolled her eyes and breathed a sigh of relief, before placing the phone back onto the receiver. Callum was sitting at the terminal in front of the phone and looked relieved to see John too. As he walked by the other Engineers, gathered for the usual morning meeting, a familiar voice piped up followed by a self-satisfying guffaw. "Where have you been John? Another cruise ship tour?" It was Luke Watson, a super numerary, or non-billeted, Second Officer who was leaning back in one of the two computer chairs. To say that he wasn't popular was too kind. Luke liked to think he knew it all and regularly suggested how the other engineers, even the vastly more experienced first officer Thomas, could do their jobs better, whilst always seeming to shy away from his own jobs. No one paid Luke any attention, having grown numb to the spiteful remarks and frequent suggestions, and John didn't even bother to look in his direction as he walked by towards Arla and Callum. John mouthed a quick thank you to Arla, who was now standing beside Callum at what was usually the First Officer's ventilation terminal, so she gave a little smile and nodded in a 'no worries' kind of way in reply. Callum reached up and clapped him on the shoulder as he arrived beside his friends. The three of them always stood together during the morning meetings, in earshot of Katherine and the others but slightly off to the side. It wasn't that they were anti-social, they just preferred each other's company on the rare occasions all three of them were on the same ship. The other engineers knew this and often teased them about it. The teasing never extended to any lewd remarks though, owing to Arla's mixed martial arts prowess. The story of how a Third Officer on a previous ship was left crying in agony, in the grips of a well-executed kimura from Arla, and apologising in a quavering voice, was widely known. The officer in question wasn't ridiculed for being humbled by a five-foot-four woman. He was ridiculed because of how stupid it was to suggest certain things in earshot of that particular woman. John still hoped for the day Luke would be equally as stupid, the two broken fingers weren't enough, he felt, for what the man did to Arla. Callum noticed Luke was staring in their direction, so he decided to provoke him by rubbing an eye with the index and middle finger of his left hand, the same two fingers Arla broke the previous week. He clearly felt the same way as John did. Luke was incensed and jumped up from the chair, pushing passed Sandra and knocking her into Thomas, spilling his morning tea over him. He was marching angrily over to Callum, who looked up in mock surprise, followed by several choice words from Sandra and Thomas. John stood motionless, arms crossed, looking bored at the scene. The possibilities of what he could do to the angry man, in the blink of an eye, were highly amusing, but he just let things play out as they weren't going to escalate any further. One little glance from Arla saw to that. She didn't even move, just looked up on hearing the commotion, and then looked Luke straight in the eye, as if daring him to carry on towards them. Luke stopped dead in his tracks mid stride, wobbling slightly as he balanced in the ungainly pose. The MCR had gone silent. Even Katherine was curious to see what Luke would do next. Normally everyone would clamour in to try and diffuse a potentially volatile situation, but this was Luke, and they weren't convinced by the story of how he'd broken those fingers. He now stood in no-man's land between the two groups of engineers. His eyes were darting around for a saving grace, something he could use to smugly explain why Thomas was now splattered with tea. Or why Sandra was being helped up from the floor by Kevin, the other Third Officer onboard along with Callum and John. Katherine was standing watching Luke intently, giving the irate Second Officer a chance to apologise before she pulled him aside quietly and reprimanded his behaviour. Luke wasn't quick enough and, much to the silent delight of everyone watching, Katherine decided to break the building tension. "Luke, can you come with me please, we need to discuss your outstanding jobs." Luke did in fact have a lot of outstanding jobs on his maintenance workload, but everyone present knew that wasn't what was about to be discussed. "You know Luke, you try to mock me for being late, yet you can't seem to complete your own jobs on time." John just couldn't resist retaliating for Luke's welcoming words a moment ago. A sharp look from Katherine, who thankfully didn't actually say anything, made him realise the remark was not appreciated. He hoped it wouldn't lead to another awkward conversation with the MEO later. The MCR remained in silence until Katherine and Luke entered the Engineer's Office. Once the door was shut, a lively conversation broke out between Thomas, Sandra and Kevin. Some of the language used to describe Luke was distinctly unpleasant, but not unwarranted under the circumstances. Arla looked at Callum and John, assuming one of the two had done something to provoke Luke. John was looking at Arla and Callum thinking the same thing. Cottoning on to the fact that their faces both bore a querying expression, they looked down at Callum who was innocently checking various screens on the terminal. Arla and John leant on the console either side of him, he was ignoring their stares and focused resolutely on the screen, trying to catch his attention. "What did you do Callum?" John cracked and asked before Arla could. He was ignored. "What did you do Callum?" Now it was Arla asking in a moderately dangerous tone. Callum flinched away but turned his head a little towards her. He was smart enough not to ignore that tone of voice. "I had an itchy eye, since when was it a crime to scratch it?" He replied indignantly. Arla raised her eyebrows in response. John felt Callum was playing a dangerous game for someone sitting well within her reach. She was rarely quick to violence, unless of course certain words were uttered or something completely inappropriate was done, but at the same time, she had very little patience for games such as this. Her bark could often be as brutal as her considerable bite, and she had a fantastic repertoire of choice words at her disposal. Callum saw sense and relented. "I may have itched my eye using my index and middle fingers." He said with a sheepish grin, leaning back from the screen, staring towards the MCR door, which Katherine and Luke had not long walked through. Arla and John rolled their eyes, stood upright and looked at one another, now both grinning like Callum. John clapped him on the back good naturedly, only for the clap to end up being brutally hard and thus worryingly loud. Arla quickly shoved Callum down against the terminal, so to hide him behind the screen, before Kevin, Sandra and Thomas noticed the silent scream on his face. The three engineers had stopped their conversation and were looking inquisitively towards Arla, the hidden Callum and John, clearly wondering what the loud noise had just been. "Sorry, there was a fly. I got it though." said John with, what he hoped was a nonchalant smile. Arla still had her hand on Callum, his mouth still wide open in a silent scream, and she was smiling in a similar manner. The three of them all shrugged. Kevin and Thomas left the MCR via the front door, discussing a job on the inert gas plant, while Sandra left via the rear door heading towards the steering gear compartments. Walking by, she didn't notice Callum sitting with his eyes shut and head resting on the terminal, neither was it noticed that Arla had hastily crossed her arms and was focused intently on the screen above his head. John had moved to his left to look at something on the next terminal screen. Once Sandra had vacated the MCR, John and Arla focused their attention on Callum again. He was banging his head lightly against the terminal, trying to distract himself from the pain caused by John's 'little' clap. John was fidgeting guiltily. He didn't mean to hurt his friend and felt awful for doing so. Arla just gave a 'what-can-you-do?' gesture, then looked back towards their hunched over friend.

Callum finally regained some semblance of composure and sat upright, although his eyes were still closed and the normally smiling mouth was a tight grimace. "Ow. Ow. Ow - So Much Ow." Callum muttered, punctuating each 'Ow' with a theatrically deep breath. "I'm sorry Callum, I didn't mean to do that." Whilst talking John very gently placed a hand on Callum's shoulder. However, it still caused his friend to flinch slightly though. "It's OK John, I know you're still adapting and all that." Whilst concerned about their friend, John and Arla quickly glanced around to make sure no one was in earshot. "But please, please don't do that again. Ow." "Honest, I will not clap you on the back like that again, I swear." "To be honest, I found it kind of funny and I wouldn't mind if you did it again." Arla said, with a slight grin, only once she realised Callum was actually OK. John looked at her exasperatedly, throwing up his hands in an annoyed gesture. Callum slowly turned towards her and, not really thinking due to the pain he was still in said; "You're lucky you're cute, or I'd never speak to you again." Before he hunched back over the terminal again, not noticing Arla bite her lips, look away quickly and blush slightly. John looked back towards the screen of the terminal he was stood beside to spare her feelings. He suspected that their years of friendship was perhaps developing into a little more for Arla. John would be thrilled to see them both together. Glancing quickly towards Arla he noticed she was no longer blushing, but looking at him beseechingly. Knowing what the look meant, he gave her a small nod of acknowledgement. John would never discuss her feelings about anyone else, with anyone else. That included with his own wife Annie, such was the respect he holds for Arla. Her small smile in return was genuine and heartfelt. Body language accounts for the vast majority of communication and Arla's face was full of gratitude. Callum had picked up on their silence and was once again leaning back in the chair, now looking between his two suspiciously silent friends. "What's going on here?" he asked, nervously eyeing John's hands while doing so. "Well, I gave you my word that I wouldn't clap you on the back like I just did ever again. It doesn't mean I won't do other things unintentionally to both of you that may hurt you. Arla seems to have realised that too, hence why we are both a bit quiet just now. And it actually frightens me." Arla was taken aback by the statement, not expecting those words at all considering what had just transpired between them. She saw the look on John's face and quickly caught on. What had started off as a diversionary tactic, to avoid an awkward moment over the silence, for John, had brought forth an uncomfortable truth. He may actually, absolutely unintentionally, injure his friends or even others around him unless he's incredibly careful. Despite having just had her own crisis of feelings, Arla stepped around the chair Callum occupied and held both of John's hands in her own. Callum stood up and placed a firm hand on John's shoulder too. They both clearly saw how frightened he was, watching his faraway expression with ones of concern. After a minute or so of standing in solidarity, John smiled weakly at his friends. He removed his hands from Arla's and embraced them both together. A tear had broken free and was slowly working its way down his face. They broke apart, Arla quickly wiping away a tear of her own, Callum sniffing loudly and clearing his throat. "We're with you John. We've both seen some of the incredible things you can do now and we appreciate how hard this must be. You've never been one for a great deal of self-control, just look at your Lego collection, so I hope you realise that we know it's not going to be easy for us either. But you know we're still going to be here with you despite that." John looked at Arla with watery eyes. She was so good at saying exactly what needed to be said. Callum nodded solemnly too, agreeing with everything Arla had just said. John's watery eyes met his gaze too. They both knew it was going to be very hard for him to reign in his strength and speed, to keep the accident and its consequences a secret at all costs. They both knew that it was going to be difficult for themselves too. Not only to also keep the shocking secret, but to try to help their colossally strong friend avoid doing unintentional damage to themselves or anything else, for that could lead to awkward questions and potentially disastrous repercussions. Yet, as Arla said, despite that, they were both going to be there for him. "Jeez, who'd have thought getting superpowers could be so emotionally draining!" Exclaimed Callum, with his typically light hearted spirit. It did the trick. Yet another emotionally charged moment had been, at least partially, diffused. Arla and John nodded in agreement. Faint smiles had crept onto all of their faces as the heightened emotions started to dissipate. Arla rounded on John. "Why were you nearly late this morning by the way?" Callum had wondered the same thing so he also looked expectantly towards John. "Ah, well you know how I now have an eidetic memory, of which your book is now stuck firmly in there - thanks Arla. Well, I was remembering my Mini JCW drive at Knockhill from last year that we all went to. Quite possibly the best gift Annie has ever gotten for me, I'll have you know. But the memory is now so vivid I was actually there, experiencing it again. I mean it felt like I was literally there. The feelings, the sights, the sounds, everything was there like it was when it happened. It was wonderful." John stared off into space happily reminiscing the drive again. Arla and Callum were smiling too at their own recollections as it had been a great day out. The three of them were smiling at one another just as Luke walked back into the MCR, looking a touch pale, fresh from a famous Katherine dressing down. John looked up towards the pale second officer, still smiling, as Luke came out of his stupor and noticed the three of them still standing together. Before he could say anything to match the apparent anger on his face, Katherine appeared in the MCR behind him, also noticing the trio still standing together. She didn't look to be in the best of moods and John decided it was best not to linger. He cleared his throat meaningfully, inclining his head slightly towards the MEO, alerting Arla and Callum to the presence of their Head of Department. They both dispersed immediately via the back of the MCR, turning left towards the workshop and a passageway that led past where they'd just hastily vacated. John decided it was best to stay put for at least a moment longer, in case Katherine did indeed wish to speak with him. A quick shake of her head followed by an expectant expression told John he was free to go but to hurry up about it. He inclined his head a touch and rounded the console to leave out of the door the MEO had just entered. Luke was standing beside one of the computers, as if about to sit down and do some administrative work, when John noticed him quickly glance out of the corner of his eye. It didn't take a mind reader or require any real imagination to figure out what he was thinking of doing. Sure enough, Luke suddenly raised a hand, 'Oh wow he must need to look at something on the console I'm just about to walk past' John thought wearily. Luke about turned and took a long stride towards John's path, leading with his left shoulder whilst staring in the direction of the consoles ahead of him. Luke was not a small man, easily outweighing John, so a shoulder check, for that seemed the plan, would undoubtedly send the smaller person sprawling to the floor. Only problem for Luke though was that John is far more agile than him. Without even trying to disguise the fact he knew what Luke had intended to do, John planted his left foot and executed a neat complete pirouette around and behind him, even going so far as smirking when their eyes briefly met during the little impromptu dance. Luke's unchecked momentum sent the larger man tumbling onto his hands and knees, while John merely carried on walking by without caring to look back. He did notice Katherine crossing her arms, closing her eyes and then sighing angrily, which made his steps quicken to almost a run, in a bout of irrational panic, thus exiting the MCR that much sooner. Although not before quickly grabbing his t-card, in order to peg himself into the forward engine room, and a pair of ear defenders. He hadn't done anything wrong, he'd only avoided walking into Luke, but it was still prudent to avoid the MEO whilst she was angry. Especially seeing as he was already not in her best graces at present. If John had lingered a little longer and turned around, he would've noticed the look of utmost fury and hatred Luke was now displaying, staring towards the door.

Later on, John was kneeling down cleaning a purifier feed pump strainer, situated on the lower level of the engine room, near a walkway running perpendicular between the ship's two diesel generators, when he heard the lower-level, or bottom plates, door open and shut. He listened to the person's footsteps as they walked around the outboard side of the port generator, appearing soon after from around the non-drive end towards the aft of the engine room. Arla's light footsteps had already given her away before he saw her. The equipment she was responsible for included both of the ship's eight-cylinder Wartsila diesel generators. John inclined his head in greeting and she gave a quick smile and wave in reply, before carrying on looking around the engine. Arla climbed the inboard ladder to open up the hot-box and inspect the fuel pumps, fuel racks and pipework, leaving only her ankles visible by sight. John closed his eyes and focused on the sounds like he had the evening before. Arla was using her torch to inspect the number two unit's fuel pump and pipework at present. He then noticed Sandra was doing her rounds on the level above him, currently looking at one of the starting air compressors. She was the Duty Engineering Officer today, John recalled from Ship's Daily Orders. Someone else was now coming down the engine room stairwell, moving past the upper-level door, down the final flight of stairs and now opening the bottom plates door, remaining hidden from view behind the bulkhead as it was closed again. As with Arla, John knew who it was before he saw them. Only this time he gave his head a resigned shake. Luke appeared from behind the bulkhead, not noticing Arla's ankles as she continued with her inspection, ominously holding a large hammer. He spotted John and made a be-line for him. John sighed with resignation over the inevitable confrontation that was about to occur, hoping it wouldn't become a violent one. Sure enough, Luke non-too-subtly bumped into John as he stood cross armed beside him. John could've very easily remained perfectly still but was mindful of Newton's Laws of Motion. In this case, a body will remain at rest, or in a constant state of motion, unless acted upon by an external force. Not a body will remain motionless, even though a larger body has exerted said external force upon it. He played up a little though, dropping the strainer basket he had been cleaning, right into the bilge under the walkway, and planted both hands dramatically on the deck to stop himself from being knocked over. John sighed exasperatedly, looked up at Luke with a raised eyebrow to express his displeasure, then looked down towards the dropped strainer basket now laying in the bilge beneath him. As he reached down to retrieve the basket Luke knocked him over again, this time by planting a boot on John's side and kicking out. “Thought you needed a little help getting down to reach that basket you carelessly dropped.” Luke said smugly, still with his arms crossed and the hammer dangling obviously from one hand. John didn’t bother looking up, instead biting his cheek and telling himself any reaction would be a waste of energy. He couldn’t quite reach the basket by kneeling down, ironically, so he decided to lay flat on the deck in order to use the full length of his arm. Just as his fingertips reached the basket's handle, the same boot as before was jammed down hard between John's shoulder blades, theoretically pinning him to the deck. Thoughts of various ways in which Luke’s foot could be removed, without raising any suspicions, were now running through John's mind. Despite his best efforts to reign in the surge of anger, all those thoughts still resulted in the foot, and the attached smug man with it, ending up grievously injured. It was only when he closed his eyes, attempting again to reign in the blossoming anger, that the words Luke spoke became clear. The foul words were about Annie. Another sound was clear too, a thud from inboard of the port generator. John's left arm, shoulder and head were just below the deck plates and Luke’s boot had him pinned too. He turned his head to the right and stared up towards the source of exploding anger dominating all other thoughts. His right hand was now moving, reaching towards Luke’s left ankle still standing on the deck. Before John's hand could reach that ankle though, footsteps were approaching at a rapid rate of knots. Arla flashed by and the air was forced out of Luke's lungs with an audible gasp, as her Shoulder drove into his midsection. Arla's momentum, coupled with impressive strength, lifted the much larger man off his feet and onwards towards the starboard side of the engine room, carried over her shoulder. John leapt up to his feet and turned around just in time to see Luke being slammed bodily against the crankcase doors of the diesel generator. His mouth dropped in shock and awe. A faint cry of surprise came from above and the torch Sandra had been holding clattered onto the deck. The sound of Luke slamming against the engine must've been quite something to be heard over the running port diesel generator. Arla disentangled herself from Luke's limp limbs and he crumpled onto the deck in a large heap. The man was out cold, knocked unconscious from the substantial impact. John approached Arla from the side, staring open mouthed. She stood rigidly straight, hands clenched by her side, staring down at the inert form by their feet with bared teeth and blazing eyes. Sandra's feet appeared on the top rung of the ladder to the right of them. She climbed down in a hurry, investigating what had caused the loud noise, only to find an unconscious Luke, a terrifying looking Arla and a dumbfounded John. "What on earth happened here? Why is Luke unconscious? Did you hear that loud crash?" The words tumbled from Sandra's mouth as she was clearly struggling to take in the scene before her. John was still too shocked to speak and just stood mouthing like a fish. Much to his further surprise, Arla spoke next. Clearly and concisely as if discussing the material state of one of the diesel generators. "Luke was squeezing by John, who was cleaning one of the purifier inlet strainers, when he lost balance and looked as if he were going to fall. I was worried he would end up injuring himself falling into the bilge, so I ran to help. Only I must've had a surge of adrenaline as in my haste to save him, I carried him into the side of the generator." Sandra joined John in mouthing like a fish. She looked towards him, seeking confirmation on Arla's outlandish claim. John nodded slowly as his jammed mind still couldn't formulate a coherent sentence. Arla turned back towards Luke and now looked strangely satisfied at her handiwork. Sandra was too busy grabbing the radio clipped to her boiler suit to notice, readying herself instead to alert the Officer of the Day to the casualty located in the forward engine room. John watched briefly as Sandra turned and walked away to a quieter spot, hearing her notifying the Officer of the Day to the casualty along with the location, then turned back around to see Arla was now staring up at him with her arms crossed impassively, a little smile showing she wasn't bothered about concealing her satisfaction. John felt Luke deserved worse, as harsh as that may sound, so he felt rather satisfied at the situation too. He looked down at Luke, hearing that he was still breathing faintly albeit with three broken ribs, then back towards Arla again and mouthed 'Wow'. She grinned and held up a clenched fist. John replied with a grin too, and bumped his clenched fist against Arla's. Seeing as neither of them were duty, and that they'd only get in the way of the duty watch carrying out the casualty evacuation, Arla looked at John and jerked her head towards the exit. He nodded in agreement and they both quickly left the engine room just as the pipe (broadcast) was made announcing the casualty. As the door to the engine room closed behind them, and after removing their ear defenders, Arla hurried up the stairs with John following behind, at a pace far less than what he would now consider a hurry. Both were sorely keen on avoiding the duty watch personnel now en-route to evacuate the injured Luke.

Having reached level one, the deck above the MCR, thankfully avoiding the duty watch, John tapped Arla on the shoulder and asked her to follow him outside for a moment. She looked quizzical but followed him without asking any questions. After exiting the accommodation block on the port side, the same side the ship was secured to the dockside, they headed towards the stern and the aft mooring deck. John was a touch wary walking past the taught mooring lines, having already gone past the sign strung across the walkway exclaiming 'caution ropes under tension', and was eyeing each one apprehensively. They both reached the stern of the ship, John feeling like he'd just walked a gauntlet, and leant on the railing, observing the activity on the cruise ship still berthed aft of theirs. Scaffolding had been erected around the damaged port funnel, much to their amusement. It was quarter to ten in the morning and therefore a little early for the first 'smoko', break time, but neither of them really cared at that moment. It had certainly been an interesting day so far, despite having only just gotten started. "That was incredible what you did back there Arla. Mind me asking though, why did you do it? You know he couldn't have harmed me." Arla looked up at him in genuine surprise. Just then the penny dropped and John figured out why just as she spoke. "I guess you forgot our conversation back in the MCR? The one about Callum and I doing what we can to help you. I saw the look in your eyes and it wasn't pleasant. I also saw your hand moving towards Luke's ankle. Now, I may have slammed him into the side of the generator, and it felt oh so good doing it by the way, but you would've probably splattered him across the engine room had you gotten hold of him. So, rather than trying to explain what would've been a horrifying scene, I thought it would be easier if I got him off you. In a manner I saw fit. By the way, it was purely coincidental, not intentional, that it happened to involve Luke ending up unconscious." John laughed aloud at the ill-disguised sarcasm in her voice. Arla was far more dignified and simply smiled airily as she looked towards the cruise ship again. John was also looking towards the pale blue and white ship now, only he was focusing on the voices coming from the weather deck at the base of the scaffolding. Arla noticed his head was cocked to one side, then saw that he was looking towards the people working around the damaged funnel. "You're listening to what those people working on the funnel are saying aren't you?" John nodded and continued eavesdropping. She waited patiently for him to finish his 'thirsting for knowledge', a phrase his mum had always used. After a couple of minutes John grimaced a little and whistled quietly. Arla stood with her arms crossed, looking at him very impatiently, wondering what he'd just heard. "Well, for a start, they have absolutely no idea what caused the damage. So that's a relief, I guess. Secondly, the ship has had to delay sailing in order to repair the damage. Lastly, it's going to cost them many thousands of pounds to fix it, plus they're also losing money from the delayed sail and additional harbour fees." Arla's jaw dropped and her eyes widened in astonishment. John was still grimacing guiltily. "Oh dear. Well let's just hope they never find out it was you who wrecked that funnel by flying into it. Then again, even if someone did see you do it, who would ever believe that a person could jump that far, smack into a solid steel funnel and wreck it in the process, rather than end up a red smear." She was right. That sort of story would have someone committed because of concern about their mental well-being. And if someone wasn't committed, such a story would be greeted by downright disbelief and mocking retorts. It would then be forgotten through the march of time. Not by all though. John knew he wouldn't forget it and felt pretty certain there would be a slight twinge of guilt each time it was recalled. He also was pretty certain that neither Arla nor Callum would ever forget it. The difference being they would most likely recall the tale, between themselves of-course he fervently hoped, with laughter, much to his embarrassment. The time was now ten o'clock - Break time. Also, now there was only two hours to go until the normal Saturday end of play. John hoped the rest of the day would pass without the excitement the last couple of hours had brought. Callum usually spent smoko walking around the flight deck above them with a cup of coffee. Sure enough, a creature of habit, John could hear him up above them. "Callum is above us having his smoko coffee." Arla looked up at the deck-head above them, then grinned mischievously towards John. "Do you think you could jump up and hit the deck head as Callum walked over it? Without breaking through it, of course?" John looked up too. Replying, "I'd rather not Arla. Knowing me I'd end up with my head poking through the flight deck. Your right that it would give Callum one heck of a good scare though. But I'd rather not try to explain to the captain why the flight deck had a hole in it. Realistically, I think it would be better if I just climbed along the deck beam there, wait until Callum is above and then give the deck-head a good thump. That should give him a scare and avoid awkward questions. Win, win wouldn't you agree?" Arla agreed with a wide smile, then shoved him towards the stairs leading up-to the mezzanine deck above them, but just below the flight deck. She was becoming very impatient lately John thought to himself as he moved in a blur, quickly finding himself holding onto the deck beam, just below where Callum was soon to step, and looking down at Arla to make sure she was watching. It took Arla a few seconds to realise he was already in position. She blinked her eyes in an exaggerated manner, as if realising 'of-course he was already there', then stood impatiently waiting for the fun. John held up his hand, showing three fingers, and started counting down as Callum approached. Three, two, one, whack! They heard a shout, a thermos falling onto the flight deck followed by a choice few curses. Arla laughed silently with glee and clapped her hands in applause. John hopped down and landed beside her, giving her raised hand a high five. They heard Callum wondering aloud what the noise was, using a word that sounded a lot like a mallard. John motioned to put his arm around Arla's waist, asking the question silently with a hesitant expression before actually doing so. She nodded, held up an arm and wrapped it tightly around John's neck as he held her close, effortlessly picking his friend up in the process. He carried Arla quickly up the stairs then vaulted over the side, grabbing onto a pipe with his free hand and sending them both upwards in a graceful arc, letting go once he knew their trajectory would land them safely on the flight deck, rather than up and then down into the water. They landed silently, with Arla looking somewhat queasy from the sudden burst of speed and vault upwards. Callum had his back turned to them, grumbling over his spilt coffee. Arla recovered quickly and walked silently towards him, John standing still and watching with an air of bemusement. To her credit, she didn't give Callum another bad shock, rather just stood silently at his shoulder and waited for him to notice. Sadly, he did still end up with a substantial shock, causing his legs to fail comically and him to end up on his backside - right in that lost cup of coffee.

"Hi Callum." Arla said cheerfully, whilst giving him a pleasant smile. Callum looked around and noticed John who gave a small wave in greeting, grimacing more than smiling at his dumbstruck friend. Arla offered her hand and Callum accepted, pulling himself to his feet then touching his damp boiler suit. "Oh great, now it looks as though I've peed myself. Thanks Arla. Am I also to assume that loud bang was your doing John?" Callum narrowed his eyes and looked between both of his friends. Arla smiled indulgently in reply, whilst John avoided eye contact and became very interested in the scaffolding around the cruise ship's funnel once more. Smoko still hadn't finished so Callum headed to his cabin to put on a different boiler suit. Arla and John followed so they could tell him about Luke once he'd changed. It took Callum a few minutes to change, largely because engineers usually have various tools, notebooks, pens and other things in their pockets to transfer over, before he emerged from his cabin again. Arla wasted no time and jumped into the story. Callum was shocked, not at what Arla had done for he knew she was incredibly strong, but at what Luke had intended to do to John. He obviously didn't know the hammer would simply bounce off whatever part of John he'd struck, and that made the thought all the more troubling. A blow from a large hammer, from a large man, would've inflicted a terrible injury. The three off them all agreed that Luke being injured, not seriously mind you, was a very good thing, for he will have to be paid off the ship due to medical reasons. If he was unstable enough to want to strike someone with a hammer, what else could he be capable of and to whom? That was the question they were asking amongst themselves. Then a pipe, a loudspeaker announcement, that goes off throughout the ship was heard, interrupting their conversation and informing the crew that a casualty evacuation was now taking place. The crew were to avoid the ship's port side one deck and the gangway was not to be used until further notice. They exited the accommodation but, rather than go down to their favourite place of late, the flight deck, they headed up towards the bridge. The bridge had external doors port and starboard for entry and exit. The three of them stopped short of going into the bridge and opted to lean on the ship's side railing, in order to watch Luke leave the ship. The wait wasn't long and passed by quietly, as the duty watch appeared bearing Luke on a Neil-Robinson stretcher between them. Somehow, they'd managed to get him down the gangway safely, and Luke was now officially off the ship thanks to Arla. "Hopefully, that'll be the last time any of us see him again." Arla stated and John and Callum completely agreed with her. Now that John knew what Luke was capable of doing to another person, he didn't want to ever be in a situation where the man intended to try and harm him again. He couldn't guarantee, he couldn't swear, that Luke would survive the encounter. The thought troubled him, despite the danger Luke now seemed to pose to others, as he didn't want to, even accidentally, take a life. Arla had seen something in his eyes back down in the engine room and it had frightened her into drastic action. Purely to avoid what John may have done had he gotten to Luke first. The only comfort for John, was that had he really wanted to harm Luke then, it would've happened before Arla could've even moved. He knew there was at least some self-control there and that was re-assuring. Smoko was now finished and there was now only an hour and a half left of the working day. They decided to head back down to the MCR, for there was bound to be a discussion regarding Luke's departure. Despite the fact it had been Arla who'd inflicted Luke's injuries, she showed no concern whatsoever. Notwithstanding, John couldn't help but admire her lack of fear. If he'd been in her position then, even with the knowledge of what Luke had intended to do, his nerves would've been completely fried from worry.

As suspected, all the remaining engineers, including the Chief Engineer, Brian, were in the MCR as they walked in. Katherine noticed their arrival and approached them, signalling for Arla and John to stop, but Callum to continue onwards. Brian came up and stood beside Katherine and it seemed the four of them were to have a conversation in private. "Let's go into the Engineer's Office next door and have a chat please you two." Brian held out his arm indicating for Arla, John and Katherine to lead the way. After closing the door behind him, Brian sat down in the remaining free chair beside Katherine and immediately got down to business. "What happened to Luke in the engine room before smoko? So far Sandra has told Katherine and I that he was about to fall into the bilge, until you stepped in and saved him Arla. But in doing so, you've caused him quite serious injuries and now he has had to leave the ship. Is that what happened?" "Yes." Arla lied, looking the Chief Engineer straight in the eye with absolute conviction. The Chief's gaze swivelled towards John. "Yes." He replied, also looking the Chief in the eye. Praying his face didn't betray the nerves he felt. "Well Arla this is quite serious as I'm sure you can imagine. Such is the nature of the accident, in that it was you who caused Luke's injuries, I'm afraid you will have to be subjected to an inquiry and be suspended from work, with pay though, until the inquiry is concluded." The Chief didn't seem at all happy about having to break the news to Arla. Brian had to adhere to policy though, as much as it pained him to do so. "Well, if you don't mind Chief, I'd quite like to ask Arla and John a few questions, before that decision is final?" Brian looked at Katherine, his face giving nothing away, as to what the reply might be. He inclined his head and allowed the MEO to ask her questions after a brief moment of deliberation. Katherine didn't ask a question though, initially, much to the surprise of everyone present. "I think you've both just lied to myself and the chief." 'Oh dear' John thought. The Chief's eyes widened at the accusation and he looked from Katherine back towards Arla and John with obvious indignation. "Even though we are a team here, I'm certain that if Luke had been about to fall into a bilge, as your story goes, bearing in mind he wouldn't have actually fallen that far and may have stopped himself by grabbing onto one of the pipes there, you would've let him fall. Knowing that, at worst, he'd only fall a short distance and get covered in dirty oil. What actually happened? No more lies please." Katherine's voice had no inflection at all, just calm and to the point. It was mildly unnerving to John the ease in which she had seen through their story and how calm her question had been. "To be honest Boss, the story you got from Sandra is a lot easier than the truth. The truth will also be as dubious as what Sandra told you, seeing as out of the three witnesses, one is currently unable to confirm what happened, and the other two are known to have a strong dislike for Luke. So, what is there to gain here except for wasting everyone's time? The Chief and yourself both know John and I, and you know we would never willingly assault anyone unless there were extreme circumstances. Plus, we've never actually been involved in any altercations in the past, nor shown any indication that we would likely get ourselves involved in one either. Now, you must be thinking, what happened for me to do something completely out of character, and get myself into an altercation?" Both Katherine and Brian were taken aback by how blunt Arla had just been, but also seemed to accept that whatever had happened, there must've been a very good reason for it. John couldn't speak. This was worse than how he'd felt during his conversation yesterday with the MEO. He knew the truth was going to be hard to believe, much like the fabricated story, but even if it was believed, would that justify Arla's actions to the MEO and the chief? John was worried for Arla, and when he worried about something to the extent he was now, words failed him. It made him physically ill and wish to hide away. 'Some-things never change' he thought wearily. "Please tell us what happened Arla." The chief asked quietly. Katherine was looking towards John. She knew him well enough to know he was worried sick right then. Brian looked briefly towards him too, noticed his stricken face, and realised something was amiss. This, of course, didn't go unnoticed by Arla. She leant over and gripped John's hand tightly, managing to at least briefly tear him from his anguish. "It's OK John, you don't need to worry about me." John wished he could believe her, his doubt written all over a pained expression. She smiled, hoping to re-assure him nonetheless, released his hand, looked towards Katherine and Brian, then told the truth. Katherine knew Luke had been carrying a hammer, for he walked past her after getting it from the workshop, and she suspected he was on the verge of doing something stupid, even going so far as to give Luke the rest of the day off to calm down. She had also seen the look he'd given John earlier, and it had given her grave misgivings as to his intentions. "I believe you. Under the circumstances, I also believe what you did was reasonable. You saved John from what could've been a horrific injury. If Luke decides he wishes to pursue the matter with the authorities, then I will support you." Katherine took a moment to explain to the Chief what had happened that morning, and what she'd felt regarding Luke's behaviour, before sitting back to wait for his decision. "If you're satisfied with Arla's explanation and the circumstances around it, and taking into consideration your observations regarding Luke himself, then I'm satisfied that no further action is required. I must ask everyone to only refer to the fabricated events in any reports or statements. I think you'll agree that an overzealous rescue attempt is a better scenario than a fellow engineer seeking to assault another." Katherine and Arla nodded solemnly. John was only just regaining his senses and recuperating from the puddle of nerves he'd just been, so he sat still as if in a daze. Brian nodded at everyone, giving John a slightly worried double take, then left the office, closing the door behind him. Even though he hadn't actually apologised there and then for his initial decision to suspend Arla, she wasn't bothered. She knew he hadn't wanted to suspend her, judging from his tone and body language, and that he was having to follow stupid policy. The MEO's intervention had clearly been a relief for him, giving him sufficient grounds to go against policy thanks to the mitigating circumstances involved. The fact the Chief also now didn't have to instigate an inquiry, for as far as he was concerned the matter had now been addressed, was an added bonus. "Are you OK John" Katherine asked with concern. She'd never seen him so worked up before and that was saying something. Arla was looking at him with concern too. John took a deep steadying breath despite not needing to do so, again some-things never change when it comes to nerves at least, and eventually nodded haphazardly. The ability to speak again followed soon after. "I'll be OK now. Just got myself really worked up worrying about what would happen to you there Arla." The words came out in a rush. Arla and Katherine looked sympathetically at him. However, he didn't find the looks demeaning or embarrassing. John had accepted long ago that it was well known how things could torture him with worry. He was just grateful that people were often patient with him when moments like this occurred. And those that weren't were simply not worth bothering with.

Midday was about to arrive so it was time to knock-off, finish for the day, then get some lunch in the Officer's Mess, or saloon as it was often referred. During the week, Katherine was content for the engineers to have lunch in the duty mess but, at weekends, unless you actually were duty, she insisted that everyone eat in the saloon. They all stood up, Katherine leaving first, heading across the passageway to go up the stairs. Arla and John returned to the MCR to find all the remaining Engineers where they had been prior to the private discussion. Seeing as they'd all been sat there for the best part of an hour, possibly signing off routine maintenance rather than just talking about the situation with Luke, they must really want to know what was going on. Callum looked especially keen to find out. "Sandra claims it was you who flattened Luke, is that true?" Thomas was the first to get the question in, looking towards Arla. Kevin was sitting in the chair beside him, keenly leaning forward and paying avid attention. Sandra stood between them, leaning on the table with her arms crossed, looking a little indignant that her words clearly hadn't been believed. Callum already knew both versions of the story and was more interested in the outcome of the discussion. "Sandra is correct. Adrenaline can make people do crazy things." Arla said with modesty. Sandra leant forward and backhanded both Kevin and Thomas across their shoulders as if to say 'told you so'.

They both shrugged and nodded glumly. "I'm just glad he's gone now. He gave me the creeps." Sandra said whilst hugging herself. "I'm gutted it wasn't me who had the chance to make it happen, especially after this morning." Thomas rubbed his knuckles, whilst making the bold statement. Kevin, a quiet man at heart but, the things he said, when he did decide to join a discussion, were often worth hearing. On this occasion, he maintained his silence but, reached up and rubbed Sandra's shoulder to comfort her. She nodded thanks, appreciating the kind gesture. Sandra, Kevin and Thomas then got up from their seats and table to leave for Lunch. Sandra headed straight to the duty mess, Kevin and Thomas to their cabins to shower and change for lunch in the saloon. Once they'd left, John, taking a moment to listen and make sure they and anyone else were out of earshot, motioned for Callum and Arla to sit in the vacated chairs and tell him what happened with the discussion. Arla told him about the Chief's initial decision, making Callum growl with frustration. Then she went on to say how Katherine had interjected, leading to the truth being revealed and stunning Callum in the process. He, like John had during the discussion, couldn't believe that both the MEO and the Chief supported, or at least begrudgingly tolerated, what she had done. After taking a moment to reflect though, he gave a firm nod as if to say the right decision had been made, and should have never been in doubt. Even if the truth hadn't come out. The truth, Callum felt, only made Arla's actions more justifiable and was probably what had swayed the Chief. An over-zealous rescue was a lot better than a fellow engineer willing to assault someone with a weapon. As it was time for lunch, they all got up and headed out of the MCR to get ready to eat in the saloon.

As usual, the saloon was a hubbub of noise with everyone talking about the day and what sites they planned to see in Miami. It wasn't often the company they worked for ventured out to this part of the world, so they were all busy planning how best to enjoy it. John also heard various different conversations centred on the recently departed second officer engineer. The fact it was Arla who had caused the departure wasn't yet widely known though as her name didn't come up in any of the talk. Arla, Callum and John sat at a table occupied by a couple of the ship's Deck Officers, who briefly interrupted their own conversation to greet them. John realised this was the first food he was about to eat since the accident. He wondered if it would affect his taste and appetite now that hunger didn't concern him anymore. With relief, he found the cheeseburger in his hands still tasted like a cheeseburger. Relaxing, John sat and consumed his food quietly, listening to Arla and Callum planning their trip ashore into Miami's famous south beach, with a twinge of jealousy. His friends seemed to pick up on his mood and abruptly stopped their conversation, but resumed after a moment's hesitation, once he shook his head dismissively and casually waved away their concerns. John hadn't read up on what to do in Miami, so knew very little of the sights and attractions, and neither did Arla and Callum it seemed as their conversation focused on nothing specific other than the famous beach itself. The ship had arranged a bus, departing at hourly intervals, to take people directly to south beach and make it easier for them to enjoy the visit.

Lunch eaten, the sensations of taste and food in his stomach a nice reminder for John that he was still himself, they headed back up to their cabins. John bade Arla and Callum farewell and asked them to get him a fridge magnet whilst they were ashore. Arla assured him they would and asked that he try to keep out of trouble whilst they were off the ship. John resented the idea that he now required baby-sitting, the engine room being gore free was a testament to that, but appreciated their concern nonetheless. As he was about to enter his cabin a sudden thought staggered him to a stop. He hadn't told Annie about the accident yet. It certainly wasn't a good idea to do that via email, and the ship's welfare phone service calls were monitored for security purposes so that was a no go too. Maybe, just maybe, it was time to try something new John thought. Maybe he should learn to fly. One of his airborne escapades the previous day had ended in a most peculiar fashion after all. He had been falling, only to find himself miraculously stopped inches above the deck after sticking his hands out to brace for impact. Seeing how quickly he'd mastered his other senses and abilities, the term 'mastered' perhaps an exaggeration, he reckoned it actually wouldn't take him long to learn to fly. If he was successful at this endeavour, then perhaps he could go home quickly, as much as that were possible from over four-thousand two-hundred miles away, and get back before anyone had realised he'd been gone. It would also be a neat thing to show Arla and Callum. The hangar would probably be the safest place to try this John felt, as it was the largest open space on the ship. He quickly changed into his gym clothes and treaded the all too familiar path to the deck below. Once in the open space, the large door was still open so he'd need to be vigilant of staring eyes. OK, it was time to get cracking. Without having a clue as to what to do because his only 'experience' at flying had been not falling. And that was only after falling first, without any degree of style or control. With that in mind, he held out his hands in front of him and braced himself, just as he had the previous evening, as if to prevent a fall. Effective for posing as a mummy or a zombie, but not for flying it seemed. Despite how absurd the scene must've looked, maybe more so than how he felt, John focused on what he was doing. Stopping himself, exerting his arms forward to brace for an impact or as if trying to bench press a weight. Amazingly, he wobbled a little, causing him to stagger backwards a few steps. "Oh my" he said aloud. A smile lighting up his face. He resumed the now not-quite-so-absurd zombie pose and focused more intently on exerting his hands outwards. He flew off his feet and slammed into the forward bulkhead of the hangar. John's eyes were as wide as dinner plates and his hands were still ludicrously held out in front of him, even though he was no longer standing. The noise from his impact with the bulkhead had not been insignificant. He remained motionless and concentrated on the many sounds around him, searching for any sign that the noise hadn't gone unnoticed. Thankfully, the majority of the ship's crew had already left the ship to go and enjoy the various attractions in Miami. Those that remained, the unlucky duty watch and a few others, showed no sign of having heard any strange noises. John blew out the deep breath he didn't realise he'd been holding. It made him shake his head and give a little chuckle. He jumped up quickly and returned to where the inaugural Campbell airways flight had departed. It hadn't been long or entirely successful, a complete lack of control will account for that, but it was a start. This time John decided to use his feet. Focusing in a similar manner as before, only now he was trying to push against something with his legs - no movement; focus a little more - still nothing. With just a little more focus, his feet left the deck and he was now hovering just an inch off the ground. "Yes" he exclaimed elatedly, throwing up his arms into a victorious pose. The excitement was premature as it cost him his all-important self-control and focus. John rocketed upwards, shouted a profanity, hit the deck-head face first, did a few back-flips but couldn't make the landing stick and once again hit a solid surface face first. At least this surface was the deck again he thought. As that had all happened in micro-seconds, his ears only just registered the sound of his face hitting the deck-head high above from where he now lay spread-eagled. After very slowly rolling onto his back and staring upwards, John came to the conclusion that flying only came naturally to birds, and that for creatures lacking wings, it was unsurprisingly difficult. Undeterred, he got back up, limbered up a little, then got to focusing again. With the intention to stay focused now too. Flying was obviously not a skill to be mastered quickly. Two more thumps into the deck-head, one leaving a worryingly noticeable head-shaped dent, three whacks into the hangar's port bulkhead, two into the starboard and finally, the most worrying of all, smashing through the reinforced glass of the office at the back of the hangar. Breaking one off the two computers in the process. That was going to be awkward to explain if he couldn't find a way to fix everything. A mad dash throughout the ship ensued. He lucked upon a new computer in a stores space up near the bow, hastily replacing the broken one which was then launched into the nearby skip on the jetty, firmly enough to bury it. The noise caused John a brief flicker of panic, as a couple of the dock workers looked around at the sound, but then thought nothing more of it and carried on about their business. The reinforced glass was a little harder. He had to search through almost every single one of the ship's many nooks and cranny's, taking him all of two minutes and two seconds, before striking gold a second time that day in the vehicle store below decks. John honestly hadn't expected to find anything to replace the broken window he'd caused, let alone an exact replacement. He wasn't about to question such good fortune and ran back to the hangar to fit the new pane of reinforced glass.

After such excitement, John thought better of learning to fly so, he meandered out onto the flight deck. Leaning on the port rail, he contented himself with watching the various comings and goings of the many people working throughout the dock. Glancing aft he noticed more activity around the funnel he'd damaged the previous night. There were several bright flares of light indicating arc-welders were at work. Shaking his head ruefully, he resumed watching the activity throughout the docks, noticing that Arla and Callum were only just leaving the ship and heading for the bus. This struck him as a little odd initially as he thought they would've gotten the bus straight after lunch. It was only when he looked at his watch and realised it was in fact, straight after lunch. All that excitement had occurred in mere minutes. Arla was looking back towards the ship, waiting for Callum to catch up, when she caught sight of John leaning on the railing. He returned her enthusiastic wave with a smile and shouted for them both to have fun. Callum looked up at the shout and finally noticed him too, giving a small wave in acknowledgement. Arla rolled her eyes at Callum's complete lack of attention and motioned for him to hurry up as the bus was now waiting for them, everyone else going ashore at that time was already onboard the bus. John laughed, watching for a few minutes more as his friends hurried onto the bus and sat beside each other near the front. The bus drove away and was lost to sight as it rounded one of the many buildings, heading towards the Port Boulevard Road that connected the docks to the Miami mainland. A minute later he heard someone coming up the external stairs on the port side and quickly realised it was today's duty engineer Sandra. She was probably coming up to have a walk around in the sunshine but, on noticing there was someone else on the flight deck with her, a fact that initially surprised her considering work had finished for the day and there was plenty to see and do ashore, Sandra headed over to stand beside him. "Ah I forgot you were confined to the ship due to your little tour yesterday." John didn't reply but smiled ruefully at her in response. He was often very quiet and just as content by himself as he was with friends whilst away from home. This often caused people who didn't know him to steer clear, something else he didn't care to change. Sandra knew him though, having sailed together on a couple of occasions, so she wasn't deterred by his typical silence or self-induced solitude. In somewhat of a paradox, he was a surprisingly good person to talk to if anything was on someone's mind, and the Duty Engineer had something on her mind. John looked over towards her as she leant on the railing beside him and offered another smile, a warmer one this time, in greeting. Sandra smiled back but, it came across as a little forced. He had a hunch that there was something troubling her despite her jovial greeting. "I'm really glad Luke is gone. He was, and is, a truly horrible person." John stiffened, dreading what he thought Sandra was about to say. "I don't have any close friends onboard like Arla does with yourself and Callum, not that she needs any help defending herself mind you, but that's not the point I'm trying to make here. What I'm saying is I often feel a little isolated as I've got no one here I can really be open with like she does. As a result, I tend to bottle things up." Now, John really didn't want to hear what Sandra was going to say, but instinctively knew this was something she needed to get off her chest so he stayed and listened. The MEO and the Chief were both excellent people to talk to and really cared about their team, but this was the first time Sandra had sailed with either of them so she probably didn't know that yet. John wasn't about to brush her off and suggest she talk to them right now though. "Luke . . . frightened me. He's frightened me a couple of times since he joined. I didn't know what to do as it wasn't something I was comfortable talking about with anyone here alone. Plus, I didn't know how people would react, maybe I'd have even been accused of lying." "I like to think I'm a good person to talk to once you get to know me. Although seeing as I'm a social hermit crab that's not easy to do I guess." John was heartbroken by Sandra's words and only wished she'd said something sooner rather than suffer in silence for so long. Good grief, Luke had been onboard for two months up until that day – poor Sandra. In trying circumstances John liked to try and lighten the mood, when things got heavy so to speak, by slipping in a little humour as tactfully as possible. Not that he'd had much success at that in the last twenty-four hours. "You are a good person to talk to alone John but, with Arla and Callum around you're either with one or both of them, or hidden away in your cabin. I also don't like to disturb people if their doors are shut like yours always is." John felt a horrible wave of guilt wash over him. He actually didn't mind if someone wanted to talk about anything, but agreed with Sandra in that his closed cabin door wasn't exactly welcoming. He thought she knew this, but accepted her preference not to disturb a closed door. People would often have their door open during the day, with the curtain behind drawn for a degree of privacy, and would only close it at night. It was a way of being approachable but, it wasn't something he did, preferring his door closed at all times. "I'm sorry you felt like that Sandra. I really am. I never knew you were suffering like this and that's my fault for not being there to talk to." John felt bad, and wished that wasn't the case. Even worse, on seeing the tears in Sandra's eyes as she looked at him, his own eyes were now watering too, threatening to spill out at any moment. He tentatively reached out and placed his hand on her shoulder, hoping to offer some small comfort. That caused the dam to break for Sandra and all those bottled-up emotions broke free. She crashed into him; her face buried in his shoulder for she was quite tall, and wrapped her arms tightly around his chest. Tears flowed freely and silent sobs were racking her body. John wrapped his arms around her in return but the guilt that had washed over him was now gone. The heart break, knowing he'd let her down, was gone too. A rising flood of fury had displaced those other emotions and his face bore a look of cold determination. He was going to defy Katherine's order to remain onboard that night. He was going to look for Luke and make him regret ever harming Sandra. John vowed, silently, to visit every hospital and look at every single patient register until he found him. His only regret was that Sandra wouldn't be there to see it, to get some sort of redemption from the torment Luke had inflicted upon her. The passage of time ceased to matter to John at that moment. All that mattered was being there for the Second Officer Engineer that he considered a friend. It was fortunate the ship was alongside and that most of the crew were ashore. During weather such as this at sea the flight deck was an often-frequented spot for people exercising, sunbathing or even just to go and walk around. As such they remained undisturbed during the several minutes it took for Sandra to calm down. She eased her arms from around his chest and took a small step back, one of her hand's settling on John's shoulder, the other wiping away tears. John let go too, allowing one hand to drop and rest by his side, lightly gripping Sandra's hand on his shoulder with the other, letting her know he was still there. She looked up at him, her pretty face red and blotchy from crying and mouthed a silent 'thank you'. He was briefly taken aback by Sandra stepping close again and kissing him lightly on the cheek. John was certain there were no ulterior motives behind such a gesture from Sandra, and smiled warmly at her as she stepped back again. It just showed him how much she'd needed to talk all that time. "Do you want to go and see the MEO or Chief about this Sandra? I know you don't know either of them very well, but I think they'll be able to help and make sure Luke is punished for what he's done. I honestly wouldn't mind if you need me to take over the duty for you today either. Regardless, even though my door is always physically shut, I want you to know that it's always open and you would never be disturbing me." John hoped this didn't come across as insincere or dismissive. She stood pensively for a moment, her feelings inscrutable to John and he began to worry what he'd said was wrong. "Yes. I'd like to go and talk to the MEO about this. I want her, and our company, to know what type of man Luke really is. Hopefully, it'll lead to his dismissal. Would you mind coming with me though?" Sandra now stood tall and confident, back to her normal self, only a brief flicker of doubt when asking him to accompany her to Katherine's cabin to talk about what happened. John immediately alleviated those doubts, happy to be there to help however he could. "I don't mind at all. Whatever you need Sandra." He immediately wished he hadn't said the last part for Sandra looked at him with suggestive eyes, making him visibly gulp with apprehension and look around awkwardly to avoid looking directly at her. To his immense relief though she laughed and smiled playfully, her uplift in mood proving how strong Sandra was. It also reminded him that she liked to joke occasionally too, and once again how easy it was for him to be duped and embarrassed. Some things never change. "Sorry John, I just wanted to see if your reaction would be as funny as I thought it would. Arla told the MEO and I on standby about how you pointedly look away if her chest is near your face, during sparring, working on equipment or even if she's leaning over to look at a screen with you. She also said that you do the same to avoid looking at her bottom if she's walking upstairs ahead of you, and it made us all laugh like crazy. I've waited for an opportunity to see if I could exploit your adorable and shy politeness for a giggle, and that was just too good an opportunity to miss even after my little outburst. In all honesty, I really needed a laugh after all those emotions." She smiled apologetically at John. He relented and allowed a resigned smile to replace his frown, accepting that she really had needed a laugh. Although, it was embarrassing to know that his mannerisms were a topic for conversation. He was going to have a little chat with Arla about that. "OK moving on from that and preferably never back to it." Sandra bit her lip and tried to look innocent. "The MEO is still on-board so do you want to go see her just now?" She looked a little crestfallen at this, maybe hoping for just a little more levity prior to discussing Luke again. Despite coming across as a little reluctant, Sandra nodded bravely and they both headed back into the accommodation. "Katherine is a really good person to talk to Sandra, I've known her for years now and she's always been there when I needed help. She was the MEO when my mum passed away a few years ago and we were actually at sea at the time with outside communications blocked. My mum didn't have much time left and Katherine went above and beyond to get me off the ship after the emergency call came through. I got to say good-bye to my mum thanks to her." Sandra had never heard this story before and walked beside him with her hands over her mouth. It took John by surprise too as talking about his mother's passing was still quite difficult for him, even with Annie. "The MEO will look after you without a doubt Sandra." John said with absolute confidence, once he'd gotten over his surprise at how freely he had just spoken. Sandra seemed to take comfort from his conviction and it strengthened her resolve that this was the right thing to do. She also wanted to let him know that if he ever needed to talk then her door was always open too. Clearly Sandra had a lump in her throat and John wasn't sure if it was because of what he'd just told her or that she was just a little nervous. In the moment they were both now stopped for words however, the squeeze she gave his hand told him what he needed to know. Before this John had never considered Sandra as a close friend, like Arla or Callum, but maybe that was going to change now. They'd both just shared an incredibly emotional and private moment together after all. Certain moments can happen during friendships that can either initiate, strengthen, weaken or sadly end relationships, and this was one such time where the bond became stronger. A line in the sand moment that signifies the start of a deeper connection between both parties involved. What a time for it to happen, John thought with a twinge of amusement. Sandra must've seen something in his face as she looked enquiringly at him. "It's a little weird just now because that horrible man has changed our relationship, from 'work-friends' to what I'd call 'actual-friends'. That's my take on this at least." He said a little self-consciously, looking at her to gauge how she felt about such a bold statement. "I think you're right there. In fact, I like to think I can consider you an 'actual-friend' now as well." She smiled and had used her fingers to make air quotations at the 'actual-friend' part. "OK fair enough. You know Sandra we're having a severe outbreak of emotion here and I have a reputation to uphold. I mean, you know 'actual-friends', well it was a little cringe-worthy, wasn't it?" They both smiled broadly at one another and a line in the sand was drawn.

It seemed all too quick, but the open door to the MEO's cabin was now in front of them. Sandra looked a little apprehensive. But as John gave her a nod of encouragement, she shook off the jitters and knocked on the door-frame. They heard Katherine stand up and walk towards the drawn curtain. She looked a little surprised to see both Sandra and John standing there once the curtain had been pulled aside. "Hello you two, is there something wrong?" The MEO asked with a concerned look on her face for the two of them. "I'd like to talk to you about Luke if you don't mind second?" Sandra quietly asked. Katherine nodded her approval but then looked at John, unsure as to why he was there too. "John suggested that I come talk to you about something we have just spoken about. Do you mind if he sits in with us?" John hadn't expected to be part of this conversation, believing he would only be acting as chaperone of sorts, and was a little taken aback. Sandra looked at him pleadingly after spotting the surprised look. He smiled, letting her know he didn't mind. Thankfully for Sandra, Katherine didn't mind either and she stood aside to let them both in her day-room. After taking their shoes off at the door, they both sat down on the fabric sofa and the MEO sat across from them on her leather desk chair. The conversation that followed was excruciating for John. Largely because Sandra had broken down a couple times as she explained, in detail, the various things that Luke had done, one of which had brought up some bile in his throat and he'd grimaced as he swallowed it back down. All he could do to help during this interview was to hold onto Sandra's hand. Towards the end, Katherine also had tears in her eyes, but she also looked furious too. John actually pushed himself further into the sofa, as he attempted to shy away from the MEO's fury. Sandra was sobbing hard by the end too, and it was clearly evident that going into the detail had been incredibly difficult for her. Katherine stood up and sat down beside her, putting an arm around the distraught young woman and rubbing her shoulder with the other hand. Without asking Sandra, she looked towards John. "Would you mind taking over Sandra's duty please John?" He agreed without hesitation but before he could stand up to leave Sandra gripped his hand firmly. Stopping still, John waited patiently for her to find the words she wanted to say. "No, I'll be OK with the duty, honestly second. It's actually a huge relief to have shared what occurred with you and I feel a lot better for having done so." "Sandra I honestly don't mi-" "No John. I'm OK now. Honestly, I'll be fine finishing the duty - please second, let me carry on? In addition, do I need to do anything else now about this? You know, what happens next?" Sandra's strength amazed both the MEO and John. He hadn't realised, until then, just how much courage she possessed. It was comparable to Arla's and Annie's, which he felt said a lot about her. Katherine dismissed him and, as he was leaving, Sandra gave him a quick hug in thanks, before the MEO went into detail with Sandra about how things were going to proceed from there with regards to Luke. John desperately tried not to listen to what was going to happen, but his curiosity got the better of him. By the time he had gotten back to his cabin, what he'd heard didn't sound too good for Luke. Even though it seemed the horrible man was going to get severely punished for what he'd done, it didn't deter John for what he was planning to do that night. As far as he was concerned, even the likelihood of a dismissal and criminal charges wasn't sufficient. All the horrific details of what had happened to Sandra were now lodged firmly in his mind, and the detailed knowledge made him feel ill. He was secretly glad Sandra was OK to finish the duty, for he would've had to remain on-board if not.

Later on, he came to the conclusion that Arla and Callum had clearly decided to have dinner ashore that evening, so John got dressed into his red-sea rig and went down to the saloon alone. As the vast majority of the crew were ashore, there were only a couple of people eating in the Officer's Mess that evening. Sandra was one of them, changed out from her boiler suit and wearing blue work clothes, so he collected some food and sat down beside her. She smiled warmly as he sat down and nudged him gently with her shoulder. "Thanks for earlier John. I don't think I could've done that without you." She said sincerely. "Ah you didn't need me there, you're plenty strong enough on your own. It was no trouble though. Well, it wasn't pleasant certainly, but I'm just glad I could be of some help." "Yea, I'm sorry you had to hear all the details. Now you know what Luke is really like." Sandra tried to make the remark sound off-hand, but the slight quiver in her voice made it obvious just how upsetting it was. They both sat silent for a moment, distractedly picking at their food. "It's hard to know how to respond here to be truthful. Hearing all those details was really disturbing, but like I said, I'm glad I could be there for you regardless." She mouthed a silent thanks and resumed eating her dinner. John went back to eating too. As he was a quick eater, he finished before her, even though she'd started first. Then, he got up and went to get a desert. Turning around, “Would you like a pudding?” He stopped and quickly asked. “It’s cheesecake, isn’t it?” She said. “Yes please then.” Remaining seated as a steward came to clear away both of their plates, Sandra politely thanked the steward once the table had been cleared. On his return, John sat back down beside her, passing a slice of cheesecake. After a quick thanks, she demolished the desert almost as quickly as he did. “Well, excuse me, I’m going to head back to my cabin. Hope you have a quiet night.” “You git John! Now you’ve gone and jinxed me. If I get any alarms during the night, you’re getting a phone call.” He mouthed ‘oops sorry’ and walked away chuckling. She stared daggers at him in response, and he silently hoped there wouldn’t be a phone call. Once his back was turned towards her, John’s demeanour changed. Now he had a face set with an angry scowl. Once back in his cabin, he changed out of the red sea rig and into the darkest clothes he’d brought - dark blue jeans and a black t-shirt of a British Touring Car team, he then sat down at the desk to wait until nightfall in a few hours’ time. Not wishing to lose track of time amongst his memories again, he powered on the gaming laptop he had with him, a sleek HP Omen, and loaded up one of the many games installed to pass the time. A few hours later, he switched off his laptop and sat back in the chair to listen, making sure everyone was either in one of the ship's bars or in their cabins, and that there was no one nearby on the jetty. Everything seemed clear so he left his cabin and went up outside to the top of the bridge. He did a full three-sixty degree turn to see if any hospitals were in sight as he needed a place to start searching. Spotting one, handily in the direction of the Port Boulevard Road that led off Dodge Island, John leapt over the railing and plummeted down, landing easily on the jetty despite the drop. One last look around, then he sprinted off and became a faint blur in the night. In a matter of seconds, John arrived at the nearby hospital, the University of Miami Hospital, hoping that it's relatively close proximity to the ship would mean Luke was inside. Avoiding the numerous security cameras dotted around, not that they would've seen him anyway for how fast he was, John worked his way through the hospital, checking out the patient registers at each nurse station he passed. Regrettably scaring the doctors and nurses at some of them, with the gusts of wind his passage brought, until he found what he sought. Luke was in his own private room much to John's delight. Two seconds later and he found himself standing at the foot of Luke's bed, after turning off the light and closing the blinds first. He also made sure the nurse's call button was well out of reach, then stood still and stared with revulsion at the sleeping man. The thoughts running through his mind of what could be done to Luke in that room were not pleasant, mainly consisting of violence, which made him question his sanity. What the hell was he doing there. Acknowledging to himself that his self-control wasn't exactly brilliant and realising that the engine room incident had been an anomaly, he was still content and pleased to see the size of the bandage around Luke's midsection. The picture of Luke in the hospital bed tempered the storm within him to manageable levels, as he currently felt less inclined to add to the injuries inflicted by Arla's efforts in the first place. Then, things got interesting as, a wheezing cough that must've proven to be quite painful, woke the injured man up and he spotted a dark silhouette at the foot of his bed. John quickly looked around for something sturdy and, not spotting anything useful for what he had in mind, instead grabbed a bar at the end of the bed with one hand. Whilst not what he originally intended; he could make do with this bar. He lifted the end of the bed, tilting it up to a steep angle but keeping himself in sight, easily. Luke's eyes widened in astonishment and he made to grab for the nurse-call button, only to find it wasn't where it had been. "Any-time you make a sound before I'm finished talking, I'll break another one of your remaining two-hundred and twelve unbroken bones. Nod if you understand." John said in barely a whisper, disguising his voice into more of a growl without realising he could. Then, tilting the bed a little further to emphasise the fact that it would be easy to do so. In response, Luke nodded urgently, eyes wide with fear. He placed the bed gently back onto the floor and crossed his arms over his chest, and let the silence build, watching with amusement as the man in the bed became visibly more agitated with each passing second. "I know who you are Luke Watson. I know how you came to be here too. I also know the whole story about the deplorable things you did to Sandra Baker, which is why I'm here." John didn't think it would be possible, but those words made Luke's eyes widen further and the man was now visibly trembling with fear. Inside, he allowed himself a small smile before continuing. "Today, Sandra had a long conversation with Katherine, your boss, after you were taken off the ship and brought here. Now your boss knows about all the things you did in great detail. I was also informed of those details, so as you can imagine, I'm rather upset, much like any decent human being would be under the circumstances. I think you can guess that you're in a lot of trouble Mr Watson and you deserve everything that's coming your way. It's highly likely that you'll lose your job, now that an investigation into Sandra's allegations against you has begun. Looking further, you'll then be subject to a criminal investigation too, due to the nature of those allegations. That, however, doesn't really explain precisely why I'm here though, as I'm guessing this information will be relayed to you tomorrow at some point anyway. I'm here because, if in the incredibly unlikely event that you somehow avoid any punishment for what you've done, I want you to know that if you ever go near Sandra, or any other woman for that matter, and do the things you did again, I will find you and once I've found you, I'll make sure you spend the rest of your life paralysed from the neck down, blind and deaf. Do you understand?" John had gripped the bar at the end of the bed again, crushing it completely flat, whilst struggling overall to keep his anger under control. At this point, the details of all the horrible things Luke had done were crashing around the very front of his mind, demanding action. He sorely wanted to hurt Luke, to make him suffer badly. But, at the same time, he wanted to have faith that justice would be served the correct way. He wanted to have faith that Luke would lose his job and be suitably punished, to the extent that no thoughts of harming anyone ever again would cross his mind. John hoped that, despite his strong desire to the contrary, he wouldn't actually have to honour the brutal promise he'd just made. Tears were streaming down Luke's face as he nodded and whimpered pathetically. The crushed bar had also caused him to urinate, with a visible pool forming and darkening the bed sheets. John hoped that this would be the last time he ever saw the, hopefully, former Second Officer. However, deep down John knew that he couldn't guarantee what his actions would be if they ever crossed paths again, and that thought frightened him. Still struggling to keep the surge of anger under control, he stepped over to the window, lifted the blinds and opened it fully. One last malevolent look back, confirmed that Luke was terrified beyond reason, and he leapt out. The ground raced up and he landed hard, staggering a couple of steps before regaining his balance. John understood that he really had been teetering on the edge of losing control in the presence of such a despicable man. One last look up towards the open window that he'd just leapt from, a drop of several floors, and that was enough – time to go.

With the swirling torrent of emotions that he had been experiencing now fully under control, John was content. He felt sure that Luke would never present a danger to anyone else again, and he'd achieved it without breaking every single one of the man's bones. Minus the three ribs Arla had already broken that is. John lifted his head, closed his eyes and took in a deep breath of the cool night air. "Time to go back to the ship." He said aloud after slowly exhaling. John then arrived back on the jetty in a matter of seconds once again, and leapt up to the flight deck, landing neatly in the centre much to his relief. It was just after midnight by the time he had re-entered the accommodation via the port external door to go back to his cabin. Surprisingly, John found Arla and Callum standing outside his door, holding a small plastic bag, asking each other 'where has he gone?' "You two only just got back?" He asked quietly, not wishing to disturb the few people already in bed. They both jumped, their backs had been turned towards him, and looked around. They had looked worried but that worry then turned to annoyance. To stop them, John held up a finger to silence the pair, then motioned for them to follow him into his cabin in order for them to talk quietly. Once they had all settled in their preferred seats, he told them about what had happened with Sandra earlier, although not going into the full details that he'd heard with the MEO. Then he explained that he had just gotten back from paying Luke a visit. Arla and Callum looked appalled. In actuality, it took Arla a couple of minutes to find her voice again. As for Callum, well he didn't look even close to speaking yet. So, as usual, it was up to Arla to ask the obvious questions. "What if he recognised you John? What if you were seen off the ship?" Fortunately, these were questions that John expected, so his response was ready. "I very much doubt he recognised me, the room was very dark and even then, I remained in the shadow from what faint light there was. I also found I could change my voice to sound completely different with ease, so there's that too. And even if he recognised me, no one and no camera spotted me while I was off the ship, so who would believe him? I remained pegged in and had only been gone for literally a few minutes anyway. It's not even possible to drive to the hospital that quickly. I know it was risky before you say anything Arla, but I just couldn't sit idly and do nothing." Arla didn't look entirely convinced but kept her feelings to herself regardless. Callum was still visibly appalled by what John had told them, so words still failed him. "Oh, please don't mention any of this to Sandra or anyone else. This was difficult for her as it was without anyone else asking questions about it." They both agreed with sombre nods of their heads. They all sat silent for a minute before John spoke again. "Well seeing as you're both here, what's in the bag there? And it may amuse you to know that I tried, very unsuccessfully, to learn to fly earlier." The bag lay forgotten as Arla and Callum both perked up, leaned forward in their chairs, and sat with expectant looks, waiting to be told of his woes. The broken glass part of the story had gone down particularly well and John was impressed at how silent they'd managed to keep their laughing. "Next time you try that you've got to make sure I'm there to see it!" Arla managed to say between fits of silent laughter. Callum was too busy wiping tears from his eyes to add anything more. John didn't mind their laughter, even at his expense, as it was the whole idea for recounting the complete fiasco and a good way to move on from Luke. Once they had both settled down again, Callum remembered the little plastic bag sitting by his feet. He picked it up and handed it over to John. As requested, there was a Miami south beach fridge magnet inside and John was thrilled by it. Arla and Callum both smiled happily as he thanked them, then jumped up enthusiastically to place it, temporarily until it was time to go home, on the door of the little fridge in his cabin. The only shame being that he wasn't actually going to get to visit the beach himself, but that was understandable owing to his 'excursion' the previous day. It was an hour into Sunday now, so Arla and Callum, both yawning impressively after a busy day ashore, got up, said goodnight to John and left for their own cabins. No more was said about Luke and John hoped nothing else would ever be again. Even the thought of that abhorrent man was enough to make him want to go back to that dark hospital room, and do something he'd later most likely regret. As he was alone now, not wishing to get stuck within his own mind again, John turned on his laptop, made himself comfy on the desk chair and picked a TV series to start binge watching. After a few episodes, the phone beside his laptop started to ring showing the MCR's number, puzzling him until he remembered Sandra's parting words from dinner time. 'Surely she hadn't been serious?' he thought with a flicker of guilt for possibly jinxing her earlier. Turned out the duty engineer had been serious and didn't sound best pleased on the phone. It wasn't common practise to call other engineers during the night, unless assistance was required, so it was still rather rude of her to do so, jinxed or not, John felt. Especially at, looking at his watch, nearly three in the morning. The alarm was for a drop in sea water cooling pressure in the forward engine room, indicative of a blocked suction strainer. Sandra had tried to change over the suction but to no avail, so she was seeking his assistance to help clean both of them. Normally, a job such as that was, classed as high risk due to one of the isolation valves being a ship-side one. Therefore, a permit for work would be required and signed for by the Chief Engineer. Understandably not wishing to wake up the Chief at three in the morning, Sandra asked him to help get the job done quickly right then. He agreed, having still been awake with no sign of any fatigue, and made his way down to the MCR. Rather than go at a blink-and-you'll-miss-it speed as normal now, John took a couple of minutes to arrive in the control room. Sandra looked surprisingly alert, for she had clearly slept well up until the alarm, very atypical whilst duty.

"Well, you took your time." She said rather haughtily, quite clearly not the 'thanks for coming down' that he had naively expected. "If that's how I'm going to thanked for getting out of bed at three am to help clean out some strainers full of fish and what-not, then you'll find yourself doing the job alone Sandra." He said, conveniently omitting that he had actually been awake, with his arms crossed impassively. The only reply from Sandra had been to lean back in the chair she occupied and cross her own arms, all the while looking indifferently at him. John shrugged, smiled and waved as he turned around to leave the MCR, intending to go back to the TV series he'd been watching. Much to his amusement, Sandra leapt up from the chair, ran towards him and seized a hand with both of hers to stop him from leaving. "OK, OK, thank you for coming down to help me John." She said with an exaggerated smile, even showing off her white teeth. Not wanting to let her off that easily though, he remained still and quiet, with an expression born out of boredom. "Please John, I'm sorry. Remember though, this is your fault for jinxing me." He laughed, feeling the score between them was now even after she'd gotten him the previous day. After breathing an audible sigh of relief, Sandra let go of his hand in a mock huff, knowing full well he'd just gotten her back, and sat back down at the terminal to shut the remote operated suction valve to the port side strainer. She had already opened the opposite valve to avoid starving the sea water cooling pump. "OK, that's the suction valve shut, can you go down and shut the outlet valve while I grab the stud gun?" Fully expecting a 'yep' reply, she had already gotten up and headed towards the workshop, without actually having gotten a response. John chuckled and offered a salute to her turned back. He decided to throw caution to the wind and employ some of his prodigious speed and strength. By the time he was back in the MCR, the full hazardous waste bag of unpleasantness had been launched into a specific skip on the jetty already, Sandra was only just coming back from the workshop with the stud gun to start the job. John was sitting at the terminal she'd used to shut the inlet valve, now setting it to open. "I just wanted to double check the pressure before we got started to gauge how bad this is going to be. Well, that's strange, the pressure looks really good, much better than it was earlier actually." He was struggling to keep a straight face by this point, but knew he had to. Sandra now stood beside him, looking at the screen completely dumbfounded. "That's the same pressure we typically get immediately after cleaning a strainer. How is that possible!?" She couldn't help the distinct rise in the pitch of her voice. John was about ready to burst, he couldn't possibly manage to contain his laughter anymore. Some quick thinking was needed or awkward questions were sure to be forthcoming. Or maybe, he could try the truth and hope for the best. “Both the strainers are done Sandra. I’ve gotten very good at cleaning them lately and I’m stronger than I look with regards to those lids by the way. The look on your face there was priceless.” He said, not managing to hide his amusement at her dumbstruck expression. “That’s not possible, I was only away there for a couple of minutes maximum.” “The pressure there says it is. Don’t worry about it, the strainers are spotless and we can both head back to our beds now.” He said while standing up and stretching out his arms. Cleaning strainers is often rather smelly work, and Sandra had only just noticed the unmistakable aroma wafting from him. Not even his speed could outrun the stench. The smell finally convinced her that the strainers were somehow clean. Either that, or she was just too tired to think up another plausible explanation. Sandra thanked him for his help, set the system back to unattended, and headed towards the exit in order to return to her cabin. She stopped at the door and turned back around, questions in her eyes. John looked nonplussed by the gaze, patiently waiting for something to be said. After a few false starts, her mouth opening and closing soundlessly trying to think of something to ask him, she just shook her head and thanked him again before leaving. John knew what he’d done had been reckless and felt slightly abashed for it. He just wanted to help and let her get back to bed quickly rather than spend the next hour cleaning those horrible strainers. His concern was whether or not she would think too much about what had just happened. If Sandra did think about it, even a little, then an awkward conversation between the two would surely follow. John hoped that she would just be grateful and forget about how absurdly quick he’d done the job. He also decided that if he was going to help people more often, greater self-control and a lot more subtlety would be an absolute must. Once back in his cabin again, after a quick shower, John settled back into the desk chair and carried on watching the TV series Sandra had interrupted. He had quite a lot of TV series on his laptop and external hard-drive to watch, and all the nights ahead to watch them it seemed now.

Thankfully for John, the next day of work passed without the excitement of the day before. There was only a brief mention of Luke, and that was with Thomas commenting loudly that he wouldn't be missed. Sandra did mention the alarm she had during the night, as part of her handover to Kevin, who was duty that day, mentioning John had helped but without any further details, much to his relief. Sunday also meant it was a roast for lunch, something he, Arla and Callum always looked forward to. After the usual after work shower and change of clothes into a collared Honda BTCC shirt and jeans, John left his cabin, met Arla and Callum at the top of the stairs, and they headed towards the saloon for the casual lunch. The three of them sat down at an unoccupied table together and dug in to their own large plates filled with roast beef, roast potatoes, broccoli, carrots and cabbage. John was happily still very fond of Sunday lunch. Some things never change. Much to his pleasant surprise, Sandra soon joined them and sat down beside him, with Arla and Callum smiling warmly at her from across the table. John smiled warmly too, pleased to see she looked happy. They ate in silence, enjoying the well-prepared food. Callum finished his food first, John finishing soon thereafter, and they both got up from the table, handed their plates to the steward with a thank you, and headed towards the table laden with various ice creams and toppings for dessert. Returning to the table, bowls pretty much overflowing with sugary goodness, they found Arla and Sandra having an animated conversation, punctuated by frequent fits of giggles. They must've been talking about one, or both, of the men that had just sat down beside them about to dig into their ice-cream, as their conversation stopped abruptly. Both of them smiling cheekily at each other, whilst eyeing John not very covertly. He sighed and decided to try and ignore them, instead focussing on his dessert. Either Arla had forgotten about his extraordinary hearing, or she'd indulged in the conversation deliberately, knowing he would hear, to try and embarrass him again. It had started with Sandra talking about the look she'd given him on the flight deck, and Arla happily added to the conversation with another moment of embarrassment she'd caused John. A few minutes later the mischievous women finished their lunch and left the table to get some ice-cream, Arla standing up and winking at John with a knowing grin. She definitely knew he'd heard. It was nice that the two seemed closer now, John thought, only after rolling his eyes at her. He just hoped the conversation between them would only feature him sparingly. Callum quickly glanced around to make sure they were out of earshot. "What do you think they were talking about?" John merely shrugged his shoulders, despite knowing that he'd been the topic. Callum glanced around again and looked at the two women with suspicion. He gave up on the thought though and went back to eating his dessert with gusto. Arla and Sandra returned with their ice-cream, their conversation continuing, much to John's dismay, and they sat down still smiling knowingly at each other. John finished his ice-cream before Callum, brain freezes no longer a concern for him, and excused himself from the table to go for a walk around the flight deck. Arla looked a little concerned, he normally sat and talked for a moment after lunch, while the others continued, oblivious to the situation, eating their desserts. However, John wanted to be alone for a bit, not wishing to listen in as they were probably about to plan another day out in Miami, maybe even with Sandra.

He went to his cabin first, changed into a pair of shorts and a t-shirt, then found himself alone on the flight deck. The pale blue and white cruise ship's funnel must've finally been repaired during the night as a different one was now in its place. Another huge and mainly white vessel with a single large red T-shaped funnel. John was feeling a little morose now, wishing he could go ashore with Arla, Callum and possibly even Sandra, to enjoy a day out in Miami. Arla came up-to the flight deck, still in her lunch clothes, to see him a couple of minutes later. She knew something was bothering him, so she had come up to check and make sure he was at least OK. "What's up?" She asked, standing at his side and looking at him intently in the centre of the flight deck. John didn't answer right away. There was much more troubling him than just wanting to go ashore. He really wanted, no, needed to talk to Annie. Arla reached out and held his hand. "John what's up?" She asked again, sympathetically. "I need to talk to Annie, to tell her what's going on in person. I just don't know if I can hang on for the next few weeks until we go home." Arla and John were both due to pay off the ship at the same time, with Callum leaving a week later. "It's not that long until we head home John. The only way you could possibly see Annie now would be to fly home yourself, but you haven't gotten the hang of that yet. Even then, a commercial flight takes hours and those fly at over five hundred miles per hour, you couldn't possibly get there and back again without being gone for a long time. I'm afraid you'll just have to wait. I'm sorry there's no other way." Arla did look genuinely upset at this. She was right though, John thought miserably, it just wasn't possible. He'll just have to wait, as difficult as that will be. "I'm sorry for burdening you with this Arla. I'm struggling here, trying to keep everything in check. Sadly, I can't read minds, you'll be glad to know, but I can tell you want to stay here with me. Please don't. Don't ruin your day putting up with my moroseness, and don't ruin it by worrying about me either, while you are ashore. Please." He said the last word with a lot of emphasis for Arla really did look as though she wanted to stay and look after him. He appreciated the gesture immensely, but didn't wish to ruin her last day in Miami as the ship was due to sail the following day. John stared abruptly in the direction of the accommodation, listening intently. "Callum and Sandra have finished Lunch and are, nope not focusing on that, getting changed in their cabins to go ashore it seems." Arla's eyes widened in amusement and she stepped back, folding her arms across her chest while giving him a penetrating stare. John didn't like the look he was getting. "Where you watching Sandra getting undressed John? I must say she is very pretty, but what would Annie think?" She asked, clearly enjoying herself. "No, I most certainly and absolutely was not watching anyone get undressed. So you can wipe that look off your face as this little play of yours is not going to bear fruit. Not this time. I'm actually surprised you would even suggest such a thing." He said a little irritably, growing somewhat tired of his mannerisms being exploited for fun. Arla looked taken aback by his abruptness, but then a little hurt too. "Sorry, I was only trying to have a little laugh to try and cheer you up. I won't bother in the future, shall I?" She turned around and headed off to her cabin without a further word. John ground his teeth and clenched his fists in silent fury. Unable to contain his overwrought emotions, he lashed out and slammed his fist into the concrete covered flight deck. The concrete and the steel deck below didn't stand a chance, cracking and buckling respectively, leaving a very noticeable indentation. The impact had also shaken the nearby area too, of which Arla had yet to vacate, causing her to stagger and then turn around in alarm. She noticed John down on one knee, with his shaking fist slowly coming back up from the damage he'd just caused. Her mouth dropped open; he'd never lashed out like that before the entire time she'd known him. Without question, she was stunned to see John lose control in such a manner. Before Arla could say a word though, John let out a growl of frustration and, not wanting to talk anymore, turned around before leaping from the flight deck, right over Dodge Island towards the blue Miami waters of Biscayne Bay. He pivoted forward and dove under the surface head first, hoping to minimise the splash, intending to proceed out towards the Atlantic Ocean, first swimming under the William M Powell bridge connecting the mainland to Virginia Key, then passing the Bill Baggs Cape Florida State Park on his left before the open waters of the Atlantic finally beckoned him. He just wanted to be alone at that moment. He didn't want to hear all sounds caused by the hustle and bustle of the busy port, he didn't want to hear what people from the ship were planning to do ashore that day, he didn't even want to talk to one of his closest friends. John didn't even look back at Arla as he leapt away. If he had, the sight of her terrified face would've only made him feel worse. John didn't know how far out he'd swam, all he cared about was minimising the sounds as much as possible, but after finding himself a few hundred meters deep, those noises he'd desperately sought escape from had all but disappeared. The quiet soothed his frayed mind greatly and he settled calmly onto the ocean floor, causing only a small cloud of silt to billow up. John sat still for several hours watching the many different species of ocean life swimming around nearby and in the far distance. Very little light penetrated the ocean surface to this depth, but John's eyesight allowed for remarkable night vision, and he could still see clearly. After a few more precious moments of peace, he decided it was time to head back to the ship. John fully intended to lock himself away in his cabin and remain isolated for the remainder of the day. Unfortunately, he wouldn't get that chance as circumstances decided otherwise.

John arrived back on the flight deck without incident, and after doing a quick lap to dry his clothes, sighed with resignation as he trudged gloomily back towards his cabin. Before entering the accommodation, he took a quick pause to see if he could hear his friends ashore. It took a few minutes to finally locate the three of them, Sandra had indeed joined Arla and Callum, as they were walking along Ocean Drive nearly two miles from where he stood. John decided to remain where he was, listening to their conversation, a little jealously, about Lummus Park Beach and some of the shops they'd visited, and watched as they turned into an alley to head towards eighth or ninth street, judging by what was being said. A group of people emerged from behind one of the buildings ahead of them and, much to his utter horror, three of them carried guns. Sound travels at three-hundred and forty-three meters per second through air, so he knew what he saw was already a few seconds in the past. Without thought, John stepped back, leapt up a couple of decks and landed with the ship's bridge ahead of him, then took a running leap towards his friends. His spike in adrenaline caused him to go far quicker than he'd planned and John soared through the air like a guided missile. Star

Island whipped by in a blur, as did the United States Coast Guard Station to his right, just before he landed close to where the MacArthur Causeway and Alton Street joined, feeding into Fifth Street. The dust cloud from his landing had barely risen an inch before he raced on, desperate to help his friends. After what felt like a lifetime, John found himself in the same alley standing behind the group of people that were now circling Arla, Callum and Sandra. Then he noticed that the head of one of the aggressor's was oddly facing skyward, the gun he'd been holding now falling from his limp hand midway towards the ground. Unsurprisingly, Arla's foot was jammed under his chin and a couple of his teeth were even flying out. Her quick thinking of getting a retaliation strike in first hadn't deterred one member of the group though. The man's gun was drawn and a muzzle flash was just beginning to escape the barrel, chasing the bullet now racing towards Arla. John sped forward himself, catching the bullet before it had even travelled a few inches along its deadly path, using the same hand to knock the gun in the direction of the man's face, before proceeding to incapacitate the remaining members of the group. There were seven in total, he only had to deal with four now though, after having already knocked down the shooter's gun, as Callum had also leapt forward, shielding Sandra from potential harm, and was in the process of landing a well-placed straight right onto the very left-handed member of the group's jaw. John wasn't exactly trying to be careful, just hoping for the best, as he went around each member of the group. Shoving the first after the shooter in the chest towards an open bin, the far right one after him also got showed towards the same bin, he then looped around behind Callum and Sandra, giving his friend's fist a little extra momentum first, then onto the man second from the left, grabbing him by the belt from behind, reaching across with his right hand, and sending him on a path towards the wall. For the final member of the group, he decided to give him a hard sweep of the legs using his left hand. John continued forward a little more and partially hid himself from view behind the corner of the building. He looked back and smiled at his handiwork which was, in a word, carnage. The gun smashed into the first man's face hard, sending him crashing to the ground out cold. The next two flew through the air and slammed into the open bin's lid. Gravity quickly took over and they were then unceremoniously deposited, where they belonged according to John, in the rubbish. The man on the receiving end of Callum's punch actually came off the ground and landed heavily, spread eagled on his back, also out cold. Next in the semi-circle saw the person fly briefly through the air, stopping abruptly with a loud thump as the wall interrupted their unplanned flight. The penultimate member of the group went face first down. John suspected the man's dentist bill was going to be eye-watering as the crunch had been remarkably loud. Last but not least, as this individual appeared to be the group's leader, the final man dropped like a lead balloon straight down in a tangled heap of twisted limbs and missing teeth. Arla was then raising her left hand and ducking instinctively away from the muzzle flash and crack of the fired gun. Callum, his left arm reaching behind him to keep Sandra shielded, had snapped his right arm back and was poised to throw another punch, before he too ducked at the crack from the gunshot. Arla and Callum cautiously stood up straight again, after realising the threat against them had suddenly stopped, and surveyed the scene. Two legs with different trainers protruded from an open bin, and five unconscious men were lying motionless on the ground around them and John was stood partially hidden behind the corner of the building. He was completely naked. Arla and Callum gawked at him in astonishment. He thought the look on their faces were because of the bullet held in his open palm. It was only when he looked down, he realised his clothes had disappeared. They had actually burnt off because of the speed that he had raced towards his friends, as was evident by the smouldering bits of fabric that were still fluttering lazily towards the ground along the path he'd taken. Thankfully for John, Sandra was hidden behind Callum, but he and Arla were both now staring wide eyed at him and his complete lack of modesty. John hastily stepped further behind the corner, with his face turning a bright shade of crimson, and signalled for them both to be quiet. He noticed Sandra was still hidden behind Callum and mouthed 'Are you OK?' to his two startled friends. They both nodded quickly, making him sigh with relief, but the grins rapidly spreading across their faces made him curse silently shortly after. Sandra was just about to move out from behind Callum, so John gave them both a quick wave goodbye and fled the scene. Running back towards the ship, he prayed the inevitable questions he'd get from Arla and Callum wouldn't solely be about his nudity. The teasing however, that was surely going to come about because of this, no amount of prayers would prevent.

Chapter 3 – Annie

John was a happy person that day. It was time for him to head home with Arla, now that the end of their trip had finally arrived and it was the start of their last day on-board. Thankfully, the past two weeks had gone by without any major incidents for John. The ship had sailed from Miami, remained at sea for just over a week and was now in Barbados. Although the days following the incident off Oceans Drive had inevitably been filled with questions. Not just for him from Arla and Callum, but also from the Miami Police Department investigating the incident. Thankfully those questions didn't concern him though as they were directed towards the only three people 'officially' involved from the ship, Arla, Callum and Sandra. Apparently, that particular group of people were well known by the Miami PD, and had been quite the nuisance around the South Beach area for some time. To find all seven of them incapacitated had been an absolute miracle for the Police, it was like the fourth of July, Christmas and thanksgiving all at once for them. The group, up until that day, had always managed to slip through their fingers for one reason or another. As a result, and a sure sign of the Miami PD's gratitude, very few questions were asked of Arla, Callum and Sandra. This had surprised all three of them as the numerous injuries sustained by the group was quite the list. John had found the hospital they'd all landed in, finally giving in to Arla and Callum's pleading, and delighted them with the various details he'd found out. He had also been rather happy about it too, not to mention a touch proud of himself for not really seriously injuring any of them. Not ones to push their luck, Arla, Callum and Sandra hadn't asked any questions of their own and bade the investigating officers a kind farewell as soon as they could. Due to the police involvement however, word of the incident had spread like wild fire throughout the entire crew. They were asked a few questions by the Captain, Chief and the MEO due to the astounding nature surrounding it: seven unconscious men; some of whom were armed with weapons; against just the three of them.

The barrage of questions from pretty much every other crew member had been horrendous though. None of them could get any peace to do any work. Everyone they bumped into wanted to talk about what had happened. It got to the point, three days later, where a note was placed on the ship's bulletin board threatening disciplinary action against anyone who continued to harass Arla, Callum and Sandra. John felt sorry for all of them as he had also been directly involved, but had to remain silent for obvious reasons, one of which being he shouldn't have been off the ship in the first place. Not that he'd paid much attention to that during those first days after the accident, he thought with a modicum of guilt. His outburst on the flight deck hadn't been forgotten by Arla either. That had been only a brief conversation between them though thankfully for John. She had apologised again for suggesting John was spying on Sandra, accepting it wasn't at all appropriate at any-time, let alone when he had been feeling vulnerable. John also apologised for his outburst, regretting the manner in which he had lost control and then hidden himself away. Arla had been really worried about him, afraid he was about to do something stupid, and hadn't actually wanted to leave the ship and go ashore. This had made him apologise profusely once again. Callum and Sandra had to beg and plead for her to go ashore with them. Unable to specifically say why she didn't wish to go, in front of Sandra, Arla had finally relented and joined them on the bus a few minutes later, worrying about John the entire time, right up until he had suddenly appeared in front of them later that evening: Completely naked. That had ended the discussion on the matter, for John hadn't even been able to explain where he'd disappeared to, because Arla had broken down into a fit of laughter at the recollection. Even though he'd given her the bullet he'd caught, the very same bullet that could've killed her, but this didn't seem to matter. As feared, the main talking point of the incident had been his lack of clothing. It didn't matter that he'd incapacitated five men before anyone blinked. It didn't matter that he'd actually caught a bullet. It didn't even matter, and this was the really sore part for John, that he'd quite possibly saved all of their lives that evening. All that had mattered was the nudity. Callum treated the matter differently to Arla, refusing to even mention it, despite his initial amused grin, and he couldn't look him in the eye for the entire week after. This didn't really bother him too much. It was certainly preferable to the near constant state of silent giggles Arla succumbed to whilst they were together.

It was a blessing for John when, four days later and after the questioning from the rest of the ship's crew had stopped, she had managed to get over her amusement, and finally focussed on other details from the incident. The bullet fascinated rather than frightened her, and she kept it safe in her cabin. Arla had been very impressed by the self-control he had exhibited as none of their attackers were accidentally killed during his intervention. Incidentally, the most serious injury had been sustained by the man Callum had punched, which had proven to be a sore point for her because she always thought of herself as the most proficient when it came to fighting. John was happy to tell her that he'd actually given Callum's punch a little extra momentum, and that her position in that regard wasn't under any threat. Their tall friend had been quite full of himself in the days after, believing he had caused the most damage of the three of them with his punch. Arla brightened up considerably after hearing this but decided to let Callum have his little moment of superiority over her. She knew it wouldn't last long. John did too and worried a little for Callum's well-being because of it. He was sure that when the time came and Arla decided to reassert her dominance, it wouldn't be pleasant for his tall friend, and that it would only end up being that much more painful, the longer his bragging continued. Arla had also been impressed by the sheer speed in which he must've been travelling. His burnt off clothes were no longer a trigger for the giggles, they were something impressive along with her souvenir hollow point bullet. Sandra had been really scared by the event, but also equally impressed by both Arla and Callum for knocking out the seven men who had sought to harm them. Arla, Callum and John had agreed not to tell Sandra of his involvement and thus keep the accident, and the remarkable consequences, a secret too. Sandra had actually dealt with all the questions with great aplomb, simply by being honest and saying she hadn't seen much. This diverted those questions onto Arla and Callum, much to their annoyance. They didn't harbour any ill feelings towards her though for it. They knew it was the truth so it wasn't her fault at all. Their resentment had been only towards the ever-incessant questions and those whom asked them. The note on the bulletin board had only come about because Arla almost broke someone's arm, after they'd foolishly grabbed her shoulder to prevent her ignoring them. Katherine had gone apoplectic at the foolish deck officer, completely ignoring his complaints of assault, and threatened to let Arla do as she pleased if he was ever stupid enough to try and stop her again. Brian had decided not get involved in the matter, believing the MEO had dealt with it sufficiently, despite not exactly adhering to policy while doing so. Rather than try to contend with a furious Katherine, the deck department's line manager, known as the executive officer (EO), whom the deck officer in question had complained to because of the MEO's spectacular dressing down, had meekly decided to publish the note threatening disciplinary action against anyone who continued to harass those involved in the incident ashore. The aggrieved deck officer tried to take his complaint further, but was immediately told to 'wind his neck in', by the captain no less, as the whole confrontation had been his own doing in the first place. One of the more surprising outcomes from the whole situation, was Callum's knew found popularity among the women on-board the ship, much to Arla's dismay. Not a day had gone by without at least one of ship's female crew members openly flirting with him. What had been most surprising to John though, was the manner in which Callum responded to the obvious flirtation. He had been polite and refused all of their advances. Unfortunately, this went unnoticed by Arla, as she always walked away each time Callum was stopped by another woman. John was starting to suspect that his friend was harbouring feelings towards Arla. Now it was a case of who took the leap first and asked the other out. At least that's what he hoped for.

The two new engineers on-board, relieving Arla and John, were now both settled in and their hand-overs complete. From this point forward, any questions relating to what was their equipment were met with a 'don't see me, see my relief' reply. Although to be fair, all joking aside, they still hadn't officially signed off the ship yet so Arla and John were helping out where possible. John's relief was a newly qualified third officer called Allaister, and he felt the young man was quite the lunatic. His stories usually culminated with him ending up in hospital because of his fascination with fast motorbikes. John's eyes had nearly popped from his sockets after hearing how fast Allaister had rode down a country road once. The main thing though, at least as far as John was concerned, was that his relief was intelligent, keen on the job and eager to learn too. Arla's relief was an experienced second officer called Joe. They'd sailed with each other a few trips back so were quite friendly with one another, plus he was familiar with the ship already having sailed on her on his previous trip. That made their handover nice and easy seeing as everything was already quite well known to Joe. Everyone was gathered in the MCR for the morning meeting and Katherine had just asked what everyone was intending to do that day. Thomas was going to be working on deck inspecting pressure vacuum valves. Arla and Joe were going to change an injector on the starboard diesel generator. Sandra was the duty engineer again much to her deep joy, as evident by the roll of her eyes. Kevin said he had to change the oil on one of the start-air compressors as part of a maintenance task. Callum, much to his dismay, was going to be working with a couple of the engineering ratings cleaning all of the main sea water strainers. John couldn't help but chuckle, knowing that particular job would only have taken him a minute maximum, and that's only if he decided to take his time with it too. Callum also knew this and also noticed his little chuckle, prompting him to utter a few choice words under his breath. These only made John chuckle a little louder, which brought Katherine's attention straight to him. The chuckling stopped in an instant and he diverted his eyes away from the MEO's annoyed gaze. Allaister hadn't paid attention to the silent exchange between the two friends, only glancing at John briefly with mild curiosity as to why he was chuckling, as he had been too busy reading something from his notebook. Allaister then informed the MEO, after pausing uncertainly at her annoyed expression directed towards John on his left, that he and the recipient of her gaze were going to go through his upcoming jobs to chase up the spares that had been ordered for them. Satisfied everyone had something to do for the day, Katherine left the MCR and headed up a deck to the Chief's office for their usual morning discussion. As the morning crowd left to get on with their jobs, John and Allaister sat down at one of the computers to interrogate the ship's stores system and find out the delivery forecast for the ordered spares. Arla and Joe were the only other people left with them and they were sat at one of the terminals changing over the ship's running generator to the port one. After a few minutes, the talk between the two pairs of engineers was interrupted by an alarm. John got up from the computer, leaving Allaister to look up the next item on their list, to see what the alarm was, as had Joe from the terminal he was sat at with Arla. John arrived first and discovered it was a bilge alarm in the aft engine room, most likely caused by Callum cleaning the sea strainers. "Rock, paper, scissors to see who goes to investigate the bilge?" he asked Joe who was now standing beside him and looking at the screen. "Rock, paper, epaulettes off you trot mate." was the Second Officer's reply, all the while smiling pleasantly at him. That was a new one John had never heard before and it made him laugh out loud. Joe gave him a friendly pat on the shoulder and he shook his head ruefully before heading off to the aft engine room, still laughing to himself over the witty reply. Arla had heard of this saying before and was biting her lip trying not to laugh at John as he trudged out of the MCR. She only buckled, letting out a quick snort of laughter, after he had looked back towards her and gave a sarcastic thumbs up.

Once out of sight, he raced off at his preferred pace of staggeringly fast, and was standing above the overflowing bilge well in no time at all. As he'd suspected, the water had come from the strainer Callum was cleaning with two of the engineering ratings called Richard and Andrew. The strainer basket was completely choked up and had acted as a very effective bucket, hence why so much water had spilled out after they'd removed it from the housing. The three of them were busy cleaning the unpleasant contents of the basket so their backs were turned to him and they weren't aware of his presence. John opened up the suction valve for the well before turning on the oily bilge pump, located just inboard of where he was standing on the starboard side of the engine room. Callum heard the pump running because the engine room was relatively quiet as both main engines were shut down. He looked up and wasn't surprised to see John standing in front of him smiling. By now he was also used to the speed at which John could move around, as much as one could be at least, but his feats of strength still shocked him every time. The most recent example had been when John lifted one the main sea water cooling pumps, as a complete unit weighing several hundred kilograms, with one hand after only taking seconds to remove all bolts securing it to the inlet and outlet flanges. Even Arla had gawped open mouthed after that. Callum rolled his eyes and got back to cleaning the basket with Richard and Andrew, leaving John to finish pumping out the bilge well. It took a couple of minutes due to the amount of water present. Once he was content no more water was flowing into the well, John stopped the pump, shut the valve, grabbed a dip tape to find out how much the contents of the oily bilge tank had risen by, and then disappeared back up-to the MCR to make an entry into the oil record book. After signing the new entry, he sat back down beside Allaister to resume their hunt for the ordered spares. Sandra had come back into the control room, having gone to the duty watch muster, so John told her about the alarm, what caused it, and that it was already dealt with. She said a quick 'thank you' before grabbing a radio and a pager, then made to leave again to start some rounds of the various machinery spaces out-with the engine rooms. She stopped abruptly, turned around and lightly gripped John's shoulder, making him turn around and look enquiringly at her. "Don't forget to say good-bye before you head off to the airport later, please. You too Arla." She stood up straight and shouted across to her friend still sat beside Joe at the terminal. Arla gave her a swift nod and a thumbs up, John smiled and said 'of course we will'. Sandra smiled back at him then left the MCR.

Arla and John had been told to go to the ship's office and sign off at half past three that afternoon. At three twenty-nine they were both waiting impatiently outside the office, eager to sign off so they could go and pack the remainder of their things, before the transport came to take them to the airport that evening. John felt a little guilty once he'd signed off. Unknown to Arla, Callum and Sandra, he'd decided that this was to be his last trip with their company and that he was no longer going to go to sea. He had already sat down with Katherine and Brian, handing them his notice of intent to leave the company, and spoken at length regarding his decision. The MEO and the Chief were both quite shocked upon reading his notice, and even tried to change his mind seeing as they felt he was more than ready to be promoted to Second Officer. John appreciated their kind and sincere words, but ultimately decided that he wished to remain closer to home due to a change in his personal circumstances, of which he obviously didn't go into a great detail about. Such was Brian's desire for him to remain with the company, the Chief even offered to speak to the shore-side appointer to try and ensure John was only appointed to ships in refit. This would mean that he would always be closer to home and be able to speak to his family everyday, something that was very important to him. As a result, he agreed that if, and only if, he could be appointed in such a manner from then on, he would remain with the company. The Chief and the MEO vowed that they would do everything possible to make it happen. John said thanks, shook Brian's outstretched hand, was unexpectedly hugged by an emotional Katherine, and left the Chief's office a little shell-shocked by their desire for him to stay. That had happened a week ago and since then, despite the best efforts of both Katherine and Brian, the shore side appointer had bluntly rejected the refit proposal, leaving the MEO and Chief feeling incredibly resentful towards the individual. This meant that John would be saying goodbye to a grey ship for the last time once he got into the transport later on. A feeling which resulted in decidedly mixed emotions, thanks to the efforts of the MEO and the Chief. He hadn't realised how much they valued his ability and experience. Having finished the last of his packing, it was now just after five o'clock and John went to find Arla, Callum and even Sandra, for they'd become good friends over the last couple of weeks, and tell them of his decision to leave the company. He'd already spoken with Annie on a video call, after going ashore to a coffee place for some WIFI, and told her of his intention to leave and be closer to home. This had come as a shock to his wife, but it was a pleasant one and made her cry with happiness, causing him to well up too. Their son Stewart had also been happy at the news, yelling 'Daddy is going to stay at home yay!' over and over again. John was still a little worried though as he'd yet to tell Annie about the accident, something he resolutely intended to do in person.

He gathered his friends and they all sat in the Officer's bar, at which point Arla, Callum and Sandra exchanged bemused looks between them. Those looks turned to ones of complete shock after John told them this was going to be his last trip with the company. The three of them sat for several minutes in stunned silence while he closed his eyes to listen to what was going on around the ship. "Does Annie know?" Arla asked through a lump in her throat. "Yea. She was as surprised as you are initially, but she is really happy about it. I've already missed two of my Son's birthdays. I'd prefer not to miss anymore. And I just want to be closer to home and be with my family as much as possible." The three of them nodded sombrely, accepting his decision and appreciating that he didn't want to miss Stewart growing up anymore. Sandra hastily wiped a tear from her face, stood up and stepped around the table between them. John stood up and accepted the hug he was embraced with, wrapping his arms around her too. Callum was now standing, waiting in line to say goodbye to his close friend. Sandra finally stepped back and held onto John's hands, looking at him with watery eyes. "Keep in touch yea?" "Of-course I will."

She nodded and smiled sadly before stepping aside for Callum, who then also threw his arms around John, gripping him in a tight embrace. "It's going to suck without my short friend around anymore, but I'm glad you'll be home with Annie and Stewart now. Be sure to keep the guest bedroom available though as I'm definitely going to be visiting as often as I can." He said after letting John go and crossing his arms to maintain some sort of dignity while sniffing. Arla had remained sitting, knowing she'd be able to say her goodbye in private when they part ways after landing at Heathrow Airport tomorrow. Then, aware of the long running joke between the two, she saw a golden opportunity present itself. Taking full advantage of the situation, she leant forward and gave Callum a swift backhand below the belt, causing him to double over and fall to his knees, accompanied by a slew of choice words. Sandra jumped at his loud outburst then looked down at him with a mixture of concern and confusion, not knowing what had just happened. She caught Arla's and John's tight grins but, was then taken aback as they burst into laughter after a quick fist-bump. "Not so tall now are you Callum?" Arla said while rocking back and forth on her chair. "Arla that was meant to be my line! I've waited years to say that! Gah!" John threw up his arms in indignation before haughtily crossing them over his chest. Arla looked completely nonplussed and shrugged at him, her eyes and smile wide with merriment as she looked towards Sandra, who still looked completely dumbfounded. John quickly explained the long running joke between himself and Callum. Once she understood what had just happened, she bit her lip in an effort not to laugh, but even the hand swiftly covering her mouth couldn't hide the loud snort she made. This only made Arla and John laugh even more, to the extent John was now on his knees, head bowed, leaning on the chair occupied by Arla, who wasn't doing much better herself and was in turn leaning on him, howling into his shoulder. Sandra couldn't stop the inevitable now and swiftly collapsed into a chair, clutching her stomach as she too started to howl with laughter. Poor Callum was still on his knees. The torrent of cursing had stopped and was now replaced by moans of anguish as he flopped onto one side in the foetal position. After a moment, while Callum and Sandra were still both distracted, Arla had gathered herself back up and took the opportunity to wrap her arms around John's shoulders in a warm embrace. They sat like that for the next couple of minutes. Sandra was wiping tears from her face and Callum started to stir feebly on the floor, prompting Arla to let John go and pat him on the shoulder as he stood up to check on their downed friend. He knelt down beside Callum and asked if he was OK, placing a hand on his shoulder and giving a gentle shake at the same time. The question was met with a baleful glare from his friend as he turned sideways to look up at him. The glare then travelled onwards to Arla who grinned in reply. Sandra was leaning forward in her chair and watched the exchange with amusement. Callum rolled back onto his hands and knees before rising slowly, and a little unsteadily, back to his feet. Not quite able to stand up straight yet, he stood with his hands on his knees panting heavily. "Surely you knew that had to happen before I left the company, right?" John said as he gripped his friend's shoulder. Callum turned his head towards John and looked at him with a pained expression before finally nodding begrudgingly. He must've agreed that after years of nothing happening, it was only fitting something would actually happen in the end. Arla waited for Callum to resume his panting, which had weakened in its intensity by now, before standing up and walking towards him. She mouthed a quick 'sorry', which got a roll of the eyes by way of a reply from Callum, and then ducked down in front of him, looping one arm around his leg before effortlessly picking him up onto her shoulders. Sandra sat back and mouthed a quick 'wow' at Arla's impressive strength, before looking towards John and pointing at the suspended Callum with an incredulous look on her face. John had crossed his arms impassively, already well aware of Arla's prodigious lifting capabilities, and shrugged indifferently as if to say 'she really is that strong'. Sandra shook her head in wonder, watching as Arla waved goodbye before turning around and carrying Callum out of the bar back to his cabin. Once the door closed behind them, Sandra stood up slowly and also waved goodbye to John, smiling sadly as she too left to go back to her cabin, leaving him standing alone with his thoughts.

The transport was due to pick Arla and himself up in fifteen minutes. John decided to go and see if Brian and Katherine were in their cabins on the deck above so he could say goodbye. Turned out they were both in the Chief's day-room discussing the appointer who had rejected the refit proposal. The conversation was full of resentment and there was also mention of taking the matter further by contacting the head of personnel operations. The talk stopped as John knocked on the door. They both stood up to say goodbye, a quick hug from Katherine and a firm handshake from Brian, telling him after that their intention was to contact someone higher up the chain shore-side. After expressing his gratitude for their efforts and thanking them both for all of their support over the years, he left with a large lump in his throat. John picked up the pace and took his packed bags down to the bottom of the gangway, grinning as the gust of wind from his passing startled the night-watchman who had been reading a book. He jumped onto the flight deck from the jetty and knocked on Arla's door to see if she wanted him to take her bags down too. After saying 'why not' Arla turned around to pick up her back pack. Before she had even taken a step towards it, the breeze that ruffled her hair announced John's return. She picked up the back pack, gave him an exaggerated eye roll, then turned around once more to give the now empty cabin a final look over. Satisfied nothing had been forgotten, Arla followed John out, switched off the light and shut the door. Rather than heading down the stairs towards the gangway, she headed up the stairs instead towards the bridge, making John do a swift about turn and look at her curiously. The bridge was empty when they arrived, not that Arla cared as she headed out the port side external door, shutting it again once he had followed her outside, now looking even more confused. John watched as Arla leant over the railing, which was quite high up from the jetty, and then looked at him expectantly whilst inclining her head towards the Jetty. He wasn't entirely sure what his friend was after and felt obliged to clarify what was clearly some sort of request. "Please tell me you're not wanting me to pick you up and jump down to the jetty with you." Much to his great displeasure, her wide grin and rapid nod of the head confirmed that was exactly what she wanted to do. After a quick look as if to say 'are you sure', which was met with another rapid nod, John shrugged, picked her up in his arms and jumped. Arla's arms tightened around his neck but, to her credit, she didn't close her eyes, instead watching wide eyed as the ground raced up to greet them with the wind whistling by. John did his best to cushion the landing but it still gave her quite a jolt, not that she complained as it didn't seem to faze her at all. The wide smile and dinner plate sized eyes told him the drop had been exhilarating for her. Arla looked back up towards the ship's bridge, mouthed a drawn out ‘wow’, then looked at John again. “That was awesome!” She said with obvious glee in her voice. “Well, who knows, if I ever figure out how to fly, we could have a go at that together too if you like?” He replied with a wide smile. Her mouth formed a silent ‘O’ and she nodded enthusiastically. John was still smiling but the smile faded slightly as he looked up at the large grey ship he’d just left. It was going to be the last time he would ever leave one of such ships. It was a bitter-sweet moment for him. He had made many good friends during the time he’d served with the company, namely Arla, Callum and Sandra too now. On the brighter side, he would never have to see people such as Luke ever again, and there were a few he had a similar dislike towards. There were plenty of great memories of the various places he’d visited throughout the world whilst sailing on those ships. Places he would’ve never had the chance to visit. Up until the accident that is. This isn’t to say all of those memories were pleasant though. Some were distinctly unpleasant and mainly involved times where something had gone wrong, resulting in very long days sweating in cramped places trying to fix whatever had broken. Those were days he would never experience again thankfully. Although, even if he had remained with the company, the broken equipment would’ve taken seconds, perhaps minutes if it were really serious, for him to fix now. Days like that would’ve still been consigned to history. All the time he had now he'd be able to spend with Annie and Stewart, that was something to cherish and wouldn’t have been possible had he not decided to leave now.

John turned his back on the ship with a contented smile on his face, happy to be moving on. Arla was watching him, also smiling, but with a tinge of sadness. He noticed the look and had an idea of how she was feeling just then, for he thought the feelings within himself were similar. John was going to miss their trips together, and with Callum, so it was likely they were all going to see each other less often now, which wasn't a nice thought for him. Arla proved his musings to be correct a minute later, saying exactly what he had just been thinking aloud. John inclined his head and sighed audibly after she'd finished talking. They both stood in silence until the transport finally arrived five minutes later, unsure of what to say to one another next, silently wondering how things between them and Callum were inevitably going to change now. He could only hope they would all remain close. The taxi taking them to the Grantly Adams International Airport stopped in front of them. John offered to put the bags in the boot, Arla agreed and couldn't help but laugh as the driver's jaw dropped at the sight of him with two large bags in each hand. He stood patiently and waited for the driver to open the boot, Arla hiding her grin behind a hand as she struggled not to laugh, even harder taking account of the still motionless driver. It wasn't until John got fed up of being gawked at and asked the driver to open the boot, making him feel a little guilty as he hadn't exactly been polite about it. The woman driving the taxi looked a little sullen, averted her eyes and opened the boot, not offering to help, which he felt was fair considering his manners, as she hastily got back into the driver's seat and slammed the car door shut behind her. John tried to apologise but only an intelligible mumble had come out in his embarrassment. Arla looked at him and shrugged before she got into the passenger seat beside the upset driver. He got into the rear seat behind her and sat silently staring out the window as the car pulled away from the ship and headed towards the airport, not wishing to upset the driver any more than she already was. It was a very quiet and uncomfortable trip as no one spoke at all. The woman had occasionally flicked her hurt eyes towards John in the rear-view mirror, but he just stared resolutely out the window, wishing for them to hurry up and arrive at the airport. Arla didn't seem bothered by the silence as she just watched the scenery go by. They finally arrived at the airport and John was out the car before the handbrake had been applied, quickly opening the boot and retrieving their bags, putting them all on a waiting trolley before the woman had even got out the car. He quickly looked up towards her, said 'sorry' and turned around to go to the departure check in desks. Arla caught up with him a moment later, falling instep beside him without a word, although it looked as if she was trying to stop herself from laughing. "Come on Arla, let it out before you burst." To her credit she didn't laugh out loud, but she couldn't do anything about the quick snort that did escape her tightly pressed lips. She looked at him apologetically and mouthed 'sorry'. It wasn't a convincing look so he just rolled his eyes and diverted his gaze towards the many check in desks out in the open in front of them. He found it curious the check in desks were actually outside under a vast roof assembly, rather than in the building. John spotted the right desk for their flight to London Heathrow with British Airways. The man at the desk was polite and efficient so the check-in was very quick, their bags were tagged and headed off down the conveyor built to disappear into the mysterious inner workings of airport luggage logistics. Airport security was never fun and more often than not involved a lengthy wait. Today was no exception as the airport was incredibly busy with thousands of people mingling around, talking and waiting for their flights. Bored by the long wait in the security line, John closed his eyes and focused on everything that was going on around him. He could see everyone within the airport at that moment and hear all of their individual heartbeats. Oddly, one individual far off to his left didn't appear to actually have a beating heart. His eyes flew open and he scanned the area off to the left, searching all the faces, pairing them up with their respective heartbeats as he ticked them off one by one in his mind. Only seconds had passed but before he could pair everyone up, a fleeting figure in the distance disappeared from view and was even lost to sound. There was a vast throng of people so he hadn't been able to make out any details of whatever the oddity had really been. He shook away the misgivings creeping up his spine and stored them away to be mused over at a later date. John was heading home to his beautiful wife and son, that was what was important. Arla was ahead of him in the line, busy looking around ahead of them so she hadn't noticed his look of disquiet.

In a rare occurrence, they both breezed through security without having to suffer the indignity of a patted search. Back packs collected, Arla and John headed towards the duty-free shopping to see if there was anything worth buying. Arla found a nice, eye-bogglingly expensive, pair of sunglasses while John was entirely predictable and bought a couple of small Lego sets, one being a junior one for his son. He also found a bottle of perfume Annie was particularly fond of so purchased one of them too, otherwise his wife might have been a trifle upset with him for not getting her anything. Arla noticed the bottle of perfume in his hand and asked where he'd gotten it from, as she hadn't spotted it during her browsing and it was one she also liked. John pointed out where he found it and she dashed off to get herself one too. After purchasing his items and carefully placing them in his backpack, John set off towards the

Starbucks coffee shop to get one of their fudge hot chocolates he spotted on the menu board. Arla caught up with him a few minutes later, new sunglasses perched on her head and old ones now in her back-pack. Now standing at the edge of the queue, Arla was still close enough to request a blonde roast caramel latte. Which was another thing she had in common with Annie, although his wife always asked for extra caramel too. The terminal building was air conditioned so a hot drink wasn't exactly out of place. Their gate wasn't to be announced for over an hour so they both decided to go and look at the other shops to pass the time.

Nearly two hours later, it was time to board the Boeing triple seven aircraft, which was going to be taking them back to the United Kingdom. The flight was scheduled for just under eight hours. John hoped there was a decent selection of movies available to watch on the in-flight entertainment system. He and Arla were sharing a row of three between them near the front of the aircraft. An extreme rarity in that they were usually lucky to be on the same plane, never mind the miracle of being in the same row on the same plane. Furthermore, for John at least, they weren't sitting over a wing. He was pleasantly surprised by this, and began thinking that his luck with regards to air travel was finally taking a turn for the positive. John was allocated the window seat while Arla, much to her annoyance, had to make do with the aisle seat. She boarded the aircraft first however and brazenly sat in the window seat, looking at him smugly and sticking her tongue out at him, before having the audacity to then hand over her back-pack for him to put in the overhead locker. His mouth agape and face set with indignation was dealt with by Arla batting her eyelids and smiling coyishly. As usual he relented with a rueful shake of the head and put both of their bags into the locker, before sitting down heavily into what should've been his friends' seat. "You know, if you had asked, I would've agreed to swap, rather than you just nicking my seat." He said quietly, looking at Arla with a surly expression. "I know you would've so I just saved us both the time and sat down here anyway," She replied, followed by a self-satisfied grin. John opened his mouth to say something scathing in return, but decided against it and merely grunted in annoyance before settling down and unpacking the headphones that were provided for the entertainment system that was built into the headrest of the chair in front. He was in the process of picking a film to watch when the entertainment service was interrupted by the typical flight safety demonstration. Having seen numerous demonstrations in the past, and despite the caution that something could be different in this one, John ignored it and looked over towards Arla, who looked just as impatient as he felt right then, as she had also been interrupted in selecting something on the entertainment system. They rolled their eyes at one another and sat back to at least pay a little bit of attention to the cabin crews' demonstration. Still bored, John looked back at Arla to strike up a conversation. "Did you know this aircraft is fitted with what are currently the world's largest and most powerful jet engines, capable of around one-hundred and fifteen-thousand pounds of thrust?" Arla was roused out of her brief stupor and looked over at him wearily. "Are you really that bored you just tried to talk about engines after I've spent the last four months looking after them?" John thought of replying but realised his friend had a point so waved off the poor attempt at conversation and tried to think of something different to talk about. Arla's weary expression proved quite distracting as she continued to stare at him though. "What plans have you got for when you get back home?" He asked. She thought for a moment before answering. "Well, I've got a holiday booked to Las Vegas for some MMA training. After that I'm looking at buying a new car as my current one is coming up-to three years old. Oh, by the way, Annie invited me to stay with the three of you once I've gotten the new car. You know, I'll break it in by driving across to stay with you." Arla replied happily with a smile. The invitation for her to stay at his for a while was news to him, plus the trip to Vegas specifically for MMA training could mean something to do with one of the sports top organisations, so he looked mildly surprised and impressed. The look wasn't missed by his friend and she feigned a look of modesty, which was ruined by the wide grin that suddenly appeared. "Annie knows about my trip to Vegas too so she invited me to stay with you to say congratulations once I get back." "And I didn't know about any of this why?" He asked with a hurt look. Arla's mouth dropped in horror at the pain in his eyes. She was just about to reach over and grab his hand when he smiled mischievously at her. "Sorry I couldn't resist that. Wow, that's awesome Arla. Are you actually going there to try out for that organisation?" Before his question was answered, he was punched in the arm with a surprising amount of force, making several people nearby look over in surprise at the sound. John didn't mind the dig to his arm, he knew she knew it wouldn't hurt him so no harm done. Arla was frowning at him as she retracted her clenched fist and sat back down properly in the borrowed-without-permission window seat. It took a few minutes for her to get over the indignation of his joke, after which she told him about the phone call she'd gotten regarding a try-out. John was seriously impressed. The organisation was widely considered as the best promotion in MMA and was home to the sport's best fighters too. For Arla to even get a try-out was incredible and a testament to her abilities. John really hoped she would be successful with the Vegas visit as he truly felt it was a just reward for her dedication and hard work. Especially considering their, well not his anymore anyway, line of work too, being away from home and her local gym for great lengths of time. John did feel a little aggrieved that Annie had kept this and the invitation from him, but he guessed it was meant to be some sort of surprise so he didn't hold onto any resentment. The surprising conversation had gone on way past the end of the safety demonstration as the plane was now taxiing towards the runway for take-off. Realising they could now use the entertainment system again, their headphones went on and they both set about finding something to watch. Before John could find something to view, he got a sudden feeling as if someone was watching him. He sat bolt upright and looked around the other seats. No one on-board the aircraft was paying him the least bit of attention. He turned and looked past Arla out the window, watching the terminal building, and the thousands of people in it, go by before it was replaced by grass and the end of the runway as the plane turned. It had been a truly peculiar feeling for him, one he hadn't shaken off until after the seatbelt signs had gone out. Arla, for the second time since they'd gotten out of the taxi, hadn't noticed the concerned look on his face since she had already started watching a film. John's uneasy feeling was washed away from seeing what film his friend was watching. In the film, he saw a pale skinned man sparkling in sunlight. Sighing heavily, loud enough to attract an annoyed glance from Arla, John eventually picked out a film for himself. Ironically, the film he chose was about a popular humanoid alien with a weakness to luminous green rocks. Arla had peered over and snorted at his choice of film, as she removed her headphones and nudged him to get his attention. "He would take you easily and is far better looking so don't get ahead of yourself." John raised his eyebrows in surprise and looked directly at her. She stuck out her tongue before putting the headphones back on and going back to the sparkly man on her small screen, all the while smiling at his wide-eyed look. He went back to his own film and silently disagreed with her. For one, Annie, as far as he was concerned, was the most beautiful woman in the world so he must've at least been quite appealing to the eye. Secondly, he knew he hadn't even scratched the surface of what he was now capable of doing, making it possible that any sort of theoretical match up wouldn't go as Arla suspected. Finally, he very much doubted a little green rock would be able to do him any harm. John smiled to himself in a self-satisfied way and settled in to watch the film.

Several hours later, John stared out the window beside Arla and watched the sprawling city of London go by as the plane circled over Heathrow airport. There were quite a few famous landmarks to be seen. The Shard, the tallest building in London and western Europe, Parliament house with Big Ben, the huge London Eye wheel and even Tower Bridge all flashed by. The plane was now just moments away from touching down; landing on home soil was always a great moment for him after being away from home for so long, and the runway was racing up to meet them. John's happiness was shattered the instant the plane's wheels touched the tarmac. Something was wrong. There had been a loud metallic crunch followed by the aircraft lurching horribly to the side he and Arla were sitting on. Time seemed to slow down for him as he turned and looked out of the windows on each side of the plane. The Sky was visible through one, with nothing but unforgiving tarmac visible out of the one beside Arla. Her eyes had opened wide in horror and one of her hands was reaching out to grab his. However, John didn't stay long enough for their hands to meet. He had snapped and tore off his seatbelt, rather than waste time unbuckling it, and was racing down the aisle to the front of the aircraft, watching as the other passengers were now ducking forward and covering their heads, or were opening their mouths to scream in terror. He had to do something otherwise Arla could die right there on the plane with over three hundred other people. Their lives suddenly weighed heavily on him and he was desperate to somehow save them all. John reached the door at the front of the plane and shoved it hard with one hand, causing it to buckle and come free of its hinges, while grabbing onto the aircraft with the other and leaning out to see how dire the situation had become. He felt like he could've thrown up after seeing just how bad it was. The massive engine was now touching the runway and sparks were starting to appear as the plane continued to tip over. Knowing the highly flammable aviation fuel was stored within the wings, John stepped out the plane, pushing aside the seemingly floating door, which gravity had yet to take a hold off, and used his hand to propel himself down the side of the aircraft's fuselage towards the wing. He noticed Arla's hand had barely moved towards where his had been as he flew by her window, then slammed hard into the leading edge of the wing, leaving a large dent. John braced his left hand against the fuselage, gripped the edge of the wing with his right, and proceeded to rip the entire wing off in one powerful movement. He turned and watched as the separated wing seemed to crawl slowly along beneath him. John had dug his fingers firmly into the plane after ripping off the wing and was now hanging on its side, the wind trying to tear off his clothes. He hung for a moment longer and realised he'd made a terrible mistake. The plane was now unbalanced and was probably going to roll the other way thanks to the weight of the remaining wing, before coming to a safe stop. The tarmac was still travelling by under his hanging feet, visible in the small gap between the fuselage and separated wing, at over a hundred miles per hour, fast enough that a major disaster was still very much a possibility, and a safe stop was still a way off yet. He used his grip to force himself down to the ground through the small gap, breaking past the now serrated broken wing edge and shredding his clothes, landing heavily and stumbling until he found his footing again under the planes vast belly. Only seconds had gone by so John prayed no one had been able to see him yet, nor any cameras catch him either. Now that he was under the plane, he saw what had caused the trouble. The landing gear on the right-hand side was completely gone and was now bouncing down the tarmac, desperately trying to keep up with the runaway plane, passing under the horizontal stabilisers at the rear. John had decided on a desperate plan. One he should've done all along, but would've significantly increased the likelihood of him being spotted, he thought regrettably. Even though the wingspan of the Boeing triple-seven was huge, the engines were still suspended over the tarmac which could spell disaster if the plane were to tilt over. Which this particular triple-seven aircraft was now starting to do. He ran towards the engine and slid under it, catching the leading edge of the outer casing with one hand, ripping off one of the panels underneath with the other and pressing it firmly into the tarmac above his head, creating a bright shower of sparks. He was hoping the dazzling display would hide his presence from view as the engine came down and crushed him into the unrelenting ground. The plan was working. Rather than the engine hitting the ground, deforming, fragmenting and being torn off, potentially resulting in a deathly fireball as the remaining fuel in the wing ignited, he was acting as a buffer. The sparks weren't a prelude to an impeding inferno, they were a harmless show as there was no way for them to ignite the still safely contained fuel. Being ground into tarmac, by the world's largest jet engine no less, wasn't pleasant and it took an unbearably long time for the aircraft to finally come to rest. John had frantically moved the now very worn panel around as the speed bled off, trying to maintain his curtain of sparks and remain hidden, until he thought it was safe to remove himself from under the engine. At that point, he discarded the panel, somewhere he felt it could conceivably have landed, and disappeared up into the open void of the missing landing gear to hide. With the plane now safely stopped, he took a moment to calm his overwrought nerves. John managed to save the lives of over three hundred people, a pretty happy thought, but by foolishly ripping the wing off in his moment of panic, rather than going under the engine like he'd just done, he had effectively written off the aircraft and cost British Airways many, many, millions of pounds in damages. Not such a happy thought. "I'm not very good at this superhero lark" he said aloud quietly, shaking his head miserably.

John realised with a start that his clothes were in tatters, which brought on a fresh wave of panic. He was amazed though that his phone had somehow managed to survive, after finding it still sat in one of his tattered pockets. Much to his relief, he spotted a hatch above him that went into the plane's cargo hold. After forcing it open, finding the bag with his civilian clothes in and changing into something that partially resembled the tatters he had been wearing. John searched around, once his phone was safely pocketed again, and found an obscure entrance into the passenger compartment. He cautiously made his way back up and found himself in the galley area towards the rear of the plane, away from prying eyes. The passengers were all in a state of fear and panic as the plane had come to rest just seconds ago. Most were still bent forward in the brace position covering their heads with their hands. Many people, including several children and even a baby, John realised with horror, were crying. Only a few were starting to stir and slowly sit upright, realising they were somehow, miraculously, still alive. He took the opportunity, granted by the passenger's disorientation, to run back to his seat, hoping his absence hadn't been overly obvious amidst the panic. Arla was already sitting upright, peering around wildly with concern all over her face, clearly looking for where he'd disappeared to. His sudden re appearance caused her to cry out in relief and she lunged at him, wrapping her arms around him in a tight embrace and burying her face into his shoulder. She wasn't crying, but her breathing was fast and shallow, indicating just how much of a fright the whole ordeal had been. John was also struggling to calm down, subconsciously taking deep, steadying breaths as he looked around at the other passengers starting to move around and check on one another. The care and compassion shown by the other passengers for each other, complete strangers they'd never met before, proved to have a calming effect on John. People can band together and do incredible things for one another during times of crisis, showing the human spirit at its finest in his opinion. Arla had released her hold of him and was now sitting in the middle chair holding his hand in both of hers. She looked around at all the people around her silently almost as if in a daze, before staring into his eyes with a look of dawning recognition once she'd noticed the different clothes he was now wearing. "Did you do this?" She asked in barely a whisper amongst the chaos of voices around them. He gave her a barely perceptible nod accompanied by a haunted expression. She mouthed 'thank you' as her eyes watered and she stretched up to kiss him on the cheek. John turned his head, grateful for a reason to avoid her gaze before he too got emotional, and accepted the thanks with closed eyes. Arla leant her head against his cheek after and they both sat motionless, emotionally drained after the harrowing experience. One that could've gone better, but could've also been so much worse as far as John was concerned. He took it as a win overall, and was content in the knowledge his bumbling actions had still managed to save a lot of lives that day.

The emergency services arrived soon after the aircraft had come to a halt and worked with the cabin crew on-board to safely evacuate everyone from the stricken plane. Flights were now being hastily diverted to Heathrow's other runway, or to other airports, by the calm and controlled people within air traffic control. John and Arla left the plane via the door he had ripped off at the front and made their way to the large group of passengers now forming under the direction of the emergency services. It was an overcast day with a cold breeze in the air and many people were wrapped in the thermal blankets that were being handed out. They looked back towards the plane, once the fireman directing them was satisfied they were at a safe distance, and watched as the remaining passengers slid one-by-one down the inflatable evacuation slides. The plane was at an odd angle resting on its left wing, the right wing was actually on fire with the debris spread over hundreds of meters down the side of the runway. The airport's huge Aircraft Rescue and Fire-fighting Vehicles were already on the scene and dousing the flames with foam. John watched silently, cursing himself for thinking his luck was finally on the up with flying, as Arla huddled against him wrapped in one of the thermal blankets. He remembered his phone, retrieved it from his pocket, and switched off airplane mode. There were several messages and missed calls from Annie. She liked to track his flight by using an app on her tablet and would've known he had landed, albeit with a crash. Stewart would be at nursery by now, so she would most likely have been watching a film while browsing social media, waiting for his flight to land so she could talk to him. He hoped there hadn't already been various 'breaking news' stories informing of the crash. That would cause her to worry like crazy until she'd managed to talk to him. John opened up the contacts list and called his wife's number. Annie must've had the phone in hand as she answered immediately. "John?! Oh my god, are you OK? Wasn't Arla on the same flight, is she OK? I saw the news about the crash and I threw up. I've been trying to call you, I'm so happy to hear your voice. What happened? The images on the news are horrific, fire stretching down the runway and the plane is missing a wing too!" Annie rushed the questions and didn't seem to even breathe, with relief clearly evident in her voice. "I'm OK Annie, Arla is too. We were really lucky as no one was seriously injured, despite how dramatic it must look on the news, especially with the fire down the runway. I'm really happy to hear your voice too, but I need to go now as I think we're all about to be taken to the terminal building as buses are approaching. I'll call you again when I can and tell you what happened from where we were sitting. I love you, bye." Annie seemed to be holding back tears as she told him she loved him too and hung up. Arla was also hanging up her phone after briefly talking to her parents and assuring them she was OK. Her phone went off again though before she could put it back in her pocket. She did a double-take and showed John the screen, prompting an identical reaction from him too. Callum was trying to call her. Arla answered the phone and must've been bombarded with questions as she couldn't seem to get a word in. Eventually, just as the buses were stopping beside them, she managed to assure Callum they were both OK, although John didn't actually hear his name mentioned at all, and that it was time for them to board a bus to the terminal building. They were taken to one of the empty hangars to be checked over by waiting medical staff. Arla and John, however, politely declined the offer. Then the cabin crew from their flight, who were now sat behind makeshift desks with laptops, saw to each passenger in order to organise onward transportation, if it wasn't possible to catch their pre-booked connecting flight. The option was also offered to organise a method of travel that didn't involve an airplane. Arla was quite happy to catch her connecting flight to Glasgow, departing in two hours' time, while John was also content to fly again as his connecting flight to Edinburgh wasn't due to take off for three hours yet. All of the passenger's luggage had been removed from the aircraft already and was in the same hangar on the small baggage trucks airports used to transport it. Arla and John were both assured by the professional staff that their luggage would be on their connecting flights, so they were now free to go and wait in the terminal for departure.

John had been very impressed by the cabin crew seeing as they had all just suffered through the same crash, yet they were all still working, courteous and helpful, whereas all he wanted to do was lie down in a dark room somewhere and relax. Both of their flights were departing from Terminal five so they got on the bus heading there and waited for the other passengers to board. Turned out there weren't many who opted to fly again, with fewer still departing from the same terminal they were in, as only three other people got on before the bus left. John had spotted hundreds of people lining the vast glass front of the terminal five building, watching the events following the crash unfold, after he'd gotten off the aircraft. Many of whom were still standing by the glass gawking at the scene, he noticed angrily, as they entered the cavernous structure. Arla saw the anger on his face and dragged him towards the Harrods store to prevent a scene. The distraction, much to her dismay, only partially worked as he kept glancing towards the onlookers and frowning each time they faced the runway. Arla bought a new handbag and made sure she kept herself between him and the source of his ire as they headed towards Starbucks for a drink. Unfortunately, even she had her limits with regards to the morbid fascination on display by some of the gathered crowd. A particularly rowdy group of what appeared to be body-builders, wearing vest tops or far too tight T-shirts, pushed past them, commenting loudly on how awesome the crash had been, and knocked her into the now irate John. Arla quickly regained her footing and marched after the group, with John following closely, and grabbed the biggest and loudest guys arm, spinning him around to face her. “Do you mind not shoving me out the way?” She was right up in his face, despite being a head shorter than the heavily muscled man. He laughed derisively and made to shove her back, clearly clueless as to who stood in front of him, but immediately stopped laughing as he suddenly found himself on his back after a swift hip toss from Arla. The man's friends stood stock still as if caught in headlights, unsure of what to do as their leader struggled to his feet again. The mountain of a man called Arla something foul, making her snarl fiercely and hold up her hands to goad him on, and then he rushed forward with his arms apart hoping to grapple the little woman and force her onto the ground. John moved closer, flanking the man's dumbstruck friends in case they were foolish enough to get involved, and watched fascinated as Arla drove her heel into the man's temple with an astonishingly fast spinning kick, making him crash heavily into the ground limp and out cold. The demise of their leader had stirred the remaining muscle-bound louts and they all started to move towards Arla, only to find themselves toppling like dominos, falling comically over one another, as John drove his shoulder into the one he was standing beside. He smiled at the mass of flailing limbs trying to disentangle themselves from each other after they'd all crashed to the floor. Arla caught his eye, also smiling widely, and motioned her head for him to vacate the scene sharpish and follow her into the gathering crowd, curious as to what the disturbance had been.

They put a good distance between themselves and the crowd before emphatically high fiving one another and laughing at the havoc they'd wrecked upon the rowdy group. Sometimes karma acted swiftly. "That kick was incredible Arla, no wonder you got that Vegas invitation." John said, not bothering to disguise the awe in his voice. "Something like that is easy when faced with an idiot who clearly had no idea how to fight." She replied modestly, waving off his compliment. "The aftermath of your timely shoulder block was hysterical though. I'll never forget all those stunned faces as they toppled over." John chuckled at the thought, although his comedy factor was from the flailing limbs rather than the shocked expressions. They went up the escalator at the opposite end of the building from the gathered crowd, now clearly visible from their elevated viewpoint. John watched with amusement as two of the group had managed to heave up their unconscious friend, supporting him with an arm across each of their shoulders, and drag the huge man off towards a first aid post. Arla was leaning on the railing beside him smiling broadly, equally as amused by the scene. She stood up again and looked around for, what he guessed due to the rumble coming from her stomach, somewhere to eat. Arla jerked her head towards one of the restaurants, and he nodded in agreement, smiled at his correct assumption, and they both went to get some lunch. The conversation between them as they ate, both were tucking into a burger with fries, branched into several different topics but was mainly about what John was now planning to do, now that he'd left the company she still worked for. He wasn't entirely sure, but wasn't shy in admitting that he may make judicious use of his superhuman abilities in whatever endeavour he undertook next. Arla had suggested boxing or even MMA, but John declined claiming it would look awfully suspicious having a complete unknown, with no apparent experience, come along and knock out or easily defeat everyone in front of him. He also felt it would be blatantly cheating, considering the insurmountable physical advantages he held over literally anyone else on earth. Arla accepted his reasons and inclined her head thoughtfully, admiring his integrity for not wanting to just turn up and dominate as he so easily would. John came up with an interesting idea after a moment of silence, by which time they had both finished their food. "I wonder if I could use my hearing to distinguish between different materials similar to ground penetrating radar? If I can, then I could actually try a bit of prospecting and sell the minerals and metals as a means to live by? I could go to places no one else could go, deep ocean, middle of the desert, frozen barren wastelands and all sorts." "That's probably one of the best ideas you've ever had John, and that's saying something considering one of your previous ideas somehow ended up with you married to your lovely wife." Arla had sat back and crossed her arms, clearly impressed by the suggestion. John was feeling rather chuffed at the compliment and agreed wholeheartedly, although he had no clue as to what idea had actually led to the ring he wore on his left hand. Like Arla said though, it must've been brilliant as he always felt extremely lucky whenever he thought of Annie. "If you do manage to succeed at prospecting, be sure to send some of the goods my way though. I'd quite like to be a lady of leisure." Arla said with a little chuckle. "I'd be more than happy to do so Arla, but come on. You would never be a lady of leisure. There will always be something you want to do. You could focus full time on your MMA if you no longer had to work though." He said, emphasising the suggestion by gesturing with his hands too. Arla looked to be deep in contemplation at this. Her eyes widened after a moment and she looked him in the eye, leaning forward and resting her forearms on the table between them. The idea had clearly struck a chord within her. "I'm going to indulge in this little fantasy here because the things you've been able to do since that accident have been nothing short of incredible, and I believe this is something you can actually do. How about we make it a joint venture though, we'll even get Callum in on it so he doesn't have to go to sea anymore. Bloody hell, with Callum and I helping, you would be able to identify: different minerals and metals; identify prospective buyers; and sort out any relevant taxes that'll arise from our earnings?" John was taken aback at how much thought Arla had put into his original idea. Her faith in his abilities and belief that they could succeed with this endeavour filled him with confidence. He reached out and firmly shook Arla's outstretched hand, sealing the deal and beginning an exciting new chapter in both of their, and hopefully Callum's, lives. John wasn't sure how to go about training his senses to detect prospective minerals and metals, but he was certain that with the help of his friends, they would be able to succeed and make a good living from it. One of the main benefits to bloom out of John's idea was that he, Arla and Callum would no longer have to rely on being on the same ship to spend time together. They were all going to set up some sort of small company and work together. There were inevitably going to be long conversations about what they were going to look for, how much to extract without raising too many questions, who to approach in order to sell the goods and how to keep their method of extraction, his bare hands, a secret. Numerous other considerations will need to be sorted out too, but these were all what he believed to be good problems to have. The main benefit of the idea for John though, was more time at home with Annie and Stewart. It was the happiest thought he'd had since the accident and he smiled at the opportunities their future together now held.

Arla's flight had now been called to head to their gate in preparation for boarding. They both stood up, having long since finished their lunch and subsequent hot drinks, and headed towards the gate together. "Well, I thought this was going to be goodbye for a while there John. As it turns out, this is now see you again soon." Arla said happily as she gave him a quick hug. "Ah, it was never going to be goodbye Arla. You live just over an hour's drive away for crying out loud! We'll sort out our little joint venture during your stay after you get back from Vegas. Good luck with that by the way, not that you'll need it. By that point Callum will have left the ship, so I'll invite him to stay too and we'll see what he thinks of our idea." "Thanks John, I'll video chat Annie after the try out and you'll find out then too. Oh, before I go and leave you all on your lonesome, do promise you'll at least try and stay out of trouble yea?" Arla smiled a little as she said it but John knew there was a serious undertone to her words. "I will do my best, but as you've seen lately, trouble seems to be quite fond of me these days." He held out his hands in a 'I can't help it' gesture. Arla smiled again and motioned her head reluctantly in agreement. Behind her, the other passengers on her flight to Glasgow were now moving forward for boarding. Another quick hug, and then Arla dashed off towards the gate to head home. John stood and watched until she was out of sight, they both gave a quick wave bye, then looked around, wondering what to do now as there was still an hour to pass before his own flight to Edinburgh. He decided another hot chocolate would pass some of the time, so he headed towards Starbucks yet again. John only just realised, with quite some guilt, he hadn't yet phoned his dad Phil to let him know he was back in the UK. He knew his dad wouldn't be overly bothered, Annie would've most likely already called him to let him know John was OK, as very little seemed to faze him. Being a retired naval officer often made his dad the only calm head amongst a panicked crowd, much like when he'd helped safely evacuate several people from a burning shop once. The wait seemed to drag by after the call with his dad ended, typical for being so close to home, until it was finally time to board his flight up to Edinburgh. Thankfully, this one went by without any incident and the plane even landed a couple of minutes early. It was a bright sunny day in Scotland and he'd been able to clearly see the three bridges spanning the river Forth prior to the smooth landing. John had to exercise a huge amount of restraint not to dash to the front of the plane and get off first once the seat belt signs had been extinguished, making do with patiently waiting his turn, whilst helping a shorter woman struggling to extract her bag from the overhead locker, before finally exiting the aircraft and heading towards the baggage reclaim hall. Annie and Stewart were waiting to pick him up and he set off at a fast run, winding in and out of the other startled passengers as he breezed by, eager to see them again after four long months away. John pretty much leapt down the stairs, avoiding the slow-moving escalator, rounded the corner and saw his wife and son sitting on a nearby bench. Annie spotted him first, pointed him out to Stewart, who then leapt from the bench, shouting 'daddy' excitedly, and then ran into John's open arms as he knelt down to hug his excited son. John stood up with Stewart in his arms, happily saying 'daddy' over and over, and ran towards Annie, who was already running over to greet him. They crashed into each other, although John was careful not to let their son get sandwiched between them, and he gripped her in a tight one-armed embrace while planting a long overdue kiss on his wife's waiting lips. He didn't know how long they stood there locked together. He would've happily stayed like that for hours, as it wasn't until Stewart cried out 'Mum, Dad!', clearly embarrassed by their public display of affection, that they reluctantly separated and smiled broadly at one another. "Hi honey" John said still holding his wife close with one arm. "Hello ex-sailor" Annie said with delight in her voice, making him laugh and bring her in close again for another quick kiss. The happily re-united family of three made their way as one to the baggage reclaim belt, which was now slowly trundling around with a large group of people gathered waiting to pick up their bags. Annie noticed the new crescent shaped scar on the side of her husband's head as they headed towards the conveyor belt, and looked mildly alarmed. John noticed her expression and said 'I'll tell you when we get home'. She briefly looked as if she wanted to discuss it there, but relented and nodded quickly in agreement. John retrieved his bags, put them on a trolley, and they headed out of the arrival's hall to their parked car, Stewart walking between them holding his hand. They had a blue Honda Civic that Annie had managed to park close by the lift on the second floor of the multi-storey car park. He put his three bags in the boot while Annie made sure Stewart was secure in the child's seat in the back, on the passenger side of their car. Once their son was safely strapped in Annie walked up-to to John as he waited by the boot, wrapped her arms around his neck and gave him another long lingering kiss. He wrapped his arms around her and lifted his wife off the ground. They eventually surfaced for air, grinning sheepishly as many people were walking by averting their eyes. John reluctantly put Annie back on the ground and she made her way round to the driver's side to take them all home, their fingers touching until they couldn't reach anymore.

Rush hour hadn't started yet so the drive home took less than thirty minutes. They lived in the Duloch area of Dunfermline in a nice four-bedroom detached house. Their home was ideally located as Annie's parents were only a fifteen-minute walk away along the road. John's dad was a short drive away in Rosyth and a large superstore was only a short walk from their front door. They had replaced their front garden with a mono-block driveway so three cars could now fit comfortably outside the house. The large back-garden had a flagstone patio area and a shed in the back left corner on a gravel quarter circle lined with smooth stone, but was mainly grass for their German Shepard Jay. The house itself had a garage to the left of the front door, and the dining room was visible through the front window on the right. There was a wash room under the stairs and a newly re-modelled kitchen and utility room on the right at the end of the entrance hall, with the stairs up on the left. Finally, the living room was at the end of the hall on the right. Upstairs had the four bedrooms, the master and second largest both had en-suites and were on the left, the main bathroom, which Annie was hoping to re-model over the next few months, was in the centre and the other two bedrooms, Stewart's at the front of the house beside the master and one for guests at the back, were on the right-hand side of the stairs. The loft had also been fully floored and had a built-in ladder that folded down when the hatch was opened. John's vast Lego collection was on a large wooden shelf at the front, installed by one of his best friends, Richard, and ran the entire width of the house. Annie didn't mind his collection and even had a few large sets of her own. John really had struck gold when he married Annie. Stewart said a quick 'hiya' to Jay, who was bounding around and whining excitedly at their arrival, before running off to the living room to play with his toys John presumed. Jay leapt up at him, a paw on each shoulder, licked his face quickly and then almost bowled over Annie as he crowded around her, clearly more excited at seeing his 'mum', who had only been gone just over an hour, than he was at seeing John who had been away far longer. This was common though, so he didn't mind at all and carried his bags upstairs to their bedroom. Back downstairs in the living room, Annie was sitting on their three-seater sofa with Jay, who was sprawled over the other two spots with his head on her lap, leaving no room for John to sit beside her, even though the currently unoccupied two-seater sofa had a blanket on it for him. He shrugged, again, as this also wasn't an uncommon occurrence, and sat down on the floor beside Stewart who started to eagerly show him some of his new toys he'd gotten while John was away at work. Annie looked on and smiled as Stewart explained to her attentive husband who each of the characters were, telling his dad the toys were based on a new tv show he enjoyed, and showed what each one did in terms of play features. While their son was busy grabbing a different toy to show him, John quickly looked up and smiled at his wife, mouthing a quick 'Love you', to which Annie mouthed 'Love you too' in return, before returning his attention to the next toy he was being shown. It was wonderful to be home.

Later that day, with Stewart fast asleep in his bed after a short story read by John, it was time for a potentially difficult conversation. Something John had dreaded since the moment he arrived back home, but knew he couldn't delay anymore. Annie was in the kitchen beside the boiling kettle, making him a hot chocolate, by the time Stewart was asleep, so he went to the fridge, picked up an open bottle of wine, grabbed a glass from a cupboard and poured her a small drink. He placed the glass beside his cup and wrapped his arms around her waist and nuzzled her neck, making her giggle and squirm a little because of his stubble. Annie looked at him affectionately, as he turned his face gently towards hers and she kissed him lightly. She kept her hand on his face, rubbing her thumb contentedly over his cheek, and finished making the hot chocolate with the other free hand. Drinks ready, they walked hand-in-hand back into the living room and sat on the three-seater sofa close together. Jay was snoring blissfully stretched out on the other sofa.

"Annie, there's something I need to tell you. I was involved in an accident while the ship was in Miami, which resulted in the scar you spotted at the airport." His wife turned her body to face him, placing an arm across the back of the sofa with her hand caressing the side of his face and the aforementioned scar, whilst lifting her legs and tucking them up underneath her. John told her everything. It took a long time and Annie sat silently throughout, her face occasionally growing alarmed and at times, he couldn't blame her, a little disbelieving. She hadn't moved during his speech, although her hand did stop on the side of face briefly a couple of times, and now she sat staring at him with an inscrutable expression. John's heart seemed to stop beating and he held his breath as he waited for some sort of reaction from her. To his great surprise, and after only a moment of stunned silence, Annie's first words were 'Show me'. John nodded and slid his hand under his wife's shapely bottom, the only woman's bottom he would ever be willing to touch at that, she raised her eyebrows and smiled expectantly, before putting her glass on the floor, and then he easily lifted her up off the sofa until his arm was straight and she was above his head, looking down wide-eyed and open-mouthed. "Oh my god." She said quietly after John had placed her in his lap and wrapped his arms around her. Annie had wrapped her arms around his neck and was looking at him in awe. "If you wanted me to, I could run to the shop, get you some flowers and probably be back before you finish your glass of wine?" He said seriously. Annie looked quizzically at him, then nodded, while saying 'OK make sure they're roses though', and picked up her glass again. She got off his lap and sat on her spot again, raised the glass towards her lips and said 'go' with a little smile. John watched for a moment, waiting until the glass touched Annie's lips, then shot off towards the shop. After his usual obligatory browse around the toy aisle, looking to see if there were any Lego sets on offer, he found some nice pink roses, wondering briefly how he was going to get back without leaving a trail of petals before deciding he could run backwards to shield them. Then he left some money on an occupied till to cover the cost, and only just made it back before his wife had finished the glass. He would've gotten back sooner but he'd tripped over a kerb and went tumbling down the road, ripping his t-shirt and nearly hitting a parked car belonging to one of their friendly neighbours. The trip had taken him four seconds and Annie nearly choked on the last mouthful of wine as he re-appeared in front of her, proudly presenting the roses he'd bought. She coughed and spluttered a little before accepting the flowers with shaking hands. Her eyes pin-balled between his smiling face, his torn t-shirt and the flowers for a couple of seconds as she tried to think of something to say. "T-Thank you. They're lovely. Wow. You're like a superhero now, aren't you?" She said once her hands settled down and her eyes locked onto his. "I have abilities that are on a par with a superhero, but I wouldn't say I was one." John then went on to tell her about the plane crash and how his actions had cost the airline many, many millions of pounds worth of damages. He digressed a little and also mentioned the incident in the terminal with Arla and the rowdy body-builders as he'd just remembered it with a chuckle. Annie laughed aloud at that but quickly became serious once more. Her reaction to this surprised him again as she put the flowers down and moved back onto his lap, holding his face in her hands and kissing him hard on the lips. "You saved all those people, including Arla, yet you think of yourself as a bungling fool? No. What you did was truly heroic. You should be proud like I am." Annie said after pulling back from the kiss, her hands still on his face. John couldn't help but smile happily at his beautiful and incredible wife. Her reaction to the news was better than he could've ever hoped. She hadn't reacted with horror, she hadn't asked all sorts of worried questions and, most importantly, she was still there with him. Annie knew that, despite the changes, he was still the same person she fell in love with and married all those years ago. John wrapped his arms around his wife's waist and rested his head on her shoulder, hugging her close. She embraced him firmly around his shoulders and kissed his cheek, hugging him just as firmly. They sat holding each other for a long time, not only because they had missed each other terribly while John was at work, but in an act of solidarity. Their love for one another had only grown and only an act of God, John decided and so did Annie he later found out, would ever separate them. Much later, their peace was disturbed by Annie groaning as Jay's cold wet nose brushed against her face. He was whining to be let out in the garden. John laughed, stood up and carried his wife over to the door to let their dog out to relieve himself. They stood at the door and John smiled slyly as he held Annie by her derrière, with their faces together and watched as Jay sniffed about the garden. "I wonder why you're smiling?" Annie asked humorously. "I'm just happy to be home with my beautiful wife." John replied innocently, making her laugh and wrap herself around him in a tighter embrace.

The next morning, John lay in bed with his eyes closed, listening to the sounds of the neighbourhood as it roused from slumber. The Filberts, a rather pompous couple who seemed to think they were better than most, were talking animatedly, trying to reason with their twenty-year-old son Jake, who he'd just heard had yet to hold a full-time job for any more than a week, much to his amusement. In addition, there was a disagreement about the son going to college to further his education. Jake sounded very sullen and complained loudly about why they couldn't just leave him alone to play his video-games, before storming off back to what John guessed was his room. The Petersons, next door to Annie and himself, were both up and about and getting ready for work. Ian Peterson and his wife Laura were lovely neighbours and good friends, often coming round for dinner and to watch movies. Laura was pregnant and soon to be going on maternity leave from her work as a nurse, while Ian worked for the local superstore as the regional manager for the area. The Petersons had even attended Annie and John's wedding and often hung out with them and their closest friends, Richard Morris and his wife Sarah, David Green and his wife Gemma and Rebecca Lee with her husband Hank. Arla and Callum stayed every so often too and were also friendly with the Petersons. Rebecca was Annie's closest friend, having known each other since childhood, and was maid of honour at their wedding. Annie had also been maid of honour at Rebecca and Hanks wedding and was also godmother to their daughter Jaimie. Richard and David had been John's ushers when he and Annie got married and had been close friends with him since primary school. Annie was still asleep lying across his chest as they had talked long into the night about some of his changes. The idea for the prospecting venture with Arla and Callum had also been discussed at length, something she had sounded very enthusiastic about. The fact that John no longer needed to sleep had initially freaked her out a little, but the feeling was quickly dismissed as she realised he would no longer snore, as she so lovingly phrased it, like a snorting pig.

John didn't need to look at his phone to know it was nine past seven in the morning and Annie's alarm was about to go off for her to get up for work. She worked as a veterinarian at the nearby clinic. His wife startled as the alarm sounded and she mumbled incoherently, while groping around for her phone. Annie managed to grab hold off the phone and silence the alarm after a couple of attempts due to her sleepy eyes. She sat upright. yawned and stretched, gave John a quick morning kiss and then got up to go to the bathroom. Stewart was also starting to stir in his room, so John got up, dressed quickly and went through to get their son ready for nursery. While they were all eating breakfast, he couldn't help but tell Annie about the difficulties the Filberts were having with their son Jake, pleasing her immensely as Noreen Filbert was a very unpleasant and snobbish woman. Her husband Victor was also a very unlike-able individual. He owned a company that manufactured various car parts and was quite wealthy because of it. They lived in the neighbourhood's largest house, a huge six-bedroom place with a twin garage, which was probably why their egos were so inflated. The next few minutes were spent very happily discussing the Filberts, and how they must be deeply ashamed of their spoilt son, as they all finished eating their breakfast. John took Stewart to the downstairs wash-room to brush his sons, and his own, teeth. He wouldn't need to leave the house and walk Stewart to nursery for another twenty minutes yet so they sat together and watched one of the children's TV channels. Annie had gone upstairs again to get ready for work. At quarter to nine, Annie came back down to leave for work, fussed Jay, kissed John and Stewart, then grabbed the car keys and her Lounge-fly Back-pack as she left the house. John helped his son put on his shoes, then put his own on, and they too left the house for the short walk to Stewart's nursery. The teachers were all pleased to see John again and also commented on his new scar, to which he told them about an accident he'd had while at work. Without going into too much detail and subtly altering the story of what really happened. Now that Stewart was in nursery and Annie at work, John wasn't sure what to do during the day until it was time to pick up his son again. He decided to take Jay for a nice long walk first and then think about the rest of the time afterwards. Doing normal routine things was good for him.

The next few weeks at home flew by for the Campbell family, without any major dramas. Until a few days before Arla and Callum were due to arrive to stay for a week. Annie had been walking Stewart home from nursery one day with Jay, who was very popular amongst their son's friends at nursery and was happy to let them fuss him, when they happened to run into Victor Filbert. Mr Filbert had been talking over his shoulder to his wife, not paying attention to where he was going, and had walked right into Jay, making the large German Shepard bark loudly in surprise. Mr Filbert had staggered back in alarm and tripped over his low fence, landing heavily on his backside. Mrs Filbert had run out shrieking like a Banshee about how Jay was a dangerous animal and should be put down, while Mr Filbert had struggled back up to his feet and started shouting loudly at Annie, making her back away in alarm and grip Jay's lead very firmly as his hackles were up. Stewart had been frightened too, silently crying as he hid behind his mother, holding her hand very tight. John had been in the loft re arranging some of his Lego layout and had heard the commotion. He raced out of the house, slowing down to a fast run once he was on the street, and quickly found himself stood beside his wife as she comforted their crying son. John told Annie to take Stewart and Jay home while he had a talk with the Filberts. It wasn't a long conversation. He had bluntly told them to shut up, with a loud carrying voice drawing curious looks from many of the neighbours nearby, and in no uncertain terms informed the stunned couple if they ever shouted at his wife and son like that again, he would pay very close attention to the work practises and safety management of Mr Filberts company, whilst casually dropping the name of a very good friend who just happened to be one of the region's most senior health and safety inspectors. Additionally, John knew of some very unsavoury incidents that had occurred recently at Filbert's companies manufacturing site. In particular the incident where one person had lost an eye, and John was pleased to see Mr Filbert turn very pale. Mrs Filbert had been about to unleash another torrent of abuse, but was humorously silenced by her husband in a surprisingly rude and abrupt manner. The look on the snobbish woman's face had nearly made John keel over with laughter, but he'd managed to keep himself together until he was safely back home. Annie had come out of the living room, still looking murderous with rage, upon hearing him burst out laughing. He quickly told his wife about what had happened, but she wasn't as easily mollified as he was. Annie was about ready to slap Mr Filbert hard across his arrogant face before John had intervened. He looked startled by this revelation, for Annie was never one to resort to violence as she always managed to diffuse tense situations with her well measured words, so she took him by the hand and marched back into the living room. John hadn't realised how frightened their son had been. Stewart was lying on the sofa, Jay's head on his legs as he sat on the floor in front of him like a sentry, crying silently with his hands covering his face. John's amusement had been immediately replaced by swelling anger.

That night, once Stewart had finally gone to sleep, with Jay on the floor beside his bed, John informed Annie that he was going to go out for a bit. It was nearly midnight so his wife looked at him like he'd gone mad. He gave her a quick kiss and then quickly left the house before she could say anything. The Filberts had two cars parked in their vast driveway, but had neglected to install any security cameras to watch over the very expensive vehicles. John was wearing dark clothes and kept in the shadows as he took a moment to make sure there was no one watching. Everyone was either asleep or had their curtains drawn anyway, so the coast was clear. The more expensive of the two cars was a sleek, brand new, supercharged Jaguar F-Type. John groaned inwardly at the thought of what he was about to do to such a fantastic looking car. After a quick shrug of his shoulders, he slipped under the car and very carefully picked it up, concerned about potentially setting the alarm off, above his head. Another quick look around to make sure no one had suddenly decided to admire the dark street, and he leapt high into the air towards the river Forth. The sudden jerk had set the car alarm off, but by the time any noise could be heard, he and the car were miles away, soaring high above the silent streets and empty fields. At the very height of his leap, John heaved the car far away into the darkness and off towards the North Sea. He landed gracefully in the small town of Kinghorn, in a dark parking area near the beach. The car park was thankfully empty and all the lights of the nearby houses were off, with none of the residents watching the peaceful night from their darkened homes. John had to wait a short while before he saw a distant splash many miles out to sea. It had been a real shame to send such a fantastic car to a watery grave, but the Filberts had gone too far with their arrogance and deserved worse as far as John was concerned. Five minutes after leaving his home, John walked back through the front door, only to be met by a quietly seething Annie standing in the living room doorway. He gulped and slowly approached his wife, cowering slightly under her furious gaze. She stood aside silently and pointed towards the sofa for him to sit down, he obliged without hesitation, and then stepped in front of him with her arms crossed. Annie didn't say a word and was quite happy to watch her husband stew in the silence. A whole agonising minute later, she finally asked 'Well?' John told her about the expensive Jaguar now sitting on the sea bed. Annie had not expected this and her mouth dropped. The tension in the air immediately vanished as she had to cover her mouth to stifle a laugh. "I can't say those horrible people didn't deserve that, but don't you ever leave the house again like that without telling me what you're doing OK?" Annie's eyes flashed dangerously as she spoke barely above a whisper. John was only too happy to agree, jumped up from the sofa, swept her off her feet to cradle her in his arms and then spun around slowly in the centre of the room. Annie shrieked in surprise and wrapped her arms around his neck while smiling jovially. Her face lit up and she looked at him wide eyed. "Oh, I wish I could see the Filbert's faces when they walk out to see an empty place where a new car once sat." John chuckled quietly and carried his wife up the stairs to their bedroom.

Sure enough, John heard a loud series of curses the following morning, as Mr Filbert had walked out of his front door, not paying attention once again with his keys out in front of him pointed towards an empty space, and only turned around when he hadn't heard the beeps of his car doors unlocking. There was quite a scene in the neighbourhood that morning. John, Annie and Stewart watched in amusement from their dining room window, as two police cars turned up and parked outside an irate Mr Filbert's house. Even without incredible hearing, the furious man could be heard screaming at the surprisingly patient police officers standing in front of him. They had been standing there for nearly ten minutes but hadn't yet been able to ask a single question, such was the tirade spewing forth from Mr Filbert's mouth. John even noticed the woman turn away briefly, disguising a snort of laughter with a cough, as Mr Filbert was starting to turn purple with rage. Almost all of the residents in the area were standing outside in their dressing gowns, many holding steaming cups of coffee or tea, chatting amongst themselves and openly laughing at their neighbour's behaviour. Most of them actually had no clue as to what was wrong, although many did notice one of the cars was missing, because all they could hear were insults, foul language, threats to sue, more insults and demands for action, even though Mr Filbert had still to give the silent police woman a chance to speak. That had been the only drama since John had gotten home, and what fun it had turned out to be. Stewart quickly got over his fright, and now had to be shushed every time he saw Mr Filbert while walking back from nursery, for he now knew him as 'purple face man'. Arla and Callum arrived a few days later, with Arla arriving just before lunch in her new Subaru, making Annie go green with envy after she had hugged her good friend. Callum arrived a couple of hours later having travelled up from his home in Newcastle. John hugged Callum as Annie and Arla were catching up in the living room, having not seen one another for many months. Upon his arrival John helped Callum take his bags up-to the guest room without the en-suite. Unsurprisingly, Arla had already claimed the other one, much to Callum's irritation. After a good long catch up, everyone knew that Arla's try-out had gone remarkably well and she was now waiting for a multi-fight contract with the organisation. Whilst Callum explained that he had just completed a confined spaces course in Portsmouth, after a short holiday to Dublin visiting his parents. Then, they all sat down in the living room in order to discuss their long-term prospective business partnership together. It was clear that they were all looking excitedly to the future.

A few days later, with discussions again going on into the early hours of the morning, they decided that a potential option could be to mine Manganese Nodules. Nodules were found in only four major areas of the world's oceans. In addition, the original proposal of using sound to find various minerals, perhaps even gemstones, was the second option that they all had a good feeling about. It wasn't all work though as the five of them spent a very pleasant day wondering around Edinburgh. The main aim of the trip was for John to visit several of the extravagant jewellery stores to see if he could learn to identify precious gemstones and minerals by sound. However, they did also visit many other popular attractions such as Dynamic Earth, the Castle, the Royal Mile and Arthur's Seat. Annie and Arla had also treated themselves to new backpacks, buying Stewart a new toy too from the same department store, while the two men of the little group visited the museum to find other materials which could hopefully be positively identified through sound with John's exceptional hearing. Overall, that day proved to be very successful as John had quite easily been able to identify many different gemstones, rare earth minerals and precious metals from sound, owing to the different material densities and how that directly affects the speed that sound can travel through them. Also, John spent some time making low frequency noises, as it appeared useful for improving the depth or range which could be explored as higher frequency noises reduced overall effectiveness, outside shops or in a different area of the museum, where they had seen a variety of different gemstones and precious metals. Callum couldn't stand the funny looks John got from passers-by and promptly distanced himself from his vocalising friend, who was now very adept at altering his voice or making, as Stewart and Callum simply described them, weird noises. Another long day of discussions followed the Edinburgh day out, and the decision was made to focus purely on gemstones. This meant that John was going to be heading deeper underground, making him chuckle as he remembered a film from the late nineteen nineties. He would have to head even further underground if Diamonds were to be the target of choice as they formed in what are known as kimberlite pipes. These pipes originate in the earth's mantle at over one-hundred and twenty-five miles deep. Callum's eyes had widened comically upon reading this, whilst Annie and Arla reacted similarly after they had gotten up to look at the screen over his shoulder, while John had about fallen off his chair once Annie eventually managed to tell him why the three of them all looked so stunned. Additional research they undertook identified that Gemstones such as Emeralds, Rubies and Sapphires are found in metamorphic rock, which is formed when incredible underground heat or pressure changes existing rocks. Larger gemstones are typically found in deeper environments where it has taken longer to cool. It would appear that if their little venture was to yield any significant rewards, then John was going to be doing an awful lot of digging. He at least hoped all this digging would be towards precise locations where he'd managed to identify specific gemstones, rather than the industrialised process of pit mining that is typically used to recover Diamonds. The four adults all contributed to buy a net reinforced with titanium, which would be securely attached to John's ankle as he dug deep into the Earth's crust, his sheer strength and resilience being the key factors, towards what they hoped would be a profitable deposit. The football sized net took three days to arrive, with the delivery time used to identify a good isolated place to start searching and begin digging, after which John set off for a very long swim. The place that had been chosen was certainly isolated as it was perhaps one of the most inhospitable places on the entire planet. Without question, they had chosen the deepest place on earth, the Challenger deep. Here John was going to be descending ten-thousand nine-hundred meters into the very depths of the Pacific Ocean, right to the very bottom of the Marianna Trench near Guam, where the pressure was an astonishing eight tons per square inch. John wished he had the same confidence as his wife and friends with regards to his resilience. The thought of being crushed by that much pressure certainly got his heart beating a little faster.

When work commenced, it took him several hours to reach the very bottom of the Pacific Ocean. Here, sunlight didn't stand a chance of penetrating to these sorts of depths, petering out after around one hundred and fifty meters, but John's remarkable eyesight still enabled him to see quite clearly. Now, he settled himself onto the desolate ocean floor and started making his weird noises. It took nearly an hour, moving around to different places, to find what appeared to be a reasonable deposit of Sapphires. However, even though John was already several miles deep, he would have to dig many more miles down to reach the precious, coloured gemstones. Concentrating hard on his work, John had been so focused on finding a gemstone deposit that his senses had failed to notice a massive form materialise as if from nowhere beside him. It was only as he checked to make sure the bag was securely fastened to his ankle that he noticed the basketball sized eye glaring menacingly at him. The words that came out of his mouth, although muffled entirely by the extreme depth, would've raised eyebrows even amongst his former marine engineering colleagues, as he reeled back in terror. The Giant Squid, hovering just feet away, was close to two hundred foot long. He never realised the almost mythical cephalopods could grow so large. Although, considering just how little is known about the earth's vast ocean depths, perhaps he shouldn't have been surprised. The animal must've sensed his unusual vocalisations, probably from many miles away, and jetted over to investigate for a potential meal. John really didn't like the idea of being bitten by a razor-sharp beak two feet in diameter, so he swiftly started digging towards what he fervently hoped would be a worthwhile prize after such a fright.

Just over a day went by before John finally walked back through the front door of his home. Annie, Arla and Callum didn't seem to have slept much, judging by their tired faces, but quickly leapt up from their seats in the living room and raced into the hallway to greet him. Annie ran straight into his arms and hugged him tightly, but stopped short of kissing him after noticing how dreadful he looked and smelt. Thousands of miles of swimming and digging combined had certainly left a mark. Arla and Callum hadn't even gotten half-way down the hall before they were halted by the stench. Callum visibly paled, turned around, quickly picked up and thus saved an excited Stewart from the horrible aroma, and ran out through the open living room doors into the garden for fresh air. Arla lasted a little longer, but still ended up joining Callum in the garden after nearly throwing up herself. Annie had grabbed her nose and clamped shut her mouth before vigorously pointing upstairs, ordering her husband to go for a very long shower and to, he guessed from her watering eyes, incinerate his clothing rather than attempt to wash them. By the time he had cleaned up, changed and disposed of his bio-hazard warning worthy clothes, all of the downstairs windows were open and a generous amount of air freshener was evident in the air. Annie had even quickly changed into clean clothes herself after running off to the utility room. John picked up the net from beside the front door, and carried it hidden behind his back into the living room where Annie, with Stewart sitting on her lap, Arla and Callum sat waiting impatiently. He deliberately paused for dramatic effect, succeeding in only winding up Callum to the point he shouted 'hurry up will you!', before theatrically unveiling what all their effort had gotten them. From within the bag, shone a huge brilliant-blue Sapphire gemstone. Their mouths gaped open and their eyes bulged as they stared in awe at the fruit of their labour. Arla stood first and held out her shaking hands, unable to speak. John removed the gemstone from the bag and she gingerly took it from his proffered hand, holding the precious Sapphire as if it were a baby. Annie looked up at John and smiled incredulously with tears flowing freely from her pale grey eyes. Their idea had actually worked. Annie, Arla and Callum had all been quietly confident the endeavour would succeed, but never in their wildest dreams did they think it would to the extent it had. Annie got up from the sofa to stand beside John, sliding an arm around his waist while carrying Stewart, who was also transfixed by the huge gemstone, in the other. He wrapped an arm around her shoulders and gently kissed her hair, smiling happily. Callum eventually managed to regain the use of his limbs, springing up quite suddenly from the sofa he and Arla had occupied, and stood next to her. John and Annie briefly looked at each other with raised eyebrows as Callum wrapped one of his long arms around Arla's shoulders. Although it was only Annie who noticed a small smile tug at the corner of Arla's mouth as her eyes briefly flicked in Callum's direction.

The five of them were silent, all eyes locked on the huge Sapphire cradled in Arla's arms, for several minutes, until Jay, with his unerring knack for interrupting significant moments, barged in on them and started to sniff the strange shiny object. They all laughed and John gave him a quick scratch behind the ears. Annie then led the way into the dining room, drawing the curtains and turning on the lights first, and they sat down at the table. Arla had put the gemstone in the centre on a folded-up towel Callum picked up from the kitchen. "This is incredible" Callum spoke reverently, eyes still fixed on the Sapphire. "I can't believe you managed to find one so large" Arla said while looking towards John. "We all worked together to find it" He replied modestly, looking at each of them in turn. But then his expression changed to one of contemplation for a moment. "Although I'm the only one who ended up looking and smelling like I'd just escaped from Shawshank Prison -" Making them all laugh "- and, believe it or not, I even saw a Giant Squid up close" Annie, Arla and Callum immediately stopped laughing after hearing about the Cephalopod and stared at him in uncomprehending silence. John explained how the giant creature had managed to scare the living daylights out of him as he'd been so focused with his search. Callum asked how big had it been, and the reply made him say 'holy -' before an elbow from Arla interrupted what was about to be a rude exclamation. Stewart stared at them curiously as John and Annie bit their lips and looked at each other with relief after the timely interruption. Part of their research had been to source a potential buyer for anything they may find. The nearest one, who supplied many of the extortionately expensive fine jewellery stores in Edinburgh and Glasgow, was a couple of hours drive away. Stewart happily joined his parents in their car, looking forward to another day out, while Arla and Callum used her new Subaru. Annie had been looking longingly towards the shiny Japanese sports-car but ended up getting in the car beside her husband, much to his amusement after seeing the jealous look she gave Callum who had jumped in ahead of her.

They arrived at the buyer's place of business at just after ten in the morning, ready for their appointment at quarter past. A kind looking older gentleman came out of his office to greet them after being informed of their arrival by his secretary. The man, who introduced himself informally as James, had looked at them curiously, clearly not used to dealing with a group such as theirs dressed so casually, but was courteous nonetheless and had showed them into his large office, with many different exotic metals and gemstones either framed on the wall or in glass displays. He had prepared for their appointment and gathered enough chairs for them to all sit around his huge mahogany desk. Annie put on some gloves then reached into the back-pack John had put down by her feet, Stewart leaned over from his seat on Arla's lap in anticipation, and she brought out the huge Sapphire and placed it on the cloth already waiting on the desk. James sat silently transfixed at the enormity of the precious gemstone now sat on his desk. The man's self-control impressed John as his mouth had only opened a tiny amount at the sight of such a large Sapphire. A few minutes of silence passed before James roused himself, put on his own pair of gloves, carefully brought the gemstone closer to him and began to examine it to ensure it was genuine, while also estimating its value. The examination took quite some time, and Stewart had started to fidget, but was now being entertained by a video on Arla's phone. As the examination continued, James made many references to a large book that sat on the desk, along with a few glances at various different things on the sleek Apple iMac computer on a smaller desk near the window. Once James was satisfied, after using an expensive looking analogue scale to weigh the gemstone, he sat back down across from them to deliver his verdict. They all sat on tenterhooks, waiting for him to speak again as he quietly surveyed each of them with an impassive face. He was certain the Sapphire was genuine, but John already knew this, and he told them the market value of what sat between them on his desk, based on its size. James then told them of the process involved in turning an uncut gemstone into fine pieces of Jewellery, often custom made to order, going into detail with respect to the various expenses, before making them an offer to purchase their item. The number mentioned was more than any of them could ever possibly have dreamed of. James took their stunned silence as a cue to leave them alone to consider his offer, so he graciously left the office. All they could do was look from one another and nod in agreement as words were lost to them momentarily. Annie clumsily got to her feet and walked to the office door to notify James that they had made a decision. He was ecstatic hearing his first offer, a rarity so it seemed to them, had been accepted and quickly stood back up from his leather chair to vigorously shake each of their hands. They finalised the financial side of things, the money was to be split equally between them, and all four of them signed a document agreeing to the transfer of possession, along with the amount accepted to purchase, to James' company. He then signed it, even kindly offering Stewart a pen and paper so he wouldn't feel left out, and got his secretary to make each of them a copy for their reference.

Their business now concluded, James escorted them back out of the building, once again offered his thanks and shook all of their hands, before bidding them farewell and safe travels. After he had gone back into the building, they could all no longer contain their excitement and exploded into wild celebrations. John picked up both Annie and Arla in a crushing embrace, and they both buried their faces into his shoulders, crying their eyes out, while Callum picked up Stewart and started running around them with him on his shoulders, whooping extatically. Once the celebrations calmed down enough for them all to talk relatively normally again, and after a quick exchange of high fives, Annie, John and Stewart got back into their car, Arla and Callum got back into hers, and they agreed to meet up in Glasgow for a well-earned shopping trip. Annie and Arla had quickly spoke to each other, making Arla laugh, before they got back into the waiting cars, drawing curious looks from John and Callum. "What was that about?" John asked Annie once she was seated in the car beside him. "I told Arla we would meet them once I had bought a Subaru of my own." She grinned indulgently, making him roll his eyes and laugh.

Chapter 4 – Not Everyone Can Be Saved

Two months had gone by since that wonderful appointment with James, bringing about several changes to the lives of the little group that had gathered opposite the kind gentleman. Annie had recently taken delivery of her brand-new Subaru, squealing with delight the moment the key touched her quivering palm. Arla was training hard in preparation for her first professional MMA fight; to be held at the O2 Arena in London. Callum was now living just along the A-Ninety-Two from Annie and John in Kirkaldy, having moved into his spacious new five-bedroom house the previous week, and John had finally been convinced by his insistent wife to buy himself a brand-new car. As a result, a shiny new metallic blue Honda Civic Type-R now sat proudly in their driveway beside Annie's Subaru. However, whilst he had initially been quite content to just having converted the loft and purchasing several Lego sets he'd coveted for quite some time, it didn´t take much persuasion to tempt him to by a new car. John had also taken stock of all the events that had transpired and he hadn't forgotten the embarrassing incident in Miami. So, he now wore underwear made from Silica fabric interwoven with the same carbon-carbon composite material used for the heat shields on the black underside of Space Shuttles. The many pairs he now owned, hadn't been cheap, but he considered them to be really good value for money. Annie, well, she still worked at the veterinary clinic to keep herself busy and because she adored animals of all kinds, albeit with reduced hours. John spent a lot of his time while Annie was working, and Stewart was at nursery, either by practising Wing Chun, his new hobby, on a specialised reinforced dummy. Or he'd spend time in what was now designated as his Lego room, adding little details here and there to the impressive layout that stretched the entire width of their home. Arla and Callum no longer worked for the company the three friends had all worked for just months prior, with Arla now focused on her professional MMA career, while Callum and Richard Morris had started a business of their own, focussing on electrical installations and manufacturing specialised monitoring equipment. It was, as Callum claimed in a thoroughly unconvincing manner during his house warming party, the main reason he had decided to move up from Newcastle. John and Annie both noticed his frequent glances towards Arla throughout the pleasant evening, although declined to embarrass their host by commenting on it, instead hoping the two would soon find a way towards each other themselves, for Arla had also been glancing at Callum quite often during the party. The business Callum and Richard started was already proving to be a great success as they had several large clients, all of whom were impressed at their professionalism and dedication to achieving the highest standards possible with each installation. They were both very much hands on when it came to the work and often carried out jobs themselves, not owing to a lack of faith in their employees, but simply because they enjoyed it and there was a lot to be done such was the demand for their services. Richard and Sarah, along with their young children Liam and Susan, always visited Annie and John at least once every couple of weeks, although Richard hadn't been able to visit as much recently thanks to the success of the business. John and Richard were both fans and collectors of Lego, and spent much of these visits up in John's little haven of plastic, while Annie and Sarah enjoyed coffee, usually accompanied by Rebekah, who lived just around the corner with Hank and Jaimie, and happily watched their children either playing in the garden, on the trampoline and the large wooden activity centre, or often ended up engrossed in the movies the little ones would pick to watch if the weather wasn't great. Today's visit was a little different, as Annie really wanted to stretch her new car's legs at Knockhill just up the road from their home. Sarah was another big fan of fast cars, so she came round to watch the British Touring Cars each race day and supported the same driver as Annie. Therefore, it was not a surprise that Sarah was also very keen on the idea to visit Knockhill and pouted at her husband until he relented and agreed to go along too. The children weren't bothered about not being able to play in the garden as they thought a day at the race track would be great fun.

John and Richard both looked longingly up towards the converted loft as they left the house last, and everyone got into their cars to head to the Scottish home of motor-sport. John had only agreed to go so long as he could take his new car, which brought about a little wager between husband and wife. If Annie could lap the circuit faster in her Subaru than John managed in his Honda, then she would get to pick where they went for their day out tomorrow. John whispered what he wanted, if he was faster, into his curious wife's ear, making her eyes widen before she hit him playfully on the shoulder. Stewart went with John and Richard in the Honda. Liam and Susan, after a quick game of musical car seats, went in the Subaru with Annie and Sarah. It was a nice warm summer day, perfect weather for driving fast cars around great race tracks. The weather had drawn a good number of like-minded car enthusiasts to the circuit and they were greeted with the sound of revving engines, popping exhausts and squealing tyres upon their arrival. Annie and John were both very big motor-sport fans and had each gotten competition licenses, easily passing the ARDS examination and far exceeding the standards required to safely compete, after the sale of the gemstone. They were both now planning on occasionally competing at a national level and had bought their own customised helmets, race suits, gloves and boots in preparation. Annie went into the circuit office and bought them some track time, paying a little extra to get transponders fitted to their cars so the lap times could be accurately timed. The extra she paid also granted them the use of brand-new cameras offered by Knockhill, so that on-board footage of their laps could be recorded and timed simultaneously. This was important as she and John were fiercely competitive, meaning the times they set were bound to be quite close. Stewart, Liam and Susan all watched fascinated as the cameras and transponders were fitted to the cars. Annie elected herself to go first with Sarah as her eager passenger. With no choice in the matter, John, Richard and the children all went to stand on the pit wall so they could watch. Their ears picked up the distinct sound of Annie's Subaru rumbling to life, so they turned to watch and wave as the gunmetal grey car appeared from the pit garage and slowly drove by, making sure to observe the pit lane speed limit. At the end of the Pit-Lane, Annie smashed the accelerator down and the Subaru roared loudly as it shot forward with a hiss of smoke from the tyres. Richard and John nodded at each other and mouthed 'phwoar' in appreciation of the screaming horizontally opposed Boxer engines note. "Wow, your wife is really giving it some. She must've been chomping at the bit to do that ever since the car was delivered!" Richard said in admiration. "Oh yes. Each time we've joined a motorway over the last couple of days, I could tell she just wanted to jam the throttle down. She actually did when we were coming back from Costco yesterday and Stewart loved it. Although her disappointment at not being allowed to go faster than seventy was pretty funny" John replied as he stood up on tip-toes, with Stewart perched happily on his shoulders wearing a new pair of Knockhill branded blue ear defenders, to watch as Annie disappeared over the crest of Duffus Dip. "I just hope Sarah doesn't end up wanting her own sports car now. Especially as her car of choice would be a BMW three series M-Sport. I'm earning better money now but certainly not that much yet!" Richard chuckled with a genuine hint of worry creasing his face. John patted him on the shoulder sympathetically with a 'what-can-you-do' sort of smile. They looked towards their right as Annie's Subaru came into view, braking hard for the final hairpin. The tyres were still a little cool so there was a wicked amount of over-steer, expertly gathered up with some sublime car control, and the engine sounded like it was sputtering as it hit the rev limiter. John and Richard almost ended up cricking their necks watching as Annie and Sarah screamed by and off towards the first turn again. The brake lights flared angrily, and the unloaded inside rear tyre locked up with a puff of smoke, as the car squirmed in a desperate effort to shed some speed and turn in towards the apex of Duffus Dip for the first timed lap. Annie and Sarah came back into the pits five laps later and parked in the garage, bringing with them a strong smell of burning rubber. The children gathered round the cooling, ticking car and enthusiastically greeted their mums as they climbed out. Annie picked Stewart up and smiled as he told her how awesome she was, while Liam and Sarah were holding onto Sarah's hands, jumping up and down excitedly, talking about how fast the car was. Annie had thrown down the gauntlet with a very quick lap, her wicked smile told him she knew it was a decent time, but John was unperturbed, welcoming the challenge with relish as he got into the Honda with Richard. The metallic blue car danced on the limit of adhesion, kissed all the right kerbs and gave off little puffs of smoke as the tyres and brakes, glowing bright orange, were working hard to keep all four wheels within the track limits. Their own five laps completed, they came back into the pit-lane and parked up again beside the silent Subaru, bringing another waft of burnt rubber with them. Annie was waiting, a little slack jawed and worried, as John gave her a devilish smile of his own. He knew those laps had been nigh on perfect, much like his wife did, hence her obvious nervousness as they walked hand in hand to the circuit office to retrieve their footage and lap time print outs. Richard and Sarah were chatting animatedly behind them, debating on who had been in the quicker car, leaving the children to run around them, while being subtly watched over by the adults, as they enjoyed a game of tag. Annie's lap times didn't make for satisfactory reading. Even though her fastest lap had only been a tenth slower than John's, it still meant she had lost the bet and she resigned herself to the agreed wager. John had been stunned by the lap times. He hadn't expected Annie to be so fast and their times so close. Richard was leaning over his shoulder and whistled at the minuscule gap. "Wow,

Annie you nearly had us beat there and that was even with John driving superbly, without any mistakes I noticed." Annie and Sarah looked up at Richard from their piece of paper, each with a rueful little smile at what could've been. John wasn't a bad winner, so even though he'd won the wager, and was eagerly looking forward to his reward later, he walked over to hug a morose looking Annie, kissed her lightly on the lips and asked where she'd like to go for their day out tomorrow. His question gave her a little thrill of surprise and she brightened up considerably. It was decided that they would go to Edinburgh Zoo and she even invited all of their friends to come along too. It had been far too long since all of them had spent the day together as a group and she fully intended to rectify that. In a rare moment of fortune, everyone was free and agreed to the day out. Arla even decided to take a day off from her intense training camp, possibly because Callum was also going, to enjoy a relaxing day out with friends. After arriving back at Annie and John's house, Richard and Sarah bade them a fond farewell, until the following day that is, and got into their own car as they were now off to a birthday party. Annie, John and Stewart stood outside and waved goodbye, readying themselves to be flattened by their whining German Shepard, who was patiently watching them through the dining room window. John picked up Stewart so he wouldn't be bowled over and decided to play the perfect gentleman, holding out a hand while politely saying 'ladies first'. Annie didn't look too impressed by the gesture but went first all the same and was promptly thundered into, amidst much slipping and sliding on the wooden floor, by the ever-eager-to-see her Jay. That night was going to be a pizza and movie night accompanied by the Greens, David,

Gemma and their daughter Claire, and their neighbours the Petersons.

It was a few hours yet before their friends were due to come round, so Annie, John and Stewart all took Jay out for a nice long walk, much to the delight of the huge fur-ball. On the way back they walked by the Filbert's house and noticed, with glee, there was still only one car in the driveway, despite all three of them being home and, from what John could clearly hear, having another argument about video games. Annie snickered after being told about their ongoing battle to encourage Jake into getting a job. At six o'clock in the evening, their doorbell rang, Jay jumped up and started barking excitedly as normal, so John got up too and answered the door to find the Greens waiting outside, with Gemma holding a nice bottle of prosecco. The Petersons were also just leaving their house to come over too as they had noticed the Greens car arrive and park in the driveway. John greeted them all warmly, except for Claire who had bolted past the moment the door opened to go and play with her best friend Stewart, and invited them all inside. Annie was up and hugged Gemma and Laura, gratefully accepted the proffered bottle, and they all went into the kitchen to get some glasses. Gemma, being good friends with Laura too, surprised her by producing another non-alcoholic bottle of something sparkling from her handbag. Laura's mouth dropped at the nice surprise and she happily accepted the third glass Gemma had gotten out. David, Ian and John went into the living room, David took a quick detour via the fridge to grab drinks, and sat down to catch up, occupying the two-seater sofa and one of the dining room chairs which John had brought in. David worked for a company based down in the Rosyth dockyard as an engineering consultant and often travelled all over the country to assist their many customers. “Those new ships your former employer has are an absolute disaster John-” something he was already well aware of having sailed on one during his last trip “- I mean, the newest one that’s currently sitting in Birkenhead has already been delayed by months, because of the problems with the main engines, and now the shipyard has just found another serious snag. This one is an absolute screamer though -” John and Ian leaned forward in anticipation while they waited for David to take a drink “Right, because the engines have been sitting dry and cold for so long, all of the cooling water seals became brittle and failed when they started to warm them through again. They now need to lift all sixteen of the cylinder heads, yup water got into the liners too, and completely take apart the jacket water rail to replace every single seal. It was like a fountain, with water going everywhere!” David leant back and waited for a reaction from his captivated audience. He wasn’t to be disappointed as John roared with laughter and Ian, who wasn’t a marine engineer but still understood the gravity of the situation, looked on in open-mouthed astonishment. “Wow, how much is that going to cost and what sort of delay are they looking at?” Ian asked as John was still incapacitated with fits of laughter. David held up his hands and shrugged, he wasn’t strictly speaking allowed to discuss the matter with anyone outside of the company, but felt it was safe enough to say ‘an awful lot and an awful long time’. The conversation moved on with Ian talking about the progress he and Laura had made in preparation for their new arrival, with David and John providing wisdom with memories of their own from a few years back when their own children had come along. They generally talked about how things have changed, with no more changing tables, bigger beds and lots more toys. Then there was the mountain of clothes that changed and grew with the children. Ian nodded gravely, thinking of his bank account. For, in his eyes, Laura was going just a little crazy, his words much to the amusement of David and John, not theirs' as he felt she was buying way too many different outfits already. Ian suddenly paled as he noticed his wife standing in the doorway, looking at him with a stare that could melt steel, flanked by Annie and Gemma who were both mouthing 'oh dear', looking at him as if now fearing for his very life. Ian looked like he wanted to melt into the sofa, but somehow managed to maintain eye contact, despite the radiating hostility from his heavily pregnant wife. Laura shook her head in a dignified manner, not before shooting her husband one last murderous glance, and sat down on the furthest away spot on the empty three-seater sofa. Annie and Gemma sat down on the empty spots beside her and waited for Laura to pick a film for them all, not wishing to provoke her any more than Ian already had. Claire and Stewart hadn't noticed the tense atmosphere now filling the room, and immediately jumped up once the TV came to life, clearly expecting to pick the film they would all watch. Laura knew a losing battle when she saw one so decided that discretion is the better part of valour, and selected the family films option, not wishing to incur the wrath of the two small children. Her mood brightened though as they picked a film she actually wanted to see.

The tense atmosphere then evaporated instantly upon the arrival of the Pizza and the remainder of the evening passed by enjoyably for all. John did decide though that he wouldn't try to listen to what Laura was going to do to Ian once they got back home, much to Annie's disappointment, in retaliation for his comment earlier. Laura bid everyone a friendly goodbye, thanked Annie and John for the pleasant evening, but then strode off angrily back to her house, leaving Ian to reluctantly follow on behind with the look of a man marching to his doom. Annie, John, David and Gemma averted their eyes and stared around awkwardly until Ian, trying and failing to catch their attention with an imploring gaze, slowly shut the door behind him. David and Gemma, carrying a sleeping Claire, then said their goodbyes and left too. Annie and John waved until they were out of sight, then retreated back inside to escape the chilly night air, although John wasn't bothered by the temperature and only hurried because Annie had dashed inside quickly and was threatening to lock him outside if he didn't get a move on. Being locked out didn't bother John, he didn't think Annie really would anyway, but her threat of not honouring the wager from Knockhill succeeded and had him back inside in the blink of an eye.

The next day dawned bright, crisp and clear. Perfect for the trip to the Zoo with all of their friends. They had all agreed to meet up at Starbucks and get drinks prior to heading over the Queensferry Crossing and into Edinburgh. The little convoy of cars, led by Arla who had also picked up Callum and left home far earlier than anyone else, arrived at the Zoo in good time as the roads were blissfully quiet. Annie paid for everyone, with their friend's objections falling on deaf ears, and John handed out the tickets. The group then left the entrance building and entered the Zoo proper, chatting keenly amongst themselves as they decided on where to go first. The decision was ultimately made for them though as Claire, Jaimie, Liam, Stewart and Susan all ran off towards the Giant Panda enclosure, forcing their startled parents to give chase. Edinburgh Zoo is a substantial place, with many different attractions such as the Budongo Trail, home of the chimpanzees, the Tigers' Tracks enclosure, with an awesome ground level viewing tunnel running through it, the huge Penguin's rock, home to Emperor, rockhopper and Gentoo penguins, and Painted hunting dogs amongst many others. By lunch time, everyone had worked up an appetite, so while the women of the group claimed tables for all of them outside in the sun, the men went inside and ordered a small mountain of food and drinks. The children talked about all of the animals they had seen so far with each other, commenting on which ones were the cutest or the scariest, while some of the adults were already complaining of sore feet from all the walking so far. Arla was suffering, her training camp was brutal, to the point Callum jokingly offered to give her a piggy-back and carry her for the rest of the day. He hadn't expected her to readily accept the offer and his instant-regret expression made all the other adults laugh. Notwithstanding, the zoo was closing soon, so it was time for them all to leave and head home. David, Gemma and Claire had already left for their home in Burntisland, in order to beat the rush hour traffic. Claire hadn't been happy about that and silently cried all the way until they were out of sight. Rebekah, Hank and Jaimie left even earlier as she was due to fly out to New York in the early hours of next morning. She worked for a popular performance arts company that regularly toured the globe. Those that remained, the Campbell', the Morris', Arla and Callum, bought a few things in the gift shop then joined the mass of people heading towards the exit and the car park beside the Zoo.

They had a reservation at Annie and John's favourite restaurant, the Sweet Chestnut, and babysitters in the form of grand-parents had already been arranged, and then they were going to see a movie at the cinema afterwards. Traffic crawled along at the usual rush-hour snail's pace. The traffic was nose to tail all the way upto, including and even after the bridge. To add to their very much delayed journey, there had been accidents on both the north and southbound lanes, meaning traffic was jammed solid stuck on the bridge. Annie and John were just behind Arla and Callum, two Subaru's in a row, with Richard and Sarah a couple of cars further behind. Stewart was fast asleep in his car seat, while Annie drummed her fingers impatiently on the steering wheel and John stared across towards the other two Forth bridges. All of a sudden, John sat upright and alarmed as he was sure the bridge had just shuddered unnaturally twice in very quick succession. Then, without warning, all the cars leapt up from the road as an almighty crash shook the entire bridge. Within seconds, the centre of the three huge towers had dropped and was starting to lean out towards the other bridges. John grabbed Annie's hand and told her to get off the bridge as soon as possible. He had gotten out of the car, ran to the edge, dived onto his stomach and peered over the side to see what had happened to the bridge, all before Annie could even reply. What he saw made his blood run cold and sent a shiver cascading down his spine. A section of the central tower close to the water was missing, leaving a large gap of around seven feet where reinforced concrete should've been. In that second, the central tower had tilted over a few more degrees and the road around it was starting to fracture. The suspension cables were also straining to break free from their anchor points to relieve themselves of a burden they were never designed for. John didn't waste any more time and launched himself towards the dark blue waters below, swam to the base of the collapsing central tower, then he leapt up into the diminishing gap where the large chunk of concrete had once been in place. He planted his feet firmly, braced his hands wide apart and heaved with all of the strength he could muster. His left hand bore the brunt of the massive weight he was attempting to support, as the towers tilting motion halted. John's jaw was clenched painfully tight as he strained to bring pretty much the entire tower upright again. Inch by agonising inch, the angle of tilt decreased until, after what felt like an eternity but was only a couple of seconds, the tower was, for anyone experiencing or watching the unbelievable events unfolding before them, somehow upright again as if by some miracle. John felt awfully exposed as he stood in the large gap, supporting the bridge with his hands, so he stamped and scraped one of his feet, destroying the shoe instantly, to create a cloud of dust to obscure him from view. This was by far the most stringent test he had yet to encounter since the accident, his arms were shaking under the strain and his breathing was becoming erratic. John forced himself to calm down, focus on breathing normally and try to see what the situation was on the road way above him. In a word, pandemonium. Cars were blaring their horns, bumping and scraping past one another, trying desperately to get off the bridge. John was growing increasingly frustrated as he was helpless to shift the ignorant drivers, at either end of the stationary traffic, who had gotten out of their cars to gawp at the collapsing Queensferry Crossing. They were completely oblivious to the danger their sheer stupidity had created, as the cars they had effectively abandoned were now blocking others from moving, thus trapping many more on the collapsing bridge. Thirteen people were potentially going to kill thousands because they had inexplicably decided to watch with some sort of twisted fascination. Each of their faces were now burned into John's memory and he made a silent vow to find all of them, repeatedly cursing foully, wishing someone would just ram the cars out of the way, preferably hitting the idiots in the process. There was a large articulated lorry on the northbound lane towards Fife who seemed to share the same opinion as John. The horn of the lorry blared, the few cars ahead moved off to the side as best as they could, and the driver inched forward in the inside lane, hitting the first of many abandoned cars. The young driver who had gotten out roared in outrage as his prized Ford Focus ST was shoved forward and crumpled as it hit the next empty car. The ST driver leaped onto the lorry's cab and hauled open the door before realising in horror that the driver was a grizzled giant of a man. A swift punch, thrown with a boiling rage, broke the young fool's nose and both orbital bones, sending him crashing back down to the road. He was barely conscious, struggling to get off the hard road, but eventually manged to get up onto his hands and knees and started to crawl towards his car. A car grazed by aiming for the gap being made by the lorry and knocked him down again. He whimpered helplessly and curled up into a ball, waiting to be hit again. Karma was busy elsewhere though. A car stopped alongside the sobbing mess, the passenger jumped out and roughly dragged him onto the back seat, before setting off again with the slow-moving line following the lorry, which by now had forced enough cars out of the way to open up a lane and allow the traffic to get off the bridge. A similar story occurred on the southbound lane towards Edinburgh. A bus had shoved several empty cars out of the way, until one of the car's owners had taken issue, a middle-aged businessman driving a Lexus, and forced his way onto the bus to confront the driver, only to be set upon by several of the angry passengers, who left him unconscious and securely tied up to an empty seat. John was growing weaker and struggling to keep his arms extended. The tower continued to mercilessly bore down on him until it eventually succeeded and gained a little ground, collapsing the weary arms that had halted its downward movement, before it crashed down onto the base of John's neck, causing his legs to buckle a little until he recovered enough to at least stand upright again. At this point, John had been supporting the bridge for nearly half an hour and only a few cars were left on it now. His wife and son, along with his friends, were now safely clear of the bridge, thankfully, as he had nearly collapsed completely with relief the moment they had and now John was just about ready to crumble. Holding on with the last of his strength, he urged the last few cars to hurry up with some extremely choice words. However, neither he, nor anyone else in the vicinity, was able to hear him because all sound was drowned out by the horrendous noises that were coming from the doomed bridge. Realising that the final car was now clear, John keeled forward completely exhausted and was brutally crushed as the bridge finally won its battle against him. The tower sat like a triumphant victor atop of his inert body for a few tortuous seconds, until it toppled over, ripping much of the road and many of the suspension cables along with it. The falling debris sending a huge wave hurtling towards the small towns of North and South Queensferry as it sank into the River Forth. John barely had any strength left, but somehow managed to drag himself off what remained of the central tower and splash down into the cold water before blacking out.

He woke up ten minutes later, after his apparently lifeless body had been pulled from the water by a RNLI Lifeboat, launched from South Queensferry. The startled crew of the bright orange craft thought he was dead to the point that one of them even crossed herself after collapsing to her knees once he had woken up. Wondering what all the fuss was about, John waved them away, insisting he was OK and struggled back up to his feet. Once up the rolling of the boat made him stagger and he gripped the bulwark for support, staring in disbelief at what remained of the ruined Queensferry Crossing. He noticed that his clothes were in tatters, but thankfully he'd left his phone in the car. Although he realised that he now had no way of telling Annie he was OK, which was a bit of a problem. The crew of the Lifeboat were watching him with trepidation and jumped at even his slightest movements. John quickly grew tired of this and headed towards the stern, hoping for some peace from their wide staring eyes. There was no one around at the back end of the boat, no one looking from anywhere else either, so he jumped over the side, swam deep down, well out of sight and made his way back to the northern bank of the river in North Queensferry. John rose out the water, rather like a scene from a horror movie thanks to his ragged appearance, and trudged his way up the seaweed strewn rocky shore towards a little car park in the shadow of the huge red rail bridge. He was still feeling fairly weak and collapsed over the small wall at the edge of the road, landing flat on his back, staring up at the graceful arch of the cantilever bridge towering high above. Within seconds though, hands grabbed at his arms, bringing him out of his brief reverie with a start as he was pulled up into a seated position. Annie and Arla's tear-streaked faces swam into focus. "Hey honey." He said weakly, making Annie burst into uncontrollable sobs as she wrapped her arms tight around his neck and hugged him close. Arla's arms soon joined those of his wife's as she too started to cry and hug him out of sheer relief. Callum was holding a struggling Stewart in his arms as he slowly walked upto the three of them, looking as if he'd suffered enough stress to last a lifetime and sat down heavily in front of John. Stewart managed to break free and launched himself towards his dad, burying himself in-between his mum and Arla. Callum let out a small croak of relief and he too joined in on the group hug, wrapping his long arms around all of them. "What happened to you after you disappeared?" Annie asked after she broke free and held his face towards hers with tears still flowing freely. Arla and Callum also let go, Stewart remained in his lap still holding him tightly, and sat down on the road in a loose circle around him. John explained how he'd leapt from the bridge and then jumped into the gap to stop the tower from toppling over right away. He told them about the thirteen idiots who had gotten out of their cars, Arla and Callum both swore angrily, and how it had cost him all of his strength to keep the bridge upright for so long, right up until the last car got off, after which he immediately collapsed, bringing the tower down on top of him. This made the three of them stare at him in disbelief and wonder how on earth he was still alive after being crushed like that. They allowed John another couple of minutes to regain some strength, but he still needed a little help to get back on his feet again. Annie wedged herself under his arm and walked him up the little hill towards her car. Stewart held onto his hand and kept glancing up at him through puffy eyes. Arla and Callum followed closely behind in case Annie needed help to support him. John was thinking about how exhausted he was and felt the ordeal had taken so much out of him because he couldn't see the sun. The dust cloud he created to obscure himself from sight had nearly ruined his chance of saving everyone. The Sun's life-giving rays had almost entirely been blocked so John's body hadn't been able to replenish the massive amount of energy he was expending while supporting the tower. By the time they all reached their parked cars, he felt pretty much back at full strength again as his body had been greedily guzzling up the sun's rays, now that they were no longer obstructed by a thick cloud of cement dust. John eased himself off his wife's shoulder and she stared at him with deep concern, but it was short lived as he stood up proud and tall then scooped her up in his arms. Annie looked immensely relieved to see John back to his new normal self, although the tattered and somewhat smelly clothes adorning him still made her nose wrinkle, much to his amusement. Stewart jumped up and down impatiently as he wanted to be picked up too. Callum stepped up and hoisted him up onto Annie's lap, so that they were both now in John's arms. Stewart looked thrilled as he sat on his mum cross-legged, very much the king of the castle. Arla put an arm around Callum's waist after he stepped back beside her, pleasantly surprising him so he wrapped an arm around her shoulders in reply and gave an affectionate squeeze.

John felt curious as to what was going on around them so he closed his eyes and took in all the surrounding sounds. The image that formed grew with each passing second and was of utter chaos. Sirens were everywhere, descending upon both sides of the ruined bridge, while cars were backed up for miles in each direction of the motorway. The surrounding towns of Rosyth, Inverkeithing and Kincardine were starting to feel the strain as cars were now having to find alternative routes across the river Forth, resulting in massive tailbacks and complete gridlock in many areas. Arla had seen this before, so she knew what he was doing, while Callum looked at him curiously, having not seen this particular skill of his being utilised before. A few more seconds passed in silence before John opened his eyes again to tell them what he now knew of everything that was going on around them. Annie and Callum hadn't known he could do this on such a large scale so they looked a little surprised at all the information. Callum jerked his head as it finally dawned on him how John had managed to find them way back in Miami. The sirens and road closure on the backroad leading to Burntisland mystified John because the chaos hadn't yet spread any further than Dalgety Bay. "I wonder what's happened there? As you said, it's still a way off from being affected by what's happened here." Arla said while Annie and Callum nodded in agreement. "At least the roads back to our houses are relatively clear. All the traffic built-up on this side of the river is trying to head south so it isn't going our way, which is a relief at least." Annie said wearily. Arla looked happier at this as she was driving Callum home. A second later a frown marred her face though as she would be staying with Annie and John that night, meaning the traffic trying to head south would be an issue after she had dropped Callum off in Kirkcaldy. John closed his eyes again as the road closure near Burntisland was nagging at him. A car had left the national speed limit road, appeared to have hit a wall, rolled over and was now resting on its roof amongst the surrounding trees. It was an ugly scene. Parts of the car had flown off and were scattered around the area. The driver and the front passenger must've been cut free from the wreckage as the roof was lying off to one side. Paramedics were attending to a woman, who looked to be in a very bad way, readying to move her into the waiting ambulance and head off to the Victoria hospital in Kirkcaldy. It looked like the man from the car hadn't survived the accident as his lifeless body was being respectfully covered-up by another, distraught looking, crew from a different ambulance parked nearby. John grimaced at the dreadful turn of events, drawing worried looks from Annie, Arla and Callum. Annie suddenly yelped in surprise, Stewart yelled excitedly as he thought it was a game, as John dropped to his knees and swayed unsteadily, barely managing to avoid dropping his wife and son. Stewart jumped off saying 'again' but Annie knelt beside her husband and stared at him nervously, waiting to find out what was so wrong. "The paramedics. I heard them on the radio as they left the scene with the injured woman. The woman is Gemma. David is dead. I .... I..... don't know what happened to Claire though." John said in barely a whisper, both hands planted firmly on the ground to stop him from keeling over again. Annie's eyes flooded with tears as she mouthed a silent 'oh no' and covered her mouth with trembling hands. Callum's hands were on his head and he looked devasted by the awful news. Arla had collapsed to the floor and covered her face, sobbing loudly while repeating 'no, please no' in a muffled, anguished cry. Stewart ran over, crying out 'Auntie Arla what's wrong?' as he knelt down and hugged her protectively. "I have to go and find out what happened to Claire. I need to know Annie. I have to know, I'm sorry." John held her face gently in his hand and his heart felt like it was breaking as he looked into her distraught eyes. She gave a small nod as she understood why. She felt the same and needed to know too. John stepped back, looked towards Burntisland and leapt high into the evening sky, glowing fiery red as the sun slowly disappeared over the horizon in the distance. He held out his arms in front of him, willing himself onwards and over the gridlocked roads far below as he was enveloped by the clouds. John didn't notice at the time that he was flying. Dalgety bay and Aberdour came and went by in an instant and he only started to descend as the blocked off road came into view during a break in the clouds.

The descent was almost instantaneous, but he still landed smoothly in the field across the road from the wrecked car.

The emergency services were no longer hurrying around the scene like frenzied bees. There was a dejected atmosphere about them all as they started to clean up the debris and pack away their equipment. A couple of police officers standing by as sentries noticed John approaching on foot through the field. They looked at each other completely bewildered at first but quickly recovered and hurried into the field to intercept the mysterious intruder. The officers, one of which recognised John as she drew closer, stopped in their tracks as they saw John's ruined clothing and filthy appearance. The man held out his hand and issued an order to 'stop right there sir'. The order went unheeded and the officer grew angry so he shouted once more. The other officer, a woman John knew as Jean, had known him for many years and was alarmed at his appearance and determined face. "John, are you ok?" She asked tentatively, her blue eyes wide with concern as she brushed aside her long blonde hair. No response came as the man jammed his hand into John's chest, only to shout out in alarm as it was like being shoved backwards by a slow-moving train. He braced his feet and jammed both hands against John's chest, but to no avail as his backwards movement continued un-checked. John only stopped because Jean was gripping his arm and pleading for him to wait. He shook his head and wondered why there was a policeman with his hands on his chest, looking like he was trying to push a car. John had been so focused on reaching the crashed car, to find out what happened to Claire, he hadn't noticed the police officers' approach, nor the shouts from the one now standing upright again, looking apoplectic with rage. "Just who in the hell do you think you are mister?" He jabbed John angrily in the chest with his finger and made to grab some hand-cuffs from his belt. "Bill please don't, I know this man, his name is John and he's friends with Gemma and David-" Jean's words cut off abruptly in her throat as she looked grief-stricken, remembering and looking over towards the lifeless body. "Shut your mouth Jean, I don't care who he is because he just assaulted a police officer!" Bill shouted the final words as spittle flew from his mouth and he continued to aggressively shove John's chest. John gazed at the crazed officer with no hint of emotion. "Get out of my way" he said quietly. Only Jean heard and she tried to shove her partner out of his way, not an easy task as the male officer was much larger than her athletic five-feet seven inches build, panicking as she picked up the hostility dripping from each syllable he spoke. Bill was having none of it though and pushed Jean away roughly, sending her tumbling to the floor. John didn't like that one bit and was already in a dangerous mood. He grabbed Bill's shirt with one hand and lifted him off the ground. The stunned officer let out a petrified squeak and tried in vain to free himself from the iron grip, kicking out and throwing useless punches, only to stop and go completely quiet as he found himself now face to face with John. Bill was several inches shorter and his feet were dangling above the ground as his terrified eyes looked into John's cold, emotionless ones. "You have a choice here. Either you agree to get out of my way and help Jean back to her feet, or I'm going to throw you out of my way" John spoke deceptively calmly as he struggled to contain his anger. "H-how dare you! Unhand me you fool. Do you have any idea the trouble-" Bill's indignant voice was cut off as he flew through the air and screamed shrilly. He landed with a loud thud over fifty feet away and the shrill scream stopped instantly. John didn't care for the trouble he was now supposedly in and resumed his march forward towards the crashed car. He hadn't wanted to really harm Bill and only flicked his wrist as if trying to swat away an annoying fly. Jean had been staring in disbelief and jumped at the loud thud from her partner's impact. No one else heard the scream or the landing though as there was still a lot of noise from all the activity going on around the scene of the crash. She stood motionless with indecision, Bill or John? Jean chose John and hurried after him. "Uh, w-what did my eyes see there John? You just threw a grown man some fifty feet like he was a toy or something!" Her voice jumped a few octaves as she spoke and glanced quickly back over towards the inert Bill with a worried expression. "I don't know what you think you saw Jean, but I do know that no one would ever believe you if that was ever repeated. I'd come up with a different story as to why Bill now has a few broken bones." John didn't like talking to Jean in such a condescending manner. He would apologise for it later, but all he cared about right then was Claire. Jean looked aghast and hurt by his callous tone and words but didn't say anything. She carried on walking alongside him in silence until they reached the road.

Jean brushed aside her feelings as she noticed the devastation on John's face. He looked like a broken man, barely able to stand so she grabbed his arm to steady him. His head dropped and he fell heavily to his knees, almost bringing her down with him as she staggered and had to let go. Jean was stunned and heart-broken to see tears fighting their way through the grime on his face as he stared hopelessly at the road. John closed his eyes and wished that this was all just a terrible dream. He tried to blot out all the sounds around him but a faint crying just wouldn't go away. John grunted in frustration and opened his eyes to try and see where the annoying crying was coming from. It took him a moment to realise the cries were coming from what sounded like a small child. "What!?" He exclaimed loudly, growing frustrated while still looking around utterly perplexed. Then it hit him. "Claire!" He gasped suddenly, making Jean and several others nearby jump, then stood up quickly and stared wildly at the trees casting their shadows over the road, behind the wall the car had hit. John ran forward, knocking over a couple of startled firemen, jumped over the wall and straight towards one of the trees several meters past the wreckage of the Morris's car. He didn't slow down and jumped once more, high up into the tree, snapping several branches as the leaves slapped his face, landing close to the top. He let out a soft moan of relief as he found Claire, still strapped safely in her car seat, having been hurled from the car during the crash and was inexplicably unharmed, bar a few small scratches across her face. Another time, John may have found himself questioning how Claire had survived, but not now. He picked up the car-seat and carefully worked his way back down the tree. Claire was still crying silently, but also stared at him sadly with puffy eyes. "My mum and dad left me. I cried but they didn't come. I miss my mum and dad." She said brokenly through her continued crying. John's voice was lost in his constricted throat and he tried desperately not to cry himself. What on earth could he tell Claire? How could he even begin to try and help her understand what had happened to her parents? John jumped the last few feet from the tree and landed lightly in amongst the silent crowd of stunned onlookers who had gathered around. A paramedic stepped forward and she couldn't believe what her eyes were seeing. "How is this possible?" Jean asked as she appeared by the equally shocked paramedic. "Take her to the hospital please. Make sure she's safe" was all John could say as his eyesight started to blur with tears. Jean and the paramedic nodded and accepted Claire into their care without hesitation. The crowd of fireman and other paramedics all followed silently as Claire was taken to the remaining ambulance, leaving John alone in the shadows.

He turned and ran further into the trees, wanting nothing more than to get away and be alone with his grief. John leapt into the clouds and flew towards the West Lomond Hill, the tallest peak in Fife, near the small town of Falklands. There was no one around as he landed near the geo-marker and sank heavily down onto his knees. John had saved thousands of lives less than an hour earlier from what seemed like an impossible situation, yet he couldn't save Gemma and David from a car crash. The injustice of it left him feeling utterly defeated and useless. He looked up towards the sky and let out a long, piercing scream of despair that shattered the peaceful silence, sent birds flying and small animals scurrying away for miles around. A couple enjoying a walk up to the summit of the East Lomond Hill in the cool evening air were startled by the scream, wondering what could've made such a harrowing sound as they looked around nervously. John sat on his knees in an almost comatose state for nearly an hour, eyes unfocused, staring off into the far distance. Darkness was now creeping in as the sun hid behind the horizon. With a heavy sigh, John got up to his feet, took a long morose look around, a further pang of despair jolted him as he saw the remaining two towers of the Queensferry Crossing, and then set off on a fast run back home.

He opened the front door to find Annie sitting on the stairs waiting for him, her eyes were red and puffy and it looked as though she had only recently stopped crying. Stewart was thankfully in bed sound asleep. Annie looked up at him and held up her arms for a hug. John bent down, picked her up off the stairs and held her close, resting his head against hers as she leant on his shoulder. He carried her through to the living room, closely followed by Jay who had been lying at her feet the whole time. Arla and Callum were waiting for them and looked up, both of them had also been crying, as John entered carrying Annie. They had remained on the sofa huddled together, too drained to move. John sat down on the sofa beside Arla and she placed one of her hands on his knee. "Are you ok?" She asked croakily. Callum looked across, lifted an arm that had been wrapped around Arla and gripped his shoulder bracingly. John took a deep breath before he spoke. "I found Claire. She wasn't hurt thankfully. Gemma is in a serious condition with a broken femur, a couple of broken ribs and a fractured skull which has caused a severe swelling on the brain. That's what I found out at the scene anyway. I don't know what's going on at the hospital though. Claire was taken there too by Jean. David-" he hesitated as his voice caught in his throat "-died on impact it seemed." A single tear escaped and crawled down his face after he stopped speaking to compose himself again. "I'm not great. I even lashed out and threw Jean's partner Bill in the field by the crash. It broke a few of his bones too." He said, starting to sound normal again. "I know him. He was the one that came round and threatened us at my housewarming party, even though there hadn't been any complaints from the neighbours. The man is a nasty piece of work so he probably deserved it." Callum said with conviction. Arla remembered the house party and the incident with Bill, as Annie had dragged her away before she flattened the arrogant and unashamedly sexist policeman after he had shoved her for no apparent reason. Bill had sneered at Arla afterwards, as if trying to bait her into doing something he could abuse his power over. The incident still irked her now so she nodded in agreement with Callum's statement. “Jean saw me do it and I was incredibly rude with her after, which I feel terrible for. She didn’t deserve how I spoke to her. I’ll get some flowers and a bottle of wine or something to say sorry.” “I like Jean. I hope you didn’t upset her too much.” Annie said as she sat up in his lap and looked at him with a worried frown. John looked away from her eyes, feeling guilty. “Oh. Well in that case I think flowers and Wine would be a good idea then. Don’t feel too bad though, you were worried sick and angry after what had happened with the bridge because of those idiots who stopped. I hope they get their comeuppance.” Annie had started gently but at the mention of the people who had gotten out of their cars, finished with a tone that matched the anger he felt towards the foolish people.

Annie gave him a quick kiss on his grime covered cheek then got up and asked if anyone wanted a cup of tea, a drink or some hot chocolate. They all requested a hot chocolate so Arla gave Callum’s knee a quick squeeze and she got up to help her in the kitchen, leaving the two men alone in the living room. “I know today has been incredibly difficult, but you should be proud of all the lives you saved today John. If you hadn’t done what you did, even though it could’ve killed you, the bridge would’ve collapsed right then and all of those people, Annie, Stewart, Arla and I included, would’ve plummeted to their deaths. Not everyone can be saved though John. Thousands of superhero comics and movies have told us that much at least. Unfortunately-” he broke off as his voice broke “-they were right. There was nothing you could’ve done for them. Which means there was nothing anyone could’ve done.” Callum looked at John and gripped his shoulder again, trying to express how thankful he was and re-assure him, but couldn’t think of any other words to do it appropriately. John had heard enough though, nodded sadly, mouthed 'thank you' and gripped Callum's shoulder in return as words failed him too. "I hope Gemma and Claire are going to be ok. I guess all we can do is be here for them if they need us." Callum said after slowly exhaling a deep breath and letting go of John's shoulder. "We'll do all we can for them. She'll know that." John said a little choked up. Annie and Arla came back in from the kitchen with four steaming cups of hot chocolate with cream, bringing with them a welcome distraction to the difficult conversation. Annie perched herself back down on John's lap while Arla sat close and snuggled into Callum, leaning into him contentedly as his arm went around her shoulder again. They sat in silence, the only sounds coming from a snoring Jay and the occasional slurp of their hot drinks, until all of the cups were empty and it was time to go to bed. Arla got up first and carried all of the cups through to the kitchen. Annie said thanks and got up to let Jay out into the garden, rousing him gently from a deep sleep. John and Callum also said a quick thanks, then they too stood up, with Callum going to help Arla in the kitchen, while John went over to Annie and wrapped his arms around her as she watched Jay in the garden. Arla and Callum came out of the kitchen carrying drinks for them all as Jay trotted back in from the garden, heading straight upstairs to his large memory foam bed in Annie and John's room. The guest rooms were already made up so there was no need to hunt around for bedding. They all said goodnight, Arla and Callum quietly closed their doors behind them, whereas Annie and John left there's open so Jay could go downstairs for a drink if he needed to. The day had been one they would never forget for all the wrong reasons, despite it having been so pleasant initially with all of the group finally catching up again together as one. A small comfort for three of them as they drifted off to sleep was that at least David's last day alive had been spent happily with close friends. There was no comforting John though. All he could think about was the thirteen people who had stopped and endangered everyone's lives, wasting valuable time and pushing him to his absolute limit. John wondered, had they not done that, could he have saved David? The thought filled him with an alarming desire to find all thirteen, and make them suffer like he was suffering.

The night was cold and dark. The group of people were strangers to one another yet they still found themselves together for some unknown reason. All of them were shivering because of the cold but they couldn't move their arms to try and generate any warmth. Their arms were all too sore and they hadn't been able to move them for nearly an hour. Faint droplets of blood were slowly working down the exposed skin of a few of the aching limbs. There were thirteen people in the haggard looking group. An unlucky number indeed as it transpired for the unfortunate souls shivering in the night. Even though the thirteen were strangers, the fourteenth member, who could still walk around, move his arms freely and looked anything but haggard, knew each of them quite well. The unfortunate thirteen were suspended by their wrists, cruelly cable-tied together and cutting painfully into their skin, dangling high above the dark and unforgiving looking waters of the river Forth. They had been hung, for reasons unknown to them, by the quiet, masked man who was pacing back and forth on the fractured road of the northern end of what was, once, the Queensferry Crossing. The terrified group consisted of four woman and nine men who had all seen what happened when the bridge collapsed. They had found themselves in what could be referred to as a 'front-row-seat' to the disaster, in a situation entirely of their own making, which is why the quiet man had abducted eleven of them from their homes, they all lived alone, and two of them from the police stations they were being held in. John stood at the very edge of jagged road, leaned forward and looked at each of his captives. He knew their names, their home addresses, where they worked and that none of them had any dependants, something he was a little grateful for, although it still wouldn't have saved them from his wrath. None of those details were really that important though. All that mattered to John, was the reason why he had even bothered to look for them in the first place. These were the thirteen people that had decided it was a good idea to get out of their vehicles, thereby effectively trapping and endangering the lives of all those that were behind them, and watch as the central tower of Queensferry Crossing collapsed. "If you haven't yet realised why you're all enjoying this pleasant star-lit night, suspended as you are, then I must ask that you take just a little longer to figure it out. If I have to tell you why you're here, even after an hour now, then I'm afraid I'll simply have to let you go and part-ways with our little assembly here." John spoke as if he were merely discussing the weather. "I d-don't know why I'm here! Why are you doing this? What have I ever done to you!" Sobbed a middle-aged woman wearing silk pyjamas. John had abducted the woman from a penthouse near Ocean's Terminal that overlooked the very same river she found herself now dangling above. Her car, an Aston Martin Vantage, had actually stopped over two lanes of traffic as she watched the disaster unfolding. John sighed loudly, stepped up to where she was suspended from and picked her up by the cable tie binding her wrists. The woman looked at him fearfully with pleading eyes, stuttering as she begged to be let go, pleading for him not to hurt her and that she was sorry for costing hundreds of people their pensions. The last little revelation certainly didn't endear the woman to John, but it wasn't why he let her go. The remaining twelve all watched in horror as the screaming woman grew smaller and smaller as she plummeted towards what could only be a certain death. The high-pitched scream stopped abruptly after a large splash disturbed the choppy water far below. "Well, I did as she asked, no one can deny that. I also proved that I'm man of my word. Now, does anyone else not know why they are here tonight?" John asked pleasantly. Eleven people soon joined the woman in the water below, much to his disappointment. He hoped the last remaining person, a young man who was a professional footballer and drove a Ford, would be the one to finally realise why he was there. "It's just you and me now-" John said a little dejectedly as he sat down and kicked his legs lazily off the edge of the road "-please tell me you know why you're here." The young man swallowed hard and looked up towards John, desperation written all over his face. He looked like he was doing some hard thinking. "Am I here because I tried to assault a truck driver after he hit my car?" The man asked tentatively. John growled angrily, reached down and picked the footballer up by his long brown hair, causing him to cry out and whimper pitifully. "As far as I'm concerned, you don't deserve to live because of your complete disregard for the lives of others." John said quietly, and the man's eyes widened in horror as he too was let go to join the other twelve that had hung out with him for the last hour or so. John watched dispassionately as the man twirled end over end, desperately flailing his arms and legs in a pointless attempt at preventing the inevitable.

But before the man hit the water, he heard Annie calling his name from a distance. He wheeled around in surprise, only to find his wife was nowhere to be seen. Completely bewildered, John hurried forward to see if she was hidden behind something. He heard Annie's voice again, louder this time, but he still had no idea as to where it was coming from. Then she called his name once more, a shout this time that startled him and he suddenly found himself staring into her concerned pale grey eyes. John was sitting upright in his bed at home, breathing heavily and shaking all over. Annie was sitting on his lap with her hands resting on his chest. "John, are you OK? I've been trying to wake you up for a couple of minutes but you weren't responding at all." She sounded frightened as she spoke. "I-I was just at the bridge, it was dark, and I-" he hesitated and looked away from his wife's eyes "-I killed them. I just killed the thirteen people who had stopped and watched the bridge collapse. What have I done?" John asked with a horrified look as he hid his face in his hands. Annie's mouth dropped and she looked stunned. She then shook her head quickly, frowned and looked towards the shut blinds. It was daylight outside. It wasn't dark like her husband had just said it was. "What on earth are you talking about? It's morning now, not night. And as far as I'm aware, you've been here the whole time." Annie looked sceptically at John, still hiding his face. "We both know I don't sleep anymore Annie so, I could've gone out during the night and come back again before. . . wait a minute. You weren't at the bridge just now, were you?" Annie crossed her arms and was clearly growing impatient with the conversation. "Of-course I wasn't, do you think I'd leave the house like this?" She opened her arms to indicate her flimsy nightdress and make-up free face. John took a moment to admire her before responding, staring openly at the pink material that did little to hide what was covered beneath it. Even though Annie had been getting annoyed, she couldn't help but laugh and tease her captivated husband by turning from side to side quickly. This moment of levity was enough to convince John he hadn't just murdered thirteen people, and he promptly collapsed back onto his pillow, breathing a heavy sigh of relief. Annie stopped with her little bit of fun and grew moderately concerned again, wondering why John had been convinced he'd just killed those people. John noticed her concern, quickly apologised for frightening her and explained why he had said those things. "That sounds like you were dreaming. But how can you dream if you don't sleep?" Annie asked with a curious expression. "I have no idea. Maybe it wasn't a dream, but an awfully worrying fantasy. All of my memories are crystal clear and are as if I'm actually reliving them as I recall them. So maybe, if I think of something, even though it hasn't happened, it's like my mind can make it seem real now, right down to tiny details such as the whisper of clothing when you move." The explanation made sense for John and, even though he was alarmed by that particular thought, he was still incredibly relieved it wasn't actually real. Annie seemed to understand what he said too and nodded agreeably. She leaned forward and rested her hands on his chest, John couldn't help but stare again at the effect this had on her clothing. "I know those people don't exactly deserve good things right now but, please no more thoughts like that. Besides, wouldn't it be more fun to think of your beautiful wife instead?" Annie said while smiling seductively. John agreed whole heartedly and pulled his wife down on to him, making her shriek delightedly. The noise woke Jay up from what had been a deep sleep, he raised his head wearily to see what was going on, then flopped back on to his bed and went to sleep again. It was a week after the collapse of the Queensferry Crossing and although there was still a great deal of sadness over the tragic events from that horrible day, John was happier now that he and Annie were both much more their normal selves again.

Gemma was still in hospital but no longer in intensive care and recovering well all things considered. Claire was being looked after by Gemma's parents and visited her mum every day. Annie and John only visited Gemma every other day, along with Callum, not wishing to crowd her, while Arla had only been once as her debut professional MMA bout was just days away and she was already in London. Annie, John, Callum, Richard and Sarah were all going to go to London the day before the event to cheer her on. Stewart was looking forward to a weekend with Annie's parents while they were away. The news still regularly featured stories about the mysterious collapse of the bridge and how it was a miracle no one was killed and that engineers still couldn't understand how it had happened. The bridge was still essentially brand new, having only opened a few years prior, and there were regular rigorous safety inspections. Interestingly, there hadn't been any mention of how the central tower had started to fall, only to suddenly return upright until the very last car was safe and clear. John also noticed that the thirteen people who had gotten out their cars were now infamous, much to his grim satisfaction. The live news coverage clearly showed them out of their cars and watching as the tower started to fall. Social media swiftly identified all of them, one of whom was a professional footballer and quite well known already, at which point the lives they had lived until then were over. The police had to get involved as the public outcry over their irresponsible and callous actions led to them all receiving death threats. There was also mounting pressure for them to be charged for endangering the lives of so many people which put the police, who were now having to protect them, in a very unenviable position. John had lost interest in his desire to punish them as he felt they had done a fine job themselves in ruining their own lives. He was however, much like the stupefied engineers who were still the subject of relentless questioning, very interested in finding out what had happened to the section of tower that somehow detached itself and caused the disaster. John found the missing section of tower the following night at the bottom of the river. The huge reinforced block of concrete looked like it was ready to be slotted right back into place as it appeared to be in good condition. Curiously, the edges were so smooth they appeared machined. Another curious thing about it were a couple of what looked like fist-sized indentations on the edge sticking upright out of the silt. Those strange indentations had John transfixed for the best part of an hour as he simply couldn't figure out what could've caused them. Annie had been equally confused, even going so far as to suggest that there could perhaps be someone else with his strength out in the world, especially seeing as he himself had been the one to observe the indentations as 'fist-sized'. The thought of someone else willing to do harm with that sort of power at their disposal made them both shudder involuntarily, so they swiftly dismissed the notion and came up with other, less frightening, theories.

The day before Arla's professional debut came around and it was time for Annie and John to drop Stewart and Jay off at her parent's house. After a quick catch up with Annie's parents, Catherine and Tam, who John got on very well with, they walked back home to make sure everything needed for the weekend away was packed and ready to go. A taxi was picking them up in an hour, along with Callum who was due to arrive at their house soon, to take them to Edinburgh airport for their flight to London Heathrow. John wasn't massively keen on the idea of flying again, especially to Heathrow, and only agreed so long as he could visit the UK's flagship Lego store at Leicester Square while they were in London. Richard and Sarah were going to meet them at the airport as they all managed to book themselves on the same flight. Richard planned to take advantage of the trip to the Lego store too, provided he could convince Sarah to let him. Once they were all at the airport, it was a reunion of somewhat mixed emotions as they hadn't seen each other since the Edinburgh Zoo visit. After checking in and passing through security, Annie and Sarah went off together to browse the shops, with a quick stop to buy coffee first and catch up. This left John, Callum and Richard free to go look at some shops themselves, ironically with a quick visit to the same coffee shop Annie and Sarah had just left. The flight to Heathrow was uneventful, much to John's immense relief, and they got into another prebooked taxi to take them to their hotel. The hotel was within easy walking distance of the O2 Arena, hence why Annie chose it rather than the one nearer the Lego shop John had been looking at. She was quick to point out that he could easily get to the store in a matter of seconds from the hotel she chose. Regrettably for John his counter argument that Richard couldn't move so speedily was conveniently ignored. Whereas, with John's choice, they would all have to get a taxi to the O2 Arena on a night where around twenty thousand people would be in attendance for the event. Unsurprisingly, Annie won that particular debate. In the interim, Annie and Sarah were treating themselves to a luxury spa treatment, which didn't appeal to John at all so, rather than being left on his own at the hotel, he went along with Callum and Richard to visit the famed interlocking brick store. He didn't get a bad deal of things though as the three of them enjoyed the afternoon visiting some of London's famous attractions, along with visits to numerous shops in which a lot of money ended up being spent. John and Richard didn't really need to worry about money, they were both very fortunate in that regard, but the amount they spent would certainly raises their wives' eyebrows and possibly provoke an interesting reaction from them. Unusually, Callum had actually spent more than either of his two friends, but at the same time he didn't have a wife or children to be mindful of. John and Richard hoped that the gifts they'd bought for Annie, Sarah and their children would be sufficient to avoid any unpleasantness. As it turned out, the gifts they purchased were very well received by Annie and Sarah, which meant that their own purchases were overlooked and safely stored away at the hotel prior to leaving for the arena.

There were a lot of people milling around outside what was once the millennium dome when they arrived and they thought they would have a long wait to get inside. However, their wait wasn't long, thanks to their VIP passes, and they were soon inside. With refreshments and souvenirs purchased, they made their way to ringside seats, ready to cheer on Arla who was on the main card for the event, possibly owing to the fact that her match up was against a highly ranked fighter, who was trying to rebuild her career after difficult back-to-back defeats. Unsurprisingly, as Arla's opponent was English, the promoters had jumped on the fact that Arla was Scottish, and billed the match up as a classic 'England Vs Scotland' bout. For the fight itself, due to her lack of experience, Arla was a heavy underdog going into the match-up but, that didn't stop her confidently marching out, to a wave of booing from the partisan crowd, climb into the cage, stand in the centre and stare at her opponent with bad intentions. When the fight commenced, it only took Arla a minute to stun the crowd into silence as a viscous combination of punches sent her opponent tumbling to canvas and into survival mode, covering up, trying to get away from the furious onslaught of follow up strikes. The referee suddenly pulled Arla off of her bloodied opponent and Annie, John, Callum, Richard and Sarah all leapt to their feet thinking she had won already. Only for them all to be left outraged as there had supposedly been an illegal blow, and Arla was deducted a point on the judge's scorecards. John was about ready to jump into the cage himself and throw the referee through the roof, but Annie had wisely grabbed hold of his hand and given him a withering stare. Callum was jumping up and down, hurling all sorts of abuse at the quite clearly biased, or completely incompetent, referee. John even noticed the organisation's owner standing up, clearly unhappy at the decision. The farcical interruption didn't seem to faze Arla at all as she never took her eyes away from the highly-ranked fighter trying to recover in her corner. The bout resumed, after the suspiciously long time it took the referee to point to each judge and notify them of the point deduction, and Arla went right back on the offensive. She landed another flurry of unanswered punches before easily taking her opponent to the mat once more with a textbook hip toss. Arla rained down more punches after passing guard and securing a full mount position, before latching onto a flailing arm and locking it in a tight armbar. Her opponent tapped out almost immediately as Arla wrenched her arm to a point it became almost uncomfortable to watch. Shockingly, the referee didn't end the fight there and then, it looked as though he was desperately trying to figure out a way to disqualify Arla. It wasn't until the opposing corner threw in the towel, the fight still hadn't stopped even though the opponent was screaming in agony, that the referee finally separated them. Even then, he still looked around as if trying to decide how he could award the victory to the woman who was now holding her badly broken arm. The five of them at ringside all leapt up with joy as Arla extatically climbed out of the cage to celebrate with her corner, then, once she had noticed her close friends, frantically worked her way past the first couple of rows in the crowd and embraced them. Tears flowed freely as all the emotions of the past traumatic weeks were finally let loose. Arla had been by far the strongest of them all in the aftermath of the disaster, keeping herself well in check in order to focus on the fight, but now she could finally let out all of those bottled-up emotions. After a good cry and many loud triumphant screams, Arla reluctantly separated from Annie and Sarah, John, Callum and Richard. As she left, each gave her a fleeting hug and a fist bump before jumping up and down celebrating again, then weaved her way back into the cage ready for the official verdict. Normally the referee would hold both fighters' wrists and raise the victors hand after the winner was announced. That didn't happen on this occasion though. John had to laugh as he heard Arla bluntly, with some choice words, tell him not to touch her. He laughed even harder as the referee then tried to hold the opponent's wrist, failing to realise it was attached to a broken arm, and was promptly punched right on the nose in retaliation. Arla's name rang out as she was announced the winner by submission after three minutes and two seconds of round one. The crowd respectfully cheered and clapped at the announcement in recognition of Arla's decisive victory despite the best efforts of the referee. There were a couple of fights on the main card once Arla's bout had finished, one being for the undisputed middleweight title, after which the five of them went backstage to congratulate and celebrate with their victorious friend. Annie, John, Arla, Callum, Richard and Sarah all fully intended to enjoy the night to the fullest extent possible, knowing that soon after their return home, they would all have to suffer through a most unwelcome and difficult day.

Lovely weather was quite often a rarity in Scotland. But rather than going out to a beach or to a park to enjoy the sunny day though, Annie and John were going to David's funeral. Gemma was at least back at home now, much to Claire's delight, having been discharged from hospital the previous day. John couldn't imagine what she was going through and he certainly didn't want to experience her pain anytime in the far future either. Sadly, he knew that you didn't always get what you wished for in life. Annie kept looking at him a little worried as she could tell something was bothering him. She asked the previous day after they had visited Gemma at her home, but John had only told her some of what was on his mind. Arla, whilst having a well-earned break from training, stayed at theirs and was going to travel with them to the crematorium. Like many long-term work colleagues, Arla knew John well and could also tell when something was on his mind. However, she had only been told the same part-truth as Annie though, that he was still thinking about the bridge and going over the disaster in his head again, and again, trying to figure out if he could've somehow saved David and prevented his untimely death. Annie lost the plot with him, sending Jay running from the room and even alarming Arla, as she almost shouted herself hoarse telling him to stop beating himself up and that if he couldn't have done anything then, no one else would've been able to either, echoing what Callum had already said the night of the disaster, but he had obviously still not let it go. Annie even clenched her fists and was strongly considering hitting him. However, rather than, most likely, breaking her hand though, she calmed down enough to tell him what she insisted was going to be the very last time, that this burden of grief wasn't his to bear alone and he shouldn't feel guilty either. Arla nodded gravely at this. "We all miss David John. As for those thirteen people who got out of their cars, yes, I know you're also thinking of them, don't bother. Don't you dare bother. You saw the accident report yourself, the crash happened seconds after the tower started to fall. Even if those people hadn't stopped, there was simply nothing that could be done, and we-" Annie pointed between herself and Arla "-are certain that there was nothing you could've done. Remember, thousands of people went home alive that day thanks to you." Arla stood beside Annie and they both crossed their arms as if to emphasise the point. John still wished he could've saved just one more, but didn't dare mention it. He reluctantly agreed it was time to move on. Arla threw up her arms and exclaimed 'halleluiah!' as Annie covered up her face and took several deep, steadying breaths before stepping up to him and gently holding his face in her hands, saying a quiet 'thank you'. Jay cautiously crept up to Annie now that the shouting was over, with worried eyes thinking he was the one in trouble. She knelt down and started to give him a good fussing, reassuring him that he hadn't done anything wrong, giving John a quick angry look, and telling him he was a good boy. Jay brightened up and gave her a few hearty licks of affection in reply. Annie blew a sigh of relief then stood up to head upstairs and get ready for the funeral, all the while thankful Stewart was staying with John's dad Phil. Arla gave John a quick dig in the stomach, looking at him with a mixture of annoyance and sadness, as she too headed upstairs to get ready. John took a brief moment to compose himself and finally put to bed his thoughts of the disaster. Jay nosed his hand thinking there was more attention to be had. John smiled guiltily then obliged by giving him a quick scratch on the nose, although his eyes still had a faraway look. Content that his nose had been scratched sufficiently, Jay jumped onto his couch and lay down to go for a snooze.

John headed upstairs to get ready and found his wife sitting at her dressing table applying some make-up as he entered their room. He walked up and knelt down behind Annie, wrapped his arms around her waist then kissed her cheek and neck as he said 'sorry' once more. She turned to face him, mouthed 'it's OK' then gently kissed his lips and rested her head against his, happy to enjoy the embrace before getting back to applying her make-up again. John got up and picked out his suit from the wardrobe, along with a white shirt and black tie. He smiled as he caught Annie stop to watch him getting undressed, holding the blusher mid-way to her face. John deliberately got changed very slowly to see how long he could distract his staring wife for. The spell broke the moment his shirt was fully buttoned up. Annie smiled sheepishly, after noticing his raised eyebrows, and returned her attention to getting ready. With make-up done, she got up and picked out a black dress with tights. Now it was John's turn to enjoy the view as he sat comfortably on the bed and openly watched her getting changed. As a result, Annie got changed very quickly then stuck her tongue out at him and smiled playfully. John got up and they hugged each other briefly before going back downstairs to get their shoes on and leave for the crematorium.

The funeral was due to start in half an hour, but they had decided to take advantage of the weather and walk because parking spaces at the crematorium were limited. Quite understandably, a lot of people were going to be attending the service as David had been very popular with his effortless charm and kindness. John, realising how much he sorely missed his childhood friend, was sure he wasn't going to get over the pain of his loss anytime soon. Callum parked at their house and accompanied them, along with Rebekah and Hank, on the short, subdued walk to the crematorium, holding Arla's hand for the entire time. The road outside the crematorium was filled with parked cars and many people were already outside the entrance of the chapel building, chatting amongst themselves quietly as they waited for the funeral procession to arrive. They saw Richard and Sarah talking with one of David's cousins and made their way through the crowd of mourners to greet them. John was distracting himself from his grief by concentrating on all of the sounds nearby. There were well over a hundred people attending the service, but there was also someone else, someone who wasn't there mourning. The hairs on the back of his neck stood on end and he craned his neck to look around, only to realise this person wasn't in sight, standing behind the main building off in the distance, or amongst the shadows of the trees in the woods. John closed his eyes to focus solely on the individual and find out who he, or she, was, only to find that the mysterious stranger was gone. Things were starting to click together in his mind, but he didn't quite manage to figure it out then as Annie nudged him in the ribs to get his attention. The hearse arrived shortly after followed by two long identical black Limousines carrying David's family. John shook his head a little ruefully and mouthed a quick 'sorry' to Annie for being rudely quiet.

The minister politely asked everyone gathered to make their way inside and wait for the service to begin. Annie and John sat in a row second from the front along with Arla and Callum. Rebekah, Hank, Richard and Sarah sat in the row behind them. The back wall of the Chapel was lined with floor to ceiling windows that overlooked the beautifully kept grounds, filled with flowers and had a narrow burn that weaved its way through the tall trees, under the little stone bridges for the paths and off into the surrounding woods. They all stood as the pallbearers entered with David's coffin, followed by Gemma, who seemed to be staring at her deceased husband through the varnished wood and elegant flowers, wishing this was all a terrible nightmare, walking on crutches. Claire came after holding onto the hands of Gemma's parents as she walked quietly in between them. The service itself was a fitting send off for such a wonderful person, with a few hymns, prayers and readings. John read a short passage, finishing with a line from one of David's favourite films, 'to live, would be an awfully big adventure'. Gemma read David's Eulogy with remarkable composure. John was in awe of her fortitude, he had struggled just reading a short passage dedicated to his friend, as she recounted David's life. There were a few touching and humorous moments, which made everyone present laugh and a few even started crying. As was customary after a funeral, the relatives of the deceased all lined up in a short corridor off to the right of the Chapel, leading to the exit, in order for everyone attending to pass on their condolences. Annie, Arla, Rebekah and Sarah were all silently crying as they each hugged Gemma, mindful of her crutches, and offered their condolences through choked up throats. John, Callum, Richard and Hank could barely speak as they followed on from the distraught women.

The wake was being held at function hall near Gemma's home in Burntisland. They stayed for an hour, mingling with all the other attendees, then bade farewell to Gemma and Claire, who sincerely thanked them all for coming, and headed back to their cars parked along Main Street. The street was lined with various shops, one of which sold particularly good ice-cream, so Annie and John, helped by Arla and Rebekah, went in to get everyone a large tub with several scoops each. The shop was just along the road from the seaside park and they all went for a little walk to eat their ice-cream, reminiscing silently over their dearly departed friend. Annie, Callum and Arla all got into John's car after saying goodbye to their friends. Then they departed taking the road that left via the top of the seaside town, avoiding the one where the accident had happened, to go back home. As far as John was concerned, he never wished to drive on that particular road ever again. Stewart was staying with John's dad for a couple of nights, which left Annie and John home alone once Arla and Callum left shortly after they got back. Annie took John's hand and led him into the living room where they sat down close together on the sofa. Jay could sense their mood and, for once, he hadn't barked excitedly when they got home. He squeezed onto the Sofa beside Annie and rested his head on her lap, closing his eyes content as she scratched his head and ears absent-mindedly. "I hope Gemma will be OK. I can't believe how strong she was today." Annie said quietly. "I wouldn't have been able to do that if I were in her position. Not a chance." John replied, staring off into the distance again. The look hadn't gone unnoticed by Annie and she frowned, but opted to remain silent, deciding to snuggle in close to her husband instead and cherish his warmth as he wrapped his arms around her. These far away looks of John's were becoming more frequent and she couldn't help but worry as to what was causing them. Annie decided that today was not a day, nor might any of the following days in the near future, be right to question him again about what was wrong. She knew that when he was ready, he would tell her. "What are you going to do tomorrow while I'm at work and Stewarts at Nursery?" Annie asked, hoping to take his mind away from whatever was troubling him. "I've got that new game on my laptop I haven't played yet, so I might actually get round to seeing what it's like. I still haven't built that big new Lego set I got in London, so that's an option too. I'll also take the fluffball for a walk first though whatever I decide to do." John replied after a brief pause to think. "Stewart is at my dad's tonight, how about we go for a meal and watch that new movie you want to see at the cinema this evening?" He asked, looking into her pensive pale grey eyes. "I would love that. I know it's not exactly the best of days, but we haven't had a date night in far too long and I do really want to see that film." She replied happily without hesitation. "It's a date then." John said and kissed her softly on the lips. Annie then got up, dragged him up too, so they could get out of their formal clothes. She smiled naughtily at the prospect of teasing her husband and even took her time walking up the stairs, laughing as he ogled her provocatively swaying hips.

John left the house before Annie the following morning to pick up Stewart from his dads and take him to nursery. Stewart ran out the house and yelled with glee as John hoisted him above his head and twirled his son around. Phil stood at the door and smiled watching his son and grandson playing around. John plonked Stewart on his shoulders then turned to face his own dad. "Thanks for watching Stewart Dad, did he behave himself?" "He was as good as gold, no trouble at all. He even held onto Zach's lead when we took the dogs out before dinner. Then we watched that monster movie with the huge lizard and ape. How are you after yesterday?" Phil asked a little distractedly as his other dog, poppy, had tried to get past to see John so he scooped the energetic tricolour King Charles Spaniel up in his arms. "It was a lovely service and a lot of people went too. Gemma was remarkable. I wouldn't have been able to cope the way she did yesterday that's for sure." John replied and his dad nodded knowingly. "Well, I better get this little monster off to nursery. Thanks again Dad, we'll see you on Sunday as usual for dinner. Stewart say thanks and bye-bye to Grandad." Stewart waved, said his thanks and bye-bye. Phil waved as he always did with both hands as John pulled out of his dad's driveway, waving back, then drove out the street and back towards Dunfermline to drop Stewart off at nursery. There was a short queue of parents waiting to drop their children off as John parked outside the nursery, so he chatted to some of the other parents to catch up a little and pass the time, keeping at least one eye on Stewart as he ran around with his friends. Once his son was inside, John turned to leave only to stop and do a quick double-take as he spotted Jean standing beside her car. She was looking right at him, face set with determination, as he walked back to his car somewhat apprehensively. John had already apologised to her for his manners, she seemed to really appreciate the flowers and wine, so that meant, his stomach dropped unpleasantly once he realised, she must wish to talk about what happened with Bill. "Good morning Jean, how can I help seeing as you've obviously taken time out of your day to follow me? May I add, this is a little unsettling and a tad stalkerish." He asked cordially before shifting to mild irritation. "Hello John, do you mind if we go somewhere quiet to talk?" She looked around a little nervously while asking. One of the wonderful things about John's hearing now was his ability to hear even the slightest mechanical sounds, such as those belonging to a tape recorder. "OK, but I'm taking my dog to Aberdour for a walk first. If you wish to join us and talk there you're welcome to." He got back into his car after saying that, not caring for a reply.

John arrived at the Silver Sands beach half an hour later and Jay started to whine impatiently as soon as he realised where he was. After a quick check to make sure no one else was around, as Jay was very good and did as he was told, but would bark a little aggressively if another dog ran straight at him. With the coast clear, John let out the impatient German Shepard who ran straight up to the nearest tree and relieved himself. Business done, Jay then trotted away with a spring in his step and started sniffing around. Jean was waiting beside her own car across the parking lot and quickly stepped over to follow him as he walked after his dog. Before she could ask any questions, John surprised her by silently signalling for her to turn around with a swivelling finger, then he plucked the tape recorder from her belt and threw it far out into the Firth of Forth. Jean had jumped as he grabbed the little machine, then stared wide eyed as it flew way out of sight. When she turned round, John met her gaze with fire in his own. "If you have anything else, and I mean anything else, capable of recording sound then put it away in your car right now or get out of my sight." John was furious and made sure his tone and expression reflected it. Jean held up her hand placatingly, slowly took out her phone and put it away in the car along with her bag. "That's all I have on me. I swear." She had both hands up now, admitting surrender to his angry demand. John nodded sharply then turned to catch up with Jay. "Bill is gunning for you. He threatened me to get you to talk and admit you assaulted him. No one at the station believed a word of what he said because of how impossible it sounded." She said immediately after catching back up with him. John stopped and blew through his teeth angrily, looking at Jean with fed up eyes. "Where is he? I'm going to drop his flaming car on him." He spoke seriously and Jean's jaw dropped, unsure if he was being genuine or not. It took her a full minute before she was able to speak again. "Well for a start that would be murder, so forgive me, but no. I'm not going to tell you where he is. Second, can you really pick up a car? Thirdly, seriously, please don't kill him." Jean said anxiously. John shrugged and carried on walking again before replying. "I've known you for several years now Jean, and you saw what I did to Bill already so I'm going to be honest with you. What I'm about to say, only three other people know, so I'm telling you, please do not repeat it. Ever. Understand?" She nodded gravely and swore it would stay between them. John told her an abbreviated version of the events that led them to the conversation they were now having. The Queensferry Crossing collapse made her jaw drop again, in utter astonishment. They walked on in silence for several minutes after John finished talking. Jean didn't initially believe what she heard was possible, but the ease in which he had thrown Bill made her think twice. "It seems that trouble has been following you around ever since your accident. You've saved a lot of lives, so why are you keeping this quiet rather than reaping the rewards of being a bonified superhero?" John felt like retorting with a phrase involving excrement and a detective, but shook his head with resignation instead and chose to answer her question politely. "How do you think the world would react, because let's be honest here, what I can do is pretty earthshattering? If the authorities found out someone with my potentially catastrophic capabilities actually existed. Firstly, my ability to do good would be considered. Then, the potential of me doing bad things would be considered, because the worst is always considered. Personally, before you answer if I may, I think there would be pandemonium world-wide." Jean bit her lip as she considered his words. Then she agreed with him. "You're right. I now know that you're trying to help people and save lives, something you're doing pretty well I might add, unless your name is Bill of course, but governments and people in positions of power and influence would most likely see you as a threat to them. They would surely know that there would be nothing, simply nothing, that could be done to stop you if they did something you disagreed with. My guess, it would shatter their egos and they would work to discredit you, have the population turn against you, to the point where you'd have to disappear." Now it was John's turn to be astonished. His jaw dropped at Jean's insightful words and he looked towards her with a newfound respect. "I hope I'm wrong though. I think the world needs someone like you. You could act as a beacon and possibly inspire people to do good like you are. Or at the very least, act as the world's biggest lighthouse to steer people away from what is bad." She sounded genuinely hopeful, although couldn't help chuckle at her reference to his previous nautical based career. At the end, John guffawed heartily and nodded appreciatively at the joke. The conversation halted for a moment as Jay came running back to make sure his 'dad' was still there. But he hadn't expected to see Jean so Jay approached a little cautiously at first until he recognised her, and saw John was still around. Jay then grabbed the opportunity to get some fussing and a quick bit of attention before he darted off again to resume his sniffing. "Ok, let's reel in the focus here a little bit to where we are just now. You know, thinking of the entire world is making my head throb, and start thinking about our immediate problem: Bill. Well Jean, what do you suggest we do about him? Putting it out there, because he's threatening you, I'm OK with a plan of action that involves gratuitous violence." John said with a decidedly evil grin. Jean ignored the last part, focused on the serious issue at hand and frowned. With a difficult and complex problem, Jean completely focussed her concentration, remaining silent for a good while. During this period of silent thought, John set about finding where exactly Bill was and subsequently found him in his car heading along the coastal road to Kirkcaldy through Kinghorn. John frowned, annoyed, because Bill may have not long driven past where they were. On the plus side, once he was out of Kinghorn there were no other cars nearby for miles. John hoped to speed the conversation up but didn't need to as Jean broke the silence. "I'm sure he's a crooked cop and abuses his power to suit those it benefits. So how about we dig into his personal life and get some dirt on him?" She answered. "Sounds like a good idea but I think it'll take too long. How about I just scare him into silence? It'll get him back for threatening you and, if he has any sense, he'll leave me alone for good too." John replied seriously, ticking away time in his head. "How would you go about scaring him?" She stopped, crossed her arms and looked at him suspiciously. "It'll take me a couple of minutes, then our problems will be sorted." He answered a little evasively, clock still ticking, whilst not quite meeting her eye. Unsurprisingly, Jean didn't look entirely convinced but, in then end she agreed reluctantly. "Awesome, watch Jay for a couple of minutes please." John said quickly, before she had a chance to regret her decision, then shot off into the air and flew towards where he knew Bill was. "You can fly?!" He heard Jean shout as she quickly faded into the distance behind him.

Within seconds, John was flying high above Bill's car and smiled to himself as he noticed there were still no other cars for miles in either direction. "Time for some fun" John said aloud and then swooped down towards Bill's hypocritically, considering his profession, speeding car. He heard a shout from inside as he grabbed the tow bar and lifted the car off the road, straight up, higher, higher, and higher still until Fife was but a patchwork quilt of green fields, towns and villages far below. Bill was screaming hysterically, pushing himself against his seat. As if moving even further away from the ground would make any difference to his current predicament, John thought with grim satisfaction. "Bill. Oi Bill! Behind you, you idiot! That's it, hello!" John had to shout to get the man's attention and be heard over the piercing screams. Bill couldn't believe his eyes as he finally spotted him, waving hello through the cars back window. "I need you to shut up just now and listen to me very carefully, OK?" John was still shouting a little to be heard clearly. Bill nodded, face a mask of dread, as he looked up, and fear as he looked down. "I'm going to give you a chance to save your own life. You're going to plummet, very quickly, towards the ground in a moment. If you don't agree to leave Jean, myself, and everyone else I care about alone, you will hit the ground and die. Obviously." Bill gaped in horror but before he could reply, the screams started up again, even louder and at a far higher pitch as John let the car go. He hovered where he was, watching with mild interest as the car grew smaller and smaller. John's logic, if the unthinkable were to happen and Bill turned into a human pancake, was that the decision as to whether or not

Bill continued to fall was entirely his own. It only took a few seconds before he heard Bill agree, shrieking like a banshee after stubbing its toe, to leave them all alone. John flew down and caught the car by the front bumper, allowing for a safe deceleration to avoid damage and setting off the airbag. He looked directly at Bill, then pointedly looked down towards the ground and back again, hoping to emphasise that they were still very high up. "I have your word now Bill that you won't bother Jean, myself or anyone I care about again. If you break that word, you won't get the chance to regret it because I'll find you. And I think we both know what'll happen then, don't we?" John looked Bill menacingly in the eye and he spoke very clearly to make sure he was understood. Bill shouted 'yes' and nodded feverishly as he cried hysterically. Another sense that had vastly improved since the accident and the subsequent changes was John's sense of smell. He'd never really paid much attention to it until then, as nothing really thought provoking or significant had occurred to bring it to the forefront of his thoughts. Sadly, that changed once Bill was safely back on the ground, still crying pathetically. John, even though the windows on the expensive BMW were shut, could tell that Bill had done something involuntary, messy and awfully smelly. It also seemed that whatever the man ate the previous day hadn't agreed with him. The resultant mess was squelching somewhat as Bill moved around in his seat. John's eyes were beginning to water from the odour so he leapt back into the air and headed back to Aberdour.

Jay was standing beside Jean, looking around to see where his 'dad' was, when John landed back beside them, making both her and his dog startle a little once they realised he was back again. Jay bounded up and pressed himself against John, demanding attention for startling him, then, once satisfied with his apologetic fussing, walked off again to wander down to the beach. Jean looked as though she was trying to catch her breath, with a hand holding her chest, and took a moment before she could talk again. "Is Bill going to leave us alone?" She asked breathlessly, not wanting to know what had happened. John looked at her, nodded firmly and smiled confidently, then ran off to catch up with Jay. She stood still and watched his retreating form for a moment before closing her eyes and breathing a heavy sigh of relief.

They finished walking Jay together, chatting amiably about how Jean was doing with her job and what John planned to do now that he was no longer working on ships. The conversation faltered a little as they got back to their cars because John, apart from the little gemstone venture, hadn't given it much thought. It occurred to him, now that he was thinking about what to do, perhaps consider his passion for motorsport. He had a competition license, along with a decent chunk of funds available, that would allow him to pursue the tantalising fantasy of working his way up the ranks and possibly becoming a British Touring Car driver. Jean sounded quite keen on the idea, because she had attended the Knockhill event of the race series several times, but also had an idea of her own too, which she had clearly been giving some serious thought. "Now that Bill is out of the way, I'll actually be able to really focus on my work and hopefully make a difference to our community. Don't take this the wrong way please John, but I think your… let's call them 'gifts', could really make a difference to that end. Do you think you could help me, to help others?" She asked hesitantly, worried that she may have overstepped a little. John looked at her thoughtfully as he considered the idea. The prospect of being able to really make a difference and help people around the community was very appealing to him. He liked the idea. He liked the idea a lot. Jean started jumping on the spot and clapping her hands excitedly, smiling broadly after he nodded with a smile. She gave him a quick, firm hug then stepped away again to calm down and think sensibly for a moment on how to achieve the goal. John cut in on her musings and deflated the happy bubble a little. “We, yes you too Jean, need to go and talk to my wife about this first. If she agrees it’s a good idea and that we can achieve it without revealing my secret, then we’ll go for it. Sound reasonable?” He asked with his hands held open towards her. Jean agreed, a little crestfallen, but she also knew it was the right thing to do and they parted ways after arranging to meet back up again at John's home, once Annie had finished work, to further discuss the proposal.

Annie finished work not long after lunch and was pleasantly surprised to find Jean sitting in their living room fussing Jay, after she was greeted with a kiss from John at the front door. There were various savouries and cakes from the local bakery sitting on the kitchen counter for lunch. Annie grabbed her favourites, put them on a plate, poured herself a glass of orange juice then went into the living room to join John and Jean, who were already tucking into their own lunch. Annie hadn’t caught up with Jean for a little while so they chatted while eating. Once lunch was finished, John cleared away all the plates then came back into the living room and sat down beside his wife, ready to discuss the idea Jean had proposed earlier. She and John spoke for a quarter of an hour, going into detail as to how he was going to be able to help with many different things yet still remain in amongst the shadows and safely hidden from the risk of exposure. Annie listened intently and didn’t interrupt them while they spoke. Jean finished off the proposal by mentioning that this could be just the start. If John was able to help and make a difference throughout the community, then the idea could expand to include the whole of Fife and maybe go further to cover the whole of Scotland too. "How exactly will John remain hidden? Won't he need some sort of disguise?" Annie asked once Jean had finished speaking. "Your husband has already proven himself to be quite resourceful with regards to keeping his abilities hidden, but I think a disguise, or an alter ego maybe, would be wise as I suspect this idea could make a lot of enemies, some of whom could prove to be potentially quite dangerous. Keeping John's identity a secret will be for the safety of everyone else involved or close to him. It will also prevent anyone from being able to gain any sort of leverage over him too." Annie seemed content with her response, "OK, so if we're thinking of an alter ego, what shall your superhero name be?" Annie asked her husband with a slight smirk, not quite able to keep a straight face, as he had just rolled his eyes dramatically, recalling a conversation with Arla. The whole 'superhero' moniker was something he had wanted to avoid, but after saving everyone from the bridge collapse, John felt it would be inevitable at some point. Not just yet though. "Let's hold off on that thought for now please. The idea is for me to stay out of sight and out of mind. There's no point in thinking up any sort of alter ego because no one should ever find out about my involvement in anything. I will wear some sort of mask though, just in case my face is spotted in suspicious areas or at crime scenes. It'll need to be made of the same material as my underwear though so it doesn't disintegrate." He said in response to Annie's question. Annie mouthed 'spoil-sport' and stuck out her tongue at him. She agreed though and didn't pursue the topic. Jean, at the mention of his underwear, looked perplexed at them from the other sofa. Annie noticed her confusion then gleefully retold the story of what happened in Miami. They were both roaring with laughter by the end, much to John's chagrin.

After wiping away some tears, Jean got straight to business and mentioned an ongoing case she was involved in. The case was regarding a brazen armed robbery that sadly resulted in the death of an employee at the bank where the crime had occurred. Annie and John, after being taken aback slightly from the abrupt change in the tone of the conversation, were both aware of what had happened and were saddened by the loss of life. John had been frustrated by the incident as they were in London at the time, meaning he had been powerless to intervene. The thieves had initially been very thorough and well prepared. They had stolen the armoured car scheduled to make a delivery to the branch, by staging an accident along the car's route, which they had memorised, ambushing the crew with what was described as 'trained efficiency' and assuming their places, then confidently entered the branch fully expecting to be able to just swan in and take whatever they could carry. This confidence came from their exhaustive efforts studying the entire money transfer routine. The violence occurred because they hadn't expected to be challenged by any member of staff at the branch. A new employee, unaware of the established routine, had asked for their identification. Something that was actually supposed to be done during each transaction. Even though the thieves had very accurate forgeries, so they could be checked to ensure everything was in order, they wouldn't hold up against the scanner. In reality, experienced branch staff had grown complacent and merely glanced at the identification. The thieves had not known that identification scanning was what should happen each time, having only observed the complacent routine.

Which meant they didn't have any contingency plans to cover the inexperienced staff member's request. The leader of the brazen group had then taken the young woman aside, apparently trying to resolve the ID issue, and hidden from view of the other branch staff members they then tried to subdue her. The young woman, however, broke free and tried to raise the alarm, only to be violently struck by a heavy object from another member of the gang, killing her instantly. The thieves then panicked because the vault was still sealed and they now had a dead body to deal with. In the end, they drew their automatic weapons, wounded two other staff members with well-placed shots, hinting at possible military training, and held everyone in the branch hostage until the vault was opened. The whole event happened very fast and they got away with several hundred thousand pounds before the police could respond. The criminal's whereabouts currently remained unknown as the armoured car was found abandoned later that day in an industrial estate near Kincardine, which suggested the thieves were no longer in Fife. John sat quietly as he mused over everything Jean had said. He was thinking about the robbery planning and timings, nearby CCTV that may have seen the vehicle the money was transferred to, the implied military training and the detail and level of research that had gone into the robbery.

It took John an hour to recover all of the stolen money, apprehend the four members of the gang then deliver them and the money to Jean at the Dunfermline police station. She had approached the Chief Inspector and quietly told her of a private investigator who had managed to apprehend the thieves and was going to be dropping them off along with the money shortly. Jean also mentioned the investigator wished to remain anonymous for his own safety and that he hadn't even told her his name, nor did she know what he looked like. The Chief Inspector was very dubious about the whole thing, but still agreed to accompany her to the holding cells external transport entrance and see what was going on. The case had proven to be a real headache and pressure was mounting for progress, so the captain was keen to investigate any potential leads, regardless of how insane they seemed. Jean opened the door and smiled with immense satisfaction upon seeing the four thieves chained together sitting atop of all the stolen money. The Chief just stood open mouthed and silent, unable to believe what she was seeing. John was standing on top of the Carnegie Leisure centre and chuckled silently at the Chief Inspector's stunned face. He then dialled Jean's number and watched as she jumped once her phone started to ring. She struggled to get her phone out of her pocket and accepted the call a little breathlessly. John had already told her to remain quiet when she answered any calls from the burner phone number so she remained silent. "Your Chief Inspector's face is quite the picture. Have fun processing that lot and I'll see you later." John hung up and smiled contentedly as Jean shook her head in wonder then put her phone away again. The capture of the thieves and recovery of the stolen money was all over the news and social media within hours. John was pleased to see Jean being credited with making a key breakthrough in the case that had led to their apprehension, but not as pleased as he was to see no mention of any other parties that had been involved. Later on, Annie was sat beside him in their living room, browsing through the stories herself until she looked at him with a radiant smile. "One hour. One hour is all it took for you to start making a positive impact." She said with pride, then climbed onto his lap to give him a passionate kiss and embrace him. Annie eventually surfaced for air and sat with her arms around his neck, biting her lip as she stared into his eyes. "If this is how you're going to reward me every time I do something positive for the community, I'm going to have the police's backlog of cases cleared in no time." He said with relish. Annie laughed and kissed him again.

Chapter 5 – Revelations

The sun was now peeking over the Edinburgh hills in the distance. Fine rays of light illuminating the two remaining bridges spanning the River Forth. It looked like it was going to be another fine day John thought. He went downstairs quietly to let Jay out as their German Shepard was now awake and had come up to him whining. Annie and Stewart were still sleeping. John didn't need to sleep now, but he still liked the routine. Lying in bed with his wife next to him is something he'll always treasure. John had been working with Jean and the police for nearly two months now. Though things were no longer just simply helping around the community. With John's help from the shadows and being finally unburdened by Bill, who had resigned from the police and actually left the country, Jean had solved a number of significant cases and she was now on a first name basis with Police Scotland's most senior officer, the Chief Constable, Kirsty McLaren, herself. The case that first got the senior officer's attention involved a series of grisly murders that had rocked the city of Edinburgh. The Scottish capital is very popular with tourists so a swift resolution had been absolutely crucial. It turned out to be anything but swift and after weeks of numerous fatalities, all of whom had been apparently beaten to death, the Edinburgh police approached the Fife division and specifically requested

Jean's assistance in the matter. Her reputation for solving difficult cases was now very well-known and it was hoped she would be able to finally solve this particular one too. The damage done had already been substantial as tourists were no longer lining the streets and filling the attractions. Even locals were afraid to go out after dark, resulting in the hospitality sector suffering a slump in fortunes. Pressure mounted and got to the point where the head of the Edinburgh police was forced to resign over his failure to stop the murders. His replacements first action was to bring in Jean. Within a day a suspect was identified and later apprehended but only because John had been there too, hiding out of sight until he had no choice but to intervene. The man who had committed all of the murders had gotten hold of what appeared to be highly advanced and experimental military technology in the form of a biologically infused Exo-Suit. The suit didn't feature the cumbersome linkages or hoses typically seen in action films. The linkages this suit did have were grafted to the man's bones and made from carbon fibre, with titanium plates inserted directly under the skin for protection. The device was powered by a miniature hydrogen cell and as long as the man kept himself hydrated, he had the strength of around thirty men and the speed to outstrip a race car. A Police Fire Arms Unit was sent in to apprehend him, with Jean following closely and John at a distance remaining out of sight. The man annihilated four of the highly trained officers before John had been able to intervene. The man even landed a significant blow that sent a stunned John through a wall as he had focused on saving the lives of the surviving officers, rather than on the maniac who had already killed the other four. John then saw red and moved with a speed he hadn't known he was capable of, savagely breaking each of the man's arms and legs before he managed to reign in his anger enough to land one final blow with enough restraint to incapacitate, rather than kill. No one had seen the intervention as the survivors of the initial assault had all started to flee. By the time they reached the exit and turned round to see if their pursuer was still chasing them, ready to unload everything they had; it was all over. The murderer lay in the centre of the abandoned building's third floor, unconscious with limbs at odd angles. They suspected the Exo-Suit had malfunctioned, overloaded the man's senses and then broken his limbs as it spasmed uncontrollably. Only Jean knew the truth after she saw John outside, watching from amongst the gathered crowd.

The fallout from the case had gone right to the first minister's desk, such was the gravity of the situation. Scores dead, military technology, dangerous human experimentation, major hits to the tourist and hospitality sectors and even accusations of a cover up from the opposition party. It was a difficult time for many key people. The Chief Constable knew of Jean's involvement and sought an urgent meeting to discuss her outstanding work. This meeting brought John from the shadows and he became officially, but still anonymous as far as records went, involved with Police Scotland. Jean opened up to Kirsty as to how she had been so successful, making the Chief Constable consider ejecting her from the building initially as her words were surely nothing but blatant lies. John had been standing behind Kirsty the whole time, having snuck in as Jean entered the room, and quietly introduced himself when things started to look bad for his friend. The most senior Scottish police officer had jumped and swore from the shock of his voice coming from behind her unexpectedly. Kirsty had her hand on her heart and was panting heavily to catch her breath as she stared wide eyed at the mysterious intruder. John had allowed her to calm down before he spoke at length of his involvement with Jean's work and the Chief Constable listened with rapt attention to every word. It was agreed that John would definitely remain involved as the results were proving to be hugely beneficial. Crime had been significantly reduced across the board. It seemed that criminals, and those considering crime, were now afraid of Police Scotland's almost mythical ability to apprehend wrong-doers. No one, except for the chosen two, had any idea as to why there had been such an upturn in fortune. Even the Metropolitan Police were reaching out for support, eager to gain just a modicum of the success their counterparts were having north of the border. John made it very clear however, that the secret had to remain between them, not that he had even shared his name, for his involvement would not be political in any sense, and that in terms of compensation for his significant efforts, he wished to remain off-the-books entirely and not be included in any operating budgets. His compensation would come from a small percentage of the proceeds gained by apprehending wealthy criminals, which still turned out to be quite a lot. Despite all the good John was doing at making Scotland itself a better place, his main priority never changed. He made it abundantly clear that if his work with Police Scotland affected his life at home, then the agreement would end immediately. Kirsty had tried dissuade him from this clause to their agreement, but as soon as the words 'greater-good' were mentioned, her words died in her throat as his whole demeanour changed in an instant. A fiery anger emerged in his eyes and the edge of her desk turned to splinters in his furious grip as he stood up and leaned over her. No words were needed as Kirsty immediately and unreservedly apologised for her insensitivity. Jean had been silent the whole time and knew the commissioner was treading dangerously as soon as she tried to change John's mind. It was best that the commissioner learned of John's unwavering priorities herself though, Jean decided, struggling to contain her mirth. Since then, their work together as a team flourished and the results continued to exceed even their most optimistic expectations.

Reminiscing over, John was proud of his work and smiled blissfully as he watched Jay out in the garden, bathed in the early morning sunlight. All seemed well and he was happy. His bliss was interrupted by a barely perceptible knock on the front door. John knew no one else would've heard it. Not even Jay had heard it and that set him on edge. First, why would someone be calling at the house at six in the morning. Second, perhaps this was John being paranoid, how did they know that such a faint knock would attract any attention from within the house? Despite his misgivings, and after he had waited a good few moments for Jay to finish his business outside so he would then go back upstairs to Annie, John went to answer the door. There was only one individual there. He could hear the heartbeat. A very slow, relaxed rhythm. The person wasn't moving at all though and stood as still as a statue. They hadn't even taken a breath in the ten minutes since the knock, further adding to those flowering misgivings. John had decided that ten minutes seemed like a fair wait for someone calling so early. There was also the secret hope they would simply leave too. John still hadn't heard the fabric of clothes rustle against the mystery visitor's chest. He was genuinely concerned now. Whoever stood on the other side of his front door, wasn't a normal person. 'Even if someone could hold their breath that long, surely there would be involuntary muscle movements of some kind as the body craved oxygen?' This was John's train of thought as he quietly unlocked, then slowly opened the door. He only opened it a few inches, just enough to peer out, and had his foot wedged firmly behind the door too. Just in case. There was man in a suit standing there. It was a very smart looking suit too. Black with faint grey pinstripes. No tie, just a white shirt with the top few buttons casually undone and rounded off with painfully shiny shoes. Seriously, they could be used as a mirror. The man was an inch taller than John. Looked like he weighed fifteen stone. A solid, fairly muscular build. Full head of shoulder length blonde hair with startling bright blue eyes. Did this man think he was a Norse god or something? John had to suppress a little chuckle to himself at that thought. "This is rather early for a house call don't you think? What do you want?" Quite clearly, John was not in a polite mood. The strange visitor hadn't taken his eyes from John's own since the moment the door had opened. He tilted his head slightly as if giving an unreasonable amount of thought to such a simple question. The silence dragged on for over a minute and John was getting irritated now. But, before he could voice his displeasure, the man spoke. "Hello Mr Campbell. Or shall I address you as John? Please forgive the early morning call, but I simply must speak with you. It's a matter of urgency. Mind if I come in?" The man had already moved as if to push John out the way and barge into his home. He had placed his hand on the door and taken a confident step towards the threshold. John didn't move. His foot was still firmly behind the door and he had his hand and thumb wrapped around the edge, at head height. The visitor stopped as he quickly realised the person standing in front of him wasn't going to be easily subdued. His hand was on the door opposite Johns. His chiselled features creasing slightly as he failed to gather himself up quickly enough, thus allowing his emotions to briefly show. He was annoyed at the obstruction. 'You've got some nerve' John thought. They both stood quietly facing one another in the small gap of the open door. The visitor was still trying to push the door open though. He was incredibly strong too. John knew that he was applying enough force with his own hand to send a car speeding down a road. Handbrake on. The strange man was obviously applying an equal but opposite force seeing as the door wasn't moving, newton's laws of motion proved right again as the door remained in a steady state of rest. There was no one on earth this strong. Absolutely no one could keep a steady state against John's own strength. John was completely certain of it. A splintering noise sounded like a gunshot going off in the uncomfortable silence between them. Jay briefly stirred upstairs. The door between their hands had cracked slightly. "What are you?" John asked abruptly. The question proved quite a shock for the man as he hadn't even tried to hide the surprise on his face. His mouth was even a little open. "What do you mean by such a blunt question Mr Campbell?" The man was angry now. His tone and expression were a clear indication as such. He'd skipped surprise, indignation, even hurt, and gone straight to anger. He'd removed his hand from the door and taken a step back, arms folded across his broad chest, but his eyes were still locked on John's. "You know exactly what I mean with that question. You're not a normal human being. You're something else, something more. I'm guessing you know I'm not normal either, hence why you weren't overly surprised you couldn't get into my home. Although you were certainly annoyed I didn't simply let you in. I guess anything other than getting your own way with things is a foreign concept to you? I must admit though, with your charming looks, smart attire and phenomenal strength, I guess things going your way is actually the norm." "Hmph". The man looked mildly impressed. He inclined his head, but still never took his eyes off John. He laughed. A derisive, mad cackling laugh that made the hairs on John's neck stand to attention. His whole body got involved. His head was thrown back, hands clapping enthusiastically. Even rocking back and forth on his feet. As sudden as the laughter had started though, it stopped just as abruptly. John tore his attention from the obstinate visitor, his front door bearing the brunt of the stubbornness, to glance up the stairs behind him, for Jay was postured up. The laughter and clapping had the German Shepard's ears pricked up and alert. After a brief hesitation, he lay back down again beside Annie on their bed though, attention now fixed on the open bedroom door. John had had a brief flutter of panic, fearing Annie's loyal guardian would come to investigate the disturbance to his quiet morning. Loud barking would've ensued, thus waking up Annie and Stewart. She would've come to investigate after retrieving their son from his room. John didn't want their house callers' predatory eyes focused on anyone but himself.

After returning his gaze to the small gap in the door, he saw the man now had an ugly, aggressive look on his face. His hands were now held open, loosely at his sides. He stood tall and straight, looking John in the eye once more. "I see there is no point in prolonging any subterfuge with you Mr Campbell. You're correct. I'm not human. You're correct, in that I know you're not a normal person too. And finally, yes. Things do normally occur as I believe they should." 'Wow, this guy has arrogance radiating from him like the heat from a raging fire' John thought. "I'm what is known as an assessor-" 'more like just the first syllable' John reckoned

"- and my job is to keep watch on creators. I believe you refer to creators as 'Gods', no? Anyway, I'm responsible for several creators. I have to make sure they don't create something that could become hostile and threaten other worlds. The work of other creators. Needless to say, I've had my eye on humans for quite some time. For such fragile, few limbed creatures, you're very destructive. Comparatively intelligent, adaptable and with considerable ingenuity. Although your creator is in a bit of trouble with me as your ingenuity seems mainly geared towards consumption and destruction-" "That's enough right there, I have to stop you…" John had held up his hand and spoke firmly. "Oh really? You think you can simply interrupt an ass-" "I do and I have again now. You're monologue there depicts all humans as pathetic, and parasitic. Like all we do is consume and destroy with no care for consequence. Almost like a disease according to you. That couldn't be further from the truth you arrogant jerk." This once again dropped the visitors jaw a little. "There are good people here on earth. Good people trying to do the right thing. Good people who help others without hesitation. Good people who are working tirelessly to make our world a better place for all." John said with a defiant tone. "Wow. That was a wonderful speech, although I don't think you said 'good' often enough…" The man paused for effect and John found the smugness on his face infuriating "… and I do believe the term you humans seem to adore, 'Cheesy' also applies. First, I must introduce myself properly, as your dismissive attitude has so far not permitted me to do so. I am Gordior of the Endless. Well, we do go by another name, but I won't burden your tiny mind with that. Now secondly, as I was saying before you so rudely interrupted, a severe crime when in the presence of an assessor it must be said, I have decided that this world needs a human of all. That is to say, a solitary figure to determine the worlds ultimate destiny. I say human, as your species is clearly the dominant one of this planet. The 'Of all' part was my own little inspiration. We assessors use our own terms when discussing the matter of why I'm here today. On this disgusting sphere of earth, rock and liquid you call home. The matter being the examination of a creator's work. Once a creator's world hits a critical point, a time in a planets lifecycle where everything is so finely balanced, the merest of nudges one way or the other can bring about the extinction of all life, or salvage it. We step in and apply this little nudge to the creator's world. To do this we examine all the life present. From the tiny, the seemingly insignificant, to the huge and blatantly obvious, then decide which single lifeform, from what we determine as the dominant species, will be given the ability to bring about the world's ultimate destruction - or become its saviour. You, Mr Campbell, are my nudge. My destroyer, as is usually the case with most examinations. Or, the planets boring Redeemer. The one who saves the day, woo!" Gordior had rolled his eyes and waved his arms sarcastically after he finished speaking again. This was a lot for John to take in. He was swaying slightly as he stood with an incredulous expression, gazing blurry eyed at Gordior. After a moment of silence, the assessor stared wide eyed at John, his facial expression changed and it appeared as if he had found John's reaction incredibly humorous. His laugh came out like a harsh bark. "Are you truly so naïve? The man I choose to be the human of all hasn't figured all of this out?" Another derisive laugh escaped Gordior's mouth. "Wow this is a first. I've never encountered something so utterly stupid in all of my existence. Haven't you figured out why all of these terrible things have been happening around you lately? The accident that somehow didn't kill you, but caused you to become super human? Arla, Callum and Sandra with the attempted mugging in Miami? The plane crash? How about the remains of that dull Queensferry Crossing in the morning haze over there? Or the best yet, David meeting his untimely demise in that freak accident you couldn't save him from? Did you really think all of that was bad luck, wrong place wrong time? Of course, it wasn't you complete fool. I orchestrated all of that. And curse this worlds Creator, you've somehow refused to reveal yourself to the population and remain hidden. You see, the unveiling of a supreme being is what tends to cause the nudge one way or another, in case you missed that point too. The planet either rallies behind the perceived supreme being, leading to its salvation, or it destroys itself trying to eradicate what it can't comprehend. And you, Mr Campbell, are making this the most difficult exam I have ever had to officiate!" Gordior had become visibly agitated now. "Normally after the supreme being is chosen, they immediately, often unwittingly, set about doing incredible things and thus reveal themselves. Even you're Creator knows this Mr Campbell! Why do you think there are fictional characters called Superheroes? Do you really think you Humans could be so imaginative and come up with such ideas? Of course not! Your creator did something very naughty …" Gordior's tone was mocking now as he once again paused for effect "… he gave various people little splashes of increased creativity. I guess it was so the world could get used to the idea that 'super beings' could exist and thus your species wouldn't lose their minds at the revelation of one. The creator wasn't allowed to do that. It interferes with my process. Muddies the result somewhat as it tips the favour towards salvation. However, despite the Creators valiant attempt to save your species, I will succeed with my assessment, because you will reveal your new self eventually. This is when the job becomes tolerable for me. The fun starts. Now, even though it's by far the more boring outcome, watching a species fawn over a supreme being, as they are led to a prosperous future and salvation, is highly amusing. The rituals, religions and societies that spawn in this sunny outcome are hysterical! The more entertaining outcome though, is destruction. It's like what the American people of your world call 'the fourth of July'. Only on a massive, global fiery scale. It's a glorious spectacle."

John had heard enough. This wasn't a time for explanations or things making sense to him. This was a being who had no value of life. It only cared for destruction, and it was going to destroy John's life. This was the time for something to be held accountable for all that had happened. All the suffering. The funeral. The pain. And John's own recent heartache. The reason why Annie felt he was so distant lately. The reason why his friends were concerned about him. He now had something stood before him that could be held accountable for it all. And this creature standing before him was going to suffer his wrath for it. "OK, thank you, I guess, for that explanation, but you've actually not given any answer as to why you're here with me specifically (Gordior actually did a little, but the look of fresh incredulity on that smug face meant that John's little bit of bait was snapped up). Surely for this examination of yours to be valid, anything that happens must be the result of the actions of my own free will. Whereas now I'm fully aware of what is going on and why such terrible things have happened, meaning anything I do from this point onwards will be influenced by your enlightening little monologue. You've strongly hinted as to why you are here discussing this with me, but you've not outright confirmed my suspicions." This might've been a step too far John realised with a sickening twist in his stomach. Now Gordior looked angry, no longer merely annoyed. John now worried about the damage this creature could cause. He looked around his street, listened to people starting to stir. Kids waking up to run into their parents' room and jump on them, Dogs barking at the foot of their owner's beds to let them out and some early risers already eating breakfast. Fife was waking up, and he didn't want it to be the last day any of these people, or animals, ever woke up to. Panic was starting to bloom within him. He had to calm Gordior at least a little, then get the assessor away from here. "Maybe you are indeed as dumb as you seem then…" It (John decided that seeing as the Assessor wasn't human, he would no longer dignify it by using any sort of masculine pronoun) spat out from between clenched teeth "…I've come here today to hurry this examination along. I'm not a fan of this creator's work. I don't like humans. The creator seems to have moulded you in the image of the very first Assessors, and I'm offended by it. So, I came here today in the hope that you would realise all of these terrible things happening were because of you…" Although John could see the Assessor's mouth moving, he couldn't hear him. It was as if the world had suddenly become muted to John. There was merely a faint ringing in his ears and he missed the creature's next words "…I could finally leave this miserable world to its destruction and remove the offending creator from existence." John was stunned into silence. This foul creature had put all of those terrible things onto his shoulders. 'How could it possibly blame me for things it had literally just admitted to causing?!' He thought furiously. His voice returning after the few seconds it took his mind to digest this incredulous statement. “Exactly how was all of that my fault?” He spoke in barely a whisper, struggling to contain the erupting volcano within. “If you hadn’t gone to such great lengths to hide your super human abilities, I wouldn’t have had to keep escalating the circumstances to force you to do so.” Came the snide response from Gordior. That flicked a switch for John. A line in the sand had been drawn. It seemed that this Assessor only wished to see the total destruction of this world and all of the life inhabiting it. He needed to get it away from his home, away from anything that could be hurt by it. He had to find a way of ending this ‘examination’ and the sick game Gordior was playing with him. “OK, how about we go somewhere away from here, away from any prying eyes and any of my neighbours who could pass by. I am quite clearly not capable of carrying out what you require me to do, so it’s obvious you’ll need to help me, help you here. I’m pretty sure any interruptions, such as a friendly ‘morning’ from one of my neighbours potentially passing by, would likely cause you to harm them such is your disdain for my species. You physically, not just verbally as of now, are interfering on earth. This should surely render any infinitesimal shred of validity this ‘examination’ of yours has null and void. As you said, I’m the one who is supposed to cause this nudge of yours, not you.” John did his best to appear calm, despite his internal volcano, as he waited for a response. Gordior looked like he was thinking hard about how to respond, or it was just enjoying torturing him with the wait. John knew it was a lame attempt to try and move this away from his family. It was all he could think of at that time, still reeling from everything that had been said. Finally, after what felt like the longest minute of John's life, Gordior let out another harsh bark of a laugh that rolled into a fit of hysterical prolonged laughter. Then, as before, the laughing ceased abruptly again without warning. "Do you really think that it matters what I do during these examinations? Creators themselves are at my mercy, never mind the pathetic life they create." Gordior laughed again. That cold derisive laugh. "Whatever, if you wish to talk in private then how about we go to the highest point in your miserable little Fife? The West Lomond Hill." John nodded and Gordior disappeared faster than a blink of the eye. Such speed troubled John, and made his next move all the more dangerous.

He moved as fast as he ever had, got dressed, kissed the still sleeping Annie and Stewart gently on their foreheads, and went to the West Lomond Hill. It took him a matter of seconds. But those seconds felt like a far greater amount of time had elapsed because of his agitation though. He had only one intention and he wasn't exactly proud of it either. Gordior was waiting. John approached it from the direction of the path between the East and West Lomond hills. The river Forth in the distance to his left, opening out towards the North Sea behind him. Dundee far away on his right. He approached Gordior as calmly as he could. Difficult considering his emotions. Gordior looked relaxed, hands inside his pockets, as if he were admiring the view. John hit him with an uppercut without warning. It was the hardest punch he'd ever thrown. A professional boxer would've been proud of it. It was the type of punch that ended fights. He threw it with venom, without any care for the consequences. At that moment, all he cared about was inflicting the most amount of damage he possibly could. Gordior wasn't in Fife anymore. He wasn't even on earth. The impact had created a shockwave that was currently rolling over fife. A sonic boom sounded as Gordior was sent accelerating towards who knew where. Car alarms were going off in all directions. Dogs were barking. People were being rudely woken up all over Fife as the sound rolled by. The tinkling of glass meant several windows had also broken as a result of the shockwave. At that moment John didn't care for the inconvenience he had just inflicted upon almost every poor soul in the region. He didn't even care if he'd killed the Assessor, such was his fury. Not his proudest moment. It was completely unexpected of him to act with such savagery and without any remorse. However, this was not the time for any such emotion, or even mercy. That would surely come later though. He hoped at least once he'd calmed down.

Gordior's heart was still beating. John heard it as the assessor left Earth's atmosphere in the direction of the moon. He was suddenly thankful for the early hour of the day. There was no one around for miles. No one the fight, he was surely about to have, could potentially injure. It was time to see just how strong, intelligent and capable he was. This was going to be a fight with an eternal, at least that's what John interpreted Gordior's 'of the Endless' to mean. A being with as of yet unknown capabilities, except for its extreme strength and durability. Gordior had survived that punch. A punch that could literally send a man, or in this case an 'Endless', to the moon. John hoped that he could keep the fight in an isolated area. He'd seen enough movies, read enough books, to know that when two beings of unimaginable power collide, chaos and catastrophe followed. He waited with growing anxiety for Gordior to return. John thought a creature of such arrogance would never accept an act of aggression from a lesser being. Never mind an act as extreme as that punch was. Not without serious repercussions. The heartbeat started to get louder, closer. It was moving at an incredible speed. Faster than even John had ever moved. He could see him now. Gordior was flying straight for him with a face of murderous intent, literally burning red as it re-entered earth's atmosphere. His suit was gone, but there was no evidence of it having burnt away. Instead, there was a black, with red highlights, bodysuit. A strange symbol on the chest, sort of an upside-down triangle with the infinity symbol in the top half and an eye artfully linking it to the lower half. John wasted no further time pondering Gordior's attire and leapt up towards it. The impact between the two shook the ground, even though it occurred at over five miles up in the sky. Gordior was faster than he was. It had ducked what John felt was a perfectly timed right hook, impacted his chest with the force of a nuclear bomb detonating, and now continued towards the ground again with its arms wrapped around him. Now John was going to really learn what he was capable of. The impact, as forceful as it was, had merely winded him slightly. He quickly recovered, and exerted all the strength he could muster to fly away from the ground. It didn't quite work as they still hit the ground with a tremendous impact, carving a huge chunk off the top of the West Lomond Hill as earth and stone exploded up into the air. The impact produced another shockwave, breaking yet more of Fife's poor residents' windows, had tiles leaping up from roofs and actually sent people tumbling to the ground. They were now in a large crater, the hill now looking like a small volcano, with debris still flying up around them. Gordior immediately reared up, grabbed John by the throat and proceeded to pummel his face with his fist. It was so fast, three punches landed before he could even react. He brought up his left arm to partially defend his face, wrist by his temple, elbow towards the centre of his chest against Gordior's arm, trying to lever it off his throat. The pressure eased slightly, but a further four punches found their mark on his face. He was hurting now. Gordior had not yet drawn any blood, but it was none the less still stronger than even John had anticipated. The punches were inflicting damage to such an extent, a skyscraper wouldn't even have been rubble by now, it would've become a fine powder. He threw a punch into Gordior's ribs with enough force to briefly upset its rhythm. The punches briefly ceased; John leapt on the opportunity and grabbed its face, with his thumb digging into its eye. Gordior roared in pain, both hands grabbing at Johns to pull it away. John applied even more force, using his left hand to grab the back of its head to further increase the pressure. He stood up, holding it bodily off the ground now. Gordior was writhing in pain, using its knees to repeatedly strike John's chest and stomach, but to no avail. All of John's suffering was now focused on driving his thumb into Gordior's eye. He bared his teeth and growled furiously as his eyes gleamed with a mad anger. The sight would've been terrifying to anyone had they been unfortunate enough to see it. He slammed it back into the ground, causing yet another small tremor to shake Fife, removed his left hand from the back of its head and grabbed the thumb of Gordior's right hand. He jerked it savagely backwards and managed to break it, thus releasing the hand from his own wrist. He pinned the arm under his left knee and started raining punches down on Gordior's face. The residents of Fife must've felt like there was a stampede of Giants running around. The force of John's punches was unimaginable. All he focused on doing was damage. Damaging the face of the being who had brought untold misery on perhaps billions, even trillions, of other creatures, on other worlds, with his 'examinations'. John's punches were now drawing blood. Grotesque black blood that looked like tar. Gordior's left hand went limp and fell from John's wrist. There will be no mercy granted here though. John decided that Gordior deserved all of the pain and suffering he was capable of inflicting upon it. He eventually stopped with the punches, most likely to much of Fife's relief as his knuckles were actually starting to hurt, pulled Gordior into a sitting position, placed its head under his right arm, which he then wrapped under its chin, gripped his left bicep and started to squeeze, lean back and stretch up all in one fluid motion. John was going to break Gordior's neck. He was applying more and more force. He could've ripped a dozen or more giant redwood trees from the ground, or pulled the Queensferry crossing up from all of its foundations. His teeth were grinding together such was the determination and effort he was applying to the vile being's neck. Surely it had to break soon. He roared with anger and exertion.

Then suddenly a new voice broke into his concentration. "Let him go now!" The voice was loud, clear, full of authority and sounded feminine to him. However, it had no effect on John though and he ignored the command. The sudden loss of feeling in his limbs did work though. Gordior collapsed, seemingly lifelessly, to the ground. John was hovering an inch and rotating slowly clockwise. He couldn't move at all. Not even his eyes. 'This is not happening' he thought furiously and it stopped him rotating in the air. A woman was standing just at the edge of his peripheral vision. Brown hair waving in the slight wind. What looked like a blue robe of some sort sliding down her outstretched arm. Her hand was open with her palm facing him as if she were using it to manipulate him telekinetically. He couldn't make out her features, but he suspected they were screwed up in concentration. His force of thought had managed to stop her telekinetic manipulation of him. He used a stupendous amount of concentration, will power and strength to slowly turn his own head to face her under his own terms. The rest of him was still motionless, hovering an inch above the earth. She was beautiful. No other way of describing her he thought. Deep brown eyes. A relatively thin face, but with strong features and high cheekbones. 'Is this what a goddess looks like?' John asked himself. He was stunned at such a sight. So was she by the looks of her shocked expression. Her hand closed suddenly and he was free to move again, landing softly on the ground, and she lowered it back to her side. The woman standing before him was six feet tall. She wore a blue robe that completely covered her, except for her forearms. She placed her hands together in front of her waist. "Please don't kill my son." John's mouth fell open. He stood facing her, stunned as the moment he'd woken at the bottom of Port Miami all over again. "My name is Sheera. I'm a supreme of the Endless, as my son called us. I am one of but a few. I know you were about to kill my only son Gordior, but please stop and allow me to speak, to explain my presence. I know of all that has happened here and it has saddened me. I was naïve. I had heard of my sons' attitude towards life and the contempt in which he treats it to satisfy his own pleasures. As his mother, I foolishly chose to treat the accusations against him as malicious lies, believing they simply couldn't be true for my son is good. I also adopted this attitude as the beings my son chose for his 'purpose' were always lone individuals, with no family ties. So there suffering was minimal, and it was the actions of the individual that had caused the suffering of countless trillions throughout the universe. Rather than the actions of my own son." These words came out like a gushing torrent, such was her eagerness to justify her indifference, John thought to himself harshly. She stopped briefly and closed her eyes. This looked to be incredibly difficult for her to say. So, John's anger faded a little and he found himself feeling sympathetic towards Sheera. To have been betrayed so brutally by your own child. He couldn't imagine what she was going through. Her eyes opened again with a hard, determined look about them. "I failed to see that it was his actions, his manipulations, that were causing these poor individuals to do what they did. I was blinded by my love for him. A mother's love. Much like Annie's love for your own son Stewart. It's only now that I've summoned the courage to acknowledge my failings and confront him. It's taken what he has done to you John, the suffering he has inflicted upon you, along with the pain yet to come, to finally accept the truth." Tears were forming in John's eyes at these words and he bowed his head slightly. The tears soon broke free, trickling down his dirt covered cheeks. Sheera approached him, so swiftly yet so silently, making him flinch a little as she unexpectedly placed a hand on his damp cheek.

He sensed Gordior was starting to stir behind him. Sheera's focus shifted from the heartbreak on his face to her son, who was now struggling to his feet. Her expression was calm. John partially opened his eyes to look at Sheera again. Her gaze shifted briefly from Gordior, to his tear filled sandy blue eyes, a picture of unbearable suffering, then back to her now upright son once more. John felt sure that there was literally fire in her brown eyes now. It unsettled him greatly and he was suddenly thankful those eyes weren't boring into his. Gordior turned groggily around to face his mother. The sight of her seemed to shake his senses. Rather than look afraid though, he seemed outraged. As if she were not allowed to interrupt whatever he was doing. He really did think highly of himself. "Mother what are you doing?

You're not permitted to interfere in my business, the business of an Assessor!" He pretty much shouted at Sheera. Her expression didn't falter. "Enough!" she really did shout. And with her shout, Gordior became rigid, standing to attention. The assessor had clearly just crossed some sort of line. A line John didn't even wish to know of, never mind approach or even shockingly cross. Gordior stood rigid, wide eyed and suddenly terrified. Maybe it wasn't as stupid as John thought. The child had finally realised the trouble he was in. "John was about to kill you. And I agree with him wishing to do so. You are only alive now because, despite the depths of your depravity, you're my son and I will always love you. And I hope I can steer you towards goodness again, rather than the evil you've become." Sheera removed her hand from John's face, gently wiping away some of the tears and dirt. It felt like a very intimate gesture to him. He turned to face both of the Endless beings. Sheera had stepped towards her son, stopping a foot in front of him, staring into his eyes. John's head tilted to the side slightly to observe them, his face the definition of confused. What was Sheera thinking or feeling to make such an intimate gesture he wondered. "I don't know why you think what you've done is acceptable. You did all of this to John, knowing the love he feels for his friends. The love he has for his father. The love for his wife Annie. And the love of his son Stewart. John knows what's happened to him, and it's even more troubling to him than the events you orchestrated. It's why he's now suffering unimaginable pain and inner turmoil. It's also the reason he wants to kill you. And why I'd let him do so, if he still wishes to." Gordior's eyes opened even wider at this. "Yes, my son. I hope you now realise your fun has actually created a unique individual. Unique even to our infinite knowledge and experience of the universe. You've created an individual capable of killing an Endless. Did you not take the time to examine the inhabitants of this particular creator's world? If you had, like you should've as an assessor, you'd have noticed long ago that humans barely use the gift bestowed upon them. Their brains are a marvel, even to me. I think their creator despises you and created humans to one day, potentially overcome your tyrannical rule of this part of the universe. This creator knows of your cruel, manipulative behaviour, and how you like to alter the base design, to create a 'supreme being' as you called them. You've made John essentially immortal. He will never grow old, never perish of natural causes. He will see his friends grow old and die. He will watch helplessly as his wife grows old and dies. He will watch his son die too. And any and all future generations that follow. Can you imagine the pain your actions are going to inflict upon him? Can you see why, in such a radical break of his character, he wants to kill you?" Sheera had her back to John, but those last words came out with a break in her voice. She truly felt sorry for him and wanted to comfort him, to apologise for what she must feel is her own mistake.

The mistake was to let her guard down with that small display of emotion. Gordior broke free from her psychic immobilisation and hit his own mother. John could barely register the assessor even moving. It had leaped towards Sheera, and struck her with what must've been the force of an asteroid strike, the creatures clenched fist landed flush on the point of her jaw, rotating her head grotesquely clockwise and down. Gravity then swiftly took over, bringing her inert form crashing down to earth in a heap. Gordior had already followed through with the punch and was standing in front of John with a look of murderous intent once again, by the time the shockwave of the impact rolled over him. He staggered back a step, completely astounded by what had just transpired. “You turned my mother against me with your refusal to be the human of all! Now you’ll watch as I kill everyone you love, then every other living thing on this planet!” he screamed at John. They both flew at each other. John didn’t want to wait for the first blow to land, and Gordior certainly wasn’t waiting for an invitation to hit him either. Once again Gordior was the quicker of the two. Not by much though now. A powerful blow landed on Johns Jaw, followed by a savage dig to the ribs. John had managed to tuck his chin slightly and rotate his torso away from the strike, minimising as best he could what was still considerable damage. He took the opportunity to land a stinging punch of his own. Rotating his torso back towards Gordior, he landed a straight punch right on the assessor's unguarded nose, breaking it and sending him staggering backwards. John leapt forward, sending his knee thundering into the solar plexus, then a superman punch whilst he was still in the air, sent Gordior bouncing off the ground, back right over onto his front. He immediately pounced again and, thinking of collateral damage, threw the assessor as hard as he could straight up. Two sonic booms sounded, although it probably seemed as only one to the reeling residents of fife, as first Gordior flew into the air and out of Earth’s atmosphere unwillingly, for the second time, then secondly as John leapt up, following him into space. He caught up with him quickly, moving faster than he believed possible, and landed another ludicrously powerful punch on Gordior’s jaw. The force of the blow sent him crashing through a satellite and eventually impacting on the moon. It took John a few moments to catch up to him again, by that time Gordior had somehow gotten back to his feet, looking bruised and battered but still formidable. John hesitated briefly, hoping Gordior would give in. Compassion and hesitation were mistakes when faced with a deranged creature such as the assessor that stood in front of him. Sheera made the error, now John did too. Before he could ready himself for hostilities once more, Gordior had leapt at him, landing a stinging punch to his cheek, an uppercut and a follow up cross to the temple sent him face first into the moons grey surface. He then felt two ribs break as a brutal kick sent him rolling into the air, landing a mile away, struggling to catch his breath. The subconscious act of panting when suffering from a severe injury caused an explosion of panic. There is no air to breathe in space, no gravity to condense the molecules of gases humans breathe, and his throat completely closed up. It took him precious seconds to get over the bloom and remember he didn't need to breathe anymore. John's ribs healed in micro seconds, but the shock of actually feeling those ribs break in the first place was immensely unsettling. Those seconds spent in a state of panic proved costly as he was barely up onto his knees by the time Gordior was once again raining down punches. There were specks of his blood now dotting the dusty moon surface. A hand grabbed his throat, lifted him off his knees, and then Gordior's head was crashing into his face. John crashed back down to his knees, his vision unfocused and his limbs shaking, struggling to keep him up. He felt those merciless hands grip his ankles, he was powerless to fight them off, then found himself hurtling back towards earth.

John was barely conscious but still felt searing heat burn away most of his clothing as he re-entered earth's atmosphere. Wind was tearing at his exposed skin and remaining clothes as the ground was rushing up to greet him. He hit the exposed rock of Ben Lomond's summit, crashing through it as if it were wet paper, sending an explosion of rock and dirt into the air, blocking out the sun briefly, before eventually coming to a halt halfway down the mountain. His body ached all over as he forced his reluctant limbs to bring him into a kneeling position. He teetered on his knees, hands gripping his thighs, trying regain control of himself. A thud in front of him announced Gordior's return. The Assessor was grinning triumphantly. Walking slowly towards John as if he had all the time in the world like a predator stalking wounded prey. This was Gordior's first mistake. And he was going to make the arrogant jerk pay for it. Those precious seconds granted by the Assessor's arrogance allowed him to recover and, of course, his body to adapt. Sheera had said it herself. If the goal was indeed to create a species that could actually best an Endless, then Earth's creator seemed to know what he was doing after all. The fight up until this moment had given John all the time he needed to become an assessor himself. An Endless assessor. Now he knew how Gordior fought, how strong it was and how quick it was. John also noticed, with savage satisfaction, that the creature stalking towards him didn't heal anywhere near as quick as he did. Gordior's nose and thumb were still clearly broken and one of his eyes was bruised and sealed shut. The time they had spent fighting already allowed for the wonder of his mutation to come into its own. John was quicker, stronger and now knew how to kick the assessor's ass. He charged forward, catching Gordior completely by surprise. Easily ducking under the assessor's punch, he sent an elbow crashing into his standing knee with such force it now bent the wrong way. Gordior's mouth hadn't even begun to open to let forth the scream of pain, before John had spun round and landed another devasting elbow to the back of its head. He had held back though as he wasn't quite ready to kill the Endless being. For all his anger and heartache, Sheera's plea was still firmly at the forefront of his mind, and he didn't wish to anger her by killing her only son. Not unless he absolutely had too. Gordior was stirring feebly, face down, in the grass at John's feet. He bent down, hooked an arm under Gordior's chin and lifted him bodily off the ground in a tight sleeper hold. He took two wide steps forward and squatted down, feet way out in front of him, resting his weight on Gordior's lower back with the assessor's legs, one bent at an unnatural angle, the other straight out and flat on the grass behind. He wasn't going to give any chance for him to break free. The Endless being was becoming fully conscious of the predicament it now found itself in and was trying to break free, legs uselessly flopping around and hands scrabbling at John's arms. "Consider this fair warning. If you do not stop, and submit to whatever punishment you deserve at the hands of your mother and superiors, I will kill you." Gordior struggled harder than ever. The Assessor's incredible arrogance unable to accept defeat at the hands of a mere human. Even if it was the human of all. John closed his eyes and applied more pressure to the sleeper hold. It was enough pressure to crush a building, although not enough to kill Gordior yet. He was hoping Sheera or some other supreme Endless would appear, but he couldn't wait long. He was certain, beyond any reasonable doubt, if Gordior broke free then that would be it. Knowing he was beaten alone, he would disappear, and return with help to destroy earth. No form of justice would be able to deter or even contain the assessor. There were bound to be others like him. Others with the same disregard for life, who would also be outraged at the idea of a species apparently created in the image of the supreme Endless. Time seemed to stand still as John opened his eyes. Loch Lomond stretched out in front of him. Twenty-four miles long and the third largest surface area of fresh water in the United Kingdom. The still rising sun only added to the beautiful scene. The Earth, his home, is a beautiful place. John closed his eyes again, prayed he would forgive himself, and snapped Gordior's neck. The sound was like a gunshot in the quiet. He could hear animals panicking and running all over. Birds were taking flight. Some people were even moving to the windows of their lakeside lodges to investigate the strange sound. Despite his intent to kill earlier, meeting Sheera had quelled that extreme desire. For all the evil that Gordior had been, he had nonetheless been a son. John had given the assessor a chance to live, but he couldn't help the creature's arrogance and its inability to accept defeat. He let Gordior's lifeless body fall to the ground and stood up to once again take in the sight of the Scottish loch. The town of Balloch was at the lochs southern edge. Luss, one of John's favourite places, was diagonally opposite from where he stood on the slope of Ben Lomond. Even though he didn't need to breathe now, it was something he still did involuntarily. John found it comforting. He took long, steadying breaths as he enjoyed the simple pleasure of this beautiful national park. He was waiting for whatever consequence his killing of Gordior was going to bring. He hoped it would only be himself that suffered from them.

John shifted his gaze northwards towards Tarbet, only to find Sheera standing next to him, also taking in the scenery. It took every ounce of restraint, and then some, not to cry out in surprise. It didn't stop his eyes briefly bulging like dinner plates though, or his breathing from becoming like that of a hot dog. After a few moments, with still no words spoken, he calmed sufficiently so as to no longer look like a child watching a horror film. Sheera turned her head slightly and their eyes met. Hers looked to be full of sadness and loss. John closed his eyes as he looked away, bowing his head slightly even though he didn't regret what he had done, which surprised him a little. 'I had no choice' he told himself. Whether or not Gordior deserved to die in the eyes the Endless was of no concern to him. The assessor would've destroyed earth if given the chance. John simply eliminated that chance. Even if another supreme endless had turned up to intervene, he felt there was still a chance the assessor would either escape their custody, or not be punished sufficiently to deter him from seeking revenge. John was never going to admit as much aloud, but he was glad there was no intervention. The only problem now was whether or not he alone would suffer for it. "I asked you not to kill my son." 'Oh dear' John thought apprehensively. "That was something I had to do. Not you John." Nine hundred and seventy-four thoughts all of a sudden raced through John's mind upon hearing Sheera's words. The expression on his face would've been right at home on that same child after the horror movie had finished. It probably would've made his friends laugh had the situation not been quite so precarious. "The Supreme of the Endless all have descendants, or Children as you refer to them. It is our responsibility to watch over them, much like they, the assessors, watch over the creators. When an assessor is guilty of genocide, as humans say, it is a terminal offence. Gordior, I finally realised, was guilty of this, and it was therefore my responsibility to administer the punishment and bring about his end. Despite the fact you just committed a murder, as I believe your world refers to it, I can see it hasn't stained your soul. I just hope it doesn't haunt your mind. I know you have been trapped in your own mind before, please don't let this stop you from living." "It won't" was John's simple reply. Yes, he had essentially murdered Gordior, but the assessor wasn't from earth, so surely that meant it was not bound by earth's laws? John also didn't feel any remorse because he felt his actions were necessary to stop Gordior from killing all life on earth. Instead, a wave of relief was washing over him. His family were safe. Annie, Stewart, his dad Phil, his brother Derek, who he guiltily just remembered and needed to call, even his German Shepard Jay were all that mattered to him at that moment. He allowed himself that tiny moment of selfishness. John fell to his knees and silent tears carved paths through the grime on his face.

John didn't know how much time had passed but, Sheera was kneeling directly in front of him when he opened his eyes again. "Would you please stop with the master ninja routine. My heart feels like it's beating out of my chest again" he said catching his breath once more. Sheera smiled apologetically and let out a little chuckle. 'OK, that's just cruel' John thought. Then to his horror, he realised her chuckle may have also been because he was now only wearing his underwear. Once again, his clothes must've completely burnt off upon his return to earth! 'Well at least I'm not naked' he thought to himself. He had purchased his custom boxers a while ago thanks to the particularly embarrassing moment where, in an attempt to save his friends, his clothes had either been torn off or disintegrated due to the friction caused by the speed he had travelled at. "I see your somewhat nervy disposition remains." Sheera laughed softly as she effortlessly picked him up onto his feet again. She turned and stood at his side, tactful enough not to stare. John and Sheera both remained silent for several minutes as they just stared into the distance. "I know you realise that sooner or later you will have to leave, or eventually lose your family." John had indeed realised this. He'd known it from the moment he realised his cells were no longer ageing or deteriorating. Sure, they could all move around to stop awkward questions. He reckoned he had maybe ten or perhaps even fifteen years maximum before such questions would arise. 'What then though?' he asked himself. It would get to a stage where he would look as if he were Annie's son and Stewart's brother, rather than her husband and his father. Then the day would come when she would pass away. The thought of losing Annie, and then Stewart too as time marched on, crippled John. The dilemma had lost him many an hour within his own mind. Annie had commented on these long periods of silence and blank stares, but had mercifully given up questioning him about them, trusting that he would talk to her about them whenever he was ready to do so. She knew something was wrong, like she always knows. John knew he should've told her the moment he realised what was going on, but he simply hadn't been able to face that conversation back then. He now realised it was something he could no longer delay. He would ask Annie's parents to watch Stewart and Jay for the day, then take her out somewhere nice and remote so they can talk. Whatever Annie decides is best, whatever she wishes to do, he would agree. It'll be the single worst conversation he'll ever have. A conversation he never imagined possible and wished, more than anything, that it weren't so. For all his gifts granted by that accident back in Miami, he'd happily give them all up to allow him to enjoy the adventure of life with his family as nature had originally intended. "I know it's going to be hard for you John. This is something no human, or any mortal creature, should ever have to go through. I can't apologise enough for what my son did to you. There are more like him though. More with his morals and beliefs. These … non humans will find out soon enough what happened here today. So, this world's creator will now need protection. You? I don't think you've reached the limit of your abilities yet; and whilst I don't think these other Assessors will be able to kill you, at least not on their own, They pose a serious threat to this planet and all of its inhabitants. You will need to protect it. Sadly, one day though, the world will see you for what you are now. My son will eventually win his cruel game." Sheera looked at John as she said this. He was worried about that too, although he'd hoped that Sheera, and the others of the supreme endless, would've protected the planet to make up for her son's actions. However, in retrospect, he supposed it was naïve of him to expect the immortals who were responsible for all life in the universe to focus solely on this little world. To protect those he loved and the world he lived in, he would deliver each and every one of them Gordior's fate. Without hesitation this time. John just hoped that the world would be able to accept him for what he was when they inevitably found out. He hoped Jean's optimistic take on his abilities would hold true. "Let them come" he said defiantly. Sheera looked into his Sandy Blue eyes, blazing with fury and a steely resolve. She felt sorry for anything that would be foolish enough to provoke and anger the man who stood before her. "May I ask one thing of you John?" He nodded enquiringly. "When the day comes for you to say farewell to the last of those you love…" His heart ached at the thought as she paused briefly "… I will return to invite you to my home. The universe will need you. As will I." With those words said, she vanished from sight. This wasn't a man dressed as a bat type look away and back again disappearance. She just literally vanished from sight. John wasn't sure what shocked him more. The words or the vanishing act. He let that thought drift away in his mind for later musings. It was time for him to go home.

Annie and Stewart were awake and had just finished breakfast when he arrived home. He still looked a mess. Face covered in mud and blood, Clothes missing except for his boxers. Before Annie could say anything, John held up his hands pleadingly. "I'll explain everything if you please let me shower and change first." Annie knew this would take less than a minute, purely the length of time it would take the shower to turn on, provide sufficient water, then turn off again. So, begrudgingly she nodded and then shook her head in utter bewilderment once her husband was out of sight. Not surprisingly, John was back downstairs and cleaned up in thirty-three seconds. "Can you ask your mum and dad to watch Stewart and Jay for today and tonight. There is something we need to talk about. Something related to how I am now." Annie had been waiting for these words for weeks now and breathed a sigh of relief. "OK, I'll ask dad when he calls. He's a bit late calling today actually, must've slept in a bit." John nodded appreciatively, kissed her good morning, and went to catch their runaway son who was making a bee line for Jay's raised water bowl.

Catherine and Tam picked up Stewart and Jay just after ten in the morning. They loved spending time with their grandson, so it was pretty much never an issue to look after him. Annie and John got in his car and left for Loch Lomond at his request. He felt it was the perfect place to say all he needed to say. It was usually nice and quiet, and it would actually show what had happened that morning too. He only hoped that no locals or hikers had already walked the seven-mile trail to Ben Lomond's nine-hundred-and-seventy-four-metre-tall summit. For if they have, then he was pretty certain the somewhat apocalyptic scene would result in many alarm bells ringing, and the quiet would be shattered by all sorts of activity. The drive was going to take around an hour and twenty minutes, not mere seconds as it would for John to travel himself. Cars were awfully slow now. They arrived at a, thankfully, still quiet Loch Lomond. No other cars were parked in the area and John couldn't see anyone in the distance. Annie found it rather fun to be carried by John, only he wasn't allowed to run at anywhere near his top speed for fear of not very nice things! It took them a minute to get to the summit and Annie saw immediately the devastation John's return from the moon had caused. There was a large crater in the path before the summit itself. Rocks and dirt were scattered all around. There was another impact crater farther down the mountain where John had come to a stop. Gordior's body was already gone. John hoped that it wasn't in the hands of an evil human corporation. Annie looked at him with an awed expression, mouth completely agape. Without a word, those were actually about to come tumbling out, he sat down beside the Geodetic marker and motioned for Annie to sit down beside him. Once she was seated beside him, he wrapped an arm around her shoulder and took one of her hands in his. He kissed the top of her head and sighed heavily. He allowed himself a brief moment to appreciate the national park's beauty. Then he spoke. He explained everything and told her what had happened that morning. Annie was quiet throughout, squeezing his hand firmly at certain points being her only outward reaction. After he stopped talking, tears were flowing freely, but silently, down both of their faces. Finally, Annie spoke. Her voice was breaking a little. These were difficult words. "What do you want to do?" They were now looking deeply into each other's eyes. "I don't want to miss a thing. When we got married, we made a commitment to one another and I fully intend to keep that. It does mean we will need to move around and abandon friends after some years. I honestly don't know what will happen though, how will this affect Stewart as he grows up or what this burden will do to you. I think we can tell our parents, your sister and my brother. I can't bring myself or even ask you to abandon them too." Annie sat quietly for a moment, never taking her pale grey eyes from his. "I suppose we're going to be moving around a little bit then." She said with a slightly strained, but genuine smile. As far as John was concerned though, it was the most beautiful smile there ever was. He knew in the end that this was going to be unimaginably painful. That was at the end though. He fully intended to enjoy all the time he had with Annie and Stewart until then. He kissed his wife softly, and hugged her close to him. They sat side by side again, quietly just enjoying one another's company. Annie broke the silence. "It's beautiful here" and John completely agreed with her. He could quite happily sit and admire the scenery all day long. Then again, he could quite happily sit anywhere all day long with Annie beside him. "I want to tell Arla and Callum. I believe, after all we've been through, we owe it to them to be honest." Annie stopped admiring the beautiful national park to look him in the eyes again. "I agree. They're family and they deserve to know. Knowing Arla, she probably won't be surprised. Callum on the other hand, will most likely need a very strong drink afterwards" Annie answered, chuckling at the end. "Shall we invite them around for a takeaway tonight, seeing as Stewart is staying at your Mum and Dad's?" "Yea. The sooner we tell them, the better. I want pizza though." John smiled warmly and nodded in agreement. He quite fancied some pizza too.

"Suppose we better head back home now. We could have a wander around Glasgow on the way and have lunch there too. I could do with some retail therapy after the morning we've had." John sounded a little deflated after he finished talking, thinking once more of everything that had happened. "Retail therapy sounds like a good plan, but let's have Lunch first once we get there. I'll call Arla and Callum when we leave Glasgow for home and invite them over for dinner." Annie said as she stood up and stretched a little. John remained sitting to admire the scenery, although it wasn't the national park that held his attention at that moment. They arrived home just before five o'clock, an hour before they'd arranged for Arla and Callum to come round. Annie picked up her iPad to order the pizza, while John went into the kitchen to make her a coffee and himself a customary hot chocolate.

They passed the time until six o'clock by discussing the upcoming BTCC race at Knockhill, of which they had VIP tickets to attend and were very much looking forward to going. Arla and Callum arrived pretty much together and bang on time as they usually did. John greeted them at the door and was surprised to see Callum had bought himself a new BMW M3 in bright orange. Arla hadn't even realised the door was open because she was too busy staring at the shiny new car. Callum stood beside her, grinning like a Cheshire cat as he greeted John then walked inside to greet Annie. Arla tore her gaze away from the BMW and jumped a little as she realised John was standing right in front of her. She smiled sheepishly, gave him a quick hug in greeting, then followed Callum inside to say hello to Annie. The pizza was ordered to be delivered an hour later, much to Callum's dismay as he appeared to be hungry. So, in the interim, John and Annie told them both about the events of that morning.

They both sat opened mouthed for most of the tale, gasping with astonishment once they realised there were forces at play that essentially governed all known life in the universe, and then looked horrified upon learning that John was now essentially immortal. Arla, as Annie correctly predicted, didn't seem massively surprised by the revelations of life beyond their home planet or of John no longer ageing. She had suspected as much once she found out he was pretty much invulnerable to harm, but hadn't wanted to say anything because of the ramifications it brought along with it. Callum had silently gotten up from the sofa, gone into the kitchen and came back with a second large glass of whisky. John actually heard him quickly drink the first one in the kitchen, then he sat down once again, staring off into the distance. All eyes were on Callum, and they were worried about how badly the revelations seemed to have affected him. "I always thought extra-terrestrial lifeforms would be tall and gangly with big heads, huge eyes and pale skin, like they always seem to be in the movies. I didn't think they would look like us. That's kinda trippy I gotta say." Callum took a small steadying drink after he finally managed to find his voice again. Annie, Arla and John looked at each other, utterly perplexed by his reaction. Of all the things he'd just found out, it was the appearance of the creatures from another world that seemed to have shocked him the most. Callum caught their silent, confused exchanges and spoke again. "What? I just thought we humans were unique in the universe, not a copy of another species. John being immortal is something Arla and I have discussed a few times because of all of his other abilities, so that wasn't a huge surprise. To be honest, the thing that got me most of all was how sadistic Gordior was. I'm really glad you killed that creature John. Who knows what else that thing would've done if you hadn't? I mean, you probably saved the lives of everyone on this planet, and that's not an exaggeration." Callum looked at John meaningfully as he finished. John felt a little embarrassed by such a proclamation and was keen to quell his friend's awe. "I don't think the Endless would've allowed Gordior to wipe out the planet. Sheera made it quite clear that her son was in very serious trouble, to the point of being executed for its crimes against life. So even if I hadn't killed it, I'm pretty sure Sheera would've once they were back on their home world again. At best, I probably saved a few hundred lives by keeping the fight between us isolated." John responded modestly, hoping to calm Callum down a little. Arla had her brow furrowed as he spoke, apparently confused by what he was saying. "Why are you referring to Gordior as 'it', rather than using a masculine pronoun? He was male after all wasn't he? You spoke of Sheera as if she were a woman, so why not Gordior?" Arla asked inquisitively after a moment of thought. "As far as I'm concerned, that creature was evil and didn't deserve to be spoken of as being male or female." John replied a little defensively. Arla looked a little taken aback as she hadn't meant to cause any offence. "I'm sorry, I didn't mean to offend you there. I get it know. You're right, something with such a dismissive view towards life shouldn't be referred to as male or female. That assessor really was a monster." She said apologetically. John smiled and waved the apology away as he felt it wasn't needed. Arla nodded in acknowledgement and took the silence that followed as an opportunity to share some news she had clearly been wishing to share since she arrived. "My next fight is in a month against the number one ranked featherweight. It's being billed as an eliminator and if I win, I'll get a shot at the title." Arla said, bursting with excitement as she clenched her fists and smiled extatically. Annie shrieked joyfully, clapped her hands and then leant over and hugged Arla. John and Callum mouthed 'Wow' at each other, then they too got up to congratulate their friend. The celebrations were cut short by the arrival of the pizza and Callum bolted towards the door as his stomach gave a very audible grumble, making Annie, Arla and John laugh. The conversation as they ate was mainly about Arla's upcoming opponent. John had heard of the fighter, who was also quite new to the organisation having only fought three times, impressively winning each fight by knockout within the first round, and therefore he knew she was a formidable foe. He also knew how talented his friend was and felt sure Arla would emerge the winner. Annie and Callum both agreed and nodded vigorously as they mumbled though a mouthful of pizza their certainty that Arla would still win, despite how good her opponent seemed to be.

After many slices of pizza, they were all full to bursting point. John still had a stomach after all and his digestion hadn't sped up to match the speed he could move at. Then, they all leaned back in their chairs, massaging their full stomachs. Annie got up, as she liked to do, and offered to make some hot beverages for everyone. Callum was first to get up, surprising Arla who had made to get up herself, and offer his help to bring them back through once they were made. John didn't even need to reply as Annie knew he would never turn his nose up to a cup of hot chocolate, and Arla asked for a caramel latte. As they all sat in silence together, enjoying their beverages, John felt a pang of heartache because he knew moments of happiness such as this would fade into the very depths of his memory due to the unrelenting march of time. Annie seemed to read his mind after noticing his vacant expression so she leant in close to whisper something. "Don't think too far ahead my darling. We have many, many more years together to enjoy moments like this." John looked into his wife's wonderful eyes, but couldn't find the words to express how much he loved her. Annie seemed to know what he wanted to say anyway, smiled happily and kissed him softly on the lips before snuggling up close so she could finish her drink wrapped under his proffered arm. John kissed her hair and decided to enjoy the moment, smiling with a look of complete contentment. Arla must've just remembered something as she sat bolt upright, making Callum jump and spill his drink, and looked towards John. "You offered to take me flying if you ever learnt how to when we left the ship all those months ago. Well, seeing as you can now fly, can we?" She asked hopefully, the words tumbling quickly from her mouth. Annie sat up too and pouted indignantly. "Hang on, how come you've never offered to take me for a flight?" She asked, feigning a look of deep hurt, to which John bit his lip nervously. "Well in my defence, the topic of me being able to fly has never come up in this context since then so I assumed no one was interested. However, now that it has, I would love to fly around somewhere with you honey. Yes, you too Arla, and even Callum if he so wishes." John replied in what he hoped was a satisfactory manner. Annie and Arla smiled in anticipation while Callum avoided everyone's gaze and stared off into the darkness outside. "Wait a minute, I forgot. You're afraid of heights aren't you Callum?" Arla wheeled around and shoved him playfully, spilling more of his drink. "I'm not 'afraid' of them, strictly speaking, just not the biggest fan of them, that's all." He wasn't fooling anyone though. Not wanting to make him uncomfortable, well more than he already was at least, they tactfully decided not to pursue the topic of his phobia. "I think, for my own peace of mind, we had better get you all some decent safety harnesses if I'm going to fly around with you." John said to divert the attention away from Callum as it looked like Arla was ready to talk about his fear of heights again. Annie picked up her iPad and started to browse for safety harnesses. Arla came over and sat beside her so they could look together, leaving Callum alone on the other sofa. John caught his attention then motioned for him to get up and go outside to show off his new car. Callum caught on quickly. "Hey John, while the ladies are shopping, do you want to go out for a spin in my new car?" He asked while standing up. John winked then stood up too, kissed Annie, who only offered up her cheek as she was busy browsing with Arla, and followed him outside.

It was a nice, pleasant sort of evening and still relatively light outside so they got in the car and headed towards the motorway for a little bit of speed. Calum's new car certainly had some kick and the seventy mile per hour speed limit came very quickly once they got on the slip road. "We all need to go on a road trip to Donnington Park or Croft so we can really let our cars loose." Callum said as he looked forlornly towards the speedometer. "Yea that would be awesome. Knockhill is great and all, but it would be nice to go to a different track for a weekend away. We'll suggest it when we get back." John replied and nodded in agreement. They were headed south on the motorway towards Edinburgh when Callum's eyes widened in horror. "Ah, I'm sorry John, I should've gone north towards Kelty and Perth." John shook his head dismissively. "It's OK, we can't avoid it forever. May as well go and see how much progress is being made with restoring the collapsed tower." He said with a shrug. Callum breathed a nervy sigh and they carried on towards the Forth Road Bridge. A truly herculean effort was well underway with the restoration of the Queensferry Crossing. The two-hundred-and-ten-metre-tall central tower was once again standing proudly on Beamer Rock in the centre of the river Forth. John hadn't been paying any attention on how the restoration was progressing up until now, and was left impressed by what he now saw. To describe the effort as 'Herculean' was very appropriate as he knew the central tower weighed a staggering twenty-two thousand tonnes. Memories of that tragic day threatened to rear their unwelcome heads, but John shook them off and instead focussed on the relaxing thump-thump of the BMW passing over the expansion joints of the Forth Road Bridge, at the reduced speed limit of fifty miles per hour, making Callum gaze sadly at the speedometer once more. They drove down into South Queensferry and parked at a place in between the rail and road bridge. The sun was slowly starting to fade away in the distance and the sky burned a bright orange. Callum and John were out of the car and leaning on the railing at the water's edge, gazing silently up at the vibrant sky. "It makes you wonder, doesn't it? How much more life is up there past the clouds, in amongst the stars." Callum said pensively. "I don't know how varied it is, but I got the impression there was a lot. We are definitely not alone in this universe, to an extent I can't even begin to imagine." John replied a little distracted as Sheera's parting words came back to him; 'the universe will need you'. He got the impression that some sort of intergalactic conflict was brewing, but he had no idea why the Endless Supreme, his serious thoughts briefly shifted to ice-cream for some reason, had said he would be needed. What could a human do to make a difference in such a situation? John shook his head again and his thoughts returned to where he was now, admiring the beauty the sun can create as it drops towards the horizon and brings about the end of the day. A sight that is so often taken for granted. Callum's phone buzzed in his pocket and he took it out to read a message from Arla. "Arla and Annie have found some decent harnesses which they've already bought and will arrive in a couple of days. Oh goody. Please forgive me if I'm not jumping for joy at the prospect of flying thousands of feet up in the air suspended by just a harness, no matter how good it is. They're also wondering when we'll be back?" John laughed at Callum's involuntary shudder. "Let's head back now. It's getting late and you've got to drive back home to Kirkcaldy yet." "Arla staying with you and Annie tonight?" Callum asked, trying to sound indifferent. John hoped his friend didn't catch him smirking. "Yea she's going to stay tonight then head back to Glasgow tomorrow morning. She would've stayed another couple of nights but her training camp is really ramping up now in preparation for her upcoming fight." John said, watching Callum to see how he'd react, only to be left a little disappointed at his friends perfectly neutral and friendly response of 'OK cool'. They arrived back at Annie and John's home all too quickly, as Callum was really enjoying driving his car, and went inside to find Annie and Arla were now watching a film about a woman being stalked by an unseen assailant. John, who had seen the film before and quite enjoyed it, sat down beside Annie and put his arm around her. She cosied up to him without taking her eyes away from the TV. Callum hadn't seen it and was curious so, after a quick glance at his watch to see it wasn't that late, he sat down beside Arla, but didn't go so far as to put his arm around her. After the film finished, Callum bade everyone goodbye and goodnight then left to go home. Annie and Arla, clearly thinking it was still too early to go to bed, picked another film to watch. This one seemed to be some sort of sequel to the sparkly vampire film so John gave Annie a quick kiss then promptly left the room to go and 'work' on his Lego layout in the loft. Annie and Arla laughed at his hasty exit then started talking as the film started. John guessed it was only going to be something on in the background so they could have a good natter over a glass of wine.

Arla left early the following morning, at the same time as Annie left to walk around to her parent's home and pick up Stewart and Jay. John noticed the two messages he'd received on his phone while Annie and Arla were leaving were from Jean, in bold letters so it must be urgent, and Sandra, who, by his reckoning, would've just joined another ship after her deservedly earned leave. He read the message from Jean first and his eyes popped wide open. Turns out, the incident in Edinburgh involving the haywire military experiment was only the tip of a very shady iceberg. According to a classified document, one Jean had access to because she had been part of the task force that captured the crazed man, a number of people had been experimented on, with varying degrees of success. The experiment they encountered; John frowned as he recalled being sent through a wall, had been deemed as one of the failures. The successful ones were stronger, faster, more intelligent and in complete control of their faculties, so they had been deployed covertly in various locations throughout the world to act as sleeper agents. John didn't like what he was reading. People with that sort of strength could be exceptionally dangerous and capable of decimating an entire unit of well-trained soldiers, meaning wherever they were, trouble would most certainly follow. Jean finished off her long message by mentioning that she was due to meet Kirsty later in the day to discuss their options because they had been invited by the first minister herself no less, to identify and capture the 'super-soldiers' before they could do any harm. John replied saying 'keep me posted', then went on to read Sandra's message, who had indeed just joined a ship down in Falmouth. Sandra's leave had been quite eventful as she had been called into a meeting to discuss her allegations against Luke, along with several other woman who had come forward following Katherine's own investigation. After a month of gathering evidence, which must've been fairly substantial knowing the depravity of the man, Sandra was invited to a formal hearing, along with all the other brave women, only to be left devastated as the case against Luke was dismissed and no further action to be taken. Katherine had gone apoplectic at the Commodore and unfortunately landed herself in some bother because of it. She had accused the senior officer of sexism and neglect, knowing full well that he was actually good friends with Luke, who had sat leering and smiling sickeningly throughout the entire hearing. Funnily enough, the commodore had not appreciated the accusation and suspended Katherine on the spot for not showing the proper respect as required when in the presence of the most senior officer in the company. To make matters worse, Luke was on the same ship as Sandra again and was openly taunting her about the hearing, but thankfully hadn't yet done anything else. John had to close his eyes and calm down otherwise he would've turned his phone into dust or thrown it into orbit.

Annie, Stewart and Jay arrived home just in time and immediately quelled the rising anger within. After a few frantic minutes of excited talk from their son and much wagging of Jay's tail, followed by a quick case of the zoomies, Annie and John set about getting ready to go out again as a surprise for Stewart, who shouted happily and dashed off to retrieve some toys for the car. Jay looked a little sad at first, thinking he was going to be left in the house alone, but barked excitedly after Annie picked up his lead. They were going to go out to St. Andrews for the day and stop off at Anstruther on the way home to get some fish and chips for dinner. John quietly showed Annie the messages on his phone while Stewart was busy choosing some toys. She reacted much the same way as he had, shocked at Jean's message then completely disgusted by Sandra's because she knew everything that had happened with both instances, up until the revelations in the messages. "I take it you're going to go out tonight and pay Luke another visit in Falmouth?" She asked grimly, knowing it was essentially a rhetorical question. "After I've paid that Commodore a visit in Portsmouth." He replied, equally as grim. Annie nodded, deep in thought. "I think they both deserve the Bill treatment. Don't you?" She asked with a knowing smile. John smiled back at her and wrapped his arms around her waist. "You read my mind honey. Let's enjoy today together as a family, then I'm going to play at being the vengeful equaliser again tonight. Don't worry though, I'll tell you all about it when you wake up in the morning." John said. Annie didn't get a chance to reply as they were interrupted by Stewart, having eventually decided on what toys he wanted to take in the car to St. Andrews.

John waited until well after dark and got changed into a matte black one-piece suit, a skin tight outfit that Annie very much appreciated. He bought and used the suit for his shadow realm police work. Almost ready to leave, John donned the matching mask, with special non reflective lenses to hide his eyes, gave Annie a light kiss on the lips then leapt out of their bedroom bay window and flew towards Portsmouth. He quickly found the Commodore, fast asleep in his wardroom accommodation, duct-taped his mouth closed, which surprisingly didn't wake him up, hoisted the somehow still sleeping man over his shoulder then bolted back outside and flew straight up into the cold night sky. The run outside woke the commodore up, the duct-tape stifled what John suspected would've been very high-pitched screams, and the pyjamas he wore meant that it was likely to become unbearably cold for him very quickly as they both broke through the clouds. John settled into a hover many thousands of feet in the air, with Portsmouth gloriously twinkling in the dark far below, and he held the Commodore by the collar of his pyjamas with one hand at arm's length, staring with an amused grin into his petrified eyes. "It's pretty cold up here, isn't it?" John asked as if it were perfectly normal to be at an airplanes cruising height without a parachute. "At this altitude, the temperature, which is below minus fifty-five degrees if you're curious, will result in the onset of hypothermia if not appropriately dressed and wearing silk pyjamas, for instance, in less than five minutes. By that point, any chance of a reasonable conversation would be lost as your speech will become slurred, you'll suffer from memory loss and eventually lose consciousness. So, let's make this quick, shall we?" John once again spoke as there was nothing particularly special about their current whereabouts. The commodore looked down fearfully, already shivering uncontrollably, then nodded quickly. "Good. Your friend Luke Watson is a monster, no other way to describe him quite frankly, yet you ignored the overwhelming evidence presented at the hearing and dismissed the case against him. That was a mistake. You will rectify that mistake by re-opening the case, and filing the appropriate criminal charges against him so that he gets the punishment he deserves. Then you will quit the company, seeing as you are clearly unfit to be in the position you are in. You will do both of these things right away tomorrow morning. If you don't, I guarantee the local police will find some very unsavoury files on your home computer in Gosport. Do you understand?" John's friendly tone flipped upside down, becoming blunt and harsh in an instant. The terrified Commodore mumbled through the duct-tape, agreeing unconditionally to the demands. John said 'good' in reply, then let the man go because he was too angry not to at least frighten him a little too. After a minute of letting the Commodore fall helplessly back down to the bright Portsmouth lights, John grunted irritably as he decided it was best not to kill again just yet, no matter how deserving of such a fate he felt the Commodore was. In the case of his fellow humans, he had no right to decide their fate, that was for the criminal justice system to decide, but he could certainly help to influence it, to make sure justice did indeed prevail. John's nose almost made him wish he hadn't bothered to stop the Commodore's fall. Needless to say, he very much doubted that those pyjamas would ever be worn again. Now that he had achieved the first part of his task, John flew off towards Falmouth to pay Luke a visit, even though he was certain the despicable man would finally get his comeuppance the following morning, because there was the small matter of a promise he made back in a dark Miami hospital room.

John was standing beside the door of the dark cabin when Luke walked in and fumbled for the light switch, trying to take off his trainers at the same time. The inebriated man managed to get one trainer off, but missed the light switch and fell into John, who then forcefully shoved him all the way onto the bench seat at the other end of the still dark cabin. Luke was badly winded by the impact and it took him several minutes to catch his breath again. He was about to shout out angrily, but whatever vile words they may have been, died in his throat once he heard a dreadfully familiar voice. "Last time we spoke Mr Watson, I made you a promise. I don't suppose you remember what it was, do you?" John asked, disguising his voice in the same manner he had back in Miami. "Oh my god, you were real?! I thought that was a nightmare because of the pain killers I was on. P-Please don't hurt me. I'm sorry, I should never have come back, I should never have gone near Sandra again, I-ack!" John interrupted the tidal wave of slurred words by leaping across the space, grabbing Luke by the throat and pinning him against the bulkhead with his feet dangling uselessly a foot above the floor. "Shut up. I don't want to hear you utter another word. I warned you Mr Watson. I warned you what would happen if you went near Sandra again. Now, it's time for your deplorable actions to be paid for." Each word came out in a growl, with John an inch away from Luke's face. A dark stain materialised and rapidly grew around the whimpering man's crotch.

Annie rolled over in her sleep the next morning, believing she had the bed to herself, and her arm swung round and smacked John right in the nose. If this had happened before Miami, John's nose would've turned into a gushing faucet of blood and he would've had to hang his head over the sink until it stopped bleeding again, otherwise the bed would look as if there had been a gruesome murder. Now though, he huffed a little indignantly and stared cross-eyed at Annie's wrist draped across the bridge of his nose, deciding not to say anything so he didn't wake her up. His wife woke up fifteen long minutes later as her alarm sounded. Annie opened her eyes and nearly fell out of bed once she realised John was lying beside her. "Why didn't you wake me up when you got back last night? You just about gave me a heart attack there!" She said, holding her chest after sitting upright quickly. "I got back after midnight and I didn't want to wake you up as I knew you were up early for work today." John replied apologetically. Annie blew out a deep breath and shook her head in exasperation. "Did you find the Commodore and Luke? What happened?" She asked quickly, remembering why he had been out in the first place. "I found them both. The Commodore is going to put right his mistake, then resign from the company. Luke on the other hand…" he paused and his brow furrowed with guilt "…got what he deserved from it. He'll no longer be working for the company either, and I very much doubt he will be able to threaten or harm anymore women ever again." He said with a firm nod of his head, as if to convince himself what he did was justified. Annie looked a little suspicious, but declined to ask any further questions on the matter as she was content both of these horrible men got what they deserved. John got up to get Stewart dressed as part of his usual morning routine, while Annie started to get ready for work. Routine was good for them both after a day like yesterday. Every so often John would look up towards the sky and wonder what else was up there, whether or not he was being watched and what was his place in amongst all of it as Sheera's parting words kept repeating on a loop. Stewart provided a welcome distraction to his latest musings as he reminded him it was time for breakfast. After dropping his son off at nursery, John was pleasantly surprised to find Jean once again standing by her car in the parking area waiting for him. He smiled warmly, inclined his head in greeting and she stepped in beside him as he carried on walking. John liked to give Jay a good walk in the morning while it was cooler and always took a detour on the way back from

Stewart's nursery. "How are you doing John?" Jean asked amicably after a few moments of silence while they continued walking. "I'm OK, but yesterday was a bit rough though. Your message though was quite surprising. I'm guessing that's why you're here, rather than this being a social call." John replied. "I wish this was a social call. Truth is, the situation has gotten very serious. There was an uprising in Beijing, of all places, against the ruling communist party. Kirsty, and the other senior members of the hastily organised team, put together a task force in order to deal with these super-soldiers. The Task Force Management strongly suspects it was one of the sleeper agents who incited it. The suspect is a woman, a former FBI agent called Bella Oceans. An unusual name I know, but it is widely believed that she was part of the mysterious 'Clean-Slate' project run by several different countries' armed forces, and she arrived in China just over a month ago according to immigration services. Unsurprisingly, our Lords and Masters have chosen Bella as the first one to be apprehended, or if capture proves impossible, eliminated as she was, according to the information we were provided, the most capable and dangerous of all Clean-Slate operatives. It's also thought to be happening because it seems she's already been activated. Being fully aware of her abilities, I don't think any sort of tactical squad will be able to capture or eliminate Bella as she's reportedly far stronger, quicker and smarter than the one we encountered in Edinburgh. Kirsty want's me, and therefore you, to go to China as soon as possible before Bella wreaks any more havoc." Jean finally finished talking with a hopeful glance towards John. It was a lot of information to take in and he was very curious about this 'Clean-Slate' project, namely, what was the main goal of it and who would stand to benefit the most. John didn't want to tell Jean of his own problems, as he glanced skywards again quickly, as it seemed she had quite enough to be dealing with as it was. "When are you leaving for China? I'm guessing you'll be going no matter what as you've got first-hand experience at dealing with these people." He asked a little distractedly, keeping his eyes ahead. "I leave in two days. Kirsty has got to make sure all the proper channels are followed so my arrival in China goes according to plan and without any surprises. My presence was actually requested, as you guessed because of my experience, so everything is being expedited in the hope we can stop Bella quickly." She answered. "OK, I'll be there. I can only spare a day though each time we do this. I don't want to keep disappearing from home and certainly not for extended periods of time." John replied evenly, making Jean breathe a sigh of relief. Bella sounded like she was going to be a terrifying prospect to deal with, and Jean didn't want to go anywhere near her unless John was there too. "Thank you John. I know your family comes first so Kirsty and I will do everything we can to make sure your involvement is kept in line with what we already have in place between us. Kirsty is an expert when it comes to negotiations and making deals, not to be confused with a politician though before you say anything, so I'm sure we'll be able to work around what you need. Let's face it, we don't have a choice in that sense, do we?" Jean laughed good naturedly at the end, although her eyes bulged and she shot him a quick nervous glance, worried her joke may be taken the wrong way. She mouthed a silent 'thank god' and looked skywards when he laughed too. John did find it funny how she remembered his refusal to be a political pawn, but was a little hurt at how she implied they were essentially at his mercy. He never wanted anyone to feel they were at his mercy, well except for maybe three people at the moment at least, but he was keen to make things right in that respect. "I know we agreed that I'd help under my own terms, but I don't want you to ever be nervous, or even afraid to ask for it. I know you will only ever ask if it's absolutely essential, like it is now. It might not seem like it, but Kirsty, yourself and I are all equal in this and I'm helping because you both convinced me it was for everyone's benefit. That may sound like the old cliché, 'for the greater-good' but I don't believe it is because we work within the well-defined boundaries of the law. My involvement just speeds everything up." John finished with a little laugh of his own. Jean looked at him thoughtfully for a moment. "You're an incredible human being John. Despite everything you can do, you just want to help. It's almost like you're the human of all, watching over everyone and making sure we're safe." She said almost reverently. John's eyes became vacant and he stumbled a few steps at her all too familiar expression. He had to stand still for almost a full minute in order to keep at bay the awful flood of memories brought on by those simple words. Jean and Jay both looked at him with concern, Jay was brushing his nose against John's hand, as he clamped shut his eyes and grimaced as if in pain. "Are you ok?" Jean asked apprehensively, placing a hand gently on his arm. John took a steadying breath, opened his eyes again and smiled tiredly. "I'm OK. Like I said, yesterday was a bit rough for me and that phrase, 'the human of all', kind of brought it all up again. I'm not some sort of supreme being Jean. I'm just me, OK? All I want to do is help, however I can." Jean looked taken aback by his reply but quickly apologised for being insensitive and that she hadn't meant to suggest he was some sort of deity. She admitted her choice of words was rather poor, and only wanted to imply that he was a watchful guardian, making sure people were safe. John smiled and put an arm around her for a quick hug to say thanks, although he was a little surprised nothing had been mentioned about the damage that occurred throughout Fife and at Ben Lomond the previous day, especially considering Kirsty's position as the Chief Constable. He was happy enough that it wasn't, but knew it would surely come up at some point. By then, he would have to consider telling her and Kirsty the truth. Jay walked on and sniffed a lamppost as if nothing had happened.

The following day was shaping up to be an exciting one for Annie and Arla. The harnesses they bought had just arrived, along with some heavy-duty thermal clothing, and John agreed to take them all up above the clouds. Annie and Arla, who was taking one last day off from her training camp as she definitely didn't want to miss this, were both talking excitedly about it, whereas poor Callum's excitement came out as more of a nervous whine. They waited until the sun was starting to go down, Stewart had been dropped off at Phil's earlier in the day for the night, so that it would be less likely for anyone else to be around when they took off. The plan was to securely fasten themselves together with the harnesses, Annie, John, Callum then Arla, and then take off from the top of the East Lomond hill, which was now marginally taller than the west, once they were certain no one else would see them. John warned them it would be quite the ride as he intended to accelerate upwards very quickly until the clouds safely obscured them from view. Callum turned a pale shade of green on hearing this little detail, while Annie and Arla both looked like it was Christmas. They knew it was going to be bitterly cold at such a high altitude, hence why their clothes looked fit for an expedition up the north face of mount Everest, but that didn't diminish their eager anticipation as they now stood waiting on the wind swept hill top. The sun was just about to complete its daily pilgrimage across the sky and fade away in the distance, which meant they were ready to lift off as there was no one else around for miles that would be able see them in the fading light. Callum held onto John as if his life depended on it and didn't manage to disguise his yelp of fear as they all shot straight up at a speed that would put a top fuel dragster to shame. Annie and Arla screamed in exhilaration as the clouds engulfed them, then seconds later set them free again, and the world appeared before their wide eyes. Words failed Annie and Arla as they craned their necks to take in all they could possibly see. Even Callum was staring in wonder at the magnificent view. Dunfermline appeared tiny, miles below them, as little pinpricks of light started to appear against the darkening sky. Edinburgh was also emerging from the darkness across the glistening river as the day retreated, to be replaced by the typically busy night life. The three imposing bridges connecting the two counties, appeared small, almost insignificant from such a height. "This is incredible John. Our home is down there, somewhere in amongst all of those shining lights. It really puts things into perspective, just how small we are in the grand scheme of things." Annie said as she looked around beneath them, trying in vain to spot their house, then looked up towards the stars above, her voice muffled by the thick balaclava. "I can't think of anything that would be worthy of describing this view." Arla said in hushed tones. John looked all around the vast world beneath them and also couldn't find any words to adequately describe the amazing, vibrant earth they all called home. He looked towards the stars with his now familiar faraway stare and vowed to do all that he possibly could, no matter what may come, to defend it. “It’s Beautiful.” Callum said quietly after a few peaceful moments. Annie, Arla and John all silently agreed with him.

CPSIA information can be obtained
at www.ICGtesting.com
Printed in the USA
LVHW081750021221
705101LV00002B/75